# Witch Ann

## M. Willard Pace

*M. Willard Pace* (signature)

Library of Congress Control Number: 2010903015
ISBN: 978-0-9723571-1-1




Published by M. Willard Pace
625 New Market Road
Tryon, NC 28782




Printed in The United States by
Morris Publishing®
3212 East Highway 30
Kearney, NE 68847
1-800-650-7888

# TABLE OF CONTENTS

# PREFACE

This story is about a lady, Ann Shepherd, who lived many years ago in a shingled covered shanty in the northern edge of Polk County, North Carolina. Her homesite was known as Ann Ridge. She was perceived by many in the region to be a witch, but after reading an article about her, I asked myself, "Was she really a witch, or had life's tradgeties caused her to be different from other folks?"

She is portrayed in this story as being born to Sally and P D Biddy on the night of the thirtyfirst of October of 1844. That's when she experienced her first tragedy, for it was on this night that her mother died after bringing her into the world.

Her great-aunt, Isa Biddy, moved in and did her best to fill the void left by the loss of her mother. She loved Ann as her very own and taught her all the things that any good mother would have taught her child.

Ann was a smart child, so her great-aunt taught her how to read and write. She taught her how to cook and how to churn milk for making butter. When she reached her teen-age years, her great-aunt taught her how to do housework, and how to care for the animals and chickens. She let her take on the responsibility of milking Prissy, the goat, a task she enjoyed, for she loved goat milk.

Two weeks passed her seventeenth birthday, Ann met her second tragedy, that of the death of her great-aunt, Isa Biddy.

Her third tragedy was when her father met and married Hassie Oddum, for her step-mother treated her very cruely.

The next great tragety was when her husband, John Shepherd, went away to fight in the civil war.

Other tragedies were the deaths of family members. First, was the death of her step-mother, whom she had learned to love after some time. Next, was the death of her mother-in-law. Then there was the death oh her father-in-law, who burned to death in his own home.

Her next tragedy was when her father was butcherd by that old "Green River boy", Brute Bates.

After the violent deaths of close family members, she began to think of herself as bewitched. For even the elderly gentlman, Eli Bailey, who had befriended her during all these tragedies was shot and killed.

The greatest tragedy of all was when she received word that her husband, John, had been killed in the war at Petersburg, Virginia.

4

# Chapter

# 1

## Facing Life's Challenges

Held fast within the clutches of Wildcat Spurr, a few miles north of Deep Gap, Ann Shepherd lived in a shingle covered shanty. She owned three black goats, two nannys and a billy. The billy had a blaze on his forehead in the shape of a bolt of lightning. She also had one huge black female cat that followed her wherever she went. When she went to the creek to fetch water for her cooking pots the cat was at her heels. When she went outside to chop wood for the mud-daubed fireplace the cat was there, chasing chips, flung from the axe she was wielding. And for sure, it was there when she went to the little barn to milk the two nanny goats, Precious and Gracious, because as she milked she would send a stream of milk to the cat's mouth directly from the goat's teat.

Besides these animals, she had three sheep, two white ewes and a black ram, which brings to mind the cliché, "Black sheep of the family." But she didn't mind the cliché, because black had always been her favorite color.

She had a pig in the pen which supplied meat for the table and lard for seasoning the vegetables grown in the little fenced in garden behind her shanty. She had a flock of chickens of various colors, which for the most part, provided for themselves and roosted in the hemlock trees surrounding the tiny shanty. The chickens provided eggs which she could swap at Bent Oak Trading Post for things she couldn't produce herself.

The chickens also provided meat for her delicious stews, cooked in the black pot, suspended from a hook attached to the side of the fireplace and swung out over the fire.

Witch Ann had only a few friends. In fact, you could just about count them on the fingers of one hand. Although she had only a few people friends, she was very fond of her animals. But to explain the fact that she was living alone and about her lack of people friends, one must begin by going back to the time when she was much younger and living with her father, P D Biddy, and her great aunt, Isa Biddy, over in Deep Gap, North Carolina.

Ann couldn't remember her mother, but her father had told her many times about what a kind person she was and that they cared very much for each other. But at half passed eleven on the night of the 31$^{st}$ of October in 1844, her mother died, but Ann had never been told why her mother had died so young.

Isa Biddy, P D's unmarried aunt, who was getting well along in years, moved in to help with the cooking and caring for Ann after her mother's death. She loved Ann as her own, but naturally, she couldn't take the place of her mother.

Ann was a smart child, so her great-aunt taught her how to read and write. She taught her how to cook and how to churn milk to make butter. She taught her how to press the butter into a mold when they had some extra to take to the trading post to trade for necessities. She even showed her how to milk Prissy, the goat. "I love goat's milk, Aunt Isa. I think I like it better'n Cow's milk," she said , as she sat milking the goat.

"You should like it, Child, 'cause you've been drinkin' it since the day you were born," Aunt Isa said, before thinking she probably shouldn't have said it just that way.

"Why, Aunt Isa? Didn't Mama have milk for me?"

"Child, I 'spet I've already said too much."

"What, da'ya mean by too much, Aunt Isa?"

"It's up to your pappy to tell you such things."

"Many times I've thought about askin'im. I guess it's about time I done it," Ann said, looking puzzled.

Late that evening, after they had eaten supper and the things were put away, she walked over to her father as he sat before the fireplace and asked, "How come Mama didn't have milk for me when I was a baby, Papa?"

"Who told you such a thing, Little'un?" her father asked, turning his head suddenly aside and looking directly into the fire.

"Aunt Isa told me. She said she thought she'd said a mite too much. She said it'ud be up to you to tell me."

"Well, Child, I hain't told you before 'cause you was just too young to understand, but now't you're old enough, I guess I can tell you. Your mama died just after you'as born, but she did get to see you and hold you afore she went," he said, as tears eased from his eyes, ran down onto his cheeks, glistening in the firelight.

"Well I've always wondered how she died," Ann said, as she wiped the tears from her father's cheeks on the sleeve of her dress.

"I know you've needed a mama, Child, but me and your Aunt Isa's done as good as we could by you."

"You've done gooder'n good, Papa, but I've always wondered how Mama died and now I know."

After going to bed, she lay for what seemed like hours, her eyes awash with tears, choking on the lump in her throat. She felt a sense of guilt for the first time in her life, because her mother had died bringing her into the world. "Why'd I have to loose the very one I needed most?" she thought to herself, as she lay with eyes wide open, staring into the darkness.

At last she realized why her father seemed so sad at times and why he often sat before the fire, long after she and Aunt Isa had gone to bed. She couldn't help but feel guilt for her mother's death, even though her father certainly didn't place any blame on her. "Sometimes things happen that we can't do nothin' about, but she give me the Jewel a my life," he'd always say.

By daybreak Aunt Isa was up and had a fire going in the fireplace. A pan of cured ham was sizzling in the large frying pan and a pone of bread was baking in the Dutch oven, sitting on a bed of coals at the edge of the fire. A pot of coffee was brewing in the cast iron pot, swung out over the fire. The smell of ham aroused Ann and she stirred from sleep. She slid off the bed and strode into the kitchen. "That ham smelled so good it woke me up, Aunt Isa," she said, as she clung to her aunt, hugging her around the waist.

"Set yerself down 'ere at the table and I'll put a piece on yer plate," Aunt Isa said, patting her on the head, leaving a dusting of flour left on her hand from making bread.

When P D came in from milking, Isa strained the goat milk and poured some into a cup and sat it by Ann's plate. P D washed his hands and they all sat down on the rough-plank benches at the table and began to eat.

Half way through the meal, Aunt Isa spoke up and said that since spring was here and after having several days of warn weather, there should be some stalks of poke sallet in the new ground patch in the holler. "How 'bout you'n me goin' down 'ere and see what we can find?" she said, speaking to Ann.

"Sure 'nuf, Aunt Isa? That'ud be a heap a fun."

So after breakfast, Aunt Isa and Ann washed the dishes and spread up the beds, swept the floors a little, took down the handled basket from the wall and headed for the new ground patch in the holler to pick a mess of poke sallet.

As they were gathering the poke sallet they heard a rustling in

7

the bushes nearby. When they looked up they saw the old Indian lady, Owatta, bending low, gathering herbs near the edge of the clearing with a young maiden at her side.

"Hope you not care me gather fresh herbs. Many sick in villiage. Me think new medcin make um all better," she said, as she stepped out into the clearing with the young maiden shying behind her.

"Help yerself, Owatta. I 'spect them herbs belongs to the God A'mighty, anyway. Is they anything I can do to help?"

"Me thank you, Kind One, but new medcin make um all better."

"I wish you'd tell me all about them herbs and what they're for, Lady Owatta," Ann said, with a slight tinge of excitement.

"Me be plenty glad to show you all I know, Young One," Owatta said, as she seated herself on a dead chestnut log and began to name and explain all the herbs she had collected.

"This milk thistle. It drive poison from body. It make well when snake bite. And this maidenhair fern. It make well when mad dog bite. And this fox glove. It make heart beat right."

After explaining the collection of herbs to Ann's satisfaction, she said, "Owatta go now. Make medcin for my people. Them plenty sick, but new medcin make um all better again."

Owatta bade them good day and as she and the young maiden disappeared into the woods, heading up the trail that leads to their village on the plateau beneath World'd Edge, rain was already spreading down the eastern slopes of the mountain toward Deep Gap. So Isa and Ann finished filling the basket with poke sallet and rushed up the hill toward the house. By the time they reached the house and stepped up onto the porch, the rain was beginning to fall. "Just in the nick a time, Ann," Aunt Isa said, as she scuffed the dirt from her shoes and sat the basket of poke sallet on the bench there on the porch. "Let's git this stuff washed and ready to cook."

After boiling the poke sallet until it was tender, Aunt Isa washed it a couple of times and squeezed out all the excess water. She raked some coals from the fireplace onto the hearth and placed the large cast iron frying pan on the bed of coals and added a couple of tablespoonfuls of lard to the pan. As soon as the pan was hot and the lard had melted, she dumped the poke sallet into the pan and let it heat up. She sprinkled in some salt and let it come to a simmer. She stirred in four eggs and let it cook until the eggs were done. The pone of corn bread, cooking in the Dutch oven was just about done. She told Ann to go and fetch her father. "Go call yer pappy, Child. This here stuff's just about done."

Ann lost no time in finding her father and telling him that dinner

8

was ready. "And we've got poke sallet, Papa," she said, clinging to his arm as they walked up toward the house.

"It ain't a minute too soon, Child, cause I'm mighty hungry."

◻◻◻◻◻◻◻◻◻◻◻◻◻

Spring went like the fleeting flight of a falcon and the Biddys found themselves locked in the heat of mid-summer.

On a warm July morning, Ann went with her aunt Isa down to the edge of the corn field to pick blackberries. When they had filled their pails and were easing out from amongst the tangled blackberry briars, Aunt Isa let out with a low moan, "I've been bit, Child. Go'n tell yer pappy I've been snake bit. Tell 'im to go fetch Owatta. I'll need some a her snakebite medicine. Hurry child!"

Ann took out up the path carrying the two pails of blackberries, leaving a trail of berries along the path as she went. As soon as she told her father about Aunt Isa being bitten, he was on his way up the hill to the Indian Village, to get Owatta and some of her snakebite medicine.

Ann hurried back down the path to help her aunt, who was now making her way up toward the house. Her leg was already swelling from the snakebite and she was in a great deal of pain. She was beginning to feel faint, but she knew she must get to the house before she passed out. Ann helped her up onto the porch and into her bedroom and helped her get into bed. She soaked a cloth in cool spring water and placed it on her aunt's head and that seemed to help some. "What kind of a snake was it, Aunt Isa?"

"A rattlesnake, Child," she managed to say.

Isa lay semiconscious as Ann did what she could to make her comfortable while waiting for P D to return with Owatta and her sack of herbs.

Owatta rushed into the bedroom, all out of breath, carrying the herbs in a deerskin bag swung over her shoulder. "Not worry, Good Woman. Me make you all better," she said, reaching into the bag to retrieve some dried milk thistle.

"Bring bowl sweet milk, Young One. Me make medcin for Good Woman," she said, sprinkling some milk thistle into her hand.

After mixing the milk thistle with the sweet milk, she lifted Isa's head and poured the mixture into her mouth. "Drink, Good Woman, this make you all better."

Isa drank it with some difficulty and when she finished drinking the milk thistle mixture, Owatta mixed some maidenhair fern into

9

another bowl of water and let Isa sip on it until she consumed it all. She made a poultice of comfry and placed it on the snakebite area. "You sleep now, Good Woman. When you wake, you be better."

"Me go now. You not worry, Young One. Good Woman be OoooK," Owatta said, swinging the deerskin bag over her left shoulder as she headed for the door.

"Thank ye, Owatta. I hope we can pay ye back for this," P D said, as he walked her to the door.

For the next two days and nights, Aunt Isa lay practically motionless with Ann watching over her day and night. But on the third day she began to stir and talk somewhat incoherently, saying things that Ann couldn't understand. On the fourth day she was wide awake and taking food and water. The swelling in her leg was gone and she was getting better. "Glad to have you back, Aunt Isa. You've been asleep for a while."

"Seems that way, Child. Sure seems that way," Aunt Isa said, before drifting off to sleep again.

Within a few days Isa was up and doing about as well as she had been doing before she was bitten, but her strength wasn't quite up to par and she tired more easily than before, but Ann helped her with the things she didn't feel like doing. This allowed her to learn more about things a grown woman should know about housework. "After all, I'm goin' on sixteen," she thought to herself.

ꗣꗣꗣꗣꗣꗣꗣꗣꗣꗣꗣꗣ

As time passed and summer went, age began to take its toll on Aunt Isa, but Ann felt fortunate that her aunt had shown her how to do all the things necessary to keep the household going. She had been a good teacher. She had not only taught Ann to do housework but she taught her to read and write as well. This made it possible for Ann to keep a written record of all the things Owatta had told her about herbs and their uses. The written record was kept it in the bottom bureau drawer in her bedroom. Her hope was some day to become a midwife and to be able to help those who were sick and to help expectant mothers when their babies were ready to be delivered.

# Chapter

# 2

## Ann Faces Many Difficulties

Ann became seventeen as October turned to November.

On the first day of November, her Aunt Isa came down with the flu. Ann used all the remedies Owatta had taught her, but nothing seemed to work. The herb, feverfew, helped to bring the fever down, but Aunt Isa's condition grew steadily worse. Ann asked her father to go up to the Indian village to see if Owatta would come down and have a look at her aunt.

Owatta tried several things, but nothing helped. Finally, feeling that they had done everything within their power, she said, "Must give Good Woman to Higher Power, Young One. Only The Great One can help when time come to go to Place in Sky."

On Wednesday, the fourteenth day of November, two weeks passed Ann's seventeenth birthday, Aunt Isa passed away in her sleep and was laid to rest on the ridge in the Biddy family graveyard.

Ann grieved over the loss of her aunt as if she had been her own mother, for she had always been like a mother to her, caring for her since the day she was born.

After Aunt Isa passed away, P D went about his chores as if in a daze. She had somehow filled the void in his life. He searched far and wide to find someone to take rer place, but his search seemed fruitless, however, after some time, without asking any questions as to what kind of person she was, he met and married Hassie Oddom. As it turned out, she was not a very nice person. But since they were already married, and having so much self pride, he couldn't bring himself to send her away. But if he had known how cruelly she was treating his daughter he would have sent her away, pride or no pride. But Ann, being threatened and not wanting to cause trouble between Hassie and her father, kept the abuse to herself.

Ann's step-mother, saddled her with most of the housework. Her father was away almost every day, working in the fields or chopping wood for the fireplace, leaving her alone with her demanding and overbearing step-mother. Hassie was very cruel to Ann and threatened to harm her and her father if she ever complained to him about how she was being treated.

◻◻◻◻◻◻◻◻◻◻◻◻◻◻

In the spring of 1847, Jacob Shepherd and his wife, Sarah, and their son, John, moved to Deep Gap from Sumter, South Carolina to escape the oppressive summer heat. Jacob had traveled through the mountains with his father when he was only a child and had always dreamed of coming back some day.

Jacob's house was a good mile from where Ann lived with her father and step-mother. And because Ann was always hard at work, washing clothes, cooking, sweeping the floor and toting wood for the fireplace, she had very little time for visiting.

In the evenings, when supper was done and the dishes washed, she carded wool for spinning and spun it on the old spinning wheel in front of the fireplace until she could barely hold her eyes open. She would then make her way into her tiny bedroom, climb into her bed atop a tick filled with shreaded corn shucks, pull the old worn quilt over her tired aching body and cry herself to sleep. She couldn't help wondering what it would be like to have had a loving mother to care for her. That could never be and she knew it, but just thinking about it helped ease the pain a little.

It seemed she had hardly gotten to sleep when the little rooster in the hemlock tree near her bedroom window began to crow and her step-mother called to her in that pretentiously kind voice, "Get up, deary, it's time to build a fire and start breakfast."

Ann slid off the bed and into her worn scuffs and headed to the fireplace. She knelt on the cold, stone hearth, unbanked the coals, lay on some pine kindling and blew on the coals until there was a blaze.

After laying on some sticks of oak and hickory wood, she wrestled the heavy frying pan from the side of the fireplace and ballanced it on the tripod over the fire, placed a lump of lard in the frying pan and begin mixing up dough for a pone of bread. When the bread finished cooking, she added more lard to the pan, stirred in some flour for making gravy, hung the large coffee pot on the hook and swung it over the fire.

Having gotten up when she did, her father out at the barn milking. Her step-mother swaggered into the kitchen before breakfast was ready, knowing that P D was out milking and wouldn't be able to

12

hear her raving, said, "Ain't you got it done yet? I'm hungry."

"It's almost done, Mother," Ann answered.

Hassie demanded that she address her as Mother, even though she knew Ann didn't want address her as such, but she did it, hoping Hassie wouldn't treat her so cruelly. But no matter how hard she tried to please her step-mother, it seemed to make no difference.

Hassie was always careful to act kindly toward Ann when P D was around, but when he was out working, awful was not the word to describe the way she treated her.

One cold, damp day, Hassie sent Ann out without a sweater to the corn crib to shuck corn, while she stayed inside and dozed before the fire, wrapped in a hand-knit wool blanket Aunt Isa had made especially for Ann.

Ann piled shucks around herself as she shucked the corn and that kept her from getting so terribly cold. When her father returned from work later that evening, he opened the crib door to get an ear of corn to feed the chickens and was startled to find Ann sitting there shivering in a pile of shucks. "What're ya' doin' out here in the cold?" he asked her.

"Well Papa, we needed some corn for meal so I thought I'd get some shucked."

"Well, get out'a there and come on in the house and warm yerself by the fire. You'll catch a death'a cold out here. I can shuck that corn when we need some," her father said, as he helped her to her feet and through the tiny crib door, holding her cold hands for a moment to warm them.

"I told her not to be out 'ere shuckin' corn. It bein' so damp and cold like this, but she wouldn't listen," her stepmother lied, as Ann and her father came inside.

"Somebody had to do it, Mother."

"You look plenty warm, Hassie," P D said, laying an armfull of wood on the hearth.

"I just set down here a minute to rest from a hard day's work," she said, as P D gave her an unbelieving look.

"I'll get some supper started," Ann said, as she lifted the heavy frying pan and placed it atop the tripod and raked some hot coals beneath it.

There was a feel of fall in the air the next morning when Ann went outside to feed the hog. "I think I'll go see if I can find us some chestnuts today," she told her father, as she came back inside, carrying an armfull of firewood.

"There's some big chestnut trees down there toward the Shepherd place. The ground should be covered up with chestnuts this

13

time of the year," her father told her.

"It 'ud be good t'have some roasted chestnuts," Hassie said, as she sat in the rocker with her feet to the fire.

"That settles it then, Papa. I'll just go down there and find out."

After finishing her regular chores, Ann told her step-mother she was going to look for chestnuts and that she would be back after while. She took the basket down from the wall of the corn crib, removed the rat's nest and dumped the remnants onto the ground. Swinging the basket over her left arm, she headed down through the woods toward the Shepherd place.

Many of the trees were beginning to shed and a layer of multi-colored leaves carpeted the forest floor. Squirrels scampered from tree to tree, carrying hickory nuts and acorns to their dens, preparing for the winter ahead, which was sure to come. There were scratched places here and there, where wild turkeys had been foraging.

She thought she heard a deer bouncing along ahead of her and thought she caught sight of one's tail as it went out of sight over the next ridge. A covey of quail burst into the air, not more than ten feet in front of her, causing her hair to stand on end and a cold chill to run up her spine.

Just beyond the ridge was a grove of giant chestnut trees, dwarfing large oaks and maples that were growing nearby. As she walked beneath the canopy of large chestnut trees, she could see that the deer had indeed been there, for their signs were everywhere.

As she began picking up chestnuts and placing them into the basket she heard a rustling of leaves. Looking up, she saw John Shepherd sauntering through the woods, whistling and carrying a basket, the handle swung over his arm. He was obviously there for the same reason she was, searching for chestnuts.

She was startled at first, not expecting to see anyone out there in the woods so far from a house. It had been some time since she'd seen John at Bent Oak Trading Post, when she had managed to go with her father, right after Aunt Isa died.

"Imagine meetin' you way out here in these here woods, Miss Biddy. But it's mighty good to see ye after such a long time. How've ya been, anyway?"

"Well, scare me to death, John Shepherd! I didn't 'spect to see nobody way out here in these woods."

"I figgered I'd come out here and see if I could find some chestnuts, but it looks like there's a god's plenty, don't it?" he said, as he sat his basket down and began filling it with the chestnuts that were so thick on the ground he could hardly walk without stepping on one.

After he filled his basket, he helped Ann finish filling hers and they both walked over and sat on the trunk of a chestnut tree that had fallen sometime during the previous winter.

Ann had often thought of John since meeting him at Bent Oak. And today they became  so consumed by each other's company that time escaped them. The sun had passed the noon hour and was drifting into the afternoon before they realized it.

"I'd better get home, John. My step-mama'll skin me alive!" Ann said, jumping to her feet and racing down the hill to retrieve the basket of chestnuts.

"That's too heavy for you to carry all the way up to your house. I'll carry it fer ya," John said, picking up the basket and taking Ann by the arm.

"Hassie'll have a fit if she sees you helpin' me carry this basket, John."

"She won't have to see me. I'll carry it to the edge of the woods and you can carry it the rest of the way."

"Well, if you insist," Ann said, half protesting, but so pleased that he had offered to carry it for her.

The sights and sounds of the forest and the scent of the newly fallen leaves gave them a sense of exhilaration as they strode side by side up the trail, chattering like two young squirrels, trying to get in all the conversation they could before reaching the clearing where John would have to turn back. When they reached the edge of the clearing, he handed the basket of chestnuts to her, touched her hand gently and said, "I'd like to call on you sometime, Miss Biddy, if you'd allow me."

"Hassie won't like it, but Papa won't mind."

"Well, Miss Biddy, that settles it. How 'bout next Sunday, after dinner?"

"Come for dinner, John. I'll fix somethin' good," Ann said, as she turned quickly and headed up the path toward the house.

"Wher've ye been all day? Yer pappy had to go back to work a'thout dinner. Just a bite a cornbread'n a cup a milk." Hassie scolded.

"Time just slipped away, Mother. I didn't mean to stay so long." "Well git in 'ere'n get sompum cooked. Your Pappy'll be starved time he gets home."

"Look at these chestnuts, Mother."

"Soon's you git supper on, you can roast me some, but you better git that supper goin' first."

"I will, Mother," Ann said, as she stirred the coals, added a few sticks of wood and swung the black pot over the fire in preparation for cooking potatoes. She placed the Dutch oven on the coals at the edge of the fire and began mixing meal for corn bread.

"As she poured the cornbread batter into the Dutch oven, Hassie scowled and said, "I'm ready for them chestnuts, Annie Bell Biddy. "Can't ye see I'm waitin?"

"Yes, Mother, I'll do it right now."

"Well, hop to it and don't be all day about it!"

By this time Ann's nerves were at the breaking point and tears were welling up in her eyes, but she bit her tongue as she placed several chestnuts near the fire and continued with preparing supper.

When the chestnuts were roasted, Hassie said, "Husk me some a them thangs. I'll eat a few afore supper."

"I found the chestnuts, Papa. The ground was covered with 'em," Ann told her father as he came inside, toting an armful of wood for the fireplace. "And guess what, Papa, John Shepherd was down there pickin' up chestnuts, too, and he asked me if he could come callin' on me. Just what do you think of that?"

"He's a fine boy, Ann," P D said, putting an arm around her.

"Prob'ly up to no good," her step-mother said, her face turning red with envy.

"He's a good boy, Hassie," P D said, as he gave her that enough said look.

"Well, ye gotta keep a tight watch on 'ese mountain boys," Hassie said, determined to have the last word.

P D looked at her as if he had a thousand words to say, but said nothing, knowing it would be pointless, but it was obvious from the look on his face that it took a great deal of strength to remain silent.

Ann hurried to get supper on the table, hoping the thought of food would clear the atmosphere and put her step-mother in a better mood, but it did nothing to quash her bitterness toward a boy she hardly knew, for she went on with her ranting and raving all through supper and even after going to bed. She finally fell asleep with her mouth open, ready to say something else, but sleep silenced her.

Ann lay for quite some time reliving the events of the day, hoping something would come of her friendship with John Shepherd.

Sometime during the night she had a dream, in which she and John had fallen in love with each other and were married in a little log church with shutters that creaked as they swung back and forth in the wind. She awoke to the sound of the wind whistling around the eaves of the house. A limb of the large hemlock tree scrubbed the wall outside her window, sounding like the sawing of a bow on the strings of a lonesome fiddle. She eased up, closed the curtains, crawled back

16

into bed, pulled the heavy covers over her tired body and lay there for some time, wishing that the dream would some day come true.

"Papa says he's a good boy," she thought to herself and she smiled into the darkness. It was the first time she'd smiled in a long time. In fact, she hadn't smiled since before her aunt Isa passed away.

The days crawled by much like a crippled snail and it seemed that Sunday would never come, but it finally did and Ann was up early, cooking breakfast and busying herself with preparing food for dinner. She baked Irish and sweet potatoes in the ashes there on the hearth. She stewed a chicken and made dumplings. A pone of bread was cooking in the Dutch oven.

"Why're ye goin' to so much trouble, "Annie Bell? You know all he's lookin' fer is sumpum to fill his belly. He sure don't care nothin' about you," Hassie scowled.

"I told him I'd cook up somethin' good and that's what I aim to do," Ann answered, defiantly.

"Well, ain't you getting' mighty sassy," Hassie said, her voice dwindling to a whisper as P D came inside.

"Smells powerful good, Young Lady," P D said, lifting the lid on the heavy cast iron cooking pot to inhale the pleasant aroma of the chicken, simmering in its ritch broth.

"Well, thank you, Papa. I hope it'll be good."

"I'm sure it will be, Child. I'm sure it will."

Hassie's face again turned red with envy, hearing words of praise heaped upon Ann by her father. But this time, she had nothing to say, or at least she didn't say anything.

John Shepherd showed up about mid-day. He and P D sat on the porch, swapping conversation, until Ann came to the door and summoned them to dinner.

"Well, John lets see what that girl a mine's got cooked up."

"It'll be good, Mister Biddy. I can smell it all the way our here on the porch."

Dinner was good, for all the chicken was eaten right down to the bare bowl. Hassie had very little to say throughout the whole time they were eating and when she did say something it was of a demeaning nature. It seemed impossible for her to be civil or to show any concern for anyone other than herself. It just wasn't in her nature.

After they finished eating the fine food Ann had prepared, P D and John returned to the front porch to engage in more conversation while Ann cleaned the pots and pans and washed up the dishes. Hassie shuffled off to her bedroom, her belly bulging from all the chicken and dumplings, baked sweet potatoes and bread she had eaten. She fell

17

across her bed and was snoring in no time at all.

When Ann finally finished washing the dishes, John asked her if she would like to walk out the road "a piece" and of course she was more than ready to go. "That's a fine idy," she said. "Would you like to come along too, Papa?"

"No, Child, I think I'll just stay here and rest a mite."

John was pleased that P D decided not to come along and off they went, out the road a piece. Of course John had other reasons for getting Ann away from the house, nothing mischievous mind you, but to continue the conversation they had started the other day when they were down there in the chestnut grove and were cut short by the swift passing of time.

They had walked only a short distance when they came to a sunny spot beside the road, a comfortable place where they could sit and continue their conversation. "I've been thinkin' about things since we talked the other day, Miss Biddy, and what I'm talkin' about is, I'd like to have you for a steady girl. How do you feel about that?" John asked, without the slightest hint of hesitation.

"I'd be mighty proud to be your steady girl, John Shepherd. Since the other day, I've thought of nothin' else."

"Seems like your step-mama is a mite harsh with you. What's wrong with her, anyway?" John asked.

"For the life of me, I can't figure her out, John. She seems to think they's nobody in the world but her. I guess you could say she's just a mean old woman. I do most all the work around the house and nothin' I do pleases her, but I don't want to hurt Papa's feelings by talkin' back to her, but sometimes I have to bite my tongue to keep from it."

"I can understand where you're comin' from, Miss Biddy. I most certainly can."

"You don't have to call me Miss Biddy, John. Just call me Ann. That's my name, you know," Ann said, looking up into his eyes.

"Well, I'll call you Ann from this day forth, since that's your name." John said. "Ann. Ann! Ann! Such a pretty name.

¤¤¤¤¤¤¤¤¤¤¤¤¤¤

In the days and weeks that followed, Ann saw John as often as she dared. And each time she saw him, Hassie was more vile and oppressive toward her than before. But Ann became more resistant with each degrading statement her step-mother made. She was determined to marry John if he'd have her and to move away from such an offensive person. She regretted having to leave her father with such a woman, but "He'll just have to work things out for himself," she thought.

Hassie tried everything she could think of to break them up. She knew if Ann married John and moved away she would have to bear the burden of housekeeping. Otherwise, P D would soon learn of her laziness, but she needn't have given that a second thought, for by this time P D already knew. One would have had to be totally blind not to have noticed.

As time went by, Hassie could see the "hand writing on the wall," so to speak, but her demeanor didn't change one iota. She continued to treat Ann as cruelly as ever and to try to place a stumbling block between her and John. But Ann was determined not to let Hassie come between them, nor to interfere with any of their plans.

The year was 1861. October had come and gone and Ann was now seventeen, but John had not yet asked her to marry him and she wondered why. But a couple of months later, on Christmas day, she was visiting with him at his parent's house when he asked her if she would marry him. It caught her so off guard that he had to ask her twice, but when she finally realized what he'd said, her arms fell to her sides and her shoulders drooped. She stared him straight in the eyes and said, "You know I'll marry you, John Shepherd, of course I will."

John took her in his arms, lifted her clean off the floor and kissed her. His father and mother were napping by the fire when he woke them to tell them the good news. "Well, Son, I thought it was about time you popped the question. I wondered what you's watin' on," his father said, rubbing the sleep from his eyes.

Sarah, John's mother, struggled to her feet to embrace Ann and to welcome her into the family. "I'm mighty proud you're gonna be my child, Child," she said.

"Me too, Mother Sarah," Ann said, as she and Mother Sarah locked in a tight embrace.

"Come next spring," John said, "I'm gonna build us a little cabin up there at the foot of the mountain. I've had a place staked out up there for some time now. The place is loaded with slim poplar trees and they're just the right size. They'll make a fine cabin. I'll hitch Jude to the wagon one day next week and we'll go up there and have a look."

"I can't wait to see it, John Shepherd."

"I guess you'll just have to, Ann Biddy," John said, smiling.

Friday of the next week, which was the third day of January of 1862, John brought the mule and wagon by the Biddy house. Ann climbed aboard and they headed up toward the foot of the mountain to

19

have a look at the place he had staked out.

P D went along to have a look at the place for himself, riding in the back of the wagon with his legs dangling. The soles of his brogans tpuched the ground when the wagon wheels ran over a low place in the rough road.

The day was clear and cold. A cloud of vapor exploded from the mule's nostrils each time it exhaled as he trotted along, pulling the wagon and its occupants up the rough road toward the foot of the mountain. Ann sat close to John, clinging to his arm and they bumped shoulders each time the wagon ran over a bump in the road.

After about an hour they came alongside a small creek, turned left and came to a stop at the crest of a ridge where John announced, "This is it, Ann Biddy. This is the place where we'll build our cabin."

He bounced down from the wagon, tied the reins to a small sapling and walked around to assist Ann in dismounting. P D stepped down from the wagon and without a word he walked out the ridge, counting the tall poplars, to see if there were enough to build a cabin and to his satisfaction there were.

"This is just about the prettiest place I've ever seen, John. What a fine place for a cabin. I can almost see it now in my mind," Ann said, still clinging to his arm. "Not too far from the creek either."

"Like I said, Ann, we'll get started on it soon's the sap's up. We'll need to peel them poplars you know. If we can get your papa to help us, it shouldn't take but a few days to build it."

"I'll help you, Son. Be more'n happy to," P D said, as he came back up the hill, after counting the trees.

# Chapter

# 3

## Ann Hopes For Happier Days

On Sunday, the twenty-third of March, John and Ann attended church at Cooper Gap with the sole purpose of arranging with the circuit preacher to "tie the knot." "What day were you countin' on, John?" the preacher asked.

"What about next Sunday, Preacher?"

"Can't do it next Sunday, John. I'll be preachin' over at Broad River that day. How 'bout Monday, the last day of March?"

"Sounds good to me," John said.

"Well, that settles it. I'll meet you and that little sweety a your'n over here at straight up twelve o'clock on Monday. That's the last day of the month. You'll miss April fools day by one whole day," he said, exploding with laughter.

The next week was pure torture for Ann, with Hassie ranting and raving and making scandalous remarks about John and about what a fool she was to even think of marrying him. Ann tried as best she could to ignore her step-mother, because she knew it would be only a few days and she'd be gone. But there was a gnawing in the pit of her stomach, knowing that her father would now bear the full brunt of Hassie's abusive attitude. "He'll just have to do the best he can with what he's got," she thought to herself, as she went about her daily chores, preparing as best she could for her wedding day.

P D appeared to be happy that she was getting married, but there was a certain sadness in his eyes as well. Perhaps he was thinking how good it would be if her mother had lived and could have been here to enjoy the occasion. "In times like these a girl needs a mama. They's nothin' like a mama," he thought to himself.

Monday morning, the last day of March, broke clear and sunny and there was definitely a touch of spring in the air. Crows were calling to each other from the ridge tops surrounding Deep Gap.

"It's a good day for a weddin'," John said, as he hitched the mule to the wagon. "It's a good day since it ain't April Fools' Day."

Ann cooked breakfast there on the hearth and after they had all eaten, she washed the dishes and poured some water from the kettle into the wash pan and went to her room to bathe, before putting on the black dress she would be wearing to the wedding.

"Why're ye wearin' black, Annie Bell Biddy?" Hassie sneered. "Looks like yer goin' to a funeral or sompum."

"I'll have you to know, black's my favorite color. It's my weddin' and I'll wear what I like", Ann said, defiantly, looking Hassie straight in the face.

"Well, ain't we gettin' to be a real smarty pants? It's a good thing you're leavin' or I'd teach you a thing or two," Hassie said, slamming the door behind her as she stomped off into the bedroom.

"You've got a hard lesson to learn, Old Woman," Ann thought to herself, as she combed her long black hair, viewing herself in the tiny mirror, set up on the table near the window.

P D emerged from the bedroom wearing his black suit and black tie. His shoes were black and shining from the tallow he had rubbed on them and buffed with a rag he had managed to find in the rag bag under the bed.

"You look like a city slicker, Papa. All dressed up in that black suit'n tie. Where you goin', anyhow?"

"Goin' to a weddin'. Where'd you think?"

"Thought you might be goin' to some kind of a convention," Ann said, as she snuggled up to her father and gave him a kiss.

"Where d'ya think you're goin', Little Girl? all dressed up like the queen a some far off kingdom."

"Goin' to a weddin', too, Papa. Gonna get married. What do you think a'that?"

"Your mama'd be right proud of you, Little Girl. She'd be mighty proud," P D said.

When tears dampened his eyes and rolled down his cheeks, he turned quickly and brushed them away with his finger tips.

"I don't see what you're so up in the clouds about, Annie Bell Biddy. Nothin' good'll come of it. You just wait'n see," Hassie said to her, each time P D was out of earshot.

Along about ten o'clock, John came up the road in the wagon and stopped in front of the Biddy house. Jacob and Sarah were in the back of the wagon, sitting on a pile of quilts, grasping the sideboards to keep from spilling over.

John stepped down from the wagon, dressed in a grey homespun wool suit. He was wearing a grey felt hat and black tie. He walked brisky up the steps and knocked on the door. When Ann came to the door, she stood staring at the man, soon to be her husband. "Grey suits you, John Shepherd, and I do like that black tie," she said, still gazing, for she had never seen him dressed in a suit before.

"Are we ready?" John asked, as he stood admiring her.

"We are, John. We are ready," Ann said, as she stepped out onto the porch with P D right behind her.

The curtains moved at the window of the front room and Hassie's half-hidden face could be seen, nose pressed against the pane, peering out through the tiny window. Perhaps she was having second thoughts about how cruelly she had treated Ann, and perhaps if she had been better to her, she would be going along, too.

The trip to the church was a joyous one, with P D and Jacob trading words and swaping jokes back and forth.

Ann sat on the wagon seat between John and her father, with thoughts running through her mind that she would now finally have someone she could love and someone who would love her. "Finally!" she said. "Finally!"

When they pulled into the church yard, the preacher was already there and even a few church members had come along to witness the ceremony. It was straight up twelve as they went inside and made their way up to the front of the church. A few sprigs of holly were placed in a vase in front of the lectern. No one knew just who had put them there, but Ann believed it was her Aunt Peggy, because she was the one who normally decorated the pulpit.

The ceremony went well and as John and Ann left the church, Aunt Peggy tossed holly berries at them as they walked down the steps.

The wind began to pick up, delivering a few snowflakes as they made their way down to the wagon. Ann turned and looked back over her shoulder at the little log church and saw the shutters swaying in the wind, creeking on their hinges. She remembered the dream of sometime ago and said out loud, "It did come true! It did!"

John looked over at her and said, "It sure did, Ann Shepherd. I don't b'lieve were dreamin', are we?"

The wind picked up even more as they made their way home. The air turned cold and clouds swirled down the east side of Wildcat Spur. At first there were only a few tiny snowflakes, but before they were halfway home, the flakes looked as large as goose feathers. Vapor rose from the little mule's rump as he trotted along. Jacob slid the quilts from beneath Sarah and himself, wrapped one around Sarah and handed the other one to Ann. "Here, this'll keep ye warm," he said.

"They say if March comes in like a lamb it'll go out like a lion," P D said, as he helped Ann spread the quilt over herself. "Seems like I

23

can hear that lion roarin' now."

When they arrived at the Biddy house they were surprised to see a pot of coffee boiling over the fire at the fireplace and a pone of ginger bread, cut into wedges and arranged on a plate at the table. "Thought you'ens might be cold when you got back so I made a little coffee and cooked some gingerbread in the Dutch oven," Hassie said, as she sat warming her feet at the fire.

"My God in heaven, is this a dream?" Ann said, standing stiff as a poker, as if in a state of deep shock.

"Looks real to me," John said, reaching over and picking up a wedge of gingerbread.

"You done real good, Hassie. How'd you know I'd been cravin' gingerbread?" P D said, as he poured himself a cup of coffee, picked up a piece of gingerbread and sat down beside her at the fireplace.

After warming themselves by the fire and feasting on coffee and gingerbread, John, Ann, and John's parents said their goodbyes, went out and climbed up onto the wagon and set out for home.

A definite change had come over Hassie and P D savored the moment. "It'ud be fine with me if things would just stay this way," he thought to himself.

ⵔⵔⵔⵔⵔⵔⵔⵔⵔⵔⵔⵔⵔⵔ

By the first week of April, the sap was up and John, P D, and Ann were up on the ridge, felling the poplar trees with the crosscut saw and peeling away the bark. Late that afternoon, when they had finished cutting down what they thought would be enough trees to build the cabin, John said, "By the time we get our stuff planted, these logs'll be dry enough to start the cabin."

"The sun'll dry 'em out perty fast, Son, but we'll have to get our crops in afore we start buildin'. We can't do 'thout our crops. We'd get a mite hongry, I 'spect," P D said.

The next several days were spent doing just that. John broke up the ground for P D and laid off the rows and didn't charge him anything, because he knew his father-in-law would be helping him build his cabin. After they finished planting P D's corn and potatoes, they all went down to Jacob Shepherd's place and did the same for him.

"Well, Son, I s'pose you're about ready to start work on your cabin, ain't you?" P D asked John, as he scraped the dirt from the soles of his shoes on the blade of his hoe.

"We've got our crops in, so I guess it's about time we got

started. How about Monday? Me and Ann got married on a Monday, that seems like a good day to start, but I do hope we won't get snow this time" John said, patting Ann on her back, saturated with sweat from working in the field.

"I don't beleive it'll snow, hot as it is," Ann said, standing in the shade, moping the sweat from her brow on the sleeve of her black dress.

So on the twenty-first of April of 1862, they were all up on the ridge, rounding up the corner stones for the cabin. John's father, Jacob, came along too, even though he was getting well along in years and was suffering from rheumatism. "I can't do much, but I couldn't go without seein' this here cabin built," He said, as he wrestled another flat rock up onto the corner pillar.

"Well, Papa Shepherd, you're gonna get to see just that," Ann said, helping him level the corner stone by placing small pebbles under the edge.

After laying the pillars, they spent the remainder of the day hewing locust logs for the floor beams, cutting them to length, fitting and pinning them together with locust pins. "I guess these thangs'll be here when the cows come home," John said, as he drove home the last locust pin and stood back to admire his handiwork. "Yeah, that looks mighty good," he said.

The following day, P D and Ann cut down a large red oak and sawed in into shingle lengths while John went down to the sawmill to pick up some lumber to frame in the doors and windows, and to pick up some one inch lumber for the flooring. It was half passed three when he got back with the load of lumber. The mule was hot and sweaty from the long trip. "Well, I finally got back. I had to stop several time to let Jude rest," he said.

"I'm ready to start splittin' shingles," P D said, as he adjusted the froe on a chunk of oak and struck it with the wooden maul. As he split the shingles, Ann stacked them in a sunny spot near the cabin to dry.

After letting the mule drink his fill of water from the creek and letting him cool off a bit, John began snaking the poplar logs up the hill to the building site

Jacob's rheumatism was acting up, so he sat in the shade a big part of the day, watching the others worked.

Along about five, John allowed as though they had better be heading home, because there was milking to be done before dark.

P D, nor Ann, nor Jacob, had any objections, for they were just about frazzled.

"We'll get started layin' them logs tomar," P D said, as he leaned

25

back against the side boards of the wagon. Nobody responded to his comment because they were just too tired and it felt good just to sit for a spell, even though the ride jostled them about a bit.

Hassie had already milked the cow and goats and supper was on the table when P D got home. He couldn't get over how much she'd changed, but he wasn't about to complain. "Sumpum smells mighty good," He said, as he stood washing his hands.

"Well, P D, I figgered you'd be hongry, so I went ahead and cooked up a little stuff."

"It's mighty good, Hassie," he said, when he sat down and began to eat.

ᙢᙢᙢᙢᙢᙢᙢᙢᙢᙢᙢᙢᙢᙢ

John and Ann were staying with John's parents while the cabin was being built. Ann was helpful to her mother-in-law, who was now beginning to feel her age. She tired quickly while performing some of the tasks that needed to be done around the house.

Aunt Isa had taught Ann all there was to know about housework, so she fell right in and started helping her mother-in-law as if she had always been there. When there was washing to do or churning or anything else, she was ready to do it. And unlike Hassie, Mother Sarah appreciated her help and told her so. "This is good, so why'd Hassie say that nothin' good would come of our marriage?" Ann asked herself.

It was hot and humid as darkness decended upon the Shepherd household. The windows were raised and the shutters thrown back, and so were the covers, as John and Ann lay watching the lightning bugs outside their bedroom window. Taillights flashed as they climbed into the night sky, looking like miniature shooting stars. John and Ann soon fell asleep and slept soundly until Mama Sarah called them to breakfast the next morning.

It was such a good feeling to Ann to have someone else cook breakfast for her, for she had always had to do the cooking after Aunt Isa passed away. She knew Mama Sarah didn't feel like doing it, but there never was, to her knowledge, anything physicially wrong with her step-mother and yet she saddled Ann with all the housework.

"Why didn't you call me, Mama Sarah? You know I would have been glad to help you."

"I know, Child, but I knowed you'as tired from all 'at work at the cabin."

26

"Well, Mama Sarah, I've been tired before, but I still had to do the cookin'."

"It's rainin' out there, Son," Jacob said, as he came inside from milking the cow. "Looks like it's set in fer a spell. Won't be no buildin' done today,"

"I guess we can use a little rest. We've worked mighty hard these last few days," John said, as he sat leaning back against the wall in the straight chair there at the kitchen table, sipping on his coffee.

After breakfast, John and his father retired to the porch to watch the rain and to talk about what they'd heard about the war. "While I was over at the saw mill yesterday, a feller said he'd heard they were gonna start draftin' men to fight in the war. I don't want to go, but if they draft me, I guess I'm duty bound to go," John said to his father.

"Yeah, Son, you're duty bound if you're called." Jacob said, as he knocked the tobacco ashes from his pipe on the porch post and refilled it.

"I know, Pa, but I don't aim to go till I get my cabin built. Ann's got to have a place to live. They owe us that much, don't they?"

"What's that you say, John?" Ann asked, as she stepped out onto the porch.

"Oh, they're talkin' about draftin' men to fight the war. I guess they can't get enough volunteers," John said.

"Don't tell me that we've just got married and started our cabin and you're gonna have to go off and fight in that war!"

"They've not found me yet, Ann," John said, as he pulled her onto his lap and kissed her. "They'll have to come and get me. But if they come, I'm duty bound to go."

The thoughts of John going away to fight in the war troubled Ann greatly, for she had just found happiness, but now, was it to be taken away? Could it be that Hassie was right after all? "Maybe they won't find you," she said.

"They prob'ly will, Ann, but I'll finish the cabin before I go."

It rained off and on most of the day, but between shorers, John and Jacob walked out to the field to see if the corn was coming up.

After an earlier than usual supper, they all went to bed, hoping that tomorrow would be clear, allowing them to get back up to the ridge, which John was now calling "Ann Ridge", to continue work on the cabin.

The following morning was clear and way before sunup they were in the wagon, heading up to Ann Ridge. Jude, the mule, seemed anxious to get on up the road. After heading that way several times, he knew just where they were going. He knew that when he got to the ridge, John would unhitch him from the wagon and stake him out, down near the creek and feed him, and for some reason or other he liked that.

John stopped the wagon in front of the Biddy house and P D rushed out, carrying his lunch, tied up in a piece of homespun fabric. He climbed onto the wagon and motioned for John to go, so on up the road they went.

After arriving at Ann Ridge and after the mule was staked out, they busied themselves with sawing and fitting the logs for the first course of the walls. "How wide a openin' do ye want me to leave for the front door, John," P D asked.

"Let's make it about three feet, Mister Biddy. I want to be able to get things through the door without havin' to tear the house down. Don't you think that's the way to go?"

"Might save a heap'a trouble if you get home late at night and need to get sompum big into the house in a hurry," P D said, grinning and pursing his lips sideways.

"You're mighty right, Mister Biddy, but I hadn't thought of it quite that way."

When they finished laying the first course of logs, leaving the openings for the front and back doors, John sawed the pieces for the door frames and nailed them together. He nailed the bottom of the frames to the end of the logs at the openings as Ann held them in place.

Ann helped Jacob bring in the flooring as John nailed it to the locust floor beams in the main part of the house.

"I'll hew out some more floor beams for the porch, John. I s'pose you do want a porch, don't you?" P D said, as he walked out toward the pile of locust logs.

"Wouldn't think of havin' a cabin with no porch, Mister Biddy."

Work on the cabin went well with only a few accidents. P D sliced into the side of his brogan with the broad ax while hewing one of the floor beams, but he didn't cut his foot. Jacob let a log get on his finger and had to wear a bandage for several days.

Ann ripped a button from her dress while helping wrestle a log high up onto the cabin wall. She broke a short willow twig and worked it through the fabric in the front of her dress in place of the button. John picked up the button from the ground and strung it on a piece of twine and looped it around his neck for a good luck charm.

John? Well, John got through the whole ordeal unhurt, except for a few scratches on his hands from handling the rough logs, but as the job progressed, his hands became tough as the leather backband on Jude's harness.

An opening was left for the fireplace and as soon as the wall logs were laid, Joseph began building the fireplace and chimney, daubing it with red mud taken from the bank above the creek. John and P D supplied him with rocks while Ann mixed the red mud.

They found two flat rocks down near the creek for the hearth and mantle and hauled them up to the cabin on the wagon.

It took a few days to build the chimney but they were lucky to have several days without rain and they hoped the rain would hold off until the red mud daubing had a chance to dry.

A couple of days before the chimney was finished, John and Ann made a trip to the saw mill to pick up lumber for the sheathing. They stopped in at Bent Oak Trading Post on their way back, to purchase nails for the sheathing and shingles. They bought sashes for two windows and sixteen pieces of glass for the panes and a can of putty for installing the panes.

While Joseph worked on the fireplace and chimney, P D and John installed the ceiling beams. They sawed and notched the rafters and had about half of them in place by the time Joseph finished with the chimney.

On Monday morning of the second week of June, the chimney was finished and John was nailing down the last oak shingle onto the roof. As he climbed down the homemade ladder he said, "When we get them winders and the doors in we'll be through."

"Sure is a fine house, John," Ann said, pleased with the good job they had done.

It was straight up twelve, on Friday, the thirteenth day of June, 1862. The windows were installed and John was driving home the last screw on the bottom hinge of the front door.

"It's our lucky day, John. No matter if it is Friday the thirteenth, it's still our lucky day."

"That's azactly the way I see it, Ann Shepherd, azactly how I see It," John said, as they locked arms and danced around the cabin three times, stopping as they passed each tiny window to view themselves in the mirrored reflection.

"You've got enough lumber left over to build a kitchen table and a couple'a benches, John. If you'd like to, we'll make them thangs afore we leave here today, and a bedstead too," P D said, sorting through the left over lumber.

"We'll do it, Mister Biddy, we sure will," John said.

So after sitting on the edge of the porch for a few minutes, eating their lunch, they got up and got to work, and by the time the sun was touching the treetops on Wildcat Spur, they had finished building the table, the two benches and the bedstead and were loading their tools in the back of the wagon, preparing to go home.

"We'll go over to Bent Oak tomor'n get us some grub, Ann. Then we'll be ready to move in," John said, as they bounced along the rough road, sitting side by side in the wagon, heading down toward Deep Gap.

"I guess we'll need to shred some shucks for a bed tick. Be kinda hard sleepin' on them planks, don't you think so, John?"

"You think 'uv everthang, Ann Shepherd, don't ye?"

"I do try to keep at least one eye open," Ann said, half smiling as she clung to John's arm.

When they stopped in front of the Biddy house, P D stepped down from the back of the wagon, gathered up his tools and said, "If you'ns need me fer anything else, ya know where to find me."

"We thank you, Mister Biddy. Don't b'lieve we could a done it without you."

"You got a good man there, Ann Shepherd. I'd keep him if I'as you," P D said, as he walked up toward the house, looking back over his shoulder, grinning.

"Bye, Papa," Ann said, as they headed on down the road toward the Shepherd place.

Jacob hadn't said a single word the whole way, for he wasn't feeling well and he knew that tomorrow his son and daughter-in-law would be moving away and that made him feel a little sad.

As P D put his tools away he glanced at the chimney and saw no smoke coming out. When he went inside, he found Hassie, piled up on the bed, asleep. There was nothing on the table to eat and she had made no effort to start anything.

"Thought you'd have some supper started, Woman. I'm just a mite hungry."

"Well, Mister Biddy, if you want sompum, I guess you can cook it. I didn't feel like cookin' nothin' noway," Hassie said, as she stirred from sleep, rolled over and sat up on the edge of the bed.

"Well, I guess I can, Hassie. I've done it before, you know. I'm just sorry ye don't feel good," he said, changing his tone of voice from one of hostility to a gentler mode. "I'll have to milk first," he said.

As he sat milking the goat, the thought came to mind, "I'll give this here goat to Ann. She don't have no milk cow and asides, she likes goat milk, anyway."

At the supper table, P D began to think that maybe there really could be something physically or mentally wrong with Hassie, "How could a person be so hateful and lazy if she wasn't touched in some way?" he thought to himself, as he watched her eating as if she hadn't had a bite all day.

"Hassie, do you hurt som'ers? Is that the reason you don't feel like cookin' er doin' the house work? Do you feel strange in the head er sompum like that?"

"Can't say as I do, Mister Biddy," she said, before cramming another bite of bread into her mouth. "Where's Annie Bell? Thought she'd be back by now. They's work to be done."

"Ann's married, Hassie. She's moved away. She won't be back no more. You'll have to think a doin' the work around here yeself."

"I ain't doin' no house work, 'cause I ain't able. Can't you understand nothin', P D?"

Choosing not to have an argument, P D finished his supper in silence and after washing the dishes, he went out and sat on the porch to ponder the predicament posed by the precarious partnership he had with his wife.

"Maybe I was in too big of a hurry. After all, she's done very little work around the house since we've been married, but she's made Ann's life a pure hell. That girl of mine won't never want to come back, long's Hassie's here and maybe not even after that," P D thought to himself, as he sat gazing at the mountains in the distance. Then suddenly the thought came to him, "Maybe Owatta'll know of sompum I can do for her. I'll have to pay her a visit!"

After breakfast the next morning, he decided to go up to the Indian village to seek Owatta's help, thinking maybe she'd be able to come up with a cure for Hassie. "It's worth a try," he thought to himself, as he hurried up the path that lcd to the village.

As he approached the village, he saw two young braves chipping flint, fashioning points for their arrows. An old lady sat on a mat in front of her hut, weaving a basket from thin willow branches. Owatta was sitting nearby, grinding herbs into a powder, using a mortar and pestle, fashioned from local stone.

"Why you come to In'dan village, P D Biddy?" she asked, lifting the pestle from the mortar and adding more herbs.

"I need ye help, Lady Owatta."

"And what that be, P D Biddy?"

"I thought maybe you could tell me what to do for my wife. They's sompum wrong with'er'n I don't know what to do."

"May be she got mean spirit, but Owatta think me know way to make bad spirit go away. Owatta come down to your house when sun rests on top of mountain," she said, as she sat in silence for a moment with a fixed look locked on the crest of Wildcat Spurr.

31

As the shade from the trees, west of P D's house lengthened, Owatta was on her way down from the village, her deer skin bag swung over her left shoulder. And by the time the sun was resting on the mountain she stepped up onto the porch.

"Owatta, what brings you down this way, this late'n the day?" Hassie asked, in a somewhat arrogant tone of voice, as she lay stretched out on the bed.

"P D say you not well. Owatta bring medcin. It make you Oooo Kaaay," she said, placing her deer skin bag of herbs on the table.

She took a cup from the shelf and dipped some milk from the churn which by now was about half clabbered, sat it on the table and added some sort of powder from a tiny leather pouch and stirred it with the quill of a turkey feather. She handed it to Hassie and said, "You drink this, Hassie Biddy. By the time sun show face tomorrow, you will be all better."

Hassie hesitated at first, but after some prodding from Owatta, she drank it all down without stopping, curled her upper lip like a billy goat picking leaves from a thorn bush and let out with a belch that could be heard half way down to the barnshed. "My God Amighty, what was that awful stuff, Owatta? I never drunk such foul tastin' stuff in my whole life."

"You sleep now, Hassie Biddy. When sun show face again, you be different woman."

During the night, Hassie talked and rolled and kicked so in her sleep that P D finally got up, made a pallet on the floor and slept there the rest of the night, that is if you could call it sleep, for at times Hassie would scream out as if she was being tortured by the devil. Other times she moved her legs as if fleeing from some gastly beast. She would open her eyes at times and roll them from side to side with an expression on her face that would have frightened the devil himself. This went on throughout the night until the wee hours of the morning. Then all of a sudden, the kicking and rolling and screaming stopped and she fell into a deep sleep.

The sun was just beginning to show its face through the trees to the east the next morning when P D felt a light tapping on his shoulder. He opened one eye and looked up. Low and behold, there was Hassie, kneeling on the floor beside him. She was tapping him on the shoulder and asking him what he would like for breakfast. "Why, anythang, Hassie, just anythang'll do!"

"Why don't you get off a that floor and get in the bed. You can't rest layin' on that hard floor. Breakfast'll be ready in a jiffy."

P D lay stone still, braced on one elbow, waiting for his brain to

32

start functioning. It was such a shock, having Hassie ask him what he'd like to have for breakfast, much less to offer to cook it for him.

He crawled up from the floor scratching his head, shuffled over and sat down on the edge of the bed and began putting his shoes on. He was in total wonderment about that powerful herb Owatta poured from her little leather pouch.

While they were eating breakfast, Hassie kept looking at P D as if she was seeing him for the very first time. Her eyes focused on things within the cabin like a baby opening its eyes for the first time to view a strange and intriguing new world. "P D, what happened to me last night? I had the awfullest dreams. Seemed like the devil was about to get me, but I managed to stay just one step ahead uv 'im. I kept runnin' and runnin' and runnin', but ever' way I turned, he'd be there."

"You did do a powerful lot'a moanin' and groanin' and movin' ye legs and you'd scream out ever' now'n 'en. Got so bad I finally made a pallet on the floor so I could get some sleep."

"Well, P D, I don't aim on goin' through that no more. Was Owatta here last night er did I dream that, too?"

"She'as here sure'nuf. She come down to see'f she could do anythang fer ye. You know you've been actin' awful strange lately. She mixed up some herbs in some milk and when you drunk it, you commenced to moanin' and groanin' and movin' ye legs like the booger man was about to get ye."

"Must'a been mighty powerful stuff. 'cause I feel like a different woman. Seems like the clouds just f-l-o-a-t-e-d away and the sun come out," Hassie said, raising her arms toward the ceiling and swimging them in a slow, wide arch.

"I'm glad to have you back, Hassie. You don't know how glad."

◻◻◻◻◻◻◻◻◻◻◻◻◻

John and Ann were up early Saturday morning, shucking corn and shreading the shucks into tiny strips and stuffing them into the bed tick. "This'll be a heap softer'n sleepin' on them hard boards, John, don't you think so?"

"It'll be softer'n a feather bed, Ann Shepherd. 'Specially with you sleepin' with me."

When they finished filling the bed tick, they said goodbye to Jacob and Sarah, promised to be back in a few days, and were on their way to Bent Oak to buy some grub so they could move into their brand new cabin and start living.

As they approached the Biddy house they saw P D out near the barn with the nanny goat tethered to a short rope and when he saw them coming up the road he hurried out to the wagon. "How's my favorite girl and son-in-law doin'? He asked, as John pulled the mule to a stop.

"Fine, Papa," Ann said, grinning from ear to ear.

"We couldn't be better, Mister Biddy. We're on our way to the tradin' post to buy some grub so we can move into that fine cabin you helped us build.

"Well, I've got this here nanny goat I'd like to give to somebody. I don't recken I'll be needin' it since my girl got married and left home. I don't recken you'd have no use fer a good nanny goat would ye, John? P D asked, grinning and pursing his mouth sideways.

"My wife loves goat milk. I 'spect we could take it off your hands, that is if she'll do the milking," John said, turning aside to give Ann a quick glance.

"We'd be glad to take it off a your hands, Mister Biddy," Ann said, teasingly. "They ain't no milk like goat's milk."

John hopped down, picked up the goat and lifted her up onto the wagon and tied the short rope to the backrest of the wagon seat. "We're much obliged to you, Mister Biddy. This here little nanny goat's the very thing we need."

"Figered it would be, Son. Yeah, I figered it would be, uh huh."

John climbed back onto the wagon and was about to tell the mule to get up when Hassie opened the door and hurried outside, carrying a biscuit in each hand, loaded with fried country ham. "Here, young'uns, this'll keep you'ns from gettin' too hongry till you can get dinner."

"Sure will, Hassie Biddie. I'm hungry now." John said.

"Ann just sat there like a statue for what seemed like three full minutes until she was finally able to say, "Thank you, Mother Hassie. Thank you so much!"

"You're quite welcome, I'm sure," Hassie said, and back into the house she went.

"What's come over her, Papa?"

"She's a brand new woman, Ann. A Brand new woman."

John and Ann were well on their way to Green River Trading Post when Ann looked back to see how the goat was doing and noticed she had gnawed a hole in the bed tick and was loading up on the shucks. "Leave them shucks alone, Precious. They ain't fer eatin', that's our bed," she said, as she drew the rope up shorter and retied it to the backrest.

"What'll ya take fer that little milk goat, John?" Uncle Henry Shepherd asked, as John pulled to a stop in front of the store.

34

Tain't fer sale, Uncle Henry. B'longs to my wife, Ann."

"Ye wife, ye say? Didn't know you had one," Uncle Henry said, as he staggered over to have a closer look at Ann.

"Yeah, we been married about two months now. Just come over here to get some grub so we can move into our new cabin.

"Well, she's a mighty perty thang. Where'd ye find her?"

"She's P D Biddy's girl."

"I know P D Biddy. Knowed him fer years," Uncle Henry said, as he took Ann by the hand and shook it so hard that she began to fear that he might dislodge her arm from her shoulder.

"Howdy do, Uncle Henry. I'm pleased to meet you," Ann said, as she struggled to free herself from the vise-grip of Henry's huge calloused hand.

"You don't know your own strength, Uncle Henry. Thought you'as gonna tear my hand clean off my wrist."

"Fagive me, Small Thang. I guess I'm not used to shakin' hands with the likes a'you," he said, loosening his grip on her hand and taking a couple of quick steps back, looking at his hand as if it had been bitten by a copperhead.

The smell of whiskey was on his breath and you could tell that he wasn't at his best behavior. He had come to Bent Oak to meet up with his budies, ready for a rip roarin' time.

"Well, we'll be seein' ye, Uncle Henry. We'd better get our grub and head on back to the cabin," John said, as he helped Ann down from the wagon.

"I'll come over'n see you'ns in a few days when ye get straightened out, John."

"Any time, Uncle Henry. Just any time."

# Chapter

# 4

## Honeymoon Cut Short

Before John and Ann could buy their grub and head back to their cabin, a stranger rode up on horseback, wearing a grey uniform and cap and heavy boots. "I'm a represenative of the Confederacy. I'm rounding up men to go fight in this war. Anybody know where I can find John Shepherd?" he asked, as he threw his right leg over the saddle horn and slid down from his mount.

"I 'spose that's me," John said, as he walked over to take a look at the list of men on the document the mustering officer was holding in his hand.

"We'll gather at the Rutherford County Court House on the eleventh of July. Be sure to be there by twelve noon. From there we'll be going up north for training. Get yourself a good pair of shoes because we'll be walking most of the way and believe me, it's a long trip. If you can get ahold of a gun, bring that along too. The Confederacy is running short of guns."

After he finished with his instructions, he mounted his horse and rode away, leaving John and Ann stunned, staring at each other, suddenly realizing they had only a few days together before John would have to go away to fight in a war that he wasn't too keen about in the first place.

"Let's get that grub and get home, Ann. We've got about three weeks. Let's make the best uvit while we've got it."

"Three weeks ain't no time at all, John. Ain't no time at all."

"I know, Ann, but It's all we've got. Let's make the best uvit."

John spent those precious days planting a garden and building a little barn for Ann, with P D and Jacob helping. She'd need a place to keep the goat and a place to milk, when summer turned to fall and fall turned to winter. "It's not much size, Ann Shepherd, but it'll have to do till I get back," he said to her, as she stood watching him nail down the last shingle on the roof.

"It's a fine barn, John Shepherd. Don't need nothin' bigger."

37

"I'll help you build a rail fence around your garden spot, Ann. It'll help to keep the wild animals out," P D said, as he climbed up onto the wagon, preparing to go home.

"You've been so kind to us, Papa, Ann said, waving to him as he went out of sight around the bend.

ⵔⵔⵔⵔⵔⵔⵔⵔⵔⵔⵔ

It was way before daylight on the eleventh of July of 1862. Ann was up preparing breakfast for John. She stuffed ham and hoecakes into his knapsack so he would have something to eat on the way to Rutherfordton.

John got up when she did, threaded his arms through the sleeves of his shirt, put his pants on, sat down to put on a pair of wool socks and the brand-new brogans he bought over at Bent Oak Trading Post the other day. As he stood up he noticed the black button, torn from Ann's dress on the day they were laying logs on their tiny shanty. It was hanging on the bedpost, suspended on a piece of twine. He removed it from the bedpost and strung it around his neck. "This'll bring me luck," he said to himself.

As he sat down at the table he said, "I 'spect this'll be the last time we'll be eatin' together fer a while, Ann Shepherd. Be a while afore this war's over."

Ann looked at him, but didn't say a word. She was fighting back tears and choking on the lump in her throat.

As soon as John finished eating, he picked up his jacket and the knapsack and swung them over his shoulder. Ann stood at the door as he picked up his muzzle loader and placed his hat on his head. He cradled Ann in his left arm for what seemed like only a few seconds, kissed her goodbye, and as he walked out of sight into the darkness he said, "Hope it won't take long."

"Bye, John Shepherd. I'll be waitin' for you. You hear me?" Ann said, as she stood in the doorway, staring into the darkness, and he was gone, just like that.

Precious, the nanny goat, let out with a blate as Ann came back inside, closed the door, walked over and sat down on the rough plank bench at the table to cry. When she looked up, she noticed that John had left a piece of hoecake on his plate. She promptly picked it up and placed it into her mouth and ate it. "I sure hope he don't get hungry."

ⵔⵔⵔⵔⵔⵔⵔⵔⵔⵔⵔ

Times were difficult for the people of the Confederate States as well as for those of the Union.

Blacks were fleeing north to escape slavery by way of the "underground railroad". With the aid of the abolitionists, they hoped to gain their freedom. Ann couldn't understand it, "After all," she said, "we were all borned into this world and we all should have the right to be here and to do what we please, long's we obey the law, and what good is a law if it ain't for everbody?"

She had been married for little more than three months, but she missed John as much as if they had been together a lifetime. "I don't know what I'll do without him. He's been gone less'n a week and already it seems like a year. Have to get ahold of myself, for he'll prob'ly be gone a long time," she told herself, as she sat milking Prcious, the goat.

Later on in the morning, she went out to hoe the little garden. She had two short rows of Irish potatoes, a few hills of cabbage and a row of corn. A few stalks of rhubarb stood in the corner of the garden and a row of beans were growing along the lower side. It pleased her to know she would have fresh vegetables right outside her kitchen door.

Thoughts had been creeping into her head lately, like: "Why do all my closest friends have to die? First, there was Mama, died when I was born. Then Aunt Isa. She was like a mama to me. Who'll be next? Will it be John? We sure ain't had a chance to get to know each other, much less anything else. He said he hoped he wouldn't be gone too long, but one day's too long."

She was talking to herself as she pulled the ritch dirt up onto the potato hills. "Can't let myself think of things like that. I'll just have to believe he'll come back to me in one piece. I must keep my hopes up and never allow myself to doubt"

She had hardly finished hoeing the garden and was hanging up the hoe in a gap between the logs of the little barn when she heard a wagon coming up the road. It sounded like Jacob Shepherd's wagon, but she knew that Jacob was getting too old to handle the mule and wagon any more. When it came in sight she saw that it was P D in Jacob's wagon and Hassie was sitting right there beside him. "What are you doin' in Jacob's wagon, Papa?" she asked, as the wagon came to a stop there in front of the barn.

"He told me if I'd do his haulin' fer him I could have his mule and wagon. It sounded like a perty good trade to me, so I decided to take him up on it."

"Good morning, Anna Bell Shepherd. How'er you this fine day?" Hassie asked, as she jumped down from the wagon, walked over and put her arms around Ann.

Ann found her actions totally unbelievable, but she managed to say, "I'm Just fine, Mother Hassie, but I think I miss John like a cat misses her kittens."

"Well, we've come up to keep ye comp'ny fer a little while. Thought you might be lonesome. We brought some chicken, roasted over the fire and a hoecake. Thought you'd like that." Hassie said, as she let go of Ann and reached into the wagon to retrieve the chicken and bread.

"You didn't have to do that, Mother Hassie, but it does sound good. You and Papa come on in. It's about dinner time. Let's try some a that good chicken."

"How's my very favorite girl?" P D asked, patting her shoulder, saturated with sweat from hoeing in the garden.

"Just fine, Papa, 'cept I do miss John awful bad. Seems like he's been gone a year and it ain't been a week yet."

"You'll have to come down to the house'n spend some time with us. It'll help ye get ye mind off that man of yourn," her father said, as they walked up the porch steps.

"May take you up on that Papa, but it'll be just fer a day, 'cause I have to take care of Precious, you know."

"Speakin' of Precious, I've got the pertiest little billy goat you ever set ye eyes on. I'd like to give him to ye, that is if you'd like to have it. It's got a white blaze on its forehead. It looks just like a streak of lightnin'."

"I'd love to have it, Papa, he'd keep Precious comp'ny. Maybe Precious'll have some little'uns. They'd be fun to have."

Ann washed the dirt and sweat from her arms and face, there at the bench on the porch and dried them on the towel that was hanging beside the door. She scuffed the dirt from the soles of her shoes and they all walked inside to feast on that roasted chicken and hoecake.

It seemed as though Hassie just couldn't be kind enough to Ann. She was a changed woman for sure. Ann remembered very well how hostile she had been to her all those years and she thought to herself, "Just don't seem like the same woman."

When they had finished eating, Hassie said, "I'll wash the dishes, Ann Shepherd. You're all tired from hoein' that garden."

"I can help you, Mother Hassie. I'm not too tired."

"No! Sit'n talk to your papa. You ain't seen him for a few days."

It was hard to believe that this woman was Hassie, but there was no denying it. So she took her at her word and went outside and sat on the edge of the porch to visit with her father.

40

"Papa, I can't get over how she's changed." Ann said.

"Whatever Owatta give her must'a been powerful stuff. I don't know what it was, but she's a changed woman," P D said, staring into space with an expression of amazement on his face.

"She never put her arm around me before, and to bring chicken and bread for me to eat and to wash the dishes to boot, well, it just turns my brain inside out," Ann whispered.

"It's a wonderment, Ann, nothin' but a wonderment."

"Well, Papa, I'll pay Owatta a visit in a few days and see if I can find out what kind of herb it was. She's told me a lot about her herbs. Maybe she'll tell me about that powerful stuff, too."

"Maybe so, Ann. Maybe so."

P D pointed toward a giant chestnut tree, lying on the ground beyond the barn, uprooted by high winds last March, and said, "If you'll help me saw that tree into rail lengths, Ann, I'll split it up and build you that fence I promised ye,"

"I believe I can do that, Papa. I'm used to that crosscut saw. Lord knows, I've sawed with it enough times to be used to it."

"I'll bring that saw up here tomar and we'll see what we can do. We'll never know till we try."

Early the next morning, Ann looked out the little window and saw her father and step-mother coming up the road in the wagon. Hassie had come along to cook dinner, knowing that Ann would be tired from helping her father pull that heavy crosscut saw through the large chestnut log. "Mornin', Ann Shepherd, hope you don't mind me tagin' along. Thought I could cook dinner while you helped your Papa."

"Land sakes, no, I don't mind a bit. Just glad you wanted to come along."

Sawdust poured from the drag teeth of the crosscut saw as P D and Ann pulled the saw back and forth, cutting deeper into the chestnut log with each stroke. Sweat was running freely as well, for the tree had taken all the surrounding smaller trees with it when it fell and the sun was beginning to bear down. When the saw had reached the halfway point, P D said, "Let's stop a minuet so I can make a couple of gluts. We don't want this saw pinchin' on us, for we'd never get it out. This tree's too heavy to lift."

He picked up his ax and chopped down a small dogwood tree and hewed out two wodden wedges and pounded them into the saw cut at the top of the log. "That orta do it, he said, as he went down on one knee and they began sawing again.

"That... That'll... That'll do it, Papa, Ann said, catching her

41

breath between each stroke of the saw.

Along about ten, Hassie came out onto the porch and called to them and asked them if they wanted to stop for a bite to eat. "The biscuits are done and there's pork belly's in the fryin' pan."

"Sounds good, Hassie," P D said, working his way into a standing position.

"Yeah, Mother Hassie, sounds good to me, too," Ann said, jerking her hands free of the saw handle as if it was too hot to hold.

They left the saw deep into the log, knowing full well it would be in the very same spot when they returned after the break.

"Well, Ann I guess if we ever get that there tree sawed up, we'll have to do it ourselves. Ain't nobody else gonna do fer us," P D said, as they returned from their break and took their positions on either side of the tree trunk.

When Ann's hands came in contact with the metal tip of the saw handle she found that it was too hot to hold. "That thing's hot enough to fry fatback," she said, quickly sliding her hand down to the wooden portion of the handle.

"Get's a little hot in the sunshine, don't it, Girl?" P D said.

By the time the sun was straight overhead, they had finished sawing the chestnut tree into rail lengths. "Now comes the fun part, Ann. I hope it splits as good as the one I done a while back. Looks like the grain runs perty straight. Well, we'll see about it ader dinner."

After dinner P D began the process of splitting the chestnut logs and his hopes were realized. All he had to do was to hack a groove in the end of the log and as soon as he started pounding the wedge into the groove, the log began to open up. "This is a good'un, Ann Shepherd. It's a good'un," he said.

The sun was resting on top of Wildcat Spurr when P D pulled the last two rails apart. "Looks like that does it," he said, speaking to Hassie, who had come out to check on their progress.

"Looks that way, P D. Yeah, sure does."

Figuring they had done about as much as they could do in one day, P D told Ann that he would be back tomorrow to put up the fence. "That's a big tree, right there, Ann Shepherd. They'll be enough in that one tree to build your little fence, I'm perty sure."

Ann was ready and waiting as P D and Hassie pulled into the yard early the next morning. She had already milked the goat, spread up the bed and straightened up the kitchen.

They got right to work and by mid-morning a large portion of the little fence had been laid. P D decided to build it about head-high, in hopes it would prevent the deer and the goats from getting into her

42

garden. He fashioned a small gate of chestnut slats and hinged it to the gate post. He sharpened the tips of the slats as a deterrent to anything trying to crawl over or under the gate.

"That ort'a keep all them critters out, don't you think? P D said, speaking to Ann.

"I belive so, Papa, if anything will. I mean everything but my cat and she'll go just about anywhere she decides to go," Ann said, laughing. For at that very moment the cat was lying streatched out on the very top rail near the gate.

"I guess you're right, Ann Shepherd. You're certainly right this time," P D said, as he looked up and saw the cat resting on the top rail just above his head.

"Supper's on the table," Hassie called from the kitchen door, as P D and Ann sat on the edge of the porch admiring the little rail fence they had just finished building.

"Sounds mighty good, Hassie. You recken you could come out here'n help us up onto the porch?" P D asked, as he and Ann struggled to their feet.

Later that evening after all the chores were done, Ann sat on the porch as darkness settled down upon Deep Gap. She was happy about the little rail fence she and her father had built and about the kindness Hassie was beginning to show her, but the sadness of John being away in the war crowded out all the pleasant things that were happening to her. She missed him every minute and if she didn't stay busy all her waking hours, she found herself wiping tears from her eyes on the sleeve of her dress. "Wonder where he is tonight. Hope he's alright," she whispered to herself, as she went inside and made ready for bed, ready again to cry herself to sleep as she had done every night since he had been gone.

ꉙꉙꉙꉙꉙꉙꉙꉙꉙꉙꉙꉙ

John was spending the night beneath a giant oak tree, somewhere up in the hills of Virginia. The new brogans had worn large blisters on the bottoms of his feet and he had punctured them with the little ivory handled pocketknife his father had given him when he was a boy. It was the very knife that his great-grandfather, Isaac Shepherd, had brought with him from Ireland, when he came to America with his parents in the summer of 1760. Isaac had carried the knife with him when he fought in the Revolutionary War and always considered it to be a good luck piece, so John brought it with him just in case. "I can

43

use all the luck I can get," John thought, as he closed the knife and put it back into his pocket.

John's shoulder was bruised from carrying the heavy musket and his legs cramped from so much walking. He lay back on the wool blanket, issued to him on the day they came together in Rutherfordton, and even though he was hungry, he soon fell asleep. All he had eaten today was a few berries he managed to snatch by the wayside as they struggled along.

It seemed as though he had hardly gotten to sleep when the platoon sergeant rousted him from his resting place, saying, "Up and at it boy. We've got a ways to go yet."

The boys complained about not having anything to eat since day before yesterday. "You'll get something when we get to Lynchburg," was the platoon sergeant's answer.

"We'll be starved to death by then, Sergeant," they complained.

"Hush up, boys, maybe we can find something along the way," the seargent said, as he lined them up on the road and they began their staggering march northward.

They did manage to find some food along the way, for they raided a corn field by the roadside and roasted the ears of corn on an open fire. They managed to kill a couple of rabbits which were cooked over the open fire as well. They were happy to have a taste of meat, for they hadn't had any since leaving home.

After filling their bellies, they lay back for what seemed like only a couple of minutes, when the sergeant yelled, "Up and at it boys, we've more ground to cover before nightfall."

And they were up and at it again, on their slow and steady treck northward, to face whatever fate awaited them. They were country boys and tough as pine knots that had been drying in the sun all summer. They were becoming accustomed to the forced march and were complaining less each day. After all, they knew the sooner they got to where they were going, the sooner they'd be coming back. At least, that's what they believed. So on and on they marched.

◻◻◻◻◻◻◻◻◻◻◻◻◻

Ann woke before sunup, thinking it would be a fine day to visit Papa Shepherd and Mama Sarah. She hadn't seen them in a few days and wondered how they were doing. She planned to stop for a short visit with her father and step-mother, since they lived on the same road that led to Shepherd place.

She rushed through breakfast and hurried out to the little barn to milk Precious. She strained the milk into the crock pot and carried it down to the creek and weighted it down with a flat rock to keep the wild animals from turning it over. She wrapped a chunk of goat cheese and a biscuit in a clean cloth and placed it into the deer skin bag that Owatta, the Indian lady, had given her after Aunt Isa died.

A small leather collar, connected to a short leash and made of leather shoestrings was hanging by the front door. Ann took it down and fastened the collar around her cat's neck. "Come on, Fidgety, we're goin' to see Papa Shepherd and Mama Sarah," she said to her cat, as she led her down the path to the gate.

She tied the short leather leash to the gate post and returned to the porch to get her straw broom and proceeded to sweep the path leading to the gate, walking backward so as to not leave any footprints. "I'll be able to know, by the tracks they leave, if anybody comes for a visit while I'm gone," she said, as she leaned the broom against the fence post.

She untied the leash, closed the gate and she and Fidgety began their journey to Papa Shepherd's house. An abundance of birds and rodents along the road kept Ann busy, as she tried to keep Fidgety going in the right direction. Curious could have been as good a name as Fidgety, judging from the cat's constant persuit of everything that came within her view. "Come on, Fidgety, we ain't on no huntin' trip. We're goin' to Papa Shepherd's," she said, pulling gently on the leash.

The cat meowed a couple of times as she trotted along behind Ann, snatching at her black dresstail, swishing from side to side as Ann walked briskly down the road.

As she came within sight of the Biddy house she could see her father and step-mother sitting on the front porch. They were peeling and slicing apples, preparing them for drying.

In order to dry apples, they were sliced thinly and spread on a smooth poplar board and placed outside where they could get the best sunlight. After a few days in the sun and they were thoroughly dried, they were placed in a wide mouth crock pot and stored in the attic.

"Looks like we'll have dried apple pies this winter," Ann said, as she cradled the cat in her arms and walked up the steps to the porch.

"They's fresh apple pie in the kitchen right this minute, Ann Biddy Shepherd. Come in and have a piece," Hassie said, putting her pan of apples aside and rushing over to give Ann a hug.

"Sounds good to me, Mother Hassie. I'm a mite hungry after that long walk."

"I could a brung the wagon up and hauled you down here if I'd a knowed you'as a comin', Girl," P D said, getting up to open the door for her.

"Walkin's such a comfort to me, Papa. It helps to ease my mind. I worry about John, up there in that war, you know. Maybe you could take me home after I visit with Papa Shepherd and Mama Sarah. That is if you don't mind."

"It'ud be a pure pleasure, Ann Shepherd. I'll hitch up the mule and be ready fer ye when ye come back this way."

Hassie took the apple pie from the Dutch oven, set three plates on the table, cut the pie, poured a glass of milk for each of them and they sat down and ate the whole pie. "That was so good, Mother Hassie. So good," Ann said, rubbing her stomach. "I hate to eat and go, but go I must, if get there and back home before dark."

"I'll have the wagon ready fer ye when ye come back by, Ann Shepherd", P D said.

Ann bade them good day and set out down the road toward the Shepherd place, with Fidgety still tethered to the shoestring leash, scampering along behind her.

"Well, would ye lookie there at who's comin' down that road," Jacob called out to Sarah, who was standing at the kitchen door, drying her hands on her apron.

"Why, it's our very own daughter'n-law, Ann Biddy Shepherd!" Sarah said, as she made her way down the porch steps and out the path to meet her. "It's so good to see you, Ann shepherd."

"It's just as good to see you and Papa. I've been layin' off to come and I finally got here. How have you both been?"

"Well, it's the same old two's and three's for us, I guess ye could say, but they's no use to complain. Who'd listen?" Papa Shepherd said, reaching over to tap Ann on the shoulder as she helped her Mother-in-law up the steps to the porch. "Question is, how've you been?"

"Just fine, Papa Shepherd, outside a bein' worried to death about John, way off up yonder, God only knows where, fightin' in this war."

"Well 'course you're worried, Child. You can't help but worry. We think about him day and night, ourselves. Just can't help it, no matter how hard we try."

"I see ye brung ye cat along. What's its name?" Mama Sarah said, reaching down to stroke it.

"Her name's Fidgety. I named her Fidgety 'cause she's never still. Always on the go. I thought a little walk might calm her down."

Mama Sarah gave Ann a drink of cold spring water and they all settled back in the big hand made rocking chairs there on the porch and talked until way passed time she should have been heading home.

"It's gettin' late. I'd better get goin' if I expect to get home before dark. Papa said he'd give me a ride back up to the cabin in the wagon. He'll be expectin' me," Ann said, as she untied the shoestring leash from the chair post, took Fidgety up in her arms, told the Shepherds goodbye and headed up the road.

P D was, in fact, waiting for her when she got back to the Biddy house. Hassie had packed her a snack for supper. "This'll keep you from havin' to cook when you get home, Ann Shepherd," she said, as she handed the food to her, wrapped in a clean cloth.

"I sure do thank you, Mother Hassie. You are so kind. So kind indeed. You and Papa must come up and see me."

"We'll do that, Ann Shepherd, and soon,"Hassie said, giving Ann a wave of the hand as she and her father headed up the road in the wagon, with the little mule in a trot.

Ann still found it almost impossible to believe that such a change had come over Hassie. It was like a dream and yet she had seen it with her own eyes. The evidence lay right there on her lap, the food that Hassie had prepared for her. "I'm bound to go up to the Indian village and ask Lady Owatta just what herb she used that made such a change in the way Hassie acts," she thought to herself, as she and her father rode side by side up the rough and rocky road toward Ann Ridge.

She was elated that Hassie was finally showing kindness, instead of all the hostilities she had been heaping upon her for the last several years. She was happy that her father could finally sit back and breath a sigh of relief.

They rolled to a stop in front of the shanty there on Ann Ridge and P D hopped to the ground like a young rabbit to help Ann down from the wagon. He didn't tarry long, for it would be dark when he got back home and the animals had to feed and there was milking to do.

"Bye, Papa. I'm much obliged to you for bringing me home."

"Just proud to do it fer my very favorite girl," P D said, as he clucked to the mule and was on his way back down to Deep Gap.

Ann checked the yard for footprints and found none. Well, nobody's been here," she said, as she released the collar from the cat's neck and hung the leash on the nail there beside the door.

She hurried out to milk the goat. She strained the milk into the crock and poured some into the cat's bowl and carried the crock down to the creek and exchanged it for the one that had been cooling all day. When she returned to the cabin, she sat down at the table to see what Hassie had prepared for her to eat. There was a hoecake with a piece of salt cured ham and a large piece of apple pie. She sat there at the table and ate the last bite of it before stopping, all except the bite of ham she had given Figety, that is. "I sure do wish John had some of this good ham," she said, as she sat rubbing her belly.

∞∞∞∞∞∞∞∞∞∞∞∞

As a matter of fact, John hadn't had anything to eat all day, except a few berries he had managed to snatch by the roadside as they marched north. As darkness settled down over the mountains of Virginia, he lay on his blanket, listening to his stomach, growling from the lack of food. "Tomorrow. Tomorrow, the sergeant keeps tellin' us, but when is tomorrow gonna get here?"

During his night of restless sleep, he dreamed of being back at Ann Ridge, sitting at the table and having a fine meal with his loving wife. He awoke suddenly to find that he was still there in the woods of Virginia with the sergeant yelling, "Up and at it boys, we're almost there. We'll have grub today."

"Where've I heard that before?" John mumbled to himself, as he forced himself into a standing position and began folding his blanket.

∞∞∞∞∞∞∞∞∞∞∞∞

Ann was up by daylight, determined to go up to the Indian villege to pay Owatta a visit, hoping she would identify that magic herb she had given to her step-mother. The herb that had made such a change in her attitude. "I can't wait another day!" she said to herself, as she scurried around, doing her morning chores.

Shortly after sunup she was on her way up the trail to the village, carrying the deerskin bag with a notebook and pencil inside. July had collided with August and sweat was pouring down Ann's face as she made haste up the steep trail to the Indian village. In places where the sun poked its face through the openings of the trees, she could feel the heat from its rays on her back, piercing the thin black dress she was wearing. But on she went, breathing deeply and with a determined stride. She climbed higher and higher up the mountainside, in the direction of Worlds Edge, coming ever closer to the village with each step she took.

As she approached the village she saw young Indian boys, practicing with their tiny bows and arrows, feigning a hunting expedition, climbing over the large boulders, strewn abundantly throughout the area and hiding behind them to surprise the imaginary

48

animals as they passed by. When they saw her coming up the trail, they immediately dispersed and ran to their individual huts to allert their parents of her arrival.

"Welcome to our village, Ann Biddy Shepherd. You have come soon. Almost beat rising sun. Why you come so soon in morning?" Lady Owatta said, as she emerged from her hut to greet Ann.

"Good morning, Lady Owatta. I've been layin' off to come for some time and now I'm finally here."

"Young Braves away. They hunt meat for our people. Without meat we go hungry," Owatta said.

"There's plenty of meat out there. I'm sure they'll find some," Ann said, lifting her hand to greet Lady Owatta.

"How your people? How Hassie Biddy?" Lady Owatta asked, motioning for Ann to have a seat on the mat in front of her hut.

"All are fine, Lady Owatta, especially Hassie. And, by the way, that's exactly why I'm here. I must know what that magic herb was that you gave her. She's a changed woman. You must tell me what it was."

"Owatta tell you, but Ann Biddy Shepherd must promise never tell another. It is secret medcin, known only to my people. It handed down many times from past. You must write down on tablet. Must use secret code when write. Owatta hold hand when you write name of secret medcin. You be first paleface woman to know, but you must forever keep secret."

"I promise, Lady Owatta, I'll never tell another living soul about your secret medicine," Ann said, as she reached into her deerskin bag to retrieve the pencil and tablet.

Lady Owatta stood and beckoned Ann to come inside. She closed the door to her hut and blocked it with a stone to make sure no one came inside while they were recording the ingerdients of the secret medicine. "No one else must know about this medcin. Ann Biddy Shepherd, you must never tell," Lady Owatta said again, as she sat down beside Ann and took her by the hand.

The tablet was barely visible, for the hut had no windows and after Lady Owatta closed the door, the only light entering the hut was through a tiny opening in the north wall.

As Lady Owatta moved Ann's pencilled hand along the paper, inscribing the secret medicine, she told Ann in a barely audible voice what she was writing. Its main ingredient was made from a plant that Ann had seen and stepped on and walked on a thousand times. She would never have dreamed that such a common plant could be so powerful. But there it was, recorded in secret Cherokee Indian code, something that she would never reveal to another person, but then Lady

49

Owatta surprised her when she said, "Owatta allow you tell only one other person about secret medcin. You will know when time come to tell, but until then, this our secret," she said, as Ann pressed the tablet close to her bosom.

Owatta removed the stone and opened the door. Sunlight, streaming through the open doorway blinded Ann temporarily until her eyes adjusted to the brightness of the light.

She sat with Lady Owatta for some time, discussing medical herbs and their uses. She was even permitted to record them in her notebook. She knew she would need this information in the future, for her intention was to become an herb doctor and  midwife.

She was getting up to leave when a young maiden rushed into the hut and said to Lady Owatta, "You must come, now!"

"Why you want me come, now?" Lady Owatta asked.

"Papoose ready to come. You come, now!" she said, as she turned and ran back the way she came.

"You come, Ann Biddy Shepherd, you need know this also," Lady Owatta said,  as she snatched her deerskin bag and headed in the direction the young maiden had taken.

This would be a totally new experience for Ann, for she had never been around when a child was being born. She watched with undivided attention as Lady Owatta came to the aid of the young lady who was about to deliver her child. She watched closely and recorded what was happening in her notebook. She noticed how, when the child was delivered, it was held up by its feet until it took its first breath. She made note of how Lady Owatta tied and cut the umbelical cord. She went with her when she took the afterbirth outside the village and burried it.

"I thank you, Lady Owatta, for letting me learn how babies come into the world. I will always be grateful to you." Ann said, as they walked back up the hill toward the village.

It was getting beyond mid-day when Ann finished her visit with Lady Owatta, bade her good day and struck out down the path toward her shanty. She felt unusually proud that she had accomplished so much  in one day. She now knew how babies made their way into the world. She could also identify the mystery medicine. She was so proud that she had been able to make notes about the birth. She had recorded a lot of information about several other herbs and their uses as well.

As she opened the gate in front of her shanty, she noticed some strange tracks. They were human tracks, but they didn't look familiar to her. "Strange tracks," she said to herself. "I can't make out who they belong to. Well, so much for that."

She went inside to prepare some food for herself and her cat, saying "I'll fix a little dinner, take a short nap and then I'll weed that garden before we get another rain. Another good rain on them weeds and I won't be able to find my garden."

She was awakened suddenly after only a short nap by a rattling knock at the door. She sprang from her bed and hurried to the door and there stood Hassie. "Well, what a pleasant surprise, Mother Hassie. You said you'd come soon and this sure is soon. Come in and I'll get you a cool drink of water."

"Sounds good, Ann Biddy Shepherd. I'm a mite thirsty and I'm sure your pappy is, too."

After P D tied the mule's reins to the shed post at the barn, he came up and sat on the edge of the porch. Ann gave each of them a drink of cool water and they sat on the porch to talk a spell. "That garden a yorn could use a little weedin', Girl a mine," P D said. "After we rest a spell, we'll get out there and help ye do it," he said, as he wiped the sweat form his forehead on his shirt sleeve.

"I was just about ready to do that, Papa, after I rested a bit."

"Well, three people can do it thrice as fast as one," Hassie said, displaying the first grin that Ann had ever seen on her face.

"You said that right, Mother Hassie. You sure said that right."

"How's that little nanny goat a doin' that I give ye a few days back, Girl a mine?" P D asked, as he sat leaning back against the post at the end of the porch.

"She's just fine. She gives plenty of milk for Fidgety and me with some left over for makin' cheese. She sure 'nuf earns her keep. I just can't thank you enough for givin' her to us, Papa."

"That makes me right proud, Girl a mine. Well let's get that garden weeded while it's in the shade uv that old chestnut tree," P D said, standing to his feet, tugging at the brim of his hat.

It was mid afternoon when they finished with the weeding. They returned to the porch to talk and rest, but after a few minutes, P D said that he and Hassie had better be heading back to the gap.

"Don't hurry and I'll fix us a bite to eat," Ann said, getting up quickly and turning to go into the kitchen.

"We need to get on, Ann Biddy Shepherd. There's things to do there at the house, milkin' and all, you know," Hassie said, as she stood up and turned to give Ann a hug.

"Well, come sooner next time and I'll cook up somethin'."

"We will, Ann Biddy Shepherd. We sure will, Hassie said, as she and P D made their way out to the wagon.

"See ye soon, Girl a mine," P D said, as he helped Hassie into the wagon.

Ann watched them until they went out of sight around the bend of the road, and as soon as they were out of sight, thoughts of John's welfare and wherabouts came rushing back into her mind. Tonight she would cry herself to sleep again, worrying about his safety and wheather he would have anything to eat.

"Wish he'd write me a letter. Just a word or two to say how he is," she said to herself, as she took the bucket from the kitchen wall, preparing to go out and milk the goat. "Guess he ain't had a chance."

She had a very restless night, for a summer rain storm moved up from Deep Gap and the thunder and lightning made her thoughts of John even more painful, knowing he would be sleeping outside on the ground with nothing to protect him from the elements. Thunder was so loud it rattled the window panes of her tiny shanty. When she finally did fall asleep, she dreamed of seeing John in the heat of battle, with soldiers falling left and right. Connon were firing rounds into their ranks, sending body parts flying in every direction. In her dream, she was right there in the midst of the battle. She saw a young man lying on the ground with his hands locked around what was left of the stump of his leg. Blood was pouring from his severed leg and seeing him from behind, she thought for sure he was John, but when she came closer she realized it wasn't him.

Another loud crack of thunder and she bolted straight up in bed. Her heart was racing and sweat poured from her forehead. Fidgety was clinging to her night gown, attempting to crawl beneath the quilt.

"That's some kind of a storm out there, Fidgety. It's enough to jar a body right out of bed, wouldn't you say?"

She gathered the cat in her arms, tucked her under the cover and pulled the quilt over her head in an attempt to shut out the loud thunder and the glare of lightning.

After an hour or so, the storm quietened and moved on down through the cove. She finally fell asleep as she prayed for the safety of her husband, who was out there somewhere, but she had no way of knowing know where.

ɑɔɑɔɑɔɑɔɑɔɑɔɑɔ

As a matter of fact, things weren't going so well for John, for he was now in northern Virginia, near Manassas. It was the night of the twenty-eighth of August of 1862, and after a hard day of marching, he discovered he had arrived just in time to join in the second battle of

Bull Run. He had a fair amount of food in his belly for the first time since the long march began and was allowed a fair night's rest, as well, but he was rousted from sleep very early the next morning and after a hasty breakfast of slosh and a cup of chicory coffee, he was rallied along with his company and marched out to the edge of Brawner's Farm, where they were to confront the Union army, comanded by General Pope.

John, having no training as a soldier and because this was his first time to go into battle, chose to fall back to the rear of the main force until he got the hang of things, but soon found himself in the midst of a retreating army.

As Union troops advanced on the Confederates, General Stonewall Jackson pretended to retreat but held his ground until he could be reinforced by Lee and Longstreet, but John's primary concern at this time was to be on the defensive until he learned the ropes, but as soon as Lee and Longstreet's armies joined in the battle, he fell right in with the seasoned soldiers and fought as hard as anyone else. Men were falling left and right as he and his comrades rushed forward. They continued their attack until the Union Army was forced to retreat all the way back to Washington.

There was no time for John to think of fear or why he hadn't been struck down, even though a musket ball did pass so close he felt it zip by his face. "Well, that was a mighty close shave," he thought to himself, as he sprang into a gallop, in full pursuit of the retreating Union soldiers.

Call it luck or call it anything you please, but he managed to get through the two day battle without a scratch. He felt as though he was being protected by some strange invisable shield. Throughout the battles, he felt a special closeness to Ann, way back in the foothills of North Carolina, on Ann Ridge to be more precise.

All day Sunday, the thirtyfirst day of August, they collected weapons and clothing from the dead soldiers to bolster their dwindling supplies. They dug shallow graves to bury their fallen comrades. Flies were swarming over the dead corpses, as they lay decaying in the hot summer sun, awaiting burial.

# Chapter

# 5

## A Loud Knock At The Door

It was the last full week of September and Ann still hadn't gotten a letter from John. There was growing concern about his welfare. She awoke early Wednesday morning of the twentieth of September, thinking, "Looks like he'd at least write and let me know that he's still amomgst the living."

She eased out of bed and slid into her scuffs and was startled by a loud knock at the door and an unfimilar voice calling her, by name, "Ann Shepherd! Ann Shepherd! You in there, Ann Shepherd?"

"Who wants to know?" Ann hollered through the door.

"Nathaniel. They call me Nat, Nat Spicer. I come by here a few days back. They'us nobody home."

"I saw your tracks the other day, but didn't know who they b'longed to," Ann said.

"I hear you study herbs. Can you catch babies? My woman needs somebody to help her. Can you do that?" He hollered back at her.

"I've only seen one birthin', but I'd be more'n happy to come with you," Ann said, opening the door and inviting him inside.

"I ain't got no buggy, just my horse, but he's big. He can carry both of us, no trouble," he said, removing his hat and curtseying to her.

"I've been walkin' all my life, but I have no problem with ridin' a horse," Ann said. "Just give me time to milk my goat and I'll be ready. May be a while before I can get back."

"I live the other side of the church, just this side a Big Level. I'll bring ye back ader the youngun's borned, and I'm bound to give you sompum fer ye troubles."

Let's not worry about pay, Mister Spicer. Let's just think about your woman and the baby."

The sky was reddening in the east as Nat mounted his horse and Ann swung up behind him and off they went, the horse in a full gallop. Ann's black dresstail flailed in the wind with each stride. Her deerskin bag, swinging from her arm, sailed along behind her like a hawk attempting to fly on a windy March day. She dug her fingers into Nat's big fat belly, holding on for dear life, trying to keep from sliding off the rump of the mighty steed as he swerved left and right around the cuves of the crooked road. "Can't we slow down a bit? If we get ourselves killed, tryin' to get to her, your woman won't have nobody to help her then, for sure," Ann said, as they rounded another curve and she came within a gnat's heel of sliding off the horse's back.

"Woah, woah, slow down big feller, better safe than sorry," Nat said, pulling back on the reins.

The horse slowed to a trot and within the hour they arrived at the Spicer house. An old lady appeared at the door waving her arms over her head and shouting, "What kept ye sa long? Molly's about ta have this youngun."

"We got here soon's we could," Nat said, as he slipped from the saddle and caught Ann as she slid from the horse.

"Well, ye didn't get here a minute too soon," the old lady said, moving aside to let them come in.

Molly, Nat's woman was lying there on the bed in intense pain of childbirth when Ann walked into the room. "Get me some hot soapy water. I'll need to wash my hands," Ann said, as she pushed her sleeves up above her elbows.

After she washed her hands and dried them on a clean towel, she examined Molly and sure enough, the baby was in the birth cannal and its head was already showing. "We'll need more hot water," she told the old lady.

"They's plenty in the pot," the old lady said.

The birth was an easy one and Ann was thankful for that. She tied the umbilacal cord with a string, just as she had seen Lady Owatta do. She severed it with a pair of scissors, after dousing them in the pan of hot water. She held the child up by the feet and he came alive with one loud cry and opened his eyes with an expression of curiosity. "Strange world huh, big boy," Ann said, as she wrapped him in a blanket and laid him on his mother's bosom.

"It's a boy! Nat was hopin' it'd be a boy," Molly said, pressing the child to her bosom and lifting the blanket to get a good look at the child's face. "Why, he's just like his pa," she said.

Ann made Molly a tonic of milk thistle to insure ample breast milk production and to aid in fighting off any infection that could have occurred during childbirth. She carried the afterbirth out to the edge of the garden spot, dug a hole and buried it. She hadn't had a chance during all the commotion to find out the old lady's name, but after Nat got settled down from all the excitement, he introduced her. "This here's Cathryn. She's my mama," he said, as he filled his corncob pipe with trembling hands, spilling some tobacco onto the floor.

"I'm obliged to give ye sumpum fer ye trouble, Ann Shepherd. I grabbled some sweet taters yisty and I'll pull ye up some turnips ta take wi'ye. They's mighty good, I tell ye."

"Thank you, Mister Spicer. That's so kind of you."

"Don't mention it, Ann Shepherd. Just proud ta do sumpum fer ye. Won't ye stay'n eat a bite with us? Ma's about got dinner done."

The invite was all Ann needed, for she hadn't had any breakfast and by this time it was getting on passed eleven thirty. "Thank you, Mister Spicer. I believe I'll just do that, if it's not too much bother."

"No bother a'tall, Little Lady," Cathryn said, as she began putting the food on the table.

It was such a pleasure to sit down to a prepared meal. It brought back memories of how cruelly she had been treated by her step-mother and how she had always had to cook the meals while Hassie sat dozing before the fire. "But she's a changed woman now. That secret herb's turned the trick," Ann thought to herself, as she sat there, enjoying the delicious meal. After eating, she checked on mother and child to see if everything was all right and it was.

Nat bagged the sweet potatoes and turnips in a tow sack and ballanced the sack over the horse's shoulders in front of the saddle. "I'm ready when you are, Ann Shepherd," he called out out from down near the barnshed.

"I'm ready, Mister Spicer. Send somebody after me if you need me, Molly, and I'll come right away," Ann said, touching the infant on the forehead and patting its mother on the arm.

"You've been so good to me and I do thank ye," Molly said, looking down at her son and smiling.

"You don't have to thank me, Molly. We got us a strong boy and that's all that matters."

The trip back to Ann Ridge was less hurried. Nat left some slack in the reins and let the horse go at his own speed, but he still set a pretty fast gait. Very little was said as they rode along. It was a good time to relax and enjoy the coloring leaves and to savor the fragrance of the roadside flowers, and to hear the chatter of a gray squirrel now and then and to see an occasional hawk circling overhead.

But no matter how pleasant the surroundings, thoughts of John's whereabouts crept back into Ann's head. She wished he'd write. "I'll go over to the trading post tomorrow. Maybe there'll be a letter," she thought, as she listened to the steady clip-clop of the horse's hooves on the rocky road.

Nat didn't dismount when they reached the shanty on Ann Ridge, but he held Ann's hand as she slid down from the horse. He handed her the tow sack of sweet potatoes and turnips and thanked her again for her help.

"Glad to do it for you, Mister Spicer. If you need me again, all you have to do is let me know."

With that said, Nat nudged the horse in the flanks and was on his way back toward Big Level.

Fidgety was sitting on the gatepost and greeted Ann with a loud meow when she opened the gate and started up the path to the shanty. As she reached to open the door she noticed an envelope lodged between the door and the jam. Her heart skipped a beat. "Who's been here while I was gone?" she said to herself as she retrieved the envelope and looked at it.

The letter was addressed to, "Mrs. Ann Shepherd, Ann Ridge, Polk County, North Carolina, In care of Bent Oak Trading Post." The name, "John Shepherd", was written in the upper left-hand corner of the envelope.

With trembling hands she opened the envelope and read the letter through tear drenched eyes: "The third day of September of 1862. My dearest Ann, I think of you always. Even in the thick of battle you are there and even when I lay sleeping, you're there in my dreams. I feel your presence always, but I know you are far away."

"In the battle of Bull Run, your prayers were surely with me, for I went through two days of blood filled fighting without a single scratch. But the war is not over and I fear much danger is still to come. I pray that I will live through this cruel war and be able to come home to you, but until then, pray for me. I will write again when I can. Your loving husband, John."

She was totally consumed by the contents of the letter, reading it over and over again, searching for something she may have missed. She had even forgotten to milk Prcious until the goat's bleat reminded her of her duties. It was pitch dark when she finally finished her chores and sat down at the table near the lighted candle to read John's letter one more time before going to bed. "He didn't say where he was. How can I answer his letter if I don't know where he is?" she asked herself.

She was delighted to hear from him, but deeply saddened that she still didn't know where he was. With heavy heart she kissed the written page, put it back into its envelope and placed it under her pillow. With tear-drowned eyes she lay for quite some time, thinking of John and praying for his safety, "Please, God, keep him safe and let him come back home to me."

She finally fell into a fretfull sleep, some time around mid-night, dreaming of being in battle alongside John. She awoke often, finding herself sitting straight up in bed panting for breath, her heart pounding.

By sunup the next day, she was on her way to let John's parents know that she had received a letter from him. Fidgety, tethered to the shoestring leash, was bouncing along behind her. It was a splended early autumn day. The multi-colored leaves of the huge oaks, maples, blackgums and chestnuts had an intoxicating effect on her as she skipped down the road with Fidgety at her heels, snatching at her flailing black dresstail.

She was so happy to know that John was alive and that he felt her presence on the battle field, even though she was so far away. She was exuberant as she skipped along, but suddenly from the bushes beside the road, a shaggy bearded man stepped out into the middle of the road and stood brazened, his hands laced through the bib of his overalls. "What's ye doin' out here traipsin' up and down the road by yeself, woman? Ain't ye afraid sumpum'll get ye?"

Feeling threatened, Ann picked up her cat, side stepped the bearded man and was about to walk passed him when he locked a rough calloused hand around her left arm. In an instant, Fidgety sank her claws into his hand and gave him a bloodletting bite to the thumb.

The bearded man let go of Ann's arm as suddenly as he had grabbed her and grasped his bleeding thumb. Ann raced down the road toward her father's house, leaving the bearded man standing in the middle of the road to deal with his scratches and bleeding thumb. "He'll know next time not to mess with me when you're around," she said to Fidgety.

"What's wrong, Ann Biddy Shepherd? Hassie asked her, as Ann bounded up the porch steps.

"A rough lookin' man tried to stop me, but when he grabbed my arm and wouldn't let go, Fidgety took care of him. I think she left him in quite a lot of of pain."

"Ah, it's one a'them old Green River boys. They ain't got no sense," Hassie said as she ushered Ann into the house.

"I'll set him straight the next time I see'im, Girl," P D said, after learning what had happened. "I'll see that ye get back home safe. You won't have to worry about him no more. I'll tell you that."

"I got a letter from John yesterday. I found it lodged between the door and jam when I got home from delivering Molly Spicer's baby."

"Just what'd he have to say?" P D asked, with Hassie echoing his question.

"He's alright, leastwise he was when he wrote the letter. He said

59

he'd been in a two day battle at Bull Run. God only knows where that is. He said my prayers were with him because he got through it without getting killed. Here, I'll let you read it, Papa. You can read it too, Mother Hassie," she said, handing the letter to P D.

"I'm mighty proud you got a letter from him, Ann Biddy Shepherd," Hassie said, standing on her tiptoes, looking over P D's shoulder to get a look at the letter.

"If this war wuzta end this very minute it'ud suit me to a fare thee well," P D said, handing the letter to Hassie.

"Me too," Hassie said, pouring over the letter as if it had some unseen message written between the lines.

"He mentioned the bloody battles. It must've been awful," Ann said, brushing tears from her eyes.

"Now don't you cry, Ann Biddy Shepherd. He's gonna be just fine," Hassie said, as she put her arms around her.

"That feels so strange," Ann thought to herself. She acts like she really loves me. I'm beginning to believe she really does!

"Remember that me and ye pappy's here when ye need us. We're family. You're obliged to know that by now," Hassie said, grasping Ann by the shoulders and looking her straight in the eyes.

"Mother Hassie, I'm beginning to see that," Ann said, getting a close up look at her bright green eyes for the first time since she had become her step-mother. "I'm finally beginning to realize that."

"I guess you're on ye way to the Shepherd house, ain't ye?" P D asked her.

"That's where I'm headed. They'll be glad to know I got a letter from John."

"I'm sure they will, Girl a mine. I'll be waitin' fer ye when ye come back up this way. I'll take ye home in the wagon."

"Thank you, Papa. I won't be down there long. There's things I need to do at the house," Ann said, as she stepped down from the porch with Fidgety cradled in her arms. "See you in a little bit."

Then off down the road she went with Fidgety again snatching at her dresstail. Her mind had been put at ease about that old Green River boy when her father told her that he would take care of things.

As Ann approached the Shepherd house, she saw sweet potatoes spread out on the front porch, sunning. Papa Jacob was leaning back in one of the large rocking chairs on the porch, smoking his pipe. Mama Sarah was sitting in the other rocker, shelling blackeyed peas onto her apron. Papa Jacob saw her first and when he stood to his feet Mama Sarah said, "Where you goin', Jacob?"

"Nowheres, Serry. Ain't that Ann comin' down the road?"

"Well, light my fire 'fit ain't," Mama Sarah said, sifting the peas, husk and all, into a small foot tub and getting up to greet Ann as she came down the path toward the house.

"Hey, Mama Sarah! Hey Papa Jacob! I got a letter from John. I thought you might like to read it."

"Why don't ye read it to us, Girl. Our eyes ain't no good no more," Mama Sarah said, standing up and offering Ann her chair.

"Keep your seat, Mama Sarah. I can sit right here on the edge of the porch."

Ann took the letter from her dress pocket and read: "The third day of September of 1862. My dearest Ann, I think of you always. Even in the thick of battle you are there and even when I lay sleeping, you're there in my dreams. I feel your presence always, but I know you are far away.

In the battle of Bull Run, your prayers were surely with me, for I went through two days of blood filled fighting without a single scratch. But the war is not over and I fear much danger is still to come. I pray that I will live through this cruel war and be able to come home to you, but until then, pray for me. I will write again when I can. Your loving husband, John."

Mama Sarah blotted her eyes on her apron. Papa Jacob puffed on his pipe. "We've been awful worried about 'im, but at least we know he's still alive," Jacob said, as he stood there, almost hidden from view in the cloud of smoke encircling his head.

"I've been prayin' fer him, too, Ann. I b'leive he'll come home safe, when this awful war is done," Mama Sarah said, easing back into her rocking chair.

"I was about ready to start some supper, Child. Won't you stay and eat a bite with us?"

"No, Mama Sarah, I'll have to get back home. I have things I need to get done and there's nobody else but me."

P D had already hitched Jude to the wagon by the time Ann arrived at the Biddy house. He and Hassie were sitting side by side on the edge of the porch, waiting for her as she rounded the bend of the road. "I fixed you a little somethin' fer supper. It'll keep you from havin' to cook when you got home," Hassie hollered to her.

"Well, Mother Hassie, you didn't have to do that."

"I know, Little Biddy, but I wanted to," Hassie said, as she carefully placed the food into the wagon.

"You're just too good to me, Mother Hassie, but I hope I'll be able to return the favor."

"Just look at all the times you cooked for me while I sat there in front of the fire on my lazy thank-you-maam," Hassie told her.

P D helped Ann aboard and climbed into the wagon on the other side, tapped the mule with the lines and they were on their way.

"Bye, Mother Hassie. I'll see you in a few days," Ann said, looking back, waving to her.

As they neared Ann Ridge, P D mentioned the large dead oak, leaning over the road near the shanty. "Cold weather's gonna be here soon and you'll need some firewood. I'll come up here next week and we'll saw that tree down and cut you up some wood. That tree'll make a pile. It's a red oak, so it orta split good," he said, as he pulled back on the reins, bringing the mule to a stop at the gate.

"I know winter's not far off, Papa. I had planned to get out there and gather up some dead limbs and stuff and not have to bother you. I know you've got enough to do, with Hassie and all."

"Hassie's ain't no trouble no more, Little Girl. She's a changed woman since Lady Owatta give her that magic herb."

"It's powerful stuff," Ann said, looking at her father, grinning from ear to ear.

"There's no doubt about it, Little Biddy Shepherd," P D said, bending double with laughter that could be heard all the way down to Britten Creek.

"Thank you, Papa, for bringing me home. I was a little concerned about that old Green River boy, but you set my mind at ease when you said you'd take care of him."

"I'll be headin' on back home now, Girl," P D said, tapping the mule with the reins.

"I'll be looking for you next week, and don't forget to bring Mother Hassie."

The sun was bearly up the following Monday, when Ann heard a wagon coming up the road and she knew who it was. "That Papa of mine don't waste no time," She thought to herself, as she walked up from the little barn, carrying a bucket of milk.

P D pulled the mule to a stop, out passed the oak tree. He jumped down, took the ax from beneath the seat and began chopping the lead notch in the tree. Hassie drove the mule and wagon up to the fence in front of the shanty, climbed down and tied the reins to the gate post. "Go on and help yer pappy and I'll cook dinner," she told Ann.

"Thank you, Mother Hassie, I'll just do that."

P D and Ann worked steadily throught the day, sawing, splitting, choping and stacking the oak wood. They stopped only a few minutes for dinner and hurried back to the job at hand. The sun was fast approaching the crest of Wildcat Spur as P D chopped the last limb into fireplace lengths. A huge pile of wood lay in the yard and Hassie had carried a week's supply and stacked it on the porch. "You'll never know how much I appreciate you helping me get some wood, Papa, unless I tell you, so here I go, I appreciate you helping me get some wood, Papa!"

"Well, you're quite welcome, Little Biddy. I'd do it any day, fer you, that is."

Hassie had supper on the table when P D and Ann staggered into the kitchen, all sweaty and tired from turning that huge oak tree into firewood. "Mother Hassie, it smells like you've cooked up a good supper," Ann said, as she stood washing the grime from her hands and face in the wash pan at one end of the kitchen table.

"We've got baked sweet taters and stewed turnips and good old corn meal mush. Now who could ask fer better'n that?" Hassie said, placing the Dutch oven of corn meal mush on the table, steaming hot from the fireplace.

The turnips, sweet potatoes and mush disappeared like a small mud puddle on a hot July day, and when they were through eating, the Dutch oven and the bowls were all empty.

"Let me help ye wash up these thangs, Little Biddie Shepherd, before we head home," Hassie said, scooting back from the table and gathering up the dishes.

"Wouldn't think of having you help with the dishes, Mother Hassie. You cooked it. The least I can do is wash the dishes."

"Well, I'd be mor'n happy to help ye," Hassie said.

"Well, if she won't let ye help her with the dishes we'd better be on our way home, Hassie. It'll be 'most dark by the time get there as it is," P D said, getting up from the table, rubbing his belly.

"If that old Green River boy gives you any more trouble, Little Biddy, just let me know."

"I will, Papa, but I'll avoid him if I can."

Hassie gave Ann a long hug, kissed her on the cheek, then she and P D climbed into the wagon and headed home.

ΩΩΩΩΩΩΩΩΩΩΩΩΩΩ

It was mid-November and Ann still hadn't gotten another letter from John. She wondered why.

In the mean time, Mama Sarah had fallen ill to a mysterious sickness, neither Ann nor Lady Owatta could diagnose. Ann would prop her up in bed each day and was able to talk her into eating a few

63

bites, barely enough to keep her alive. She did her best to nurse her mother-in-law back to some degree of health, but nothing she did seemed to work.

She moved in with her in-laws, bringing her goat and cat along with her. It was just too far to travel back and forth each day to take care of them. She left the chickens at home, knowing they could fend for themselves.

Papa Jacob was becoming so feeble, he was hardly able to care for himself, much less take care of Mama Sarah, but Ann certainly didn't mind taking care of them for they had been so kind to her. After all, they were her husband's parents and she would do anything for him. "He's away fighting in that terrible war, that is if he ain't dead already," was the thought that came to her mind, time and time again, as she went about her daily chores. "If only he'd write."

On Saturday of the last week of November, Hassie and P D came down for a visit and to lend a helping hand. Hassie offered to take care of Mama Sarah while Ann and P D went to Green River Trading Post, to get some much needed supplies and to give Ann a chance to get out of the house for a little while. Ann thought it was a good idea, so she placed a small bag of dried apple fruit in the handled basket along with a dozen eggs to be used in bartering for coffee and flour at the store. They climbed into the wagon and away they went.

As they walked throught the door at Bent Oak, the proprietor said, "They's a letter here from yer man. Been here fer sev'al days. I meant to bring it to ye, but I jest ain't got around to it yet, been so busy, you know."

"Well let me have it. I've been worried sick about him," Ann said, snatching the letter from his hand and breaking the seal. She looked at the front of the envelope and saw John's address in the upper left hand corner. The thing that caught her eye was 'Richmond, Va.'

"Well, at last I can write to him," she said, as she pulled the letter from the envelope with trembling fingers and began reading silently. Her lips moved, but no sound came from them. As her eyes moved down the page, huge tearsdrops filled her eyes, broke over her lower eye lids and spilled down onto her cheeks, and onto the letter.

After she finished reading the letter, she blotted her eyes on the long sleeve of her black dress and said, "He's been bad sick, Papa. Let me read it to you," and she began reading the letter aloud.

"My dearest Ann, I have not been able to write you because for the last several weeks I have been deathly sick. Matter of fact, they thought I was dead. They had already covered me with a sheet, ready to take me out to the burying ground when one of the men on the burying detail found that I was still breathing as they were loading me onto the wagon.

Now that was a mighty close call, but I soon recovered and now I'm as good as new."

"I have been assigned to a special brigade to defend the Confederate Capitol. I don't know how long I'll be here, but I hope I'll be stationed here till this awful war's over. My mailing address in on the envelope. Write me as soon as you can. I long to hear from you. It seems so long since I've seen you. Please let me know how Mama and Papa are doing. Bye for now, I must get back to the business of war. I made time to write you 'cause they'll pick up the mail today. I miss you, my dearest one. Love, John."

While P D did the bartering, Ann seated herself on a nail keg and began a letter back to John. She told him how much she missed him and how she was praying for his safe return. "Your mother is bad sick and seems to be getting worse every day. Your papa is barely able to take care of himself. I've been so worried about you, thinking you might be dead. I'm sorry you have been so sick and glad to know you are well again. I think maybe you should ask the officer in charge to let you off on furlugh. I fear that if you put off coming home till this war is over, you will not see your mother again alive. I am caring for her as best I know how, but nothing I do seems to help. I will not rest till I hear from you. Remember that I love you always. Stay safe and come home soon. Love, Ann Biddy Shepherd."

She addressed the envelope, folded the letter, stuffed it inside, sealed it and handed it to the proprietor and told him to be sure it went out in the very next mail.

"I shore will, ma'am," he assured her.

Ann climbed into the wagon and P D was about to climb aboard when he bounced back to the ground saying, "I'as about ta fergit. Papa Jacob wanted me to get him some backer. He'll be as nervous as a rattle snake if he don't get his backer."

While P D went inside to get the tobacco, that same old Green River boy approached the wagon and started harassing Ann. He threatened her for letting her cat bite him on the thumb the other day. Ann sat steady as a rock, looking straight ahead, saying nothing. This angered the Green River boy and he came even closer, flailing his arms and voicing obsenities. When P D emerged from the store, he immediately saw what was happening and rushed out to confront him.

"If you thank 'at cat bite was bad, maybe you'd better try this on fer size," P D said, as he drew back his big knotty fist and let fly a blow to his nose.

Blood eased from the Green River boy's nose as he crumpled to his knees, got up staggering, found his footing and took off out the road like he'd been struck by lightening.

"Let 'at be a lesson ta ye!" P D hollered at him. "You'll get sompum worse'n 'at if ye ever bother my girl agin," he said, shaking his fist at him as he went flying down the road and out of sight.

"My cat wouldn't have hurt him if he'd a stayed in his place," Ann said, as P D climbed into the wagon, his face flush, the muscles in his arms taut as the strings on a bass fiddle.

"I hope he's learned his lesson," P D said, his voice cracking with anger. "If he ain't, I'll give him another'n, at no charge."

Very little was said as they made their way back from the trading post. P D sat staring straight ahead, trying to recover from being so angry, his eyes focused on the mule's ears as they moved forward and back with each step.

Ann sat with her hands folded in the lap of her dress, thinking of John and hoping he would be able to convince the officer in charge to let him go on furlough so he could come home to see his sick mother, perhaps for the last time.

"Sorry ye had ta see all that, Girl, but that's the onlyest thang them Green River boys understand. I figered it wuz better he learned sooner than later," P D said, reaching over to touch Ann's hand. "Anyhow, we'll wait'n see how the shoe fits."

"Papa, it was the only thing you could do."

"I know, Little Girl, but it would be a heap better if he'd come to his senses."

As the days crawled by, Ann continued caring for Mama Sarah as best she knew how, but she seemed to grow weaker with each passing day. Papa Jacob held his own, well sort of, but Ann noticed he was having trouble getting to his feet and he was moving more slowly when he tried to walk. "I think I'm gonna have my hands full if things get much worse," she thought to herself as she sat by the bed, spoon feeding her mother-in-law. "I'll take it as it comes and that's that."

As fate would have it, things did get worse. Papa Jacob got down with his back and was unable to get out of bed one morning when Ann called him to breakfast. "Get up, Papa Jacob, breakfast is ready,"

"Can't get up, Child. My back just won't let me," he said, attempting to turn onto his side, grimacing with pain. No matter how hard he tried, and try he did, he couldn't lift his feeble body from the bed. "Maybe'f ye rubbed my back with some a that liniment from down 'ere't the barn 'at I used on the mule afore I give him to yer pa, it'd straighten me out," he said, feeling totally helpless for the first time

66

in his whole life.

"Well, just hold what you got, Papa Jacob, till I get Mama Sarah cleaned up. She's had a little accident sometime during the night."

"What kind'uva accident, Child? Did she git hurt?"

When Ann threw back the covers, she said, "That kind of accident, Papa Jacob."

Right away he knew just what kind of accident she'd had. If he had only waited a couple of seconds, he wouldn't have had to ask.

Ann poured some warm water from the cast-iron kettle into the washpan, added a dab of soap from the soap dish and gently washed her mother-in-law and cleaned up the mess. She dried her and fitted her with a diaper, fashioned from a piece of an old worn out bed sheet she had managed to find by rummaging through the rag bag.

"Now, Papa Jacob, just what can I do for you?"

"Some a that old horse liniment from down there in the barn'ud limber me up some," he said, looking up at her through pitiful eyes.

"I'll be right back," she told him, as she rushed out the door and raced out toward the barn with Fidgety loping along behind her. "I'm not ready to milk yet, Fidgety. Gotta get Papa Jacob on his feet."

When she returned with the bottle of liniment, she turned her father-in-law onto his belly, poured some liniment into her cupped hand and gave him a good working over.

"That stuff's workin' a'ready, Child. You're some kind of a doctor. A man won't need no doctor, long's you're around."

"I'm not a doctor, Papa Jacob, but I wish I was. All I know's what I've learned from Lady Owatta," Ann said, as she pulled his nightshirt down and helped him roll over so he could sit up on the edge of the bed.

"Well Ann Biddy Shepherd, you're as good as airy other doctor. I'll tell ye that."

"I'll take that as a compliment, Papa Shepherd. I guess I can take it to court, or anywhere else for that matter."

Back at the Biddy house, P D and Hassie were sitting before the fire after eating breakfast, trying to decide what to do about Ann and the predicament she had inherited.

"P D, you know that girl of our'n can't handle them two old people all by herself. I b'leve I'll just pitch some clothes in a sack and go on down ere'n see what I can do to help her. I b'leve I owe her that much. Just look at all the thangs she's done fer me! And I could a helped myself if I hadn't a been so crazy."

"You just do that, Hassie. I'll hitch old Jude to the wagon while you get ready. I'll take my ax and saw. We'll get her some firewood while we're at it," P D said, threading his arms through the sleves of his coat as he headed for the door.

No sooner than Jude was hitched to the wagon and P D had put the saw and ax beneath the seat, Hassie came outside, carrying the bag of clothes and a dried fruit pie she made the day before. "She likes dried apple pie. This'll lift her spirits," she said, as she threw the bag of clothes onto the wagon, climbed up and sat down beside P D, carefully balancing the pie on her lap.

"It sure it will, Hassie. I'm glad you took a likin' to our girl. It makes thangs a lot better."

🞪🞪🞪🞪🞪🞪🞪🞪🞪🞪🞪🞪🞪

"Why don't ye get out of this house a little bit and go out there'n help yer Pappy get ye some wood. I'll take care of ye in-laws fer ye and start some dinner," Hassie said, grasping Ann by the shoulders, looking her straight in the face, blaring her jade green eyes. "It'll give ye a chance to get a breath of fresh air, too."

Ann needed no extra proding, for she treasured the thought of spending some time with her father, even though sawing, spliting and hauling wood was not an easy task, but hard work wasn't new to her. God knows, Hassie had allowed her plenty of experience. "But all that's changed now," Ann thought to herself.

They strolled out to the edge of the woods, with Ann hanging onto his arm as if she were only a child. "I'm so glad you're here, Papa," she said.

Papa Jacob and Mama Sarah took to Hassie like bees to a blossom. She fussed over them as if they were her own parents. She combed Mama Sarah's hair, rubbed Papa Jacob's back and helped him on with his shoes. They both revelled in all that special attention.

After sawing and splitting wood all morning, Ann and P D came inside to warm up a bit and to get a bite of dinner. When Ann walked into the bedroom to check on Mama Sarah, she found her sitting up in bed, smiling as though life had never been better.

"Well, ain't you a sight fer sore eyes, Mama Sarah. Mother Hassie's done wonders for you," Ann said, stroking her freshly combed hair. "And look at you Papa Jacob. You're gettin' around here like some young rooster."

"I b'lieve we'll keep Her," Papa Jacob said, speaking of Hassie. A cloud of smoke filled the room as he puffed away on his pipe. Mama Sarah only grinned, for words didn't come so easily to her any more.

68

She may have had a light stroke, but there was no way they could have known, for she had been bed-ridden for quite some time.

"I guess you can keep her fer a little while, but I want her back soon's you're through with her," P D said, as he stood washing his hands. And from the look on his face one would have thought someone had just stolen the deed to his property.

"We'll take good care of her," Papa Jacob assured him, the bowl of his pipe bobbing up and down, the corner of his mouth twitching, eager to break out with laughter.

After eating the good dinner Hassie had prepared, Ann and her father were back at work, splitting and hauling wood. They worked till almost sundown, when P D said "I thank that'll keep ye goin' fer a while, Little Biddy,"

"Sure will, Papa," Ann said, smiling.

Hassie had supper on the table when they came inside, all tired and aching from the long day's work. "I b'lieve I'm gonna need some of Papa Jacob's liniment," P D said, as he eased down onto the rough-sawed plank bench beside the table.

"Soon as you eat yer supper I spect I'd better give ye a workin' over. I guess we'll need to see if we can't get some more of that stuff from over't the tradin' post. The bottle's about half empty," Hassie said, winking at him.

After they had eaten supper and Hassie had rubbed his back with liniment, P D tucked his shirt-tail into his britches, kissed Ann and Hassie goodbye and promised to be back in a day or two to see how they were all doing. "Thank you, Papa, for helpin' me get some wood," Ann hollered to him as he went up the road, the little mule in a trot.

"Any day, Little Biddy, jist any day," he hollered back at her.

Since Papa Jacob and Mama Sarah seemed to be doing so much better, Hassie decided to go home the following Saturday. "They're doin' so much better, I b'leive I'll just go on home when ye papa comes," Hassie told Ann, as they sat at the fireplace warming their feet.

"Mother Hassie, you've done wonders for the both of 'em. It's hard to believe, but the proof's there," Ann said, pointing a thumb in the direction of the bedroom, where Papa Jacob and Mama Sarah lay fast asleep. "They were a handfull, but you sure have proved to be a blessin' in disguise."

"I'll keep a close check, Ann Biddy Shepherd, and when ye need me, I'll be back," Hassie said, laying her arm around Ann's shulders, her green eyes sparkling, as the flames flickered in the fireplace.

"Why don't you tell me about your younger days, Mother Hassie, just what were they like?" Ann asked.

"Ain't much to tell, I mean of the thangs I'd like to talk about," Hassie said. "My papy died when I was just a little thang. I can barely remember him. I remember he'd hold me on his lap in the evenings, sit in front of the fire and he'd sing me them little songs. Seems like I can hear him now. He'd sing to me till I got sleepy and then he'd put me to bed and pile enough quilts on me till I couldn't hardly turn over. He'd kiss me good night and in no time it seemed he'd be calling me to breakfast. "Mother never seemed to care nothin' about me. I never did find out why.

As I said, my pappy died when I was just a little thang, fell off of a rock cliff tuther side of the mountain while he was up there huntin'.They told me that him a'dying when I was so young crippled my mind. That's what they'd always say. And after my mother married my step-daddy, he didn't do me no good neither. He treated me worse'n a dog. He'd beat me with a stick and he'd do other thangs to me that's too bad to mention. After such a shabby start, seems like I turned out perty bad, but Owatta's secret herbs sure straighten me out."

Shifting a bit in her chair and giving Ann a sideways look, she said, "Ann Biddy Shepherd, you don't want to hear all that stuff. I 'magine some thangs are better left unsaid. Let's get to bed, I know you're dog tired after cuttin' wood all day."

Ann lay for quite some time, thinking of what her step-mother had told her about her upbringing. "At least I've got a papa that loves me, but she don't even have that," she thought to herself, as she lay wide awake, staring into the darkness.

But in no time her thoughts turned to John. She hoped he would be able to persuade his commanding officer to at least let him come home for a short stay.

ꙮꙮꙮꙮꙮꙮꙮꙮꙮꙮꙮꙮ

John and his brigade had been building reinforcements and digging entrenchments around Petersburg for the last several weeks. General Lee believed the only way to save Richmond from Yankee invasion was to crush it at Petersburg.

John had finally gotten the letter from Ann, imploring him to beg his superiors to let him go on leave, so he could visit his sick and aging parents, perhaps for the last time. He had made the request and was waiting for permission from his commanding officer. If he had done like so many others, he would have struck out for home without asking, but he had a strong sense of responsibility which had been instilled in him at a very early age.

On New Year's Day, 1863, the army of the Potomac was encamped at Fallmouth, Virginia, on the northern bank of the Rappahannock. The men had not been paid for several months and even though the army warehouses in Washington were filled with food and supplies, very little of it was reaching their encampment. The camps were filthy, littered with decomposing rubish and heaps of manure lay close by. A very high percentage of the Union soldiers encamped there contracted dysentery and medical care was primitive, to say the least. Hundreds were dying from scurvy, dysentery, typhoid, diphtheria, and pneumonia.

Word of their plight had somehow reached the Confederate Capital in Richmond and this information was then passed down to the officers in the field around Richmond and Petersburg. "Private Shepherd, I believe I can let you go home for a while. There's not gonna be much fightin' goin' on here this winter, anyway. Seems like them Yankee boys are comin' down with a real bad dose of the back door trots," John's commander told him. "But be sure to be back here when spring comes around, 'cause we'll be back at it by then for sure."

"Well, Sir, you know that Polk County, North Carolina's a long way off. It'll take some time just to get there'n back," John told his commanding officer.

"I'm aware of that, Private Shepherd, just make sure you're back by spring."

"I'll be back, Sir, I promise you that. Come hail or high water, I'll be back."

# Chapter

# 6

## John On Leave To Visit His Parents

After filling his haversack with hardtack and jerky, and making sure his canteen was full of water, he checked to make sure his furlough paper was in his coat pocket. He threaded his arm through the cord attached to his bedroll, ballanced his muzzle loader over his shoulder and struck out down the road on foot.

By way of Richmond he traveled southwest toward Amelia, retracing the steps he had taken the previous July, when he was inducted into the army and marched off to fight in the war.

The day was clear and cold. The wind was brisk and blowing from the northeast. He turned up the collar of his coat to protect the back of his neck from the biting cold. At times, the legs of his britches billowed in the wind and flailed like a ship's sails in a wintry gale. Even though the wind was bitter cold, it seemed to benefit him in one way. Since it was at his back, it at least gave him a boost in the right direction. He walked at a fast pace which increased his heart rate and body temprature.

He only met two travelers along the way, an old man, driving a team of mules hitched to a wagon, hauling a load of corn and another man who appeared to be in his late forties, riding a fine looking little filly, sporting what looked to be a brand new saddle. Neither stopped to make his acquaintence. They only nodded good morning and continued on their way.

He stopped to rest for a few minutes around two in the afternoon, or at least judging from the position of the sun, that's what he calcuated the time to be. Stepping over to a sunny slope beside the road, he sat down in a bed of leaves, carried there by the winter wind. After eating a few bites of  hardtack and jerky, he took a swig of cold water from his canteen, and after relieving himself of the excess fluid in his bladder, he was on his way again.

The sun had eased down behind the Blue Ridge Mountains as he approached a farm house on a little knoll on the right side of the road.

A barn stood nearby and an elderly man had just finished milking the cow and was walking up the path toward the house when he looked back over his shoulder and saw John coming up the road. "And who're you sposed to be, Young Man?" he asked, turning and facing John as he came closer.

"I'm John, John Shepherd, that is."

"You from around here, John?"

"Afraid not, Sir. I'm from down there in North Carolina, Polk County, North Carolina."

"What's you doin', goin' this a'way? Why ain't ye up there a'fightin' them damn Yankees?"

"I been up 'ere but they ain't much fightin' goin on now, so I got a furlough to go home and visit my folks a little. They're old and sickly and my wife wrote me and told me I'd best come home if I wanted to see'em alive again."

"Well, it's about to get dark on ye and you aint a'gonna get home tonight noway. Wh'on't ye come in the house and have a bite a'supper with us and they's a extry bed in 'ere too. My boy's off up 'ere somers a'fightin', hisself. No use to let a good bed go to waste."

"I'm mighty obliged to ye, Sir, but I'm a mite too dirty to sleep in a straingers clean bed."

"You ain't no strainger to me. You're a neighbor, long's you're on our side. 'Sides, a little dirt never killed nobody, nohow. Come on in," the old man said as he opened the door and stood back, letting John go in ahead of him.

"John, I'm Lum Luger. Come on in'n meet my wife, Lailer."

"I thank you, Sir, you are certainly a kind man," John said, as he removed his hat and curtsyed to the old lady, standing near the fireplace, stirring stew  in the large black pot with a long handled wooden spoon.

"Welcome to our humble home, Young Man. I'll have a bite to eat fixed in a bit. Won't ye stay'n eat some with us?"

"Nothin'ud please me better, Ma'am," John said as he stood at attention, waiting to be asked to have a seat.

"Lailer, this here's John Shepherd. He's from down 'ere'n North Carolina, Polk County, that is."

"Pleased to meet ye, John. Won't ye sit down. I 'magine yer about give out after walkin' all day," Lady Lailer said, sliding a chair out from the table and motioning him to sit down.

"Feels so good to sit in a chair for a change," John said, leaning back and savoring the almost forgotten feeling.

Lady Lailer set the table with four soup bowls and four large spoons. She filled the four bowls with stew from the pot and they each took their places around the table. "I all'as set a extry place, in case that boy a'mine was to show up. Can't never tell, ye know."

"Sure can't, Ma'am," John said, as he sat motionless, waiting to see if Lum was going to say the blessing.

"Bless this stew and the hands that made it. Shield our boy from them damn Yankees. Bless our neighbor, his wife and family. Keep us honest, humble and sober. Save us all when this thing's over. Amen."

"Amen," John said, feeling shocked that Lum had used the curse word in his prayer.

John ate stew and hoecake and had seconds. When he emptied his bowl the second time, Lady Lailer offered him more.

"No thank you, Ma'am, I've had a plenty," John said, as he wiped his mouth on the cuff of his sleeve, placed his spoon in the bowl and pushed back from the table. "It sure was good, though."

After they had eaten, Lady Lailer began washing the dishes as Lum and John moved their chairs over near the hearth and Lum began a long drawn out story of the hard life he had experienced there in the hills of Virginia.

"Now, John, you've got to understand, they wuzn't nothin' here but woods when we come into this part of the country. Had to chop down trees to build the house. Built the chimney out of poles, too. Didn't have time to go lookin' around fer rocks. Coated that chimney with red mud to keep it from catchin' on fire, 'cept it did catch on fire a time er two. Toted water up on the roof'n poured it down that chimney to put out the fire."

"You sound just like my pa. He moved up from Sumter, South Carolina, up to Deep Gap, North Carolina, when I was just about eight years old. Built his house from trees he cut down right there on the place," John said, feeling proud that he and the old man had things in common. "Makes me feel like we're real neighbors after all," he said.

"Worked real hard to make somethin' of this place," Lum said, "and now my boy's off up 'ere som'ers a fightin' so we can keep it. Don't know what this country's comin' too, noway. I had no quarrel with them people up there in Washington, D C. Only wanted to live out my life in peace and go on to meet my Maker in some kind of a shape. You know what I'm tryin' to say?"

"I b'leive I do, Mister Luger. I'm sure I do. I was never too keen about this war myself, neither, but Pa said if they called me, I was duty bound to go. They called me and I went."

"Guess they ain't no use'n thrashin' it around all night. I know you're tired after walkin' all day, so why don't we try to get a little

75

shut-eye."

"Ye bed's all ready and the cover's turned down, Son. Hope ye get a good nignt's sleep, a'fore ye have to strike out again tomorrow," Lady Lailer said, as she emerged from her son's bedroom.

"I'm eternally grateful to you, Ma'am. It'll be like sleepin' on a cloud. I'm sure you'll have to shake me awake in the mornin'."

"Goodnight, Son," Lum and Lady Lailer said, as John went into the bedroom and closed the door.

John didn't have to be awakened the next morning. The smell of ham, cooking in the large frying pan at the fireplace, aroused his stomach and it in turn, opened his eyes. "That's ham I smell. I ain't had ham for a long time," he said, sitting on the edge of the bed, threading his legs into his britches.

By the time John got dressed and into the front room, Lady Lailer had breakfast on the table. "Thought I'd let ye sleep as long as ye could, John. Didn't know how long it'ud be a'fore ye get to sleep in a good warm bed again."

"The smell of that ham woke me up, Ma'am. I ain't had a mess of ham in many a day."

Lum's out 'ere milkin' the cow. Soon's he's back we'll be ready to eat, Lady Lailer said, laying another stick of wood onto the fire.

When Lum came inside from milking he looked over at John and said, "I've got a big black stallion out 'er'n the barn. Got a brand new saddle, too. B'longs ta my boy, but he won't be needin' it fer a while. Why don't ye take 'im wiye. He'll get ye down 'ere to where yer a goin' a lot faster. He needs the exercise, anyway. Won't do him a bit a good, standin' around in the barn all winter. Just so you bring him back when ye come back this way next spring."

"Are you sure, Sir? What makes you think I won't take him off and you'll never see no more?"

"I think I'm a right good judge a character, John. You wouldn't do such a thing."

"No, Sir, I sure wouldn't. I could never do that, but what if somethin' was to happen to him?"

"Ah, quit tryin' to make excuses and say you'll take him. You're welcome to him, you know."

"Well, I'll take him, Sir, and be thankful to have him. I'll bring him back early next spring. I have to be back in Richmond by then."

"Now you're talkin', John. Just take care of him and see that he gets fed. That's all I'm askin'."

"I will, Sir. I'll guard 'im day and night, won't let nothin' happen to him", John said, as they all sat down to breakfast.

After breakfast, Lady Lailer fixed up a bag of food for John while he and Lum went out to the barn to saddle the stallion. The horse was full of fire and more than ready to get going. Lum had shelled about a peck of corn into a tow sack. He ballanced it evenly over the stallion's back along with a couple of bundles of fodder. "This'll come in handy when ye can't find nothin' else fer'im to eat, but go sparin' with it. You'll prob'ly to be able to find stuff aong the way to keep 'im from gettin' too hungry," Lum said, as he made sure that everything was tied securly onto the horse's back.

"I will, Sir. I promise you I'll take real good care of your boy's horse and I'll see that he gets fed, I promise you that."

"I b'lieve ye will, Son. I'm sure you will."

John slid his musket into the holster and led the stallion out of the barn and up the path to the house. He tied the reins to the hitching post and walked up onto the porch to thank Lady Lailer for her hopitality and for the delicious food she had prepared for him. "I can't thank you enough, Ma'am, for all the good food and a good night's sleep in that wonderful bed. I'll always be greatful to you."

"You're quite welcome, Son. Here, I fixed ye up a little somethin' to take with ye. I hope it'll keep ye from gettin' hungry fer a while," she said, handing it to him in a cloth bag.

She turned quickly and rushed back into the house, for tears were burning her eyes and she didn't want John to see her crying.

"Much obliged, Ma'am. I'll see you next spring," John said, as he mounted the stallion and without saying another word he was on his way down the road.

Lum had stayed in the barn, for he was having trouble keeping his eyes dry as well. They were obviously very worried about their son. John didn't know his name. They hadn't mentioned it to him for some reason or another and he hadn't asked.

The day was cold and crisp, but at least, the wind wasn't blowing. It was Wednesday, the fourteenth day of January. John had remembered looking at the calander at the Logan's the evening before.

The stallion was a fine riding horse and he moved as if on a mission, going at a reasonably fast pace.

As the sun was resting on the mountain top to the west that evening, the stallion had covered several miles. Before darkness set in John selected a little cove, sheltered by giant hemlocks. A small stream was flowing nearby, a likely place to spend the night. He removed the saddle and bridle from the horse and replaced the bridle with a halter. After watering the horse, he secured the halter rope to a small maple tree and fed him some corn and fodder.

He selected a place to sleep, a place where the leaves lay dry and deep. He rolled out his bedroll and covered it with a thick layer of leaves. He brought the saddle over for a headrest and slithered his slender body beneath the blanket and settled down for a night of rest. For sure, it would not be as comfortable as the night before, but comfortable enough. He would stay reasonably warm under the blanket beneath the bed of leaves. As he lay listening to the call of a nearby screech owl and the stallion chomping on the corn and fodder, he soon he fell fast asleep.

He slept soundly throughout the night, but the next morning, as the sky to the east took on a faint glow of pink, he thought he was dreaming when he heard young voices.

"S'my horse. I see'd him first."

"Tain't so. I see'd 'im first."

"S'mine I tell ye. Git ye hands off him."

Suddenly, John realized he wasn't dreaming. He raised his head slightly from the saddle and was surprised to see two young boys wrestling for posession of the stallion. "I beg to differ with the both of you," he said, as he sat up, pointing his musket in their direction. The leaves, peeling away from his body in the dim light of dawn took on the appearance of someone rising from the grave and when the two young boys saw him sitting there with half his body covered with leaves and the barrel of his musket, looking to them the size of a cannon, they tore out through the woods like two scared rabbits and disappeared from sight with their coattails flailing in the wind.

The stallion nickered as John rose to his feet and prepared for another day's journey. He fed the stallion some fodder and a hand full of corn and after eating a few bites of the food that Lady Lailer packed for him the day before, he mounted the stallion and they were on their way again.

There were two occasions on his trip south, when he saw Yankee scouts, but he quickly got out of sight and covered the stallion's head with his blanket to keep him quiet until the scouts moved on.

He met several friendly folks along the way. Most were willing to give him the hand of welcome and provisions for himself, as well as for the stallion and an ocasional offer of the barn, in which he might spend the night. "Just hope my woman's alright and Ma and Pa, too," he said, as he bedded down in a kind farmer's barn.

As he crossed the state line into North Carolina, he felt a real sense of relief. "Shouldn't take too long now," he said, as he nudged the stallion in the ribs and he took off in a full gallop.

It just so happened that his woman and Papa Jacob were doing

78

alright, but Mama Sarah's condition had worsened considerably over the last few days. Ann watched over her night and day, and all the while, wishing that John would make it home before she passed on.

She hadn't gotten a letter from John for several days and figured he must be on his way home. Days passed as Mama Sarah seemed to hang suspended between life and death. Ann told her she believed John was on his way home and that seemed to keep her hanging on, hoping to see her son one last time.

But as the days came and went, she grew weaker and weaker. And then she seemed to be coming down with pneumonia. In the middle of the night, Ann was kneeling at the fireplace, warming a piece of wool cloth, soaked in oil of camphor to place on her chest, hoping to relieve some of the congestion. Her mother-in-law was wheezing and struggling so to get her breath that Ann was beginning to believe she might not make it through the night. Papa Shepherd lay sleeping on the far side of the bed, too old and frail to realize how sick she was.

Deep into the night, Mama Sarah's condition seemed to get some better, at least she was breathing better.

Ann sat dozing in the rocker at the fireplace, thinking her mother-in-law was comfortable and would be able to sleep the rest of the night. But sometime before sunup the next norning, she was jarred awake with Papa Shepherd yelling at the top of his voice, "Serry! Serry! Wake up, Serry! Ann sumpun's wrong with Serry!"

Ann jumped to her feet and rushed to the bedside, felt of Mama Sarah's forehead and it was cold. She placed her fingers to the side of her neck to see if she could feel a pulse and there was none. "She's gone, Papa Shepherd."

"What's you mean, she's gone," Jacob said, as he stood barefooted by the bed, dressed only in his woolen drawers.

"I mean, she's dead, Papa."

"Well, what'd ye let her die fer?" You'as 'sposed to be lookin' ader her, wuzen't ye?"

"I done all I could, Papa. It was her time to go and she went. I'm sorry, but that's the way things are. We can only do so much and then it's up to God A'Mighty."

"I beg ye pardon, Child, I guess I lost my head there fer a spell. I didn't mean to scream at ye."

"It's alright, Papa, I understand. I've been through this sort of thing a time or two myself, you know."

"But still, I had no call a hollerin' at ye that way, Child."

"It's alright, Papa. Put your clothes on while I make us some coffee. Maybe that'll help to calm us down."

"Maybe so, Child, maybe so."

Ann filled the pot with water, added some coffee and swung it over the fire. "Let me check to see what day it is. We'll need to mark down in the bible the day she died," she said, taking a pencil from the shelf and checking the date on the calander. "Thursday, Februrary the fifth, eighteen sixty-three," she said, as she wrote it down in the bible.

There was a chill in the air as they sat drinking their coffee. The fire at the fireplace popped and cracked as if warning of inclement weather. "Fire's talkin' snow, Child. Hope it don't snow afore we get Serry buried," Papa Shepherd said, as he took another sip of coffee.

He struggled to his feet, walked over to the window and looked out. "It's a blowin' snow out 'ere right now, Child, but I can still see a few stars. Maybe it won't get too bad."

"Soon's we get Mama Sarah laid out and get her dressed, I'll go up and get Papa and Mother Hassie to come down and help us, Ann said, as she rummaged through her mother-in-laws bureau, looking for her best dress.

"It's a shame I ain't in no shape to help you, Child. When a man gets old, he just ain't no count no more."

"You are too, some count, Papa Shepherd, so don't be sayin' that no more. You took care of Mama Sarah, long as you's able and that's all that can be expected of anybody."

Ann poured some water from the cast iron kettle into the wash pan, added some lye soap and bathed her mother-in-law. Her legs and arms were beginning to stiffen a bit, but Ann managed to dress her. She straightened her body and crossed her arms over her chest. She pinned the old familiar broach onto her dress, the broach Mama Sarah had worn for years.

When she finished preparing her mother-in law for burial, she made up some dough for a hoecake and fried some ham and eggs. She filled Papa Shepherd's plate for him and then her's. When they had finished eating, she threaded her arms through the sleeves of her black coat, wrapped the wool scarf around her head and face, barely leaving her eyes exposed. Papa Shepherd's walking stick was leaning against the wall near the door. She grasped it as she walked out the door and struck out up the road toward her father's house.

She had hardly gotten out of sight of the Shepherd house when she saw that same old Green River boy who had harassed her last fall. He was coming down the road toward her, but when he lifted his eyes from the ground and saw her, he promptly moved over to the far side of the road and stood there with his head down until she had gone out of sight around the next bend. "If he had bothered me, I would have wore him out with this here walkin' stick," she mumbled to herself, as she quickened her pace.

When she came within view of her father's house, she saw him standing on the porch, gazing up at the threatening clouds, sweeping down from the crest of Wildcat Spur. "What brings you out this early and in this kind of weather, Child?" he asked, as she mounted the steps to the porch.

"I need ye help, Papa."

"And what might that be, Girl?"

"Need ye to help me dig a grave, Papa."

"Grave? Fer who?"

"Mama Sarah. She died last night and Papa Shepherd ain't in no shape to be diggin' no grave."

"What's wrong, Ann Biddy Shepherd?" Hassie asked, opening the door and walking out onto the porch.

Mama Sarah died last night and I need somebody to help with the buryin'."

"Well, come in here and get yeself warmed up. We'll go down 'ere'n help ye with it. You know that," Hassie said, putting her arms around Ann, ushering her into the house.

P D followed behind them and they all seated themselves before the fire for a few minutes to warm up. Ann brought them up to date about the happenings at the Shepherd house. "I think Mama Sarah took pneumonia. She was caughing and wheezing something terible. I done all I knowed to do, but I guess she was just too old to get better. Sometime passed midnight, she seemed to be a little better. That's when I dozed off, sittin' there in front of the fire. The next thing I knowed, Papa Shepherd was hollering and calling her name, saying something was wrong with her, and when I felt of her forehead, it was cold. I felt for a heartbeat and there wasn't any. Papa Shepherd wanted to know why I let her die. I told him I'd done all I knowed to do."

"Pore thang's better off, I s'pose," Hassie said, holding Ann's hand, assuring her that she had done all she could do.

"I'm sure you done everthang you could, Girl. When the Man upstairs calls, they ain't no trace chain in the barn that'll keep us here," P D said, as he came inside after hitching the mule to the wagon.

He took Ann by the hand, helped her to her feet and said, "Now I reckon it's up to us to give her a good send off. She's been a real good woman. Nobody can take that away from her."

"She was a peach of a woman. I just wish she could have lasted till John got home," Ann said, as she pulled her wool coat over her shoulders once again and threaded her arms into the sleeves.

81

"Is John on his way home?" Hassie asked.

"I don't know for sure, Mother Hassie, but since I've not heard from him in several days, I figure he must be."

"I hope he is, Ann Biddy Shepherd, but won't it be a sad time fer him when he gets here?"

"We're living in a sad time, anyway, Mother Hasie, with our men off in that war, shooting each other down like dogs."

"It's a bloomin' shame that people can't learn to get along with one another," P D said, as he helped Hassie on with her coat.

As they made ready to climb into the wagon, Hassie said, "You set in the middle next to yer pa, Ann Biddy Shepherd, you'll stay warmer that way."

"Thank you, Mother Hassie. You are so kind."

They sat wordless for some time, as Jude trotted along, pulling the wagon down the road toward the Shepherd house. Death was never taken lightly and if there was nobody outside the family to bury the dead, it was up to the immediate family to do it.

When they arrived at the Shepherd house, Papa Shepherd had somehow made his way down to the barn and stood motioning for P D to pull the wagon up to the front of the barn. "The pine box is up there in the loft," he said, pointing up in that direction. "I've had it cut out fer a long time. All we'll have to do is nail it together. I cut out two of 'em, one fer me and one fer Serry."

"Well, you go back to the house, Papa Shepherd, we'll take care of it for you," P D said, as he stepped down from the wagon, there in front of the barn.

He climbed up into the loft and sure enough, the pieces for the two pine boxes were there, stacked neatly in two separate piles. A small cans of nails sat on each stack, enough to fasten them together.

"The little one's fer Serry," Papa Shepherd called to them from the porch.

P D began handing the pieces down as Hassie and Ann stacked them onto the wagon.

When they finished loading the pieces onto the wagon, P D guided the mule up to the porch. "We'll put it together out here on the porch" he said, as he sat the can of nails on the porch and went inside to ask Papa Shepherd where he kept his claw hammer. After locating the hammer, he busied himself with assembling the pine box. When he finished nailing it together, Ann helped him carry it into the house. Hassie placed two straight chairs facing each other, but far enough apart to rest each end of the pine box on the seat of each chair.

Papa Shepherd came into the room, carrying a quilt that Mama

Sarah had made several years ago. It had been a favorite of her's. "Let's spread this here quilt into the coffin. It'll bring her comfort. She loved it so much,"he said.

"I'm sure it will, Jacob. I'm sure it will," P D said.

After spreading the quilt down into the coffin, leaving folds on each side, P D and Hassie lifted Mama Sarah and placed her body inside the pine box. Ann spread the folds over her lower body, leaving her arms and face exposed. "How's that, Papa Shepherd?"

"Looks mighty good, Child. She'd be proud of it."

"If you'll tell me where you want her burried, Jacob, I'll get on up there'n get started on digin' the grave," P D said, as he placed the claw hammer back on the mantel.

"Right out 'ere on the ridge, P D. Out 'ere where it can catch the risin' sun."

"I know just where you're talkin' about, Jacob. I'll get started on it right now."

"I'll help ye, Papa, Ann said, sliding her slender arms into the sleeves of her wool coat once again.

"I'll start some dinner while you do that," Hassie said, as she stirred the fire in the fireplace and pulled some coals onto the hearth, preparing to roast some potatoes.

It was blowing snow and the ground was frozen, as P D and Ann made their way up to the ridge in the wagon. "Ground's gonna be kinda hard the first few inches," P D said, as he selected a nice place on the eastern slope of the ridge and struck the ground with the pick.

"Seems so, Papa, but we can do it. We've done a heap a things together, you and me."

After marking off the area for the grave, P D began to attack the frozen earth with a vengence. The ground was frozen to a depth of about four inches but after he had pried the first chunk of dirt from the grave sight, it became easier to remove the remaining frozen ground. Once he got through the frozen crust, the soil was soft enough to spade with the shovel.

"Rest a spell, Papa, and let me shovel some of that dirt," Ann said, as she stepped down into the foot deep hole and grasped the shovel handle. "How'll we get out of here when we get down far's we're going, Papa?"

"I nailed some cross pieces onto a two by six. It's there in the wagon, Girl."

"Oh! Well, I was just wondering, Papa."

They worked steadily, taking turns shoveling the dirt from the grave and by a little passed mid-day they had reached the proper depth.

P D climbed out of the pit on the ramp he had made, and looking down into the opening said, "That'll do it, Ann Shepherd."

"Let's go see what Hassie's cooked up fer dinner," he said, as he loaded the tools onto the wagon and helped Ann climb aboard.

"Didn't know if you was comin' er not. Must be nigh on to two o'clock," Hassie said, standing at the door, as Ann and P D scraped the dirt from the soles of their shoes on the edge of the porch.

"Wanted to get it done afore we eat dinner, Hassie, asides, we'll have to hurry if we get her buried afore dark anyway."

"Well, come on in and warm yerselves. Dinner's been ready for a good while."

Ann and P D washed the dirt from their hands and they all gathered around the table. Hassie had set a plate for Mama Sarah out of respect for her, even though she knew she wouldn't be eating at that table, ever again.

They each bowed their heads as Papa Shepherd, seated at the head of the table, uttered a short prayer. "Thank ye fer the grub, fer family and friends. Save us from ourselves and from our sins. If Serry brings as much joy there as she did here, nobody there'll ever shed a tear. John didn't make it, but bring him home d'rectly. Ye promise in Ye Book not to put on us more'n we can bear, but I think we've had a little more'n our share. Amen."

Immediately after dinner, they all gathered around the coffin to have a last look at Mama Sarah and to shed tears of grief for her departure. "You'as a good'un, Serry, you sure wuz," Papa Shepherd said, as he thumbed the tears from his eyes.

Ann, very gently, pulled the folds of the quilt over Mama Sarah's body. P D placed the cover on the pine box and began the task of nailing it in place.

As Papa Shepherd, Ann and Hassie stood in a huddle, trying to comfort each other, P D went outside and backed the wagon up to the edge of the porch to shorten the carrying distance as much as possible. He knew it would be difficult for Ann and Hassie to lift and carry their end of the box. "Its snowin' harder out 'ere folks. We'd better get started afore it gets any worser," he said, as he stomped the snow from his shoes.

Ann and Hassie each chose a corner of the light end of the box as P D lifted the heavy end and they carried it slowly out to the wagon. Resting the heavy end of the coffin on the back of the wagon, he rushed back to help the ladies slide it the rest of the way in, almost catching Hassie's forefinger between the box and the wagon bed in the process. "Let's leave a little stickin' out the back, so we'll have somethin' to hold to when we get ready to unload it," P D said.

"Who's that feller on the black hoss?" Papa Shepherd asked, as he stood staring up the road.

Ann shielded her eyes from the falling snow and looked in that direction and let out with a scream that echoed throughout Deep Gap, "It's John! It's John! It's John!" she exclaimed, as she raced up the road to meet him, fast as her legs would carry her.

John slid from the saddle and like hot butter, they melted into each other's arms.

"Missed you, my Woman."

"I've thought of nobody but you since you've been gone, John."

"Where you fixin' to go somewhere? Looks like you've got the wagon all loaded up," John said.

"Up to the ridge, John. You didn't get here in time. Your mother passed on last night. She held on long as she could, but she just couldn't hold on any longer," Ann said, her voice breaking.

"Well, I simply must see her one last time," John said, as he and Ann walked, arm in arm, back toward the house, with the black stallion trailing along behind.

John spoke to P D and Hassie, then embraced his father, who was visibly touched by his son's arrival. Jacob was elated that he was finally home, but saddened that he had not arrived in time to see his mother before she passed away.

"Son, ye mama passed on late last night, but she must a went peacable, cause she didn't make a sound. Leastwise, I didn't know she was gone till this mornin', when I woke up and she wadn't movin'. I kept hopin' you'd get to see her one more time afore she went on to meet her Maker."

"Well, I sure tried, Pa, but I just couldn't get here a day sooner. If Lum Luger hadn't let me use his horse, I wouldn't of made it this soon. Anyway, can ye take the lid off and let me see her one last time?"

"Give me a few minutes, John, and I'll open it fer ye," P D said. They carried the casket back inside and he pried the lid free with the claw hammer. John leaned over the casket, sobbing deeply, while touching his mother's cold, pale, boney hand. Ann came close and put her arm around him and led him over to the bench at the table and sat with him for several minutes, cradling him in her arms. When he finally regained control of himself, he motioned for P D to refasten the lid.

"We'd better get movin' if we 'spect ta get done afore dark," P.D said. "I 'spose it's half passed three by now and dark comes early this time a'th year, ye know."

P D drove the casket-ladened wagon as the others walked slowly

85

behind, with Hassie steadying Jacob, as he struggled along.

When they reached the gravesite, P D took the two ropes from beneath the seat and strung them across the grave, one on top of each board, placed over the grave opening to support the coffin.

John helped P D carry his mother's casket to the grave and rested it on the snow covered boards over the opening, until words could be said over her:

"Here she is, Lord. You let me have her fer a spell, but now I give her back to ye. I hope you'll be as good to her as I was. Good bye, Serry. You've been a goodun." Papa Jacob said, as tears trickled down his face, moistening his beard.

They all said Amen as P D, John, Ann and Hassie took hold of the ropes and lifted the coffin slightly, so Papa Jacob could remove the boards. When the coffin settled to the bottom, P D and John pulled the ropes free. By now the snow was blowing in the wind, with some flakes as large as a man's thumb. As John and PD began shoveling dirt into the grave, the dirt that had been easy to spade earlier in the day, was now beginning to freeze.

"You'd best get you back to the house, Papa Jacob, before you get a dose of 'newmony'," Hassie said, as she turned him around, took him by the arm and walked him slowly down the hill.

Maybe you'd better go, too, Ann. Me'n ye pa'll finish up here," John said, as he threw another shovel full of dirt into the grave opening.

When they finally finished filling the grave, it was snowing so hard the ground was white, except the spot where they had dipped up the last few shovelfulls of dirt.

Ann and Hassie helped Jacob up the porch steps and brushed the snow from his hat and coat. They supported him as he made his way into the house and over to the fireplace, where he eased down into his favorite chair. Ann stirred the fire and added a few sticks of dry wood.

"Warm yourself, Papa Jacob, and I'll start us some supper," she said, as she moved the big cast iron skillet over to the front of the fireplace and settled it onto a bed of coals.

"We'd better get home, Hassie. It's snowin' harder out 'ere'n the animals there't th house'll be waitin' ta be took care of," P D said, as he and John came in from the porch, after scuffing the mud and snow from their shoes.

"I'm ready, P D," Hassie said, as she wrapped her shawl around her head and face, tucking the tails inside the collar of her coat.

They said their goodbye's to Ann, John and Jacob, brushed the snow from the wagon seat, climbed aboard and headed home, the little mule in a trot.

Ann was so happy to have John home. She had worried about him, night and day, since he had been away, fighting in the war. "It's good to have you home, John. I didn't know if I'd ever see you alive again, but I prayed you'd make it back, all in one piece."

"It's been bad, Ann, but I've somehow managed to dodge the bullets. It was good to know that you were back here, prayin' for me."

When supper was over, Ann got Jacob tucked away for the night. Then she and John went to bed, where they whispered to each other well into the night about things they had encountered since they had been apart.

As the shadows from the andiorns at the fireplace danced about the room, they lay in a tight embrace and everything else in the world vanished as their hearts beat in unison to their oneness.

"It's so good to be back with you, Ann Biddy Shepherd, so good indeed," John whispered, and soon they both drifted off to sleep.

Three inches of snow lay on the ground the next morning. The call of a lone crow resounded throughout Deep Gap, as the sun sparkled through the snow covered treetops to the east.

Ann bounded from bed, slid her feet into her scuffs, and hurried over to unbank the fire at the fireplace. John stirred restlessly as he lay dreaming, positioning his arms as if holding his musket, moving his forefinger as if pulling the trigger and saying, "Take that, you Yankee, that's what you get for killin' my buddy."

He woke in a sweat, breathing rapidly, sitting straight up in bed with a piercing, steely look in his eyes.

"Wake up, John. You're at home. Don't you remember?" Ann said, turning suddenly and rushing to his side.

"I realize that now, Ann," he said, running his fingers through his thick, black hair. "I see that now."

"You just lay still, John. I'm fixin' to cook breakfast. Lay still. You deserve some rest."

"I'll help you with it, Ann," he said, as he swung his legs off the side of the bed, slid his legs into his britches and his feet into his brogans. "It's so good to be home, my Love."

They were standing in a tight embrace in front of the fireplace when Papa Jacob roused from sleep and asked, "Where's Serry?"

"She's dead, Papa Jacob, don't you remember? We burried her yesterday."

"Now I do, Son. I dreamed she was here and we wuz out ere cuttin' firewood."

"Papa Jacob, I'll have some breakfast in a jiffy. No need to get up yet," Ann said, as she mixed the batter for a pone of bread.

After a breakfast of flour pone, white gravy, pork, pear preserves and hot coffee, John went outside and swept a path to the barn with a stiff pine brush. He put the halter on the stallion and led him down to the branch for a drink of water. As he came back into the breezeway of the barn, Ann had already finished milking Precious, her goat, and was about finished with milking Gracious, Papa Jacob's goat. "You're a fast milker, Ann," John said.

"This cold weather puts a little hurry in your hands," she said, as she sat on the stool, milking with both hands, the steam rising from the bucket, clutched between her knees.

Because the weather outside was uninviting, much of the day was spent with John and Ann sitting near the hearth, consumed by each other's company and conversation. But of course, Papa Jacob broke into their conversaton occasionally, his mind dwelling on the time when he and Sarah first met and got married. "Way down there in Sumpter, South Carolina, I remember it like it 'as yisty," he said. "I thought she was the pertiest thang I'd ever set my eyes on. That was back 'ere in thirty-two. Seems like only yisty," he said.

A tear twinkled in the corner of his eye, when a stick of wood in the fireplace dropped down into a bed of coals and blazed up. But most of the day he sat gazing into the fire, puffing on his pipe with the smoke trailing up and over his shoulders and back through the snow illuminated room.

By mid-morning, the sun was shining brightly outside and the temperature was rising. John went out to the porch to bring in some wood for the fireplace and noticed that all the snow on the path to the barn had melted, where earlier in the day he had swept most of it away with the pine brush.

"If it's weather fit tomorrow, maybe you'n me can go up to the cabin and see if it's still in one piece," John said to Ann, as they sat eating their evening meal.

"Should be a good day, John. A lot of the snow melted today."

"You think you'll be alright, stayin' by yourself while we go and check on the place, Pa?"

"Why shore I will, Son. You'ns need a little time together anyway," Papa Jacob said, after taking a sip of coffee from his cup and wiping his mouth on the cuff of his sleeve. "Don't mind a bit, Son. I'll just sit here hunkered down at the fire till you'ns get back."

The sun was barely up the next morning when John saddled the stallion, slid his muzzle loader into the holster and after climbing into the saddle, Ann swung up behind him and they were on their way up to Ann Ridge to check on the little shanty. Ann clung to John like a leech,

88

happy to be able to be this close to him, after being alone for so long. She wished they were going back to their little shanty to stay, but she knew, come spring, he'd be going back to fight in that awful war and she knew that Papa Jacob would be depending on her now for sure, for he had no one else.

Aside from a few small tree branches that had fallen on the roof of the shanty, it was pretty much as Ann had left it, though they did see some very large shoe tracks in the yard and evidence of someone sitting on the porch, chewing tobacco and spitting out into the yard.

"That's him, that old Green River boy, Brute Bates. I'd know them tracks anywhere. They ain't nobody in this part of the country that wears shoes that big," Ann said, pointing to the tracks and then measuring them with three spans of the hand.

"There's one thing about it, he'd better stay away from here, if he knows what's good for him", John said, the veins in his neck swelling with anger.

"Papa's already give him one bloody nose. He promised him another'n if he ever bothered me again."

"What'd he do to you, Ann?"

"Oh, he stopped me on my way to your Papa's place, when I went down there to read them the letter I got from you. He asked me what I was a doin', trapsin' up and down the road by myself. When he laid a hand on me, Fidgety dug her claws into his hand and nailed him on the thumb with her teeth."

"Well, he'd better watch his step when it comes to messin' around with my woman," John said, becoming even more angry.

"I think he's learned his lesson," Ann said. "Because the other day when your mother died, I met him on the way down up to give Papa the bad news. He moved over to the side of the road and just stood there, all sulled up, till I went on out of sight around the bend."

"Well, I hope he has, Ann Biddy Shepherd. If he knows what's good for him, he has."

John and Ann went inside the shanty and built a small fire to warm up a bit. They decided to roast some chestnuts in the meantime, and when the chestnuts had finished roasting, John removed the husks with his ivory handle knife. They sat for a few minutes, eating chestnuts and enjoying the precious little time they were able to spend alone together.

"We'd better be headin' back, Little Woman. Pa'll be walkin' the floor by the time we get back, anyway."

"He'll be hungry too," Ann said, as she pulled the ashes over the fire at the fireplace, killing all the flames.

89

John climbed into the saddle and Ann swung up behind him. The big black horse was full of fire and ready to go, so John let him go at his own speed. The tail of Ann's black dress flailed in the wind. She wrapped her arms around John's thin waist, as the mighty steed sped down the road.

They had gone only a short distance when they saw a giant column of smoke rising into the sky. It looked as though it was coming from the Shepherd place. "That smoke looks like it's comin' from Pa's house,"John said, as he nudged the stallion in the flanks, urging him to go faster.

"Sure does, John. It's bigger'n any brush fire I ever seed, too."

As they passed P D's place, it looked as if he had gone that way with the mule and wagon and it looked as if the mule had been forced into a gallop, for his hoofs had dug deep, slinging snow as he galloped along. "Papa's already on his way down there," Ann said, holding on for dear life, as John urged the stallion to go even faster.

When they came into view of the Shepherd house, their worst fears were realized. The house was totally engulfed in flames and the roof had already collapsed. After retrieving the two rockers from the porch, P D and Hassie were standing helplessly by, as the fire comsumed the house.

"Where's Pa?" John asked, as he brought the panting stallion to a standstill in the yard beside the wagon.

"Ain't seed 'im, Son. Must still be in 'ere," P D said, with a frightened look in his eyes. "No way to know till the fire burns out."

A large can that Jacob used for storing coal oil was sitting on the ground some distance from the house. A clutter of huge shoe tracks were pressed into the snow around the coal oil can and trailed off in the direction of Wildcat Spurr.

"That's Brute Bates' thacks right 'ere," P D said, his face turning red with anger, while ashes and cinders from the burning house settled on the brim of his hat.

Finally, after the fire had consumed the house, P D and John tried, but failed to locate Jacob's remains amongst the smoldering cinders, so they decided to send Ann and Hassie home in the wagon, while they went in pursuit of the Green River Boy. "He'll pay fer this, one way'er tuther," P D said, as he and John mounted the stallion.

They traced the tracks to the base of Wildcat Spurr, where they took an abrupt turn to the left and headed up the steep side of the mountain. They knew the horse would not be unable to climb the steep terrain, so they dismounted and tethered him to a small sapling and continued their pursuit on foot.

"Looks like he's headin' fer the cliffs," P D said, breathing heavily from the exausting climb up the snow covered mountain.

"Seems so," John said, as he clambered along behind P D, crawling on his hands and knees.

As they neared the cliffs, they heard the blood curdling scream of a man and a thud at the base of the cliffs. "He must'a fell off'a them rocks up 'ere," P D said, as he and John continued crawling on hands and knees in the direction of the scream.

When they reached the spot where the tracks ended, they saw him. There on a jagged boulder sprawled Brute Bates' lifeless body at the foot of the cliffs. It appeared as if he had just walked to the edge and stepped out into open space, or perhaps he had lost his footing and slipped, but there was no sign of that. Either way, he had met his fate. He had crossed that great divide and met his just reward. "No way to get down 'ere. 'Sides we couldn't carry 'im out, noway. Must weigh nigh onto two hunderd pounds," P D said, as he leaned back on his haunches, breathless from all the tragic happenings and the climb up Wildcat Spurr.

"The buzards'll pick him clean. At least, that a'way, he'll be worth somethin'," John said, wiping the sweat from his forehead on the sleeve of his coat.

Knowing full well it would be almost impossible to retrieve the body, they began inching their way back down the slipery, snow covered terrain. "How'd we ever git up this mountain, John? We must'a been out'uv our heads," P D said, as he and John slid on their backsides down the mountainside.

"We must have gone a little crazy, P D," John said, as he went sliding along on his butt, slamming into the trunk of a large oak tree, knocking him almost senseless.

"Well, we had to make sure it was him. If we had waited till the snow melted, we might of never knowed fer sure," John said. "But now, we know fer sure it was Brute Bates, that old Green River boy."

"You're right, John. Now we know, but it won't bring ye pa back, now will It?"

"Afraid not, P D. I'm afraid not," John said, as they made their way back down to where the stallion stood tethered to the sapling.

As they viewed the remains of the Shepherd house, they stood in silence for a few minutes, then sifting through the ashes and charred timbers near the hearth of the fireplace, John found the skelatal remains of his father. On the hearth lay his old clay pipe and nearby lay his pocket watch, the crystal broken into a thousand pieces. The hands of the watch were stopped dead at nine forty-seven.

John and P D went down to the barn and as John handed down the pieces to Jacob's coffin, P D placed them on the feeding trough there in the breezeway. "I'll nail his coffin together, Son, while you look fer the rest uv his bones," P D said, as he picked up an iron wedge from the bottom step of the stairs to the barn loft. "Guess this'll do fer a hammer, since his hammer , no doubt, got burned up in the fire."

When John was satisfied he'd found all his father's bones, he put them into a tow sack and brought them down to the barn and placed them gently into his coffin and placed the lid on top. P D nailed it shut with the iron wedge and said, "He'll be safe here in the barn tonight, 'specially since we don't have to worry about Brute Bates no more,"

P D fed and watered the cow. She didn't need to be milked because she had gone dry a few days back. Ann had carried the goats with her in the wagon when she and Hassie went up to P D's earlier in the day. "I'll take the cow up to my house in a day er two and take care uv her till she comes in," P D said.

"I sure do appreciate all you've done, Mister Biddy."

"Don't mention it, Son. We were  just proud to do it," P D said, as they climbed astride the stallion and headed up the road toward the Biddy house.

As they walked into the front room at P D's, Ann and Hassie were sitting in front of the fire. The old tattered Shepherd bible was resting on Hassie's lap. She had been looking at the recorded information of the births and deaths of members of the Shepherd family.

"Where'd ye get that bible, Hassie?"John asked.

He was very surprised to see it again, for he thought it had been consumed by the fire that had taken the life of his father.

"I must'a stuck it into my carry bag by accident, the day ye mother died. I was flippin' through it to see'f anybody'd put down when she died."

"Well that's one accident that paid off," John said, as he lifted the bible from Hassie's lap and thumbed through it's tattered and tearstained pages. "Looks like Mama shed a bunch of tears through the years, readin' this good old book," he said. "Hope it brought her some comfort."

"I'm sure it did, Son," Hassie said.

"She loved that old bible, John," but my concern is, did you find Papa Jacob? " Ann said, eagerly awaiting an answer.

"Found his bones right there next to the fireplace. His pipe was layin' there on the hearth. Found his watch, layin' next to his bones. The crystal was broke into a thousand pieces. The hands stopped at

92

exactly nine forty-seven. The fire must have started around nine o'clock," John said, as he stood staring at the fire in the fireplace.

"What'd ye do with his bones, Mister Shepherd?" Hassie asked.

"We put his coffin together and put his bones in it. Left the coffin out there in the barn," John said.

"Ain't ye afraid that old Green River boy'll try to do sompum with him tonight while nobody's lookin'?"

"We don't have to worry about him no more, Hassie. He fell off'a that big cliff, up there on Wildcat Spurr. Met his maker right then and there. Guess everbody's better off with him gone. Anyway, I'm sure Pa's bones'll be there in the mornin' when we go down to burry him," John said, gazing down at the page in the bible where Ann had recorded the death of his mother.

"Two days ago we burried Mama. Tomorrow we'll burry Pa," he said, as he handed the bible to Ann and asked her to record his father's death.

"I've got a pot a soup beans simmerin' over the fire. I hope you and Ann are thinkin' about stayin' here tonight," Hassie said, as she lifted the lid from the pot, the steam rising up the chimney.

"Well, Mother Hassie, we don't have much choice. We don't have a thing to eat there at the cabin," Ann said.

"Well that settles it. Drag yer chairs around the table and I'll take up the bread and set the pot of beans on the table and we'll be ready to eat. I guess you're 'bout starved. You ain't had nothin' to eat since early this mornin', have ye?"

"All we had was a handfull of chestnuts up there at the cabin, Mother Hassie."

"I guess we ought to say a few words to the Man upstairs," Hassie said, as they all sat around the table in silence, waiting to see who would be saying those words.

Hassie bowed her head and said, "Lord, I ain't no good at this sort of a thang, but I'm mighty gratefull that them that's left of us is still together. We'll try to do better in the days to come than we've done in the past. At least, that's what I aim to do. Amen."

They all echoed the amen as they each broke a piece of bread from the pone as it was passed around the table. Hassie ladled some beans onto each plate and they all began to eat.

Not a single word had been spoken since they began eating. As a matter of fact, P D hadn't said a single word since he came inside, but he broke the silence when he said, "Guess his mama'll be worried about him,"

"Who's that, Papa?" Ann asked.

"Brute Bates' mama. You know she's bound to love him in spite of all he's done, 'cause he's all she had left. Her old man died three summers ago. Slipped off a rock down there in Green River and drowned."

"I'll tell her just what happened to him when I see her," John said. "And I'm bound to tell her what he did to my pa, too."

"Well, I wouldn't make no special trip down 'ere to tell her, Hassie said, looking P D straight in the eye.

ꛯꛯꛯꛯꛯꛯꛯꛯꛯꛯꛯꛯ

Darkness was settling down over Deep Gap as P D came in from taking care of the animals. Ann had helped Hassie clear the table and was drying the dishes while Hassie washed.

Ann was still astonished to see how much Hassie's personality had changed. She had been such a strange person in the past, but Ann was now beginning to think of her as a mother, something she had never dreamed possible.

Long after they had gone to bed and all the others were fast asleep, Ann lay awake, thinking about how all those whom she loved had been taken from her.

"There's my mother, died when I was born. Then Aunt Isa and then two days ago, Mama Sarah and now Papa Jacob, burned to his bare bones in his own house. That's one-two-three-four," she counted silently on her fingers. "Why should all this be happenin' to me? I'm afraid it's a curse," she thought to herself, as she lay, wide eyed, staring into the dead of night.

The deaths of family members and especially that of her mother began to weigh heavily on her mind, gnawing at her very soul. So after the deaths of John's parrents, she decided to withhold her affections from those she loved. Perhaps if she pretended not to care so much for them, nothing bad would happen to them, or at least that's what she was thinking.

Hassie was up by daybreak the next morning, mixing dough for a hoecake. A large pan of fatback was frying on a bed of coals on the hearth at the fireplace. Coffee was boiling in the big castiron pot, suspended from the hook over the fire. "Why didn't you call me, Mother Hassie. I would have been more'n happy to help you cook breakfast," Ann said, sidling up to Hassie, much like a child would do with its mother.

"No need, Ann Biddy Shepherd. Look at the times you've

cooked for me."

"I know, Mother Hassie, but this is here is another time and another place."

"May be another time, Ana Bell, but it's the same place. Believe me, I've thought long and hard about the way I treated you. I'm ashamed of myself. I hope you can find room in your soul to forgive me. I know I don't deserve it, but I do hope you can."

"I do, Mother Hassie. I surely do," Ann said, as tears flooded her eyes and eased down her cheeks.

She hugged Hassie around the waist, then backed away suddenly, remembering the promise she made to herself about not getting too close to those she loved. It was painful for her to do this, for it was totally against her nature, but she believed it would be less painful in the long run if she kept her distance. So that's what she began to practice almost religiously.

"Will you and John be stayin' here with us now't Jacob's house is gone?"

"No, Mother Hassie, we'll be stayin' up at the cabin, soon's we can get over to Bent Oak to get some stuff."

"Well you know you're more than welcome to stay here with your pa and me if you'd rather."

"I know, Mother Hassie, but we'll just feel more at ease if we're in our own house. Besides, John'll be goin' back to that god-awful war in a few weeks anyway. I sure do dread that day."

"I know, Ann Biddy Shepherd. I do hope and pray that he makes it through it without gettin' all shot up," Hassie said, staring into the fire, her jade green eyes sparkling in the firelight.

"I pray every day, Mother Hassie. It's the only thing that keeps me from losin' my mind."

After breakfast, P D hitched Jude to the wagon and he and John went down to the Shepherd place to dig Jacob's grave, where only three days ago, they had buried his wife.

It was twelve noon when they returned to P D's and after they had eaten dinner, they all prepared to make that sad trip to the ridge at the Shepherd place to burry Jacob's bones. "Seems so sad, but at least they're back together again," Hassie said, as she emerged form the bedroom, after donning her black dress.

"They were both such good people. Why'd they have to go this way?" Ann asked, brushing the tears from her eyes with her fingertips.

"Noboby can answer that, Ann, but it happened and we'll carry on the best we can," John said, in an attempt to say something that would give Ann comfort in her time of sorrow, for within only a few weeks they had begun to feel like her very own parents.

It was such a sad occasion as John and P D lowered Jacob's bones into the grave, for Mama Sarah's grave was still fresh. "Lord, I've seen a lot of men die, but I've seen nothing so sad as this. Be with us in our time of sorrow," John said, as he tossed a handful of sand and gravel onto pine box at the bottom of the grave. "God rest their weary souls."

Ann and Hassie sat in the breezeway of the barn as P D and John filled in and rounded up the grave. John broke two sprigs from a nearby holly tree, placing one on Jacob's grave and the other on Mama Sarah's. "Rest in peace, Ma and Pa. I'm gonna miss you both," he said.

John and P D turned their backs to the grave and walked slowly down the hill toward the barn.

"What about the cow, P D," are we gonna take her with us?" Hassie asked.

"Guess so. Can't leave her down here, Hassie," P D said, as he tied the cow's halter rope to the standard at the back of the wagon.

John saddled the black stallion, mounted the big black horse and Ann swung up behind him. The sun was resting on Wildcat Spurr as they headed up the road toward P D's house.

"Ann, if ye pa'll let us borrow old Jude and the wagon for a day, we'll go over to Bent Oak and get us some grub. Then we'll go up to our place and spend a few days together, before I have to go back up north," John said, as he walked into the kitchen the next morning.

"I don't see how he can rightly turn you down, John, since the mule belonged to your pa in the first place."

"I think you're right, Ann Shepherd. I think you're right."

A little after mid-morning, after borrowing the mule and wagon from P D, they were on their way to Bent Oak, with Jude in a trot. A loose board in the bed of the wagon made a slapping noise as the wagon bumped over the rocky road.

John and Ann sat close to each other, just like two peas in a pod, taking on the flavor of two newlyweds. After all, they hadn't had a chance to spend very much time together since they were married. Even though Ann knew she had promised herself to keep her distance from those she loved, it was impossible to hide her true feelings for John. "You know I worry about you when you're up there fightin' in that awful war, John," she said, clinging to his arm.

"Let's not talk about it, Ann. We've got a few days. Let's forget about the war for a while."

When they walked up onto the loading dock at the store, Brute Bates' mother, Maudie, stepped outside, her face mottled and stained with tears. She had been crying day and night since her son went missing. "Have ye seed my boy?" she asked John. "I been lookin' everwhere fer 'im. Hain't nobody seed 'im."

"Maudie, I'm bound to be honest with you. I have seen your boy. When I saw him last, he was sprawled out on a jagged rock up there on Wildcat Spurr. Me and P D Biddy followed his tracks in the snow, after he burned Pa's house to the ground. We heard him scream when he fell off of that big cliff, up there on this side of the mountain."

"You'ns prob'ly thowed him off, yeself. I wouldn't put nothin' a'passed you'ns," Maudie screamed, pointing her bony finger straight into John's face.

"I've nothin' else to say, Maudie. What I've told you is the very way it happened. You can go up there and see for yourself, if you want to. Better yet, ask P D, he'll tell you the very same thing I've told you."

"He'd tell the very same lie's you've told, John Shepherd. You's all liars. All liars!"

"Think whatever you want, Maudie, but it's the God's truth or He may strike me dead."

Maudie headed down the road toward home, sobbing into her apron as John and Ann made their way into the store. "I'm sorry about her boy, but it's a little late to change things now," John said.

"In her own way she loved him, but look at what happened to him," Ann thought to herself. "Maybe if she hadn't cared so much for him, things would have been different."

Ann and John didn't have a shopping list, but they pretty well knew what they needed to buy, or at least they knew what they could afford. They picked up the things they needed, paid for them and were soon on their way home to the little shanty on Ann Ridge.

"John, it's so good to be heading home, but it seems so strange. We're not dreaming, are we?"

"No, we're not dreaming. It's all real. This is me and that's you, and that's old Jude, out there pulling the wagon," John said, first pointing to himself, then to Ann and then the mule. "Should I pinch you to make sure you're awake?"

"No thank you, John, I'll take your word for it," Ann said, clinging to his arm and smiling up at him.

After unloading their supplies at the shanty, Ann started supper while John returned the mule and wagon to her father's house. He didn't linger long at the Biddy's and after bidding P D and Hassie goodnight, he mounted the black stallion and headed back toward Ann Ridge, for he knew that darkness would arrive soon after the sun went down behind Wildcat Spurr, especially at this time of the year.

The big stallion carried him effortlessly, his mighty muscles flexing with each stride, but when the horse saw something on the bank above the road that looked like a bobcat, he stopped abruptly, slamming John's groin against the pommel, leaving him in a great deal of pain. The horse's nostrils flared and he let out with a loud whinny. "What's the matter with you, big'un?" John said to the stallion, when the pain finally subsided enough so he could speak.

It was beginning to get dusky dark and when John looked up at the bank above the road, he saw what had frightened the horse. A half rotted poplar log lay a few feet up the embankment, taking on the appearance of a large bobcat, stretched out and ready to pounce on anything coming up the road. The log had been decaying for some time and two spots at one end glowed with fox fire, looking much like two burning eyes. "That's just a rotten log, big boy. Nothin' to be afraid of," he said, patting the stallion on the side of his neck.

With a little urging, John persuaded the horse to move on, but the horse galloped sideways, keeping an eye on the log until John tightened the reins, forcing him to look straight ahead. "It's alright, big boy," John said, as the horse sailed along, his hoofs barely touching the ground with each stride.

John had heard many tales of horses being spooked, throwing their riders and racing home with empty saddles, but this was his first encounter with anything of that sort.

When he reached the foot of Ann Ridge, he stopped at Britten Creek to let the stallion drink. When the horse's thirst was satisfied, John led him up to the barn where he removed the saddle, put him into the stall and fed him some corn and fodder.

The fire at the fireplace flickered, casting a ghostly shadow of Ann against the far wall as John walked in from the tiny porch. "Hope supper's ready, Ann. I'm hungry enough to eat a horse."

"Well, sit down there at the table and I'll get you somethin'." Ann said, dipping stew from the heavy cast iron pot and ladling it into John's bowl. "There you are, John. Dig in."

They ate stew and corn pone and drank hot coffee until they were stuffed and as they sat facing each other at the table, John said, "You're a delight to behold, Ann Biddy Shepherd. You're what makes my life worth while."

Ann smiled at him, but made no reply. In her heart, she knew he meant everything he had said, for he was not the kind of man to waste words.

After the dishes were washed, they sat before the fire, gazing into the glowing embers and swapping small talk and just enjoying each others company.

It was the tenth of July of the previous year when they last spent the night together, and on the very next day John went away to fight in the war.

They talked deep into the night and finally fell asleep, sometime around midnight. The fire at the fireplace flickered for a while longer, then faded into a faint orange glow, as john and Ann lay sharing the warmth of each other's bodies on this cold Febuary night.

They treasured the precious few days they had left before John would be off again to fight in that awful war, but they stayed busy there at the little shanty, cutting wood for the fireplace and preparing the ground in the  fenced in garden spot, so Ann would only have to lay off the rows and be ready to plant, when spring rolled around.

They made several trips to visit P D and Hassie, but today they were heading to Bent Oak Trading Post, riding on the back of that big, black stallion.

"This here horse sure has come in mighty handy, John," Ann said, as the stallion carried them swiftly down the road.

"Don't know what we would have done without him, Ann. Guess we could have borrowed old Jude," John said, smiling.

The soles on John's brogans were wearing thin, so he figured on buying a new pair at the trading post. He wanted to make sure they were broken in before leaving to go back to the war. He remembered how the new shoes he had worn on his first trip wore large blisters on his feet and how he punctured them with his grand-pa's pearl handled knife. He didn't want to go through that again. He knew he would be riding the stallion, but if something happened to the horse he could end up walking.

They dismounted at the trading post and as John was about to attach the bridle reins to the hitching post, Henry, his uncle, staggered down from the loading dock. "Imagine seein' you here today. I thought you'as up 'ere a'fightin' 'em damn Yankees, John", he said, clinging to John's arm in order to maintain his balance.

"No, Uncle Henry, I'm home for a few days, on furlough. I guess you didn't know that Ma died a few days back, and your brother got burned up when Brute Bates set the house afire, did you?"

"Why no, I didn't know. How could I? Nobody never tells me a thang. Ye say Brute Bates set Jacob's house afire? I'll kill 'im fer that," Henry said, as he seemed to sober a bit and his face went blood red with fury.

"I'm afraid you're a little late for that, Uncle Henry. He fell off that big clift, up there on Wildcat Spurr. Met his just reward on that big jagged rock, about a hundred feet down the mountain side. Me and P D followed him up there. We figured he either misstepped or slipped in the snow. Anyhow, he fell off and got hisself killed and I say good riddance. Mean should have been his middle name."

"Well, he saved me a lead ball and some gun powder," Henry said, as the red began to fade from his face.

"We all thought you'd gone back to Sumter, Uncle Henry."

"Nope, John, I like it up here in 'ese mountains. It's a lot cooler up here in the summer than it is down 'ere in that stifling heat of South Ca'lina. Asides, I've got work up here. I do."

John didn't ask him what kind of work, but he felt sure he could guess without too much effort.

"Well, I'm real sorry to hear about my brother. Wadn't no better man in 'ese parts. Shore wadn't," Uncle Henry said, letting go of John's arm and grasping the hitching post to steady himself. "He didn't deserve to die that away."

They left Henry standing, babbling to himself, leaning against the hitching post, and went inside to buy the few things they needed, including a new pair of brogans. There were only a few to choose from, but John was fortunate to find a pair that fit his feet fairly well and after paying for them, he sat down on a nail keg and put them on his feet and laced them up.

"How do they feel, John."

"They're a little tight, Ann, but they'll limber up in a few days. I'll break 'em in before I head back to the war."

He tied the laces of his old brogans together and swung them over his shoulder and picked up the sack of other things they had bought and when they walked outside, Uncle Henry was gone, so they climbed astride the stallion and struck out for Ann Ridge.

As the horse galloped along, carrying them on their way back to the shanty, Ann asked in broken words, "When — will you — be headin'— back — north, —John?"

"Sunday, — th' eighth — of March —, Ann."

"That's a mighty short time", Ann thought to herself, as she clung to John's waist so tightly that he reached down with his left hand and loosened her grip a bit.

Indeed, it was only a short time before John would be returning to Virginia, for today was the last day of Febuary. They had only one full week to spend together before he would be leaving. That precious week faded like a raindrop on a bed of sand in a mid-August sun.

# Chapter

# 7

## John Goes Back To The War

Ann couldn't hold back the tears as John mounted the black stallion and headed out the road, going back to that awful war and to whatever fate awaited him, but she knew as well as he that he must go, for he had promised his commaning officer he'd be back by spring, come hail or high water, and he was a man of his word.

She made her way back inside the tiny shanty, viewing things through a veil of tears and sat down in the straight chair at the fireplace. She sat for some time, blotting the tears from her eyes on the sleeve of her black dress.

Finally, after shedding all the tears her eyes could produce, she stood on her tiptoes to reach the note pad on the shelf beside the fireplace. The note pad contained all the information she had recorded about herbs and about birthing and the secret ingredients Lady Owatta had used to cure Hassie of her oppressing malady. She seated herself at the table on the rough sawed bench and poured over the notes until the sun was halfway till noon. If she was ever to become a midwife or an herb doctor, she would need to learn all she could about such things. "It's comin' spring and when things begin to turn green I'll go up to the Indian Village and see what else Lady Owatta can tell me," she said, as she placed the note pad back on the shelf.

The bleating of the nanny goats, Precious and Gracious, reminded her that she was all alone again and the fact that the duties of providing for herself and her animals had fallen on her shoulders once again. She was well versed on the duties of caring for herself and she didn't hesitace a moment in resuming that duty.

She released the bucket from the nail on the wall and walked hurriedly out toward the barn, with Figety trailing along behind her, snatching at her long, black dresstail. "Come on, Figety, let's get some milk", she said, as she walked into the breezeway. "Mornin', Precious, and you, too, Gracious. You ready to give me some milk?"

And so began another chapter in the life of Ann Shepherd. Pain and dread and lonliness had become an unavoidable part of her life. It had been a little over a year since Aunt Isa passed away, but it seemed a lot longer to her. "Time passes so slow when a body's in a dread, waitin' for somethin' bad to happen," she whispered to herself, as she sat on the tiny milkstool.

She had endured so much pain and humiliation from her mother-in-law, Hassie Oddum, but she wasn't about to let things of the past dominate her life. "Good things are ahead, I'm sure of it," she said.

Fidgety brushed against her leg and let out with a loud meow, reminding her that she was ready for her usual squirt of warm milk. "Move back a little and I'll squirt some in your mouth, Fidgity."

The squirt was somewhat off its mark and caught the cat squarely in the left eye. Fidgety stepped aside, brushed the milk from her eye and proceeded to lick the milk from her paw as if that was the way it was supposed to have been done. "Well, Fidgety, that was a little off the mark, but you got it anyway."

"Meow," the cat answered.

Except for the company of her animals and chickens, Ann was now alone again. She began to talk to her animals as if they were human. Even though she got no answer when she talked to them, it helped her overcome her lonliness. She had names for all her chickens, her sheep, her goats and of course her cat. They were her friends, and at times, it seemed, they were her only friends.

Word had gotten around about her aiding in the delivery of Nat Spicer's baby boy last September, and now folks throughout the community were calling on her for help when they had sickness in the family or another child was about to be born. People began addressing her as 'Doctor Shepherd'. She knew she was far from being a doctor, but it made her proud that they placed that much confidence in her.

As the days became warmer and the wild plants began to spring up, she made arrangements with Lady Owatta to spend time with her, gathering and identifying plants and herbs and making notes about their uses. Lady Owatta was very obliging and when Ann didn't have other chores that needed attending, they were out in the woods, doing just that. They gathered belladonna, an extremely toxic herb, but an ointment made from this plant could be used in the treatment of gout and rheumatism.

She and Lady Owatta made several small bags of deer skin, in which to store the various herbs.

They stored the toxic herbs in small bags and identified them as being poisonous by marking the bags with an "X", using pokeberry stain as ink. These were kept separate and carried in a larger bag marked with an "X" also.

During the spring and summer and even into the fall, they gathered Belladonna, Bindweed, Boneset, and Coltsfoot. They gathered Comfry, Dandelion, Elder, and Fairywand, and a host of other herbs. They gathered herbs until all the bags were filled with the precious herbs she would need to treat any ailment she might encounter.

She wrote the names of each herb on small scraps of paper and placed them inside their individual bags, so she would have no trouble identifying the herbs later on.

Letters from John came far and in between, but each time Ann received a letter from him, her hands trimbled with excitement. In his last letter he told her he was stationed at Petersburg, a few miles southeast of Richmond, and that he was attached to a unit that was responsible for defending the Confederate capitol against Yankee invasion. He said he was very lucky to be stationed there, for most of the fighting was being done elsewhere at that time.

The war had been going poorly for the Confederates during the summer of 1863. Vicksburg had surrendered to the Yankees on the forth day of July. Gettesburg was lost to the Yankees at about the same time. And now, the last full week of November, Chattanooga was about to go down in defeat.

"It can't be too long before them Yankees'll be starin' down our our throats," John thought to himself, as he worked to reinforce the walls of the trenches with wooden stakes, lacing them together with small tree branches.

Ann was concerned for John's safety every waking hour. She prayed for him each night before going to bed, "May he be spared and be returned to me, safe, sound, and soon."

As she lay on her shuck filled mattress, the fire in the fireplace fading and dying, she could hear the wind, moaning outside the shanty. She could hear it roaring across the crest of Wildcat Spurr. Snow was sifting through the cracks in the walls as smoke from the fireplace belched back into the little shanty. "I might as well bank that fire," she said, as she slid off the bed and into her scuffs. "Won't get no heat from it noway, long's the wind's blowin' like this."

After banking the fire, she crawled back into bed and pulled the heavy covers over herself. Fidgety curled up under her chin and they were soon fast asleep. They slept soundly through the night, but were awakened at daybreak the next morning by someone pounding so hard on the door she feared it might fall off its hinges.

"Doctor Shepherd!" came a lady's voice from the other side of the door. "My man's broke his leg, right above the knee, and I need ye to come'n fix it."

Ann bounded from bed, sending Fidgety flying. She rushed to the door and lifted the latch.

"Sorry to rouse you from bed at this earley hour, Ma'am, but my man's in a lot of pain and I didn't know what to do fer'im," the young lady at the door said.

"Well, come in, out of the wind and cold. I'll build a fire and make a pot of coffee. That'll warn you up a bit," Ann said, as she took the young lady by the arm, guiding her over to the chair in front of the fireplace.

"I'm Matilda Blanton," the young lady said, as she eased her tired shivering body down into the chair. "I hear say you're a knowin' doctor."

"All I know is what Lady Owatta has told me, but I'm always obliged to help in any way I can. Where is your man? Is he in the warm?"

"He's there at the house, but I guess the fire's gone out by now, I've been walkin' most of the night to get here, and he can't stand up, let alone keep the fire goin', and they's nobody there to see about him," Matilda said, blotting a tear from her.

"Soon's I get this fire built, we'll fix us a bite to eat, but I'll have to feed and milk the goats before we can go," Ann said, as she knelt on the cold hearth, placed some fine kindling onto the coals and blew until there was a blaze and swung the kettle over the fire.

As she released the milk bucket from the nail on the wall, she said, "I'll milk the goats while the water's gettin' hot."

After feeding and milking the goats, she and Matilda sat before the fire, drinking coffee and munching on a piece of day old bread.

"Matilda, I don't mean to be nosey, but would you mind telling me where you live?" Ann asked.

"Down on Green River, out passed Deep Gap. It's a good piece down there, doctor."

"Well we best be goin'. Your man's in a lot of pain and he may be cold, too," Ann said, while selecting the things needed to treat a broken leg.

At sunup they bundled up as best they could and headed down toward Deep Gap. The weather was clear, but each puff of wind brought with it a flurry of fine ice crystals that stung their exposed faces. About an inch of powdery snow lay on the ground in low places along the road, but none lay along the ridges where the wind could get at it. Their feet made a crunching sound on the frosty roadbed as they trudged along, heads bent low, facing into the wind.

104

Further on down the road they stopped to rest in a sunny spot, sheltered from the wind by a high bank. They stood in an embraced stance, sharing each other's armpits as an incubator for warming their hands. As soon as their hands were warm and the feelings returned to their fingertips, they stepped back, pulled their coat collars around their faces and headed on down toward Green River.

"The wind's slowin' down some," Ann said, in a somewhat labored utterance because of her facial muscles being so cold.

"Yeah, but it's still plenty cold," Matilda replied.

It was sometime passed noon when they finally reached the Blanton house. They rushed inside and found Skip Vaughn Blanton, Matilda's husband, shivering beneath a pile of quilts. "Thought you'd never get back," he whined.

"Went and come as fast as I could. It's a long way up to Doctor Shepherd's house and back," Matilda said, as she reached over to stroke her husband's forehead.

"Guess you're in a lot of pain, Mister Blanton," Ann said, as she removed the covers to have a look at his broken leg. "I should say you are. You've got quite a bend in that leg. We'll need a couple of boards for splints," she said, looking over at Matilda. "But first we'll have to line up the bones and that'll take some doing."

"How are you at handling pain, Mister Blanton? Have you got any likker in the house?"

"Got some sittin' in a jug under the bed," Matilda said, as she went down on her knees to retrieve it.

"Well, give him a good snort of the stuff, it'll help dull the pain when we pull the bones back in line."

Skip took three big swallows of the corn likker, took a deep breath, lay back and closed his eyes.

"We'll give the likker a little time to take affect before we try to set the bones. You'll have to get up there at the head of the bed and hold him down while I pull on his leg. No, on second thoughts, I guess it'd be better if we rolled up a couple of bed sheets, looped them under his armpits and tied 'em to the bed posts. Could be, I'll need you to hold his leg straight while I put the splints in place," Ann said, pointing toward the bureau, where she figured Matilda kept her bed sheets.

Matilda reached into the bureau drawer, took out two bed sheets and fashioned the ropes. She laced the rolled up bed sheets under his armpits and tied them to the bed posts.

"Now get me two narrow boards, about twice as long as your arm for the splints, and we'll need some soft rags, somthin' to keep the splints in place when we get the bones lined up," Ann said, running her

105

hands along Skip's leg to locate the spot where the bone was broken.

Matilda rushed out to the shed where her husband stored scraps of lumber and picked out two narrow pieces of the same length and brought them back into the house. "Will 'ese do, Doctor Shepherd?" She asked.

"They'll be fine, Matilda. Now comes the hard part. Crawl up there on the bed and hold him down while I pull on his leg. He's gonna holler some, but don't let it scare you none. I'll go as easy as I can," Ann said, grasping his ankle with her right hand while holding onto his foot with the other. She would use his foot as a leaver to align the leg bone, once she had the two segments end to end.

Skip moaned and tried to sit up in bed as Ann began pulling on his leg, but Matilda, being quite heavy, threw all her weight on his chest and held him down as Ann continued working with him. After several hard pulls, she heard the broken bones snap into place. "Well, that wasn't so bad, now was it?" Ann said.

She kept a firm grip on Skip's leg until Matilda could get down from the bed and come around to hold his leg steady while she applied the splints.

When Ann finished with Skip, he looked as if he had the leg of a mummy, wrapped with rags from his hip to his ankle. "I think that'll do it," she said, stepping back to admire her handiwork.

"Looks good, Doctor Shepherd, good indeed." Matilda said, mopping sweat from her brow with a piece of shredded bed sheet. "We'll let him rest while I cook us a bite of dinner."

"I'm afraid I won't have time for that, Matilda. If I head out this very minute, it'll be dark before I get home." Ann said, as she searched through her deer skin bag, looking for some pulverized comfry.

She sprinkled some of the precious herb into a coffee cup and told Matilda how to administer it. "Mix a big spoonful of this herb in a dab of warm water for a poltice, put it on his leg where the bones are broke and tie a rag around it. It'll help the bones heal. It's right here where I've tied this peice of cloth into a bow, I left it open so you'll have no trouble finding the place," Ann said, pointing to the piece of cloth Matilda would need to remove in order to apply the poltice.

"We ain't got no money, Doctor Shepherd, but when my man gets well, he'll be obliged to pay ye fer ye trouble," Matilda said, as she reached into the Dutch oven and pulled out a sweet potato and a chunk of cornbread. "I guess this'll keep ye from starvin' till ye can get somethin' better."

"He'll have to stay off that leg for a little over a month, Matilda. It'll take that long to heal. Maybe you can whittle out a crutch from a sapling for him and he can hobble around in a couple of weeks, but tell him not to put any weight on that broke leg. Do you think you can take care of things by yourself till he gets better?"

"I'm a strong woman, Doctor Shepherd. My man's been sick before and I took care of things by myself."

"Well, I best be going. If you need me, feel free to send somebody after me."

"Thank you, Doctor. I'll forever be in your debt."

"Goodbye, Matilda", Ann said, as she struck out for home, with her dresstail flailing in the wind as she made haste up the frozen road, now covered with a thin dusting of snow.

The trip back home was long and arduous, climbing hill after hill, facing into the cold north wind. She didn't have Matilda's arm pits for warming her hands, but as she trudged along, she remembered the times when she was living with her father and Hassie, how she would get up on those cold mornings and build a fire in the fireplace and cook breakfast, while her step-mother lay in bed, weighted down with heavy quilts and yelling at her to hurry up and get breakfast ready.

Even though those days were painful, they had toughened her and prepared her for life in ways she never dreamed of. "You never forget tough lessons," she whispered to herself, her breath fogging into the cold air.

The muscles in her legs ached as she struggled along the frozen road, with World's Edge coming slowly closer with each step. The sun had dropped down behind Wildcat Spurr. The stars were twinkling in the darkening sky as she turned left off Judes Gap road and started up toward Ann Ridge. "Home at last", she said, when she heard the bleating of the goats. Fidgety was waiting for her, perched on the split-rail fence, outside the tiny shanty. Home had never felt so good to her. "Fidgety, I guess you're about starved. Have you been able to catch anything to eat?"

"Meow," the cat answered, as she followed Ann into the shanty, pawing at the tail of her dress.

"Guess I'd better get them goats milked," she said, as she released the milk bucket from the nail on the wall.

After all the chores were done and after fixing and eating a few bites of supper, she sat at the fireplace, staring into the flickering flames. Her thoughts were of John, wondering how he was doing.

The flames at the fireplace had a soothing effect on her, and being so tired from such a strenious day, she soon fell asleep, leaning back in Papa Jacob's rocking chair.

107

As a matter of fact, John was not doing so well. With supplies dwindling, he and his fellow soldiers had to make do with very little food. To make bad maters worse, two fifths of his comrades were absent, with or without leave.

But John was not about to shirk his responsibilities as a soldier, for he remembered the words of his father, "Yeah, Son, you're duty bound to go if you're called."

John was in this thing to the finish. He knew he could never have respect for himself, nor could he expect others to respect him if he left his post just because things were tough.

So he was still there, hunkered down in the trenches at Petersburg. He knew he would be there until the Yankees were defeated, or until, God forbid, they were overrun by their foe and forced to give up their stronghold. So he learned how to survive on the bare necessities, living outside in the trenches, in the cold and snow.

To escape the harshness of the wintry weather, the soldiers dug small caves into the banks of the trenches and covered the openings with whatever material they could find.

One could hardly expect an animal to live in such harsh conditions, but John and his fellow soldiers did. They spent the winter months, living in the trenches like rats and longing for springtime, when they would be able to bask in the sunlight. But for now, it was just a matter of staying alive.

At night when he was unable to sleep, he would lay in his dugout and caress the large black button, attached to the string around his neck. Somehow, it brought him comfort and gave him a sense of closeness to his wife who was so far away.

The backstick in the fireplace burned through and dropped down into the smoldering coals and as it did, it popped and sent a firecoal flying through the air that landed on Ann's lap. She woke suddenly from a dream she was having about John, that of being in the midst of a fierce battle. She jumped to her feet and brushed the redhot coal from her dress, scaring Fidgety about half to death in the meantime. The cat stood in the corner of the room, her tail straight up in the air. It looked as if every hair on its back was standing on end as well.

"I didn't mean to scare you, Fidgety, but it don't take long for a live firecoal to get you hoppin'!" Ann said, as she examined the scorched spot on her dress.

She banked the fire in the fireplace and turned down the covers on her bed. After she and her cat climbed in, she pulled up the covers and closed her eyes. Fidgety curled into a ball under her chin and in no time they were fast asleep.

The wind calmed down about midnight and snow began to fall. By morning, six inches of the white stuff lay on the ground outside the tiny shanty. Everything looked so pure and clean. The blanket of snow was undisturbed, except for the corner of the garden spot, where a rabbit had ventured out before daybreak. Snow stood in a piramid on the gate posts. A blue jay, finding refuge beneath the hemlock below the barn, was searching through a bed of leaves for something to eat.

It was daylight when Ann woke from sleep. She slid into her scuffs and walked over to the tiny window and looked out. "We got us a snow out there today, Fidgety. I'll have to sweep us a path to the barn, otherwise you'll not be able to go out for your morning feast of goat's milk."

"Meow," the cat answered, brushing up against her leg, causing a volly of miniature fireworks to explode from the static electricity generated from rubbing against Ann's wool nightgown.

"You're full of fire this morning," she said, as she knelt before the fireplace, raking the ashes away from the glowing embers.

After breakfast, Ann laced up her high top shoes, slipped into her black coat and went outside to clear a path to the barn. She broke a small branch from the hemlock tree and swept the soft snow from the path. Precious and Gracious were blatting at the top of their lungs, ready to be fed and milked. "I'll be right back, darlings," Ann said, as she rushed back into the shanty to get the milk bucket. "Come on, Fidgety, if you want some warm milk."

The cat didn't have to be told twice, for she was a mite hungry, but being a cat, she wasn't as fond of snow as a dog might have been. She sniffed at the snow and cowered closely behind her master until they reached the security of the barn.

Ann had hardly finished milking the goats, when she heard the muffled sound of a wagon coming up the road. She looked and saw that it was her stepmother, Hassie, riding alone in the wagon. A cloud of vapor exploded from Jude's nostrils each time he exhaled.

"What brings you out in this kind of weather, Mother Hassie?"

"Your Pa. Your Pa's sick. Your Pa's bad sick, Ann Biddy Shepherd. I come up her yistydy and you wasn't here."

"Bad sick? In what way is he sick? Ann asked, as Hassie pulled the mule to a stop, there in front of the barn.

"Newmony. I fear he's got newmony. He can't hardly get no breath. Just about smothered last night, in spite uv ever thang I done. Thought maybe you'd know somethin' we could do fer him."

"Let me get this milk strained and I'll get my bag of herbs and we'll get down there fast as we can," Ann said, rushing up onto the porch and into the shanty.

In very short order, Hassie and Ann were on their way back to the Biddy house. "Maidenhair fern should help him if anything can," Ann said. "I made sure I had some in my deer skin bag."

"I hope it'll help him, Ann Biddy Shepherd, 'cause he's mighty bad," Hassie said, swatting Jude on the rump, urging him to go faster.

When they walked into the Biddy house, they found P D scrunched up in the bed, shivering with a very high fever. "Pa, I'm here to help you," Ann said, as she placed her hand on his forehead. "You're burnin' up. We'll have to get that fever down."

She stirred some maidenhair fern into a cup of warm water, added a teaspoon of molasses and began spooning it into her father's mouth. He was reluctant to drink it at first, but Ann insisted and with a little persuasion, P D drank it all down. Next, Ann stirred some pulverized willow bark and crushed dandelion leaves into another cup of warm water and spooned that into his mouth as well. "This'll make you feel better and help with your kidneys, Pa."

Ann and Hassie sat by his bed all morning, waiting for signs of improvement. Finally, around noon, he began to relax a bit. He looked up at Hassie through half-opened eyes and whispered, "Git me the pot, woman, I'm about to run over."

Hassie reached under the bed and withdrew the blue enameled chamber pot, while Ann helped her father to the side of the bed. Before he was through, the chamber pot was almost running over. "That ort'a take a load off you, P D," Hassie said, laughing and almost spilling the contents onto the floor.

"Pa, are you feelin' better?" Ann asked, as she helped him back into bed and pulled the covers over him.

"Yeah, Child, and I'm a mite hongry, too."

"We can take care of that, can't we, Mother Hassie?"

"I b'lieve we can do that, Annybell Biddy."

By the time Hassie and Ann got the meal cooked, P D had managed to get up, get dressed, and was sitting at the table, fork in hand. "I do believe you're hungry, Pa."

"I ain't eat a thang in two days and I'm ready for some grub," he said. "Them herbs you give me sure brung on th hongrys."

"Well, here it is, P D Biddy," Hassie said, as she placed a plate of ham on the table, followed by a bowl of fried eggs. "The hoecake's about done."

Hassie was a bit surprised that P D had recovered so quickly. "It's just like a miracle, Ann Biddy Shepherd. You sure know how to doctor," she said, as she loaded P D's plate with ham and eggs and a chunk of hoecake.

"I owe all I know to Lady Owatta, Mother Hassie, she sure is a good teacher."

When they finished eating, Ann said she'd better be going. "The animals'll be waitin' for me," she said.

"Don't think for one minute I'm gonna let you walk all the way home by yerself, Annybell. I'll haul you up there in the wagon."

"That's so kind of you. Mother Hassie, but shouldn't you stay here with Pa?"

"I'll be alright, Ann. I'm feelin' a heap better since you doctored me," P D said.

"Well, if you're sure," Papa, "but let me leave you some herbs. I think another dose will straighten you out."

Hassie hitched the mule to the wagon while Ann was saying her goodbyes to her father and soon they were ready to go.

"Don't worry, P D. I'll be back in a little," Hassie assured him, as she and Ann climbed into the wagon.

On the way to Ann Ridge, they had a heart-to-heart talk.

"Mother Hassie, I don't remember my mother, but you have begun to feel like a real mother to me. I couldn't ask for a better one, and let me say, I never believed I'd ever be saying this, but I've grown to love you. You hear that? I love you!"

"And I love you, too, Ann Biddy Shepherd. I treasure you as my daughter, and there again, there couldn't be one better'n you."

Hassie stopped the wagon at the gate, just long enough for Ann to step down and unload her bag of herbs. She said goodbye, tapped the mule with the reins and was on her way again, back down to the Biddy house to take care of P D.

"I'll See you in a few days, Mother Hassie. If you need me, let me know."

Hassie tapped the mule with the reins once more and he broke into a trot. Snow was plentiful and the road was rough. It was dangerous to be traveling so fast, but she was anxious to get back home to check on P D.

Hard ice was forming in places along the road which made it even more risky to be going at that speed and as they rounded the turn

111

and started across Britten Creek, the mule lost his footing and stumbled head first into the cold water. The wagon careened to the left and landed upside-down in the frigid water. Hassie was trapped face down in the cold water beneath the wagon. The singletree disengaged as the wagon overturned, allowing Jude to regain his footing and he clambered up the bank and out of the creek. The mule sensed that something was wrong, because Hassie was not moving, and seeing that he was no longer attached to the wagon he raced on down the road with the singletree and reins dragging along behind him.

When P D heard the noise and  looked out the window, he saw the mule galloping up the road, his frightend eyes flared when he came to a stop in front of the house. P D grabbed his heavy coat and rushed outside to find the mule soaking wet and breathing hard. "What's wrong, Jude? What's happened to Hassie?"

Of course, the mule couldn't answer him, but P D knew that something was terribly wrong. He unhooked the singletree and led the mule down to the barn and dried him off as best he could, threw a dry towsack onto his back, mounted him and went flying back up the road to see what had happened to Hassie.

When he approached Britten Creek and saw the overturned wagon and Hassie's legs sticking out from beneath it, he yelled, "Hassie! Hassie! What happened?!"

He waded into the cold water and using all his strength, lifted the wagon off his dead wife's body, sending it crashing over the falls. He knew she was dead when he pulled her limp body from the icy water and carried her up the bank and eased her down onto the snow.

He dropped to his knees and cried, as he gently smoothed her eyelids over her paling green eyes and brushed the hair from her face with his fingertips.

He had lost the love of his life and he knew it. "Why did this have to happen? She was  just tryin' to help somebody, so why did it have to happen?"

When he finally regained his composure, he led Jude over to where Hassie was lying in the snow, lifted her limp body and draped her over the mule's back. Ice cold water dripped from her dress and hair as he led the mule down the slippery road toward the Biddy place.

P D's head hung low and tears flowed freely. His mind traveled back to the times he and Hassie had shared together. "There were good times and there were bad times," he remembered. "And now she's gone. That makes two wives I've lost, and did I deserve it? I don't think so. What have I done to be punished this way?"

Arriving at home, he led the mule up to the porch, and again using all his strength, carried Hassie inside and placed her on the kitchen table. By this time it was getting late, so he decided to put the mule into his stall. After feeding the mule, he decided he might as well fed and milked the cow.

After taking care of the animals, he began the task of preparing his wife's body for burial. After bathing her, he searched through the bureau drawer for her black dress. "She always looked so nice in this here dress," he said to himself, as he worked her stiffening arms through the sleeves.

He pulled her stockings onto her feet and worked them up onto her legs and smoothed out the wrinkles. He wiped her high top shoes with a cloth and put them on her feet. He placed a pillow beneath her head, brushed and combed her raven hair, straightened her body and placed her arms across her chest. "You're a good lookin' woman, Hassie. Why'd you have to leave me so soon?"

Ann turned in early, feeling good about her father's speedy recoverery and proud that she was finally able to tell her step-mother that she loved her. "I really do love her," she said to herself, as she drifted into a peaceful sleep that lasted clear through the night.

But again, the next morning, she was awakened by a knock on the door and a familiar voice calling, "Little Biddy, you awake?"

"Is that you, Pa? What are you doin' up here so early? You're supposed to be sick. Don't you know that? You should be in bed." Ann said, rubbing the sleep from her eyes, as she unlatched the door to let him in.

"I'm afraid I've got some bad news, Child."

"And what might that be, Pa?"

"Your strep-mother's dead," P D said, as he reached to cradle Ann in his arms.

"She can't be dead. She was just beginning to feel like a mother to me, and now you tell me that she's gone! It can't be. It just can't be! Just yesterday, I told her how much I loved her. Why, Pa? How did it happen?"

"Th mule must'a slipped on the ice down there at Britten Creek and the wagon turner over. Trapped Hassie under the water and she drowned," P D said, as he and Ann stood in a tight embrace.

"Why is it that ever'body that I get close to has to die? Can you tell me that, Pa? Can you!?" Ann said, as she went limp in her father's arms. "First, there was my mother, she died when I was born, then Aunt Isa, then Mama Sarah and Papa Jacob. And now, just when I was able to tell her that I loved her, Mother Hassie had to die. When will this thing ever stop?"

113

"Thangs happen, Child, and we don't always have the answers, but we can't ever give up. We have to keep goin' no matter what life throws at us."

"I know, Pa, but it ain't easy! It just ain't easy!" Ann said, sobbing, as she pressed her face to her father's chest.

"Can you come down and help me put her away?"

"I can help you, Pa. I'll do anything you ask me. But what'll we do for a coffin?"

"They's some pine boards in the barn loft. Shouldn't take too long to put one together."

"Well, sit down and let me fix you some breakfast. I know you've not had any."

After they had eaten, Ann put on her high top shoes and coat and went out to feed and milk the goats. She told P D to sit by the fire while she was doing that.

"I can help you, Girl."

"No, Pa, you're just gettin' over the flu. You'd best take care of yourself. You don't want to get a backset."

So P D did as she wished, and sat warming himself by the fire while she took care of the animals.

"Well, Pa, I'm ready if you are," Ann said, after straining the milk into the crockpot.

The sun was well up into the sky and there was a warmth in its glow, as P D and Ann walked side by side down the narrow road. "Gonna be a perty day today, Ann. The sun'll take a lot of this snow away today."

When they approached the crossing at Britten Creek, Ann looked down below the falls and saw the overturned wagon. Vapor was rising from the melting frost on its underside. "How'll you get the wagon out from down there, Pa?"

"I'll have to get somebody with a strong team to pull it out. I hope it didn't break nothin'."

As they stood for a moment, observing the overturned wagon, Ruffus Ruff and his son, Willie, rode up on horseback. "What'ye lookin' at, P D? Did ye loose sompum er nother down 'ere?

"Just my wife and the wagon." P D answered.

What'ye talkin' about. Shorly ye wife ain't down 'ere, too."

"No, Ruffus, she got drownded yistydy when the wagon turned upside down in the creek."

"We're awful sarry, P D, we didn't mean no disrespect. Really we didn't."

"It's alright, Ruffus. They's no way you could'a knowed."

114

"As I said, is she still down 'ere, P D?"

"No, I found her and took her home. I aim to burry her today. I ain't dug no grave yet and I'll have to make somethin' to burry her in."

We'll help ye, P D. We ain't got nothin' else to do. We wuz just out ridin' around. Thought we'd go down to the Shepherd place, may try to buy it, that is if it's fer sale," Ruffus said, sliding down from his horse to shake P D's hand.

"We'll help ye get ye wagon out, too, Mister Shepherd," Willie said, cutting his in Ann's direction.

"Who could ask for better neighbors than that," Ann said.

"Can we offer you and yer girl a ride? These hoses er big. They can carry two people, easy."

"Thank ye Ruffus, we'll take ye up on that. I'm a mite under the weather. Had a bad case of the flu." P D said, as he helped Ann up onto Willie's horse, and then climbed up behind Ruffus on his horse.

"We'll come back down here'n pull 'at wagon out fer ye ader we get ye wife burried," Ruffus said, as the horses carried them swiftly down the road toward the Biddy house.

Ann could feel Willie's heart pounding beneath her hands, as she wrapped her arms around him, the mighty steed carrying them effortlessly along the frozen road. It was such a strange feeling, having her arms around a young man her own age, but suddenly, her thoughts were of John and how she had clung to his waist so tightly, while riding that black stallion. Oh, how she wished Willie was John, but John was many miles away and it would be a long time before she would have the opportunity to wrap her arms around him again, if ever.

Arriving at the Bidy house, Ann went inside and walked over to where Hassie was laid out on the kitchen table. She touched her cold, pale hands and with tears streaming down her face, said, "Mother Hassie, I'm so sorry, just so sorry. Why did it have to happen? Why did you have to go this way? We were just gettin' to know each other."

Just then, Ruffus and Willie came inside, with P D trailing along behind them. They each removed their hats and after standing in silence for several minutes, Ruffus turned to P D and said, "If you'll tell us where you keep yer tools, we'll start diggin' that grave."

"Out in the barn, Ruffus. I'll show you," P D said, as he donned his hat and walked toward the door, beckoning to Ruffus and Willie to follow him.

Ann stood at the table, weeping for her step-mother for several more minutes. She finally decided that she must try to pull herself together for her father's sake, "After all, this is the second wife he's lost," she said, as she turned aside, dried her eyes and began looking for

115

something to put together for a meal.

"I'll start makin' some kind of a coffin while you boys're up there diggin' the grave," P D said, as he climbed into the barn loft to retrieve the lumber.

Don't worry yeself none, P D. We'll take care'a that grave fer ye," Willie said, balancing the shovel over his shoulder.

Ruffus picked up the mattock and they headed up the hill toward the Biddy graveyard.

P D picked out some wide, straight boards from the barn loft and tossed them to the ground and climbed down. He took the framing square and handsaw from the wall and began measuring and sawing the planks to length. When he finished cutting the boards for the coffin, he reached into the nail keg beneath the loft steps and brought out a handful of horseshoe nails. "Guess these'll have to do, because they're all I have," he said, as he began nailing the boards together.

As he was driving the last nail into the coffin, he heard Ruffus and Willie coming down the path from the graveyard. "Them boys sure are fast grave diggers," he thought to himself.

"We done alright, P D. We dug down right beside a big boulder. Didn't hit another single rock," Ruffus said, as he scraped the dirt from the soles of his shoes on the bottom loft step.

"That's just pure luck, Ruffus, because that graveyard is plumb full of bolders."

"That's a right nice coffin you've made 'ere, Mister Biddy, Willie said, as he stood admiring P D's workmanship.

"Thank ye, Willie, I could'a done better, but there just wasn't enough time. Anyway, if you'll help me get it up to the house, we'll see how it fits," P D said, as he hung his framing square and handsaw on the wall.

"Me'n Willie'll carry it fer ye, Mister Biddy. You can open the door fer us."

P D stepped up onto the porch and opened the door as Ruffus and Willie carried the pine box inside. He placed two straight chairs near the wall, facing each other, just far enough apart to support each end of the coffin.

"Is there somethin' you'd like to wrap her in, Papa?"Ann asked.

"That old wool throw, Little Girl. Hassie loved it. She spent many hours, wrapped up in that thang, sittin' there in front of the fireplace at night. I can almost see her now."

Ann lifted the throw from the back of the rocker and spread it down into the pine box. P D eased the pillow from beneath Hassie's head and placed it at one end of the coffin. Ruffus and Willie gently lifted Hassie from the table, carried her over and eased her down into the coffin. Ann arranged her raven hair around her pale face and smoothed her black dress down over her legs. "We'll miss you, Mother Hassie, she said, as tears eased down her chapped cheeks.

P D helped Ann spread the throw over Hassie's body. They stood in silence by her side for a while and after saying their goodbyes, P D placed the lid on top of the coffin and nailed it shut.

A loud knock at the door startled them and when P D opened the door, there stood Eli Bailey, clad in brogans and a long overcoat. He was clutching the brim his wool hat between his thumb and forefinger. "P D, they's a wagon layin' down below the falls on Britten Creek. Looks zackly like your'n."

"It is mine, Eli. It tumbled down there when I lifted it off of Hassie yesterday."

"Do tell. Did she get hurt?"

"Killed her," P D answered. "She drowned in that ice cold water. We're fixin' to go burry her right this minute."

"Can I be of any help to ye?" Eli asked, glancing at the pine box.

"Of course you can. Eli. If you don't mind, you could help us carry her up to the graveyard."

"Don't mind a bit, P D, just glad to be of help."

Ann threaded her arms through the sleeves of her heavy, black coat and wrapped her wool shawl around her face and head. P D put on his coat and hat, saying, "I guess we're ready folks, as ready as we'll ever be. I'll never be ready, far's that goes, but it's somethin' that's got to be done."

Each of the four men took hold of a corner of the coffin and carried it outside. Once outside, they hoisted it onto their shoulders and went marching up the path to the graveyard, the edges of the pine box biting into their shoulders.

Ann trailed along behind, carrying the two ropes to be used in lowering the coffin into the grave. She couldn't keep her mind from wandering back to the times when Hassie treated her so cruelly, but she was thankful that she had finally come to her senses and began treating her like a person instead of a despised animal. "I guess we have Lady Owatta to thank for that," she thought.

Once they arrived at the grave site, they rested the coffin on the ground and P D noticed right away that the grave opening was about six inches too short. "Looks like we've got a little more diggin' to do, men. Looks like it's a mite too short," he said, removing his hat and scratching his head.

"We'll take care a that in short order," Willie said, as he picked up the shovel and began shaving the dirt from one end of the opening.

The soil was soft and since there were no rocks to hinder him, it took only a few minutes to make the opening long enough to receive the coffin.

P D asked Eli if he would say a few words and maybe a short prayer, which he did. When he finished with the eulogy, they lowered the coffin into the grave. "You've been a puzzlement, Hassie, but you turned out good, real good," P D said.

"Amen to that," Ann said, smiling. "She turned out real good."

"P D picked up a clod of dirt at his feet and tossed it into the grave, "We're gonna miss you, Woman. We're gonna miss you for a long, long time."

Ruffus and Willie pulled the ropes free and stepped back for a moment to let P D and Ann have their last look at the coffin. "We'll finish thangs fer ye, P D. You'n Ann go on back ta th house. You look like you're all tuckered out," Ruffus said, as he began shoveling dirt into the opening.

"Thank you, Ruffus, you're a gentleman. We're mighty obliged to you."

Ann clung to her father's arm as they made their way down the hill. "It's been another sad day, Papa. I sure do hope we don't have another'n any time soon. I do b'leive we've had our share of bad days," she said, looking up into her father's sad eyes.

"We've had our share, Ann Biddy Shepherd. Indeed we have."

"I'll have somethin' fixed to eat, soon's you men get through up here," Ann said, looking back over her shoulder.

"Thank ye, Miss Biddy, We'll shore be ready fer sompum to eat when we get all 'is dirt moved," Willie hollered back to her.

"He called you Miss. Don't he know you're married?" P D said.

"Won't take me long to let him know, Papa."

"What day is this, Child?"

"It's the last day of November, Papa."

"Time sure passes in a hurry," P D said.

"Not for me, Papa. Time just creeps by, with John off up yonder, fightin' in that awful war."

I know it pains you, Child, but maybe the war won't won't last too much longer."

"I certainly hope you're right, Papa, I've had a bellyfull of it."

As she helped her father up the steps to the porch, weakened from his bout with the flu, he said, "I'm a mite weaker'n I thought I was. I think I'll lay down fer a bit. See if I can get my strength back."

"Go ahead, Papa. You rest and I'll get some dinner started."

By the time Ann finished cooking dinner, P D had gotten up and was sitting at the table, waiting for the other men to come down from the graveyayd.

As Ruffus, Willie and Eli came inside, after scrubbing the dirt from the soles of their shoes, P D said, "I'm ready fer dinner, men, and I'm sure you are."

"We sure are, Mister Biddy. I'm so hungry I could eat a rattlesnake," Willie said, looking Ann straight in the eye and winking.

Ann blushed as she stooped to lift the pot of Irish potatoes from the fireplace.

"I'll git that fer ye, Miss Biddy. That's pot's just too heavy fer a little gal like you to be pickin' up," Willie said, struggling to free Ann's hand from the pot handle.

"I can do it, Willie. I've been doin' it since I was a child. Besides, I ain't Miss Biddy. I'm Ann Shepherd, John Shepherd's wife. He's off fightin' in the war, and while I'm thinkin' about it, why ain't you up there?"

"Ain't gonna fight in no war. I'll hide out in a cave and drink muddy water and eat spring lizzards afore I'll fight in this crazy war."

"Well, Willie, what makes you any better than my man?"

"Ain't no better, Missus Shepherd, just got more sense, I guess. And while I'm at it, I 'polagize fer callin' you Miss Biddy. I didn't know you'as married."

"That's alright, Willie."

They all gathered around the table and ate until the cook pot was empty. "That shore wuz a good dinner, Miz Shepherd," Eli said, as he cleared his throat and pushed his chair back from the table. The other men agreed.

ロロロロロロロロロロロロロ

Time would heal the pain of the loss of Hassie, or so P D thought, but it hovered over him like a ghost on a dark night. He spent many winter evenings, sitting before the fireplace, wondering what he could do to break the spell, but nothing came to mind.

When spring finally arrived he kept himself busy, working in the fields, grubbing stumps and sprouts. He cleaned the mule's stall and replaced the missing shingles on the barn roof, but the lonliness continued day after painful day. "I'll go up and see'f Ann can give me somethin' that'll straighten me out," he said one morning, as he sat at the table, forcing down a few bites of hoecake and a slice of pork belly.

119

It was a beautiful Wednesday morning, the forth day of May, 1864. The woods were alive with birds, singing and chirping, as the wagon bounced along the rocky road, carrying P D on his way to Ann's shanty. A crow was cawing, sitting on the top branch of an oak tree, high up on the ridge to his left. A grey squirrel scampered out to the end of a dead limb of a chestnut tree, sprang through the air as if it had wings and landed on the trunk of a hollow tree and disappeared into a knothole. "Thangs seem to be goin' good fer the critters, why can't they go good fer me?" P D thought.

He tapped Jude with the reins, prodding him into a trot. He was now in a hurry to get up to his daughter's shanty.

"It's good to see you, Papa. Where've ye been keepin' yeself?" Ann said, opening the door and curtsying to him.

"I've been down in the dumps, Doctor Shepherd. Been like this all winter long, and now't spring's here, it ain't no better. Do you think you might have sompum in that bag a'yourn that'll straighten me out?"

"I could try some of the stuff that Lady Owatta gave Mother Hassie, that is, if you think you're man enough to take it," Ann said, waving her hands above her head and laughin.

"I believe I'm man enough, Ann Shepherd. Let's try it and see'f I am. I'm ready to try anythang."

"We'd better wait till tonight to try it, just in case you go into a fit," Ann said. "If you can stay the day with me, I'll go back down with you and after we take care of the animals, I'll give you a dose of that stuff and we'll see what happens."

"You got yerself a deal, Girl."

About mid-afternoon, Ann raked some coals from the fireplace, covered them with a thin layer of ashes and lay on two large sweet potatoes, covered them with a sifting of ashes and raked another layer of firecoals on top of that. She took the wooden bowl from the fireboard and measured out enough cornmeal for a hoecake. "Won't take long to fix us a little supper, Papa, and after I feed and milk the goats, we'll be ready to go."

After Ann fed and milked the goats and she P D had eaten a bellyful of sweet potatoes and hoecake, they sat out on the porch for a little while and rested. "Are you about ready to try some of that secret herb, Papa?"

"I'm as ready as I'll ever be, Ann Biddy Sherpherd."

"Well let's go and get it done," Ann said.

So along about sundown they pulled to a stop in front of the barn at the Biddy place. P D unhitched the mule from the wagon, gave him some water and fed him. He milked the cow and brought the milk

120

inside where Ann strained it into the crock.

"Well, Papa, if you're ready, you'd best get into bed. I don't b'lieve I'd be able to lift you off the floor."

"By the time you get it ready, I'll be ready," P D said, as he loosened the laces of his shoes and shucked them from his feet, socks and all.

Ann dipped the tin cup into the churn and brought out a cupful of half clabbered milk and sat it on the table. It was perhaps the same spot where Lady Owatta had placed the cup, when she mixed up the concoction she gave Hassie. She stirred in some of the secret herb with the quill of a turkey feather and brought it over to where her father lay stretched out on the bed. "Here it is, Papa, drink it down and we'll hope for the best."

P D gulped it down in three swallows, then belched even louder than Hassie had done when she drank some of the same stuff. He moaned and said, "Great God in heaven, what did you give me? I never put such foul tastin' stuff in my mouth in my whole life."

"You'll sleep now, Papa, and when you wake up in the morning, you should be a heap better."

P D slept, but not very well. All through the night and until the wee hours of the morning he was tormented by dreams. He climbed trees, swam in a muddy river, almost drowning a time or two. He tracked rabbits, went squirrel hunting, cut and carried in wood for the fireplace until he was exhausted. He was chased by ghosts and goblins, scared about half out of his mind.

His eyes rolled back into their sockets. He held his hands in front of his face in an apparent attempt to ward off some grotesque being. This went on till three in the morning when he finally drifted off into a deep sleep.

Ann, deciding the worst was over, made a pallet on the floor and prepared to get some sleep. "Sure is powerful stuff," she said, as she she closed her eyes. "Mighty powerful stuff."

The sun was already up the following morning and Ann was still stretched out on the pallet on the floor, asleep and snoring.

P D had been awake for only a few minutes. He was sitting up in bed, looking at objects in the room as if seeing them for the first time. He gazed at Hassie's wool scarf, hanging on the wooden peg beside the fireplace, "Wonder who that b'longs to," He said, as he swung his legs off the edge of the bed and reached for britches.

"How do you feel this fine morning, Papa?" Ann said, as she rolled over on the pallet and propped up on one elbow.

"Who might you be, young woman? and what are you doin' here

121

in my house?"

"Why, I'm your daughter, Papa. Don't you remember me? I'm Ann Biddy Shepherd."

"It's comin' back to me now, but it's like I've been in a thick fog, or flyin' on a cloud. What happened to me, noway?"

"I gave you some of Lady Owatta's secret herb last night. Don't you remember?"

"Now I do and I'll tell you another thang, I'm powerful hongry. Is they anythang in this here house to eat?"

"I'm sure I can find something, Papa. I'll get some breakfast started right now."

"I feel right strange, Ann, I feel like I'm somebody else," he said, counting the fingers on his hands, forward and back, as if checking to make sure none were missing.

"Got some fingers missin', Papa?"

"No, I've got eight fangers and two thumbs. I b'lieve that's all I ever had," P D said, grinning.

"Well, do you feel better or worse?"

"Better a'course, Miss Biddy," he said.

"Now you know quite well I'm not a Biddy any more, Papa."

"Of course I know, Child a'mine. I know you're married to John Shepherd. I remember that like it wuz yistydy."

They both broke into a fit of laughter that lasted for several minutes and when they finally regained some control of their emotions and were wiping tears from their eyes and faces, Ann said, "Been a long time since we laughed like that, Papa."

"Shore has, Child, and It shore does feel good, too."

"Well, Papa, when we get a bite to eat, why don't we go up by my place and take care of the animans and maybe go over to Bent Oak Tradin' Post and see'f they's a letter there from John?"

"Nothin' else'ud suit me better, Ann. Nothin'."

P D fed and milked the cow and put her into the pasture. He fed Jude, gave him some water and hitched him to the wagon. "You ready to go, Girl?"

"Sure am, Papa," Ann said, as she came bouncing down the porch steps, ran down and climbed into the wagon.

They were in seventh heaven, as they sat side by side in the wagon, the little mule in a trot. When they reached Ann's shanty she milked the goats while P D mended the fence gate in front of her house. The top hinge was pulling away from the post.

"Would you like a drink of water before we go, Papa?"

"I'm alright, Ann. Let's go. Time's a wastin'."

So, off they went, heading down toward the trading post. "Let's put the past behind us, Papa. Maybe things'll be better if we look ahead instead of lookin' back all the time."

"By Jove, I thank you're right, Ann," P D said, tapping Jude with the reins.

When they reached Bent Oak, a crowd of folks were standing out front and it seemed as if something unusual had happened. "What's goin' on?" P D asked, as he pulled up beside the crowd and climbed down from the wagon.

"Sylus Ruff's boy's dead, killed off up yonder in Vaginny, som'ers. He was up 'ere fightin' 'em dam Yankees. Got hisself killed. His pa got word today that he wuz dead," an old man in the crowd said. "Makes me mighty sad and dam mad, too,"

"Makes me sad and mad, too," Ann said. "And just how can we look to the future for any kind of hope, with this damnable war goin' on. Can you tell me that?"

"It's mighty hard to hope, Maam," the old man spoke up, the bowl of his clay pipe bobbing as he spoke.

Ann jumped down from the wagon and ran into the trading post to see if there was a letter from John and sure enough there was. She broke the seal, pulled the letter from the envelope with trembling fingers, plopped down on a nail keg and began to read it:

"My dear Ann, there is not much to tell. We're still hunkered down in these trenches at Petersburg, waitin' for them Yankees to make up their minds, wheather to fight or quit. I'm sure glad spring's comin'. Livin' in these ditches ain't fit for humans. I can tell you that first hand. I do hope you are well. I can't wait till this war's over and I get back home to you, but until then, stay safe and keep prayin'. I will be looking for your next letter. I sure do miss you. Love, John."

"Well that's a load off my mind," she said, as she reached into her bag, pulled out the writing tablet and started a letter: "My dear John, I'm so relieved to hear that you are still amongst the living. Word was received today that Sylus Ruff's boy, Toddy Joe, was killed, somewhere up there in Virginia, and his little wife is big, waitin' on that baby to come. The notice didn't say exactly where he was killed or how, so make sure you keep your head down when the bullets start whizzin'. I can't tell you how much I miss you. I hope this war is soon over and you're back home where you belong."

"Papa is well, but Hassie is dead. The wagon turned over and killed her, down there in Britten Creek last winter. There was ice on the road, you know. Will stop writing now and get this letter sent. Write when you can and come home soon. Forever your Love, Ann."

She dropped the letter into the mail basket. Those standing around noticed her wiping the tears from her eyes on the sleeve of her black dress. When she handed John's letter to her father, he stood straight as a fence post while he read it.

They bought what few items they could afford, for money was scarce and practically worthless. Goods were in very short supply. Coffee was scarce, but they were able to buy a few ounces of the brew.

"I 'spect I'd better be gittin' back over to Deep Gap, Ann. They's work to be done, like plowin' the fields and they's corn to plant. Are you ready to travel?"

"I'm ready. Papa," Ann said, gathering the things she had bought in one hand and holding onto her father's arm with the other. "What in the world's gonna happen to Cathy Ruff, with that baby on the way and nobody to help her take care of it?"

"Willie'd make her a good man," PD said, with a salting of sarcasm in his speech.

"He ain't worth killin', Papa. That coward'ud run and hide if that baby uttered one little whimper and you know it."

"I know it, Child. I just said it 'cause he seems so all fired crazy to git hisself a woman."

"God forbid that such a thing would happen to that poor girl," Ann said, as she climbed into the wagon.

"I b'leive she's got more sense'n that, Ann, but you can't never tell about people these days."

Nothing else was said about the subject on the way home.They tried to put the bad things out of their heads, and to just sit back and enjoy the beauty of nature and the coming of spring as they rode along.

Jude, the mule, seemed to enjoy the coming of spring as well, looking from side to side as he trotted down the road, his long ears moving forward and back, like the wings of a dragonfly.

"Will you be plantin' yeself a garden this year, Girl?"

"Soon's it warms up I'll be out there plantin', Papa. I couldn't make it without my garden. Guess I'd get pretty hungry."

"If you'll let me know when you're ready, I'll come up and help you. Soon's the ground gets dry I'll come up there and git it broke up."

"Well ain't you the nice'un, Papa. I'll cook up a good dinner and we'll have us a good old time!"

Fidgity was sitting on the little garden gate when the wagon came to a stop. Ann bounced to the ground like a ten year old girl. "Get down and come in for a while, Papa. I'll get a poke and pour you out half a'this coffee. We gotta have our coffee, you know."

"How well I know, Ann Biddy Shepherd," P D said, laughing.

"I'd like to stay a while and talk, but I'd better get on home and start doin' that fun thang, like diggin' up stumps and grubbin' sprouts."

"I'm Glad you think it's fun, Papa. That should make it seem a little easier."

Ann went inside and poured half the coffee onto a scrap of old bed sheet, tied it up with a piece of twine and brought it out to her father, who was still sitting in the wagon.

"I'm obliged to you, Girl. I'll see you in a few days." He tapped the mule with the reins and they were on their way down the road toward Deep Gap.

Ann waved to him until he went out of sight. Then she lifted Fidgety from the gate post and carried her in her arms up the path to the shanty and sat down on the edge of the porch. She sat there for quite a while, stroking her cat and listening to the birds. But the chirping of the birds couldn't steer her mind away from thoughts of her husband. "If John was here, I'd parch some of that coffee and we'd sit right here and drink coffee and talk till dark," she said.

ロロロロロロロロロロロロ

"Halt!" came the order from the Confederate soldier in the trench. "Who goes there?" he demanded, as the form of a man advanced toward him.

He could see the silhouette of the approaching man clearly, for there was a full moon overhead.

"Private John Shepherd," the approaching man answered.

"What's your password?"

"Mud puppy," came John's reply.

"Come closer so I can see you," the soldier in the trench ordered.

"I've come to relieve you for a while," John said, climbing down into the trench.

"Wher've you been hidin' out these last few days. I thought you'as dead or somthin'."

"Had sores on my feet from standin' barefotted in these muddy ditches. Had to have 'em looked at. My shoes rotted off my feet, but anyway, they're better now," John said.

After some small talk, John took up the position of sentry as his comrade settled into his dugout to get some sleep. The night was warm, for it was now the eleventh day of June.

Even though things were now calm, the preceding day marked the last day of the bloodiest six weeks of the war. General Grant's plan had been to get around the right flank of Lee's army, destroy it, then move on to Richmond and bring an end to the war. But Lee had managed to out maneuver Grant on each of his attempts.

There had been heavy losses on both sides. In the first two days of fighting in the wilderness, Grant had lost seventeen thousand of his troops. Two hundred men had been burned alive in brush fires that raged throughout the wilderness. The battles continued along a hundred-mile crescent before the two exhausted armies settled into the siege at Petersburg, a few miles southeast of the Confederate capital.

# Chapter

# 8

## John Meets His Childhood Friend

John could hear his comrade snoring as he stood guard, looking out toward the enemy lines. Half way between where he was standing and where he perceived the enemy trenches to be, he saw a man coming toward him. As the man stepped from beneath the shadow of a large tree into the bright moonlight, John saw that he was a young black man. He looked to be about his own age.

John knew that black men were serving as soldiers in the Union army. He had no way of knowing how many, but as a matter of fact, thirty-eight regiments of black troops took part in the Petersburg siege. These men lived in shallow trenches called bomb proofs. They were always out in front of the regular troops. It was their task to warn the men in the trenches of enemy movement.

"Zat chu, John Shepud? Is you fum Sumta, Souf Calina?"a voice stole through the night air.

"And who wants to know," John asked in a hushed voice.

"Fust, is you fum Sumta?" the voice in the night asked again.

"I'm not tellin' you till you say who you are."

"I beezs Goge Washintun Wiggins," the voice in the night resounded.

"You better keep your voice down if you expect to keep on living," John called back to him, barely loud enough to be heard.

"Yes I'm from Sumter, South Carolina, but are you who I think you are?"

"Fraid so, John Shepud."

"Well, George Washington wiggins, what the devil are you doin' way up here in Virginia?"

"I stolt away on a ship. Sided since I be free now, I'd gwon up noth an heah I beez, jis a settin heah atwixt two awmys, bout ta git masef kill."

George Washington Wiggens was John's childhood friend. They had grown up as neighbors in Sumter, South Carolina, and hadn't seen

127

each other since John's father moved to the mountains when Jonn was a young boy.

Living in Sumter, even though they were from different races, they were like brothers, playing from sunup till dark, or until their mothers called them to supper. Sometimes George would stay and have supper with John, sitting at the family dining table. There were times when John ate with George, especially when the Wiggens' killed hogs and chitlins would be on the menue.

All those wonderful days of childhood came flooding back into John's head. He had always treasured those days, even though he hadn't talked much about it. "What's all this hatred that's tied up in the hearts of white folks against black people? I just can't understand it. For the life'a me I can't," he thought to himself.

"Meet me out there under that big oak tree and we'll talk a spell," John called out softly.

"I's ready if yo is, John."

They met beneath the oak tree and talked until way passed midnight. George Washington Wiggens had a few hard tack in his pocket which he shared with John. They gnawed on them as they talked and when they stood up to return to their posts, they still hadn't consumed their rock hard biscuits. They were so hard, it was said, they could stop a bullet.

"I bez keepin a peel eye out fo yo. We do dis agin soon, maybe."

"We'll have to be careful, George. We could be killed if we're caught," John said, before carefully making his way back to his post.

The following night, John and George met under the same oak tree. George had a large apple in his pocket. "Iz got a apple here'n my pocket. Be morn glad to vide it wif yo, but'a haint got no knife."

"Don't let that bother you none, George. I've got one right here in my pocket," John said, reaching into his pocket and bringing out the pearl-handle knife his father had given him.

"Dat be a powful good lookin' knife yo got ere, John."

"Belonged to my grandpa. He carried it with him through the revolutionary war. Gave it to my daddy and he gave it to me. Said it'ud bring me good luck."

"Looks like he wuz right. Got you haf a'dis hea apple, didn't it?" George said.

John opened the blade and handed the knife to his friend. George held it for a minute, taking a close look at it there in the bright moonlight. "Sho is a niceun. Dis knife sho is nice."

George sliced the apple in half, wiped the blade on the leg of his trousers and handed John his half. He closed the pearl-handle knife and without thinking, dropped it into his own pocket.

"Sho is good to see yo agin, John Sheppud. Many be da times I've thought uvya."

"I didn't know if we'd ever meet again, George, but here we are in this God forsaken place. Who would'a thought it? Just who would'a thought it?"

When they finished eating the apple, they shook hands and each returned to his post. They looked forward to their next visit there under the canopy of the old oak tree, but little did they know that this very day, the massive army of the Potimic began crossing the James River, on the pontoon bridge that had been strung across the river in only eight hours. The army was so massive that it would take four days for the last man to cross the bridge.

After his comrade relieved him, John crawled into his dugout and quickly fell asleep. Things had been so tranquill the last few days, except from a few misguided artillery rounds that totally missed their mark, he had been lulled into a false sense of safety.

So many Confederate soldiers had just walked away and gone home, it left the lines of defence in the trenches pitifully inadequate. The town of Petersburg was defended by a thin line of about three thousand Confederates under General Beauregard's command.

On the fifteenth of June of 1864, sixteen thousand Union troops under General W.F. Bailey Smith attacked the lines of defence at Petersburg and by nightfall it looked as if Petersburg was within the Union's grasp.

Windfield Scott Hancock urged Smith to launch a moonlight assault, but Smith begged off and ordered a withdrawal, remembering Cold Harbor. His decision enraged the enlisted men and while the Union soldiers cursed and waited, Beauregard was reinforced. Thus General Smith had missed the opportunity to take Petersburg and perhaps bring an early end to the war. Because of Smith's hesitation, the war was prolonged, as repeated attacks were beaten back by the small Confederate army.

The burowing continued for months. The men survived in the trenches, exposed to the rain and hot Virginia sun and plagued by flies. They were also exposed to mortar fire, and no one could say with confidence at any hour that he would be living the next.

And so the war continued and John was still there in the trenches and all the while wishing the war would soon come to an end, allowing him to go home to the wife he loved so dearly.

Things had become so dangerous outside the trenches that John never tried to contact George Washington Wiggens again. There was no way to know if Wiggins was still alive. "Maybe he's been killed in the fightin'. After all, he was right there in the middle of it. So many of our brothers have been killed. When will we ever learn! When will we ever learn!"

ꙊꙊꙊꙊꙊꙊꙊꙊꙊꙊꙊꙊ

"That shore wuz a good dinner, Ann Biddy Shepherd," P D said, pushing back from the table.

"Glad you enjoyed it, Papa. We've been blessed with just the right amount of rain this summer. My little garden's been a blessin'."

"Well, the corn's about the best I've ever eat. The green beans er good too. My stuff's done good this summer. Only thang is, I don't have no little woman to cook it fer me," P D said.

"Would you want me to help you find a woman, Papa? I'd be more'n happy to help you out," Ann said, laughing.

"I'm not ready just this minute, Little Lady. I've had nothin' but bad luck when it comes to women. I think I'll wait a while if that's alright with you."

"I'm not rushin' you, Papa. Sounded like you were in a hurry."

"Not quite, Child. Not quite."

Being mid-June, the weather was hot, so after dinner they retired to the cool porch to rest and let their food digest. The sound of water trickling over the rocks in Britten Creek was soothing and soon P D was snoring, sitting in a straight chair, leaning back against the wall beside the door.

Ann didn't disturb him, but went inside to wash the dishes while he took his nap. After finising with the dishes, she walked back out onto the porch and when she did, her father awoke suddenly and jumped to his feet. "How long've I been asleep, Girl? I need to get back down to the gap and hoe out my sorghum cane. I planted a good size patch down on the Shepherd place, but the crabgrass has just about got it smothered out."

"It's so late in the day, Papa, you wouldn't get much done, anyway. I'll come down tomorrow'n help you. That is, if you don't think a little woman would get in your way."

"You could never get in my way, Child. I'll come up and take you down in the wagon. We'll make a day of it," P D said, as he stepped down from the porch and struck out for home.

"I'll be waitin' for you, Papa," Ann said, as she settled down in the straight chair, her bonnet draped over her lap.When she found

130

herself nodding in the summer heat, she picked herself up and staggered into the shanty and fell across her bed, thinking she would rest her eyes a bit, but in no time at all she was fast asleep. As she slept, she dreamed of John, and in her dream she had received a letter from him saying he would soon be coming home. She became so excited she awoke and when she realized it was only a dream, tears came to her eyes. "Is it a sign? Maybe the war is about over and he'll finally be comin' home to me," she said, as she rolled over on her side and sat up on the edge of the bed. It was only wishful thinking, for the war was not soon to be over. She and John would have to endure many days of lonliness before they could expect to see each other again.

ⅩⅩⅩⅩⅩⅩⅩⅩⅩⅩⅩⅩⅩ

It was very hot in the trenches as John lay in his dugout, trying to get some sleep before he would be relieving his comrade of his watch at midnight. He thought he could hear tapping, deep within the earth beneath him, as he held his breath and pressed his ear close to the ground, but after a few minutes of straining to hear, the tapping stopped. He had some hearing loss and a constant ringing in his right ear after a morter round exploded just outside the trench a few days back. "Maybe I'm just hearin' things," he told himself, as he turned onto his back and stretched his legs.

He lay there for some time thinking of Ann, wondering how she was doing. She was always the last thing on his mind each night before he fell asleep. In fact, thoughts of her occupied his mind most of the time, day or night. "I sure wish these generals would make up their minds wheather to fight or just quit. I think quittin' would be better for all of us," he muttered to himself before falling asleep.

ⅩⅩⅩⅩⅩⅩⅩⅩⅩⅩⅩⅩⅩ

The sun was hot on their backs as Ann and P D bent low, chopping and pulling crabgrass from the sorghum cane. Sweat trickled down their faces and their backs ached from so much bending and stooping. "This is hard work, Papa, but it'll be worth it this winter when we pour some'a that sorghum on a hot hoecake, smear on some butter and just sit back and have a feast."

"Shore will, Girl. Be nice to have a little sweetnin' in our grits, too," P D said, sweeping the sweat from his brow with his forefinger, leaving a smear of mud from his soiled hand.

131

At mid-morning they walked down to the edge of the sorghum patch and sat in the shade of a blackgum tree to cool. They had only been sitting there for a few minutes when they heard the sound of hoofbeats coming down the road. P D stood up to see who was coming and saw Eli Bailey astride his big red stallion. "Mornin' Eli. What brings you out this way on such a hot day," P D asked.

"They's deserters in these parts and they're stealin' anythang they can git their hands on. They broke into Cathy Ruff's house while she'as out hoein' her little garden and stoled all her corn meal and all the salt pork she had in the meat box, and her big as a cow, expectin' that child any day now. What kind of a dog would do a thing like that to a poor helpless woman?" Eli said, his face red and twisted with disgust. "Now, how's she gonna get by with nothin' to eat and nobody to help her?"

"That kind of a person ain't worth a musket ball, but I'd feed him one if he tried that on me," Ann said, goose bumps welling up on her sweaty arms.

"I felt it my duty to warn everbody. It'ud pay to untie the latch string on your doors at night and keep a gun handy, cause they'll be back fer shore," Eli said, as he steered his horse back onto the road and went galloping on his way to warn others of the impending danger.

"Thank you, Eli," P D said, sitting down beside Ann, his face turning red with anger. "A man that's too no-account to fight fer the cause ain't worth killin', but I'm ready to waste a bullet if I catch somebody doin' a deed like that."

"Girl, you need somethin' bigger'n a cat to take care uv you. With you livin' by yeself and all. They's a feller over in the cove that's got some big hounds fer sale. I'll get you one if you want me to."

"Don't sell that cat of mine short. She took care of that old Green River boy, didn't she?" Ann said, smiling with confidence.

"I worry about you, Child. A papa worries about his girl."

"We'll be careful, Papa. I don't sleep too solid since John went off to fight in the war."

It was some time passed mid-day when they finished hoeing the sorghum. P D hitched Jude to the wagon and they climbed on board and headed up the road to the house. "I've got a pone of corn bread and some good fresh churned buttermilk. That ought to cure the hongrys, don't you thank?" he said, looking over at Ann.

"Just about anything would taste good right now, Papa. Makes me feel guilty having something when Cathy Ruff ain't got nothin'. She's my cousin and I can't help worryin' about her."

"We'll gander off down that way after we eat a bite and see'f they's anythang we can do fer her. I'll take her some corn meal and a piece'a fatback meat. That'll keep her from starvin' fer a day er two. She'll not starve long's we've got grub," P D said.

After they had their fill of corn bread and buttermilk, Ann scooped about a gallon of corn meal from the bin while P D went out to the smoke house to cut off a chunk of fatback. "We'll wrap her up a piece'a corn bread and take a jug'a milk," P D said, as he came back inside carrying the slab of fatback.

"Sounds good, Papa, you're a good man."

"I'm shore she'd do the same fer us."

"You're right, Papa. You're sure right about that."

P D pulled the drawstring inside, closed the door, and as they walked out toward the barn, he said, "Can't be too careful these days. Never know when you'll get a visitor."

They loaded the stuff onto the wagon, climbed aboard and were on their way.

When they arrived at Cathy's house she was down at the spring, washing the dirt from a few small Irish potatoes she had grabbled for supper. "Hey, Cousin Cathy, I heard about that dirty scoundrel stealin' your stuff," Ann said, jumping down from the wagon and reaching to embrace her. "Hey, you're gettin' mighty big. When's that baby due?"

"Any day. I expect it just any day now, and I hope it's a boy. If it's a boy, I'll call him Toddy Joe Number Two. I think his daddy would have liked that," Cathy said, with a little break in her voice.

Fear was in her eyes, for she wondered what she would do if the baby decided to come in the middle of the night. She couldn't deliver it by herself, or at least she didn't think she could.

"You'll go back with us. You can stay with me till after the baby's born. I'll help you to get that baby into the world,"Ann assured her. "I've helped deliver babies before. I know how it's done."

Cathy's eyes lit up and tears eased down her cheeks as she hugged Ann and kissed her. "Thank you ever so much. I was hopin' you'd say that, but I don't have one red cent to pay you for your services."

"You're my cousin. Besides, who needs money when you've got friends and kin?" Ann said, as she stepped back for another look at Cathy's protruding belly.

"Well, they's no use in leavin' this meal and fatback meat here fer one'a them scoundrels to steal. You can just take it on over to Ann's place," P D said, patting Cathy on the shoulder.

"Mister Biddy, you're the kindest man. I don't know how I'll ever repay you!"

"P D's my name. They all call me P D."

"I know it's P D, but you're Mister Biddy to me," Cathy said.

"Well, let's get some sheets and blankets and get on over to my place," Ann said, as she helped Cathy up the porch steps.

"Might just as well take these Irish potatoes with us. Stuff to eat's a little hard to come by these days," Cathy said, as she tied them up in a towel that was hanging on the wall outside the kitchen door. "You brought me some cornbread and buttermilk. We might as well take it on with us, too."

"Let me untie the latch string on this door," P D said, as he loosened the leather string on the outside of the door and pulled it inside. "You can open the door with a knife er sumpum flat like that, Cathy. Do ye carry a knife wiyi?"

"I do since that devil stole my meat and meal the other day."

It was difficult for Cathy to climb up into the wagon, so P D took her by the hands as Ann gave her a boost from behind. "That was a lot'a help. When you get as big as I am, your arms seem to get shorter," she said, laughing.

As they rounded the bend at Britten Creek and headed up the hill toward Ann Ridge, they could hear Ann's goats blating and as they rolled into the yard in front of the tiny shanty, Fidgety let out with a loud meow! "Guess she thought I'd never get back. We've been gone since early this mornin'," Ann said, Bouncing down from the wagon and reaching up to help Cathy climb down.

Ann held Cathy's arm and as they made their way through the gate and up the porch steps, and as usual, Fidgety was snatching at her dresstail. After lifting the doorlatch with the blade of her knife, she struggled to walk inside. The cat's claws had become entangled in her dresstail and was unable pull free. "Well, Fidgety, can't you get along on your own? You've got four feet. That's twice as many as I have," Ann said, as she bent down to free the cat's claws from the frayed hem of her dress.

"Papa, I'll fix us a little supper soon's I milk the goats and feed the chickens."

"Naw, Child, You've got your hands full. I'd best be gittin' home. The cow'll have to be fed'n milked. Old Jude's itchin' to git out'a them harnesses. Mules git tired , too, you know."

"I know, Papa, but if you eat here you won't have to fix sometnin' when you get home."

Well, just fer supper'n I'll have to go," P D said, as they made their way out to the little barn, and again, Fidgety was right there behind Ann, snatching at her dresstail.

134

"Cathy's gettin' mighty big. Looks like she'll have that baby just any time," P D said, as he opened the barn gate for Ann.

"Yes, Papa, she said just any day now."

After the goats were milked, Ann and P D were making their way back to the shanty when Cathy stuck her head out the door and shouted, "This baby's on its way! The pains are gettin' closer every time!"

"Well, Cathy, get in there and lay down on the bed."

"Papa, put some more wood on the fire. We'll need plenty of hot water," Ann said, as she sat the bucket of milk on the table.

She washed her hands and dried them on a clean towel and examined Cathy to see how far along the baby was. "Her water's already broke, Papa, bring me a pan of hot water."

All of the excitement drove P D into a tizzy, and instead of dipping water from the water pot, he soused the dipper into the stew that Ann was warming up for supper. "Papa, that's the stew. Get me some hot water!"

"I'm gettin' it, Doctor," P D said, as he rinsed the dipper in the washpan, sitting by the fireplace, dried it on the dish towel and began dipping water from the water pot.

"Any time today'll be good," Ann said, as she tied a bed sheet around her waist.

"Here's your hot water, Doctor. Is it alright if I go out on the porch'n get a breath'a fresh air?" P D said, as he sat the pan of hot water on the straight chair next to the bed.

"Go ahead, Papa. I don't want you faintin' on me. Delivering the baby's about all I can handle at a time," Ann said, looking at her father and grinning.

Ann knew this birth was going to be an easy one, for the baby's head was already in the birth canal. "This is gonna be a good'un, Cathy. Yeah, it's gonna be a real good'un."

A few hard pushes and the baby was here. Ann held it up by the heels and tapped it a couple times on the buttocks with the palm of her hand and it commenced crying. "Is it a boy or girl?" Cathy asked, raising up on one elbow to have a look at the child she had just brought into the world.

"Le'me look. Well, it's a girl, Cathy. Wouldn't you just know?"

"Is it alright? Is the baby alright?" P D asked, as he came rushing back into the house, his face white like cotton.

"It's fine, Papa, and wouldn't you know, it's a girl. Did you pick a name for a girl?" Ann asked Cathy, as she laid the tiny infant on its mother's belly and proceeded to cut and tie the umbilical cord.

"Didn't think a single time about a girl's name. Thought it'ud be a boy for sure, but since it's a girl, I think I'll call her Mary. That was my mama's first name, you know. And if you don't mind if I use your first name, I can't think of a better name than Ann. I'll call her Mary Ann, Mary Ann Ruff. That's a right pretty name. Now, don't you think so? Cathy said.

"I think it's perfect," Ann said, as she wrapped the infant in a blanket and placed her into her mother's arms.

The baby latched onto its mother's breast and began feeding as if it were starving. "That's the way to do it. You didn't have to be showed, did you, Mary Ann?"

"That's a right perty name," P D said, as he sank into the straight chair at the side of the bed, feeling a bit faint.

Ann finished cleaning up and P D carried the afterbirth out passed the barn and burried it.

"You ready for some of that stew, Cathy? You'll need to eat if you're gonna make milk for that baby. I mean, the way she's goin' at it," Ann said, as she dipped some stew into a bowl and broke off a piece of corn pone.

"I guess you're about to starve, too, Papa."

"Not so hungry, but I do need to eat and git on home. It'll be dark afore I git the cow milked as it is," P D said, as he sat down at the table and began eating in haste.

On his way home, he stopped the mule in mid-stream at the Britten Creek crossing, allowing Jude to drink his fill of water, before heading on down toward Deep Gap. "Guess you've been needin' a drink fer some time, ain't you, big boy?" he said, as the mule lifted his head and shifted the bits in his mouth, spouting water back into the creek. The mule snorted a couple of times and stepped off with extra vigor, forcing P D against the backrest of the wagon seat.

As he brought the mule to a stop in the breezeway of the barn, he sensed that something was wrong, but he didn't find out just what, until he let the cow out of her stall and noticed that her bag was empty. "Them dam thievin' deserters has done stole the milk right from your bag, Betsy," he said, standing there in astonishment.

After feeding the cow and mule he walked up the path to the house and as he did, he said, "I hope they didn't steal nothin' else," but as he pushed on the door, he realized that the wooden latch was still in place. "Well if they did they had to crawl in the winder."

He lifted the doorlatch with the blade of his pocket knife and stepped inside and made a quick survey of the darkened house, but didn't see that anything was out of place. "I guess they didn't git in.

136

Leastwise, I don't see anythang missin'," he said, after striking a match and lighting the lamp.

He reached up and lifted his muzzle loader from the rack over the door and checked it to make sure it was loaded and ready to fire. "Can't never tell when them thieves'll come back, but I'll dang shore be ready fer 'em," he said, as he laid the gun across the foot of his bed.

After going to bed, he worried about Ann and Cathy having to spend the night alone, especially with a new-born baby in the house. "Shore would be good if John wuz here to take care uv'em," he thought.

But just before falling asleep, he remembered what Ann had said, "Don't sell Fidgety short. She took care of that old Green River boy, Didn't she?"

ᙢᙢᙢᙢᙢᙢᙢᙢᙢᙢᙢᙢ

It was nearing the end of July of 1864. John and his fellow soldiers were still manning the trenches there at Petersburg. The war was still dragging on and it seemed to them as if it would go on forever. They were growing weary of the war, having to lay in the hot muddy trenches, their clothes rotting and literally falling off their backs. Barefoot and hungry, many had simply slipped away and gone home, but John stayed. The words his father had said to him as they stood on the porch, way back in Deep Gap, "Yeah, Son, you're duty bound if you're called," rang constantly in his ears, and he was determined to see it through to the end.

John's fears that George Washington Wiggens had been killed in battle were very real to him, but they were unfounded, for Wiggens had somehow survived the gruesome battles that raged around the trenches, but there was no way John could have known that.

Likewise, Wiggens' fears that John may have been killed were unfounded as well. The battles were so fierce they could not help but have such thoughts. So many had been killed on both sides.

ᙢᙢᙢᙢᙢᙢᙢᙢᙢᙢᙢᙢ

Cathy's baby was now about two weeks old and she had been thinking of going home. She and Ann were awakened early this morning by the baby's cooing as it searced for its mother's breast. "You stay hungry about all the time, don't you, Mary Ann", Cathy said, steering the baby's mouth in the right direction.

There was a gentle knock at the door and without first checking to see who it was, Ann lifted the wooden latch on the door, thinking her father had come for a visit. But when she opened the door, a heavyset man with a dirty rag covering his face stepped inside, shoving her asside and grasping her arm. "I'm here to git some grub. Gimme sompum to eat and you won't git hurt," he said in a very demanding voice. "And besides that, I could use a little 'sugar', too, if ye know what I mean."

He threw Ann across the bed, barely missing Cathy and the baby. He held her arms out to the side as he pinned her down, forcing himself upon her.

With the sound of a wildcat, Fidgety screamed as she sprang from the top of the bureau and landed on the intruder's head. She sank her claws into his scalp and locked onto one of his ears with her incisors. She clung to his head, looking much like the coon-skin-cap worn by Daniel Boone, except for her tail, which by now was half the size of her body.

The intruder scrambled to his feet and reached up to free the cat from his head, but when he did, she sank her teeth into his thumb, bringing a stream of blood. He made a mad dash for the door and as he ran outside the cat leaped from his head, bringing with her a clump of his hair as she sailed to the floor, landing on all fours.

Ann ran to the door to get a good look at the intruder in order to identify him if she ever saw him again, but by the time she reached the door, he was already rounding the bend, heading down toward Britten Creek. "I bet he'll not try that trick again," Ann said, as she came back inside and closed the door.

"That's not likely," Cathy said, as she held her baby close, her heart pounding.

After having a bite of breakfast, they went out and sat on the front porch to rest and to give their nerves a chance to settle down. They hadn't been sitting there but a short while when they heard a wagon coming up the road. "That's Mister Biddy, I bet," Cathy said. "If it is, I think I'll ask him if he'll take me home. Do you think he'd mind doin' that, Ann?"

"I'm sure he wouldn't, but are you sure you're ready to go?"

"Yeah, I'm ready, I think I'll be alright at home," Cathy said, as she shifted the baby to the other breast.

P D agreed to take her home in the wagon, so after they had eaten the mid-day meal, he helped Cathy and the baby into the wagon, climbed up on the other side and down the road they went.

Later on in the afternoon, Ann took care of the animals and

138

retired to the front porch to rest. She sat down in the straight chair, leaned back against the wall and immediately she was nodding, and after a few minutes she was asleep. She dreamed of John, and in her dream she saw him in the midst of battle. His clothes were worn and ragged. His shoes were barely hanging onto his feet. He looked skinny and pale and his face was covered with a dark shaggy beard.

Ann had the habbit of leaning back against the wall in the straight chair to nap, but this time the back legs of the chair were sitting a little too far from the wall, and to make bad matters worse, one leg was resting on a greasy spot left on the floor where she had fed Fidgety a piece of chicken the day before. In her dream of John, she saw him flying through the air as a result of a terrible explosion. In that very instant, the chair slid from beneath her and she came crashing to the floor, barely missing Fidgety's tail, as the cat lay sleeping on the floor beside her. Fidgety jumped to her feet, arched her back with every hair standing on end, her tail bristled like a hair brush. "Well excuse me, Miz. Fidgety, I didn't go to scare you," Ann said, scrambling to her feet, looking around to see if by any chance anyone had witnessed the incident. "Why don't I fix us some supper and we'll eat and go to bed?"

After supper, she fluffed up the cornshuck mattress and she and Fidgety climbed into bed for a night of rest. But the night was far from a restfull one, for she kept dreaming the same dream over and over, seeing John flying through the air from that terrible explosion.

# Chapter

# 9

## John Is Caught Up In The Explosion

In reality, John was spending another restless night in the trenches at Petersburg. He had open sores on both feet and earlier in the day he had all but demanded that his platoon sergeant allow him to go thc the infermary, yelling at him loud enough that it was certain he could have been heard by the black Union soldiers who were nearby in their 'bombproofs'.

In fact, he had been heard by George Washington Wiggens, for he was one of those soldiers. He recognized John's voice. It gave him a great deal of pleasure to hear his voice and to know that he was, in fact, still alive. For he had convinced himself that John had been killed in the heavy fighting in mid-June, but it saddened him to know that he was having trouble with his feet. "I shoo wush dis wau'd git ova. I'as had a plenty uvit," He said, reaching into his pocket to see if John's pearl-handle knife was still there, and it was.

John had gotten no sleep the whole night through, because of the painful sores on his feet. As night began to turn to day, he could see the sky beginning to redden in the east. "Another scorcher," he said to himself, as he sat resting his back against one of the timbers in the trench and fumbling with the black button strung around his neck.

It was Saturday, the thirtieth day of July, 1864, and his thoughts were of Ann and how he would love to be back in the foothills of North Carolina, sitting on the porch of the little shanty, making small talk with her and listening to the crowing of the game rooster, perched on the lower branch of the hemlock out beyond the barn. It seemed he could hear the chirping of the birds down near Britten Creek. He could almost hear the blating of the two nanny goats, Precious and Gracious. In his mind he could see Fidgety, snatching at Ann's black dresstail, as she made her way out to the barn to milk.

He was locked in a hipnotic state of mind, but he was suddenly jarred back into reality when the ground began to quiver and colvulse. The timbers along the sides of the trench began to give way. And then

141

in one belching, billowing second, the earth rose up and he suddenly found himself carried aloft on a carpet on dirt and debris and when he heard that god-awful explosion, he felt numb all over as he went flying through the air amongst splintered timbers, choking smoke, and body parts. He was aloft for only a few seconds, but to him it seemed more like an eternity.

The next thing he knew, he was working himself from beneath the mutilated body of one of his comrades. When he finally worked himself free and looked around, he found himself on the edge of a massive crater. He reached up to touch his scalp and found that his hair had been burned away by the flames of the explosion. His face, hands, and feet were badly burned as well.

He heard moans and groans from his fellow soldiers as they lay gravely wounded, scattered hither and yon as if thrown about by a great storm. He called for help, to no avail, but after the initial shock of the great explosion, the soldiers who had escaped unhurt saw what had happened and began the task of rescuing those who were trapped beneath the debris.

When John saw his comrades approching, carrying a makeshift stretcher, he waved to them with his blistered hand and they immediately came to him and lifted him onto the makeshift canvas stretcher, knotted at the corners to allow the rescuers a firmer grip. Four men carried him out of the carnage and out to a waiting wagon and as he was being loaded onto the wagon, he passed out from the pain. "Is he dead?" one of the soldiers asked.

"No!" another soldier answered. "He's still got a pulse. I think he passed out from all the pain."

"Get him to the infermary pronto," the sergeant in charge ordered the rescuers.

ꗠꗠꗠꗠꗠꗠꗠꗠꗠꗠꗠꗠꗠ

"Good Gawd in Heabum! What'uz dat?" George Washington Wiggens said, as he stood transfixed by the sight of the gaping crater. He was standing only a few feet from the edge, with debris and body parts falling all around him.

He was frightened clean out of his wits as he stood mesmerized, staring at the unbelievable sight. And then in an instant he decided that he had had enough of this war. He hesitated for only a moment, just time enough to get his bearings, before striking out on foot. He headed south and never looked back. No one noticed that he was gone, for they were in such a state of shock from the event that had just taken place.

Wiggins had heard rumors of a regiment of coal miners from Pennsylvania, who were attempting to dig a five-hundred-foot tunnel beneath the Confederate lines, which were to be packed with eight thousand pounds of gun powder and then ignited. It was a scheme thought up by General Burnside and the object was to rip a hole through the Confedereate defense, then all they would have to do would be to rush through and take the town. But Wiggens could not, in his wildest imagination, conjure up in his mind that an explosion of this magnitude could ever take place, for the whole scheme was generally laughed at by the soldiers. But it had happened and he had seen everything he wanted to see and more.

So he was ready to face whatever perils he would have to encounter to get back home. "Ize shoa John be daid. He be one a dem mens what done flung apart in dat sploshun. Ize bound to trabel down ta da little woman's house'n tell'er he done gwone on," he said, as he made his way through a corn field, keeping close to the road, but making sure he stayed out of sight.

Even though he would be traveling through his own friendly states, so to speak, he knew he would still be in a great deal of danger. For there were those who would shoot him on sight and he knew it. He was very aware of his color, but he was proud of who he was. One thing for sure, he had had at least one friend amongst the white race and that was John Shepherd.

Tears came to his eyes as he reached into his pocket to grasp John's pearl-handle knife. "He be gwone, dat's foa sho," he thought to himself, as he walked steadily through the edge of the woods. The sun was sinking down behind the mountains and he cound feel that sweet southern breeze on his face as he trudged along.

As the curtain of darkness closed down around him, he searched for a comfortable place to spend the night, finally settling down on a bed of moss. He lay there in the deafening silence, interrupted only occasionally by the haunting call of an old hoot owl.

ꙨꙨꙨꙨꙨꙨꙨꙨꙨꙨꙨꙨ

Ann finally did get to sleep, but was awakened early the next morning as she dreamed of John, kissing her on the face, but when she awoke, she discovered that it was only Fidgety, standing on the pillow, licking her on the chin. When she opened her eyes, the cat let out with a loud meow, bit her lightly on the nose, then leaped to the floor. "You can't be that hungry, Fidgety! I fed you good last night," she said, as she swung her legs off the bed and slid her feet into her scuffs.

The sun was already up and shining brightly through the tiny window. The goats were blatting. The rooster was crowing and the wild birds were singing cheerfully throughout the woods.

When Ann reached into the can for a scoop of coffee, the scoop scraped the bottom. "I 'spect it's about time to make a trip to Bent Oak," she said, as she emptied the contents of the can into the kettle. "Should be enough eggs to trade for some a'th things I need, that is if there's anything to be had. If this hateful war goes on much longer, there won't be a thing to be had."

She stirred up some batter for a hoe cake, poured it into the Dutch oven and sat it on a bed of coals to cook, while she went out to the barn to feed and milk the goats. And of course the cat had to go along, too, hoping for a squirt or two of warm milk. And of course, the cat's hopes were fulfilled.

After breakfast, Ann swung the the wicher basket onto her arm. It contained seventeen eggs, which she hoped to trade at Bent Oak for some coffee and salt.

With walking stick in hand and Fidgety teathered to the shoestring leash, she headed down the road toward Britten Creek. She had hardly gotten under way when she heard a wagon in the distance. She knew it had to be P D. She could tell by the familiar slapping of the loose board in the wagon bed. As it approached, the first thing that came into view was the mule, his long ears moving forward and back with each step. And yes, it was Jude, and yes it was P D's wagon, but the person sitting in the seat was unfamiliar to her. "It wasn't P D, but who was it?" she wondered. And then she noticed that he was wearing that same old dirty rag over his face that the deserter was wearing when she was attacked a few days back.

As they met, the man in the wagon seemed to recognize her. He whacked Jude on the flanks with the reins and went racing up the road as fast as the mule would take him.

"What is this about?" Ann asked herself, as the wagon went flying up the road. "Just what can this mean?"

She was caught up in a three-way dilemma. Should she return to her shanty, to make sure nothing happened there? Should she hurry down to her father's house, to see if he was alright, or should she go on down to Bent Oak? After all, she had seventeen eggs in the basket she was carrying, with hopes of trading them for coffee and salt. "I'll hurry on over to Bent Oak and then I'll check on Papa," she said to herself, as she set out in a trot, with Fidgety scampering along behind her.

As she stepped up onto the loading dock at Bent Oak and was about to go inside, Eli Bailey met her at the door. "Miss Shepherd, they's been more trouble 'round 'ese parts," he said.

"Tell me about it. How well I know," Ann said, as she sat the basket of eggs on the counter and massaged her forearm, where the basket handle had left its mark. "Some low-down scum has stole my Papa's wagon, and his mule, too."

"How'd ye know that?" Eli asked.

"Cause I met him on the road. He thrashed the mule with the lines when he went by me, and tore out up the road like he thought I might recognize him. He was wearin' that same old dirty rag over his face that he was wearin' when he tried to take advantage of me the other day. Soon's I get my stuff, I'm goin' down to Papa's, to see'f he's alright."

"Gitche business done here'n I'll take ye down on my hoss," Eli said, his face turning crimson with disgust.

"Won't take but a minute," Ann said, uncovering the eggs, allowing the proprieter to count them. "I'd like to trade these for some coffee and salt, that is if you have any," she said.

"Got very little salt'n and just about no coffee, but I'll let ye have a little uv each," the proprieter said, removing the eggs from the basket and placing them into the wooden box under the counter. "You still didn't get a letter from John," He said.

Ann wrapped the coffee and salt in a piece of cloth and placed it into the basket without a single word in reply to the storekeeper's statement about not having a letter from John. "Let's go, Eli, I'm worried about Papa."

Eli mounted his horse, and Ann, standing at the edge of the loading dock, climbed up behind him. She cradled the cat and basket with one arm and off they flew "like the down of a thistle," so to speak.

She locked her free arm around Eli's big belly in order to keep from sliding off the horse as his strong muscles flexed beneath them, carrying them swiftly down the road toward Deep Gap. Fidgety let out with a loud meow and hissed when Ann unintentionally squeezed her a little too hard, as she clung to Eli, tight as a tick on a dog's back.

"Don't let'at cat get ahold'a me. She needs to save her strength fer later, when we meet up with that thievin' deserter," Eli said.

"I'm doin' my best, Eli. She's a big cat, you know."

"At's what bothers me, Ann."

As they approached the Biddy place, there was no sign of P D. They called out to him, but no answer. The front door was open and as they walked up onto the porch Ann called out, "Papa, are you in there?"

"Where in th name'a sense are ye, P D?" Eli yelled, and still there was no answer.

As they intered the house they found things in a mess. Corn meal was spilled onto the floor next to the meal bin and the lid was thrown aside. The cupboard was empty and the table cloth was missing. The jar, used for storing molasses was gone from the shelf beside the table.

There were blood spatters on the floor at the kitchen table and the chair that P D usually sat in was overturned, with a pool of blood beneath it. There was a smear of blood, trailing through the house and out the back door, like someone had slaughtered a hog and dragged it outside. "My God in heaven, Eli, What's happened to my papa?" Ann said, reeling from the thought of what might have happened to him.

"Don't know, Child, but it don't look good."

The trail of blood continued on through the yard and into the edge of the woods, and there they found him, lying in a pool of blood, looking much like a slaughtered hog. Ann fell on him, screaming at the top of her voice, "Oh, Papa! Why? Why did he have to do this? Why didn't he just take the stuff and go?"

After crying until she couldn't, she pushed herself up into a kneeling position. The side of her face was smeared with her father's blood. She raised her arms skyward and swore to avenge her father's death. "I'll kill him if I find out who did it, Papa. I'll put that rogue out of his misery as sure as the sun comes up in the east and as sure as Britten Creek runs into Green River."

She was so distraught, everything seemed a blur. A thousand images of tragedies she had experienced throughout her life pranced through her brain. She had lost so many who were near and dear to her and now, her very own father lay dead there before her, all the blood drained from his body. How could she continue to go on and still act like a normal person? "How much more can I take and still be human?" she asked, looking up at Eli, with a look of desperation on her bloodstained face. "Just how much more?"

Eli placed his big rugged hands under her armpits and gently lifted her to her feet and steadied her until she could stand on her own.

"My dear, I know it's not easy, but you'll have to brace up. There's nothin' else you can do. "Nothin'," he assured her.

They stood for several minutes, staring at P D's mutilated body. A large open gash on the left side of his throat oozed blood and he had cuts in the palm of his left hand where he had apparently tried to ward off the attack. "Who ever killed him must'a slipped up behind'im while he wuz eatin'," Eli said.

As they stood, mulling over who could have done suce a

146

dastardly thing, they heard a wagon coming down the road. "That sounds exactly like Papa's wagon," Ann said, as the muscles in her arms tightened and she began to tremble. "You got a gun, Eli?"

"Got one richeer in my saddle bag," Eli said, as he reached inside and withdrew a long barreled pistol. He checked to make sure it was loaded and said, "Let him come. I'm ready fer'im."

But when the wagon rounded the bend, they recognized the driver. It was Willie Ruff. His horse was tethered to the rear standard of the wagon and Ruffus, his father, was trailing along behind him astride his horse.

"Where'd you get Papa's wagon?" Ann asked, her voice quivering with anger. "Is that blood I see on your shirt?"

"It was up there this side'a Britten Creek, headed this way," Willie answered, looking directly into the barrel of Eli's pistol, his hands flittering above his head. "All I've done was to brimg him back where he b'longed. Yeah, this blood on my shirt's where I wrung that old rooster's neck, yesterday. Had 'im under my arm, now don't you know. Must'a bled a quart. Squirted right out on my shirt."

"Did ye see anybody 'round th wagon?" Eli asked.

"Nope, won't nobody in sight," Willie said, staring at the smear of blood on Ann's face.

"Are you hurt?" Ruffus asked.

"No, it's my papa. He's been butchered like a hog. He's layin' over there in the edge of the woods."

"Well, who could'a done such a thing? Must'a been them thievin' deserters," Ruffus said, as he walked over to the edge of the woods and stood, staring at P D's body.

"If I ever find out who did it I'll put him out of his misery," Ann said, trembling, with tears streaming down her face.

"I'll do it fer ye, if I find out first, Little Lady, Ruffus assured her, as he turned and looked at Eli, still pointing the pistol at his son.

"You ain't gonna shoot me, are you, Mister Bailey?" Willie asked, his hands still held high in the air.

"You can put your hands down, Willie. We know who you are," Eli said, as he put the pistol back into the saddle bag. "But I think we'd better, all of us, keep our eyes open day and night. Looks like they's a killer loose."

"I think we'd better get started on some kinduva coffin. Is they any lumber layin' around here any where?" Ruffus asked.

"Papa made a coffin for hisself, after we burried Mother Hassie," Ann said. "I think he put it up in the barn loft."

"Go'n look, Willie," Ruffus said. "It'll be dark afore we can get him burried, best we can do."

Willie leaped from the wagon and ran out to the barn and climbed up into the loft. And sure enough, there it was, lid and all, half hidden beneath the fodder. "It's up here, Pa," he hollered to Ruffus.

Ruffus and Willie slid the coffin down from the barn loft while Ann went inside the house to get a clean bed sheet to shroud her father's body. She didn't attempt to bathe him, because she knew she couldn't bear to to look at him in that condition any more.

She felt so alone. She had only one other person in the whole world, it seemed, that loved her and that was John. At least, she hoped he was still in the world, even though she hadn't heard from him in quite a while.

After they wrapped P D's body in the bed sheet and placed him into his coffin, Ruffus and Willie took the mattock and shovel from the barnshed and headed up the hill toward the Biddy graveyard to dig the grave, with Eli trailing along behind.

"I'll try to find somethin' I can fix to eat," Ann said, as she walked down toward the branch to wash her father's bloodstains from her face.

To her surprise, she found a crockpot sitting in the middle of the branch, weighted down with a rock, and inside was a freshley dressed chicken. "Papa must'a planned on havin' this chicken for Sunday dinner," she thought to herself, as she washed the blood from her face.

She looked at her reflection in the still water at the edge of the branch and her face looked clean. After drying it on her dresstail, she stepped back into the bushes to relieve herself, for she hadn't had a chance to do that since early this morning. "Well, that's a relief," she said to herself, as she rinsed her hands in the stream, removed the rock from the top of the crockpot, picked it up and started up the path toward the house.

"Me-ooow!" Fidgety screamed, as she sprang from behind a laurel bush.

Ann was so startled, she came close to dropping the crockpot.

"Fidgety! You about scrared the life out'a me. Don't you think I've had enough surprises for one day?" she said, standing for a moment to collect her wits.

"Me-ow!" her cat said, brushing up against her dresstail, purring.

The scare was somewhat therapeutic in that it helped her look at the situation with a clearer head. "I'd let some people know about Papa, but he'd be stinkin' by the time they got here, 'cause the weather's so hot," she thought to herself. "Anyway, a body's got'a do what a body's got'a do."

148

She carried the crockpot into the house and sat it on the kitchen table, picked up the bucket and went back down to the spring to fetch some water. She placed the chicken into the cast-iron cook pot, covered it with water and rekindled the fire beneath it. "I guess it was a good thing that I went over to Bent Oak first," she said.

For the thief hadn't left a grain of salt nor a trace of coffee in the cupboard. She did find a scraping of lard in the bucket beside the meat box, just enough to season the chicken. She had no flour for bread and none for dumplings. "Well, we'll at least have chicken," she thought.

The chicken stew was simmering in the pot when the men returned from digging the grave. They got a whiff of its aroma clear out in the yard. Coffee was boiling in the kettle, sending out a pleasant aroma of its own. "Come and get it, men. There's chicken stew and coffee and that's all I could find to cook. Grub's a little short these days, as you all know," Ann said, as she placed four bowls on the table.

She had manage to find four spoons, and searching around, she found four coffee cups. "They're chipped, but they'll serve the purpose," she thought to herself.

"Grub might be a little short, but it shore does smell good," Willie said, removing his hat and tossing it into the corner near the woodbox.

He picked up his bowl and began dipping chicken stew from the pot, filling his bowl to the brim. He filled his coffee cup, sat down at the table and began eating as though he was the only person there.

"Can't ye wait on th rest uvus, Willie? 'sides, they's a lady in our midst, jist in case you hadn't noticed," his father said, scolding him.

"I'uz hongry, Pa. Takes a lot'a sap out'uv a man, diggin a grave in this August heat. I meant to say July," Willie said.

"Well, you could at least have a little respect fer th lady," Ruffus said. "She cooked it. At least she should have th first go at it."

"I 'pologize, Missus Shepherd. I guess I thought uv you as one'a th boys," Willie said, placing his spoon beside his bowl and folding his hands in his lap, staring up at the ceiling.

"That's alright, Willie, You men've been out there diggin' in the hot sun. At least I've been in the shade," she said, as she went about filling Ruffus and Eli's bowls with stew.

After she finished filling their bowls and pouring them some coffee, she emptied the pot into her bowl. She ended up with a little over half a bowl. There was about a third of a cup of coffee left in the pot, so she said, "I think I'll have a cup of water with my stew."

Willie emptied the coffee kettle, pouring it into his cup. "Ain't no more coffee," he said, sitting back down at the table. He dipped up

149

the last drop of stew in his bowl and said, "Shore wuzen't a nuf, but I guess it'll have to do."

"I guess we'd better git busy," Eli said, as he took the last sip of coffee from his cup. "Are you ready to bury ye pa, Child?

"I'm not ready, Eli, but it's got to be done."

"Willie, bring th wagon around and we'll load him up, Ruffus said, pushing back from the table and reaching for his hat.

"He acts like Papa's just another chunk of wood," Ann thought to herself. "But I don't know what I would have done without his help. I guess you don't look a gift horse in the mouth."

Ruffus and Eli loaded the coffin onto the wagon, then Eli held Ann's hand as she climbed up and sat down on the seat beside Willie.

"Whache got in at'ere box?" Uncle Henry Shepherd asked as he came strolling up the road with a pint whiskey bottle tucked away in his back pocket.

"It's P D Biddy," Willie said. "Some thievin' deserter cut his thoat'n left 'im to bleed to death."

"Well, thangs'er goin' to the dogs around here 'ese days. We're gonna hafta find 'ese scoundrels and put'em outa ther misry," Henry said, thrashing the ground with his walking stick.

"We're fixin' to take him up to the graveyard'n bury him. Would you like to come along?"

"Well, I never had a hankerin' fer funerals, but I guess I'll come along, since he's my brother. It's the least I can do fer him. He wuz a good man, you'ns all know that."

Eli, Ruffus, and Uncle Henry sat at the rear of the wagon, facing backward, their feet dangling, and off they went, the little mule straining to pull the heavy load up the steep hill to the graveyard.

They had hardly gotten under way, when Willie reached over and laid his hand on Ann's leg. She jerked away quickly and gave him a stern took, but that didn't stop him, for he did the same thing again. She took hold of his hand and slung it away. "Keep your hands to yourself," she said, her eyes blazing with anger.

"I didn't go to touch you Missus Shepherd. My hand must'a slipped," Willie said, lying.

It was mid-afternoon when they reached the Biddy graveyard and unloaded the coffin onto the ground. "Who'll say some words over 'im? Uncle Henry asked, his hat pressed tightly against his chest. "How 'bout you, Eli?"

"I'm not muchuva speaker, but I guess I can say a word er two. After all, they ain't nothin' bad that can be said about 'im. He had a hard life. He lost his first wife when Ann wuz borned. Then he  lost

Hassie, down 'ere in Britton Creek last winter. But he was a good man. He'd give you th shirt right off'en his back if you needed it. If you got in a bind, he'd be right 'ere to help ye. It was just too bad he had to go this'a way. God bless his soul, he wasn't a religious man, but he shore did take care uv his own , and his neighbors, too, if I may say so. But as fer th scoundrel what killed him, may God have mercy on his soul! For if I find out who done it, I shore won't show no mercy on what's left of him!"

"Amen," Willie said, wiping the sweat from his forehead on his shirt sleeve.

Uncle Henry took a sip from the bottle he had stashed away in his back pocket.

Ruffus motioned to Willie and they lowered P D into the grave with ropes they had looped around each end of the coffin. Loose dirt and small pebbles dropped onto the lid of the coffin, as it scraped the sides of the opening, settling to the bottom of the grave.

Tremors traveled up and down Ann's spine, hearing the rattle of the pebbles falling onto the lid of the coffin. Her mind traveled back to the time her father told about how her mother had died, and she remembered about wiping the tears from his cheeks on the sleeve of her dress. She remembered how happy he was on her wedding day, dressed in his black suit and black tie. His shoes were black and shining from the tallow he had rubbed on them and polished with the piece of cloth he had managed to find in the ragbag under the bed.

She remembered him splitting shingles for her shanty, from the large red oak she had helped him saw down and saw into lengths. Shingles that now keep her dry when it rains. "Yes indeed, he really was a good man," she thought to herself.

"Ashes to ashes and dust to dust," Eli said, as he tossed a clump of dirt onto the coffin.

"Amen," Willie said.

"Uncle Henry, if you'll take Ann back down to th house, Me'n th boys'll git'im covered up," Ruffus said, as he began to shovel dirt into the opening, with no more feeling than if burying a dead animal.

"Crawl up in th wagon, Girl'n I'll take ye to th house," Uncle Henry said, taking another sip from the pint bottle.

There was about an hour of sunshine left in the day, when the men finished filling in the grave and headed back down toward the house. Ann was sitting on the edge of the porch, holding Fidgety on her lap when they came up from the barn shed, after putting the tools away.

"What ye gonna do with that milk cow, Missus Shepherd?" Willie asked, as he walked up and sat down beside her on the edge of the porch.

Fidgety hissed as the hair stood out on her entire body, looking much like a giant porcupine. Willie promptly stood up and shuffled out into the yard. "That animal ain't the friendliest thang, is it?" he said, pointing nervously at the cat.

"She takes care of things," Ann said.

"I'll take the cow off'a yer hands. Give ye three dollars, Confederate money fer her. She ain't worth more'n 'at," Willie said, reaching into his pocket, as if reaching for the money.

I suppose I'll have to let her go. There's no way I can take care of her. She's worth more than any three dollars, but you can have her for that," Ann said.

"Well it's a done deal," Willie said, handing the money to her at arms length, making sure not to come into contact with the cat.

"We'd be obliged to ye, if you'd rent this place to us. Willie's got hisself hitched up with that Ruff gal and she's got a young baby, now don't ye know." Ruffus said, pawing in the dirt with the toe of his shoe. "We'd give ye seven Confederate dollars a month. That comes to about a quarter a day. I don't thank ye can do better'n 'at," he said.

"What Ruff gal?" Ann asked.

"Cathy Ruff," Willie said.

"Well I pitty her, Willie!"

Willie's face turned blood red, but he didn't dare say anything.

"You'll have to pay me in advance," Ann said.

"What does 'at mean?" Willie asked.

"That means you'll have to pay me at the first of the month instead of at the end."

"We can do that," Ruffus said, taking seven dollars from his pocket and handing it to her. "And we're obliged to ye."

"You'll have to promise me that you'll bring half the fodder in the barn loft and half the corn from the crib up to my place," Ann said.

"It's as good as done. We'll bring it up to ye tomar," Willie said. "But what about th mule and wagon."

"You can keep the mule and wagon, but you'll have to promise to do any haulin' that I'll need to have done," Ann said.

"We'd be more'n happy to do that, Missus Shepherd. "More'n happy," Willie said, feeling that he had come out of the bargining with everything very much in his favor.

"I'll be back down here tomorrow, to pick up Papa's clothes and other things, and while I'm thinkin' about it, I'll take his muzzle loader with me today," she said, as she got up from the porch and went inside to retrieve her father's gun from the rack above the front door. "Can't

152

never tell when I might need it," she said.

The smile on Willie's face turned to a frown, for he had hoped she would leave P D's clothes and if he couldn't wear them himself, he could sell them outright, or trade them for other things he would be needing. For some strange reason, he hadn't thought of the gun.

"I'm ready if you are, Eli," Ann said.

"Well let's go then, while they's still daylight." Eli said, guiding the big horse over to the porch.

Ann handed the gun to Eli and he slid it into the holster while she climbed astride the horse. She cradled Fidgety in her arms and the horse galloped away.

Eli stopped the horse at the gate in front of the little shanty and held Ann's hand as she dismounted. Fidgety sprang from her arms, leaped over the gate, and went straight for the front porch, scenting along the path as she went, the hair on her body bristling. "What's eatin' at that cat?" Eli asked.

"Somebody's been here while I've been gone and she knows it, and it's somebody she don't like," Ann said, as she grasped the stock of the muzzle loader.

Eli dismounted, pulled the long barreled pistol from the saddlebag and said, "You'd better let me go in first. Can't tell, he just might still be in 'ere."

But when they went inside they couldn't see anything that had been disturbed. "Can't see no signs uv nobody bein' in here," Eli said.

"Looks just the way I left it," Ann said. "That's a miricle in itself, but what about my goats and chickens?"

"Don't know. Let's go check onum," Eli said, returning to the porch and heading for the barn.

"What's 'ese feathers a doin' piled up on th ground here?" He asked, stooping down to pick up a handfull.

"Looks like they're from my best rooster, Eli."

"They's plenty a blood here on th ground, too, Ann."

"Some scoundrel's done killed my very best rooster," Ann said, the veins in her neck swelling and her face burning with anger.

"Looks 'at way, Girl. Sure does."

When they entered the barn they found the goats standing in their stall, munching on some fodder. "I didn't feed these goats any fodder today," Ann said. "Only a ear of corn apiece."

"Well afu didn't, who did?"

"It's that thievin' deserter. Look! He's milked Precious and Gracious. No more'n a teacup left between 'em," Ann said, dropping to her knees there in the stall. "If that don't beat all! He'll be back for

153

more. I feel sure about that."

"You'll need to be awful kerful, Girl, you here all by yesef. Can't never tell when he'll come sneakin' around. I'll fix up ye pa's gun, so's it'll be ready to shoot. Don't be afraid to fill'im full a lead, if he does. He's got no business messin' around here anyway," Eli said, getting angrier by the minute.

"Papa's already showed me how to load and shoot that gun, so I know how to do it," Ann said, as they walked back toward the shanty. "I know how to use it and I will if I have to!"

"Well, I'm gone," Eli said. "I need to check on my place, and they's milkin' to be done when I get home, that is, ifen 'at scoundrel ain't done it aready."

"Keep ye door fastened," he said, as he mounted his horse and rode away, with darkness closing in around him.

"I'll take care of myself," Eli.

Ann walked up the steps, crossed the porch, and went inside, with Fidgety at her heels. "I'll never be scared as long as you're around," she said to her cat, as she closed the door and pulled the drawstring inside.

There was a piece of hoecake on the table, left over from this morning's meal. She broke off a chunk and fed it to her cat and sat munching on the rest of it, washing it down with water that had been standing in the bucket all day.

Sleep would be elusive for her tonight, for she felt as though the whole world was caving in around her. Sounds of the pebbles falling onto her father's coffin rattled in her brain. She clasped her hands over her ears, but she couldn't muffle the sound. When she closed her eyes, the sight of her father, lying in a pool of blood, was clearly visible and when she opened them and looked about the dark room the image continued momentarily. She felt as though she would loose her mind. And then Fidgety bounced up onto the bed, crawled over and snuggled up under her chin, purring. "Fidgety, I don't know what I'd do without you, and that's a fact," she said, stroking the cat and listning to the snapping of static electricity as her hand moved over the cat's thick fur.

As she lay, way into the wee hours of the night, she attempted to evaluate her life. She wondered if life was still worth living, but suddenly, thoughts of John flooded her brain and eased her troubled mind for the moment. "I still have John," she said. "I still have John, or at least I hope I do."

But it was difficult to to keep her hopes alive. The stories of the bloody battles being fought in and around the Confederate Capitol of Richmond were very troubling. There were stories of soldiers who had lost arms and legs and so many had been killed.

It was getting harder each day to keep believing that John was still amongst the living, for she hadn't received a letter from him in quite a while. "I do wish he'd write me," she thought.

Sometime after midnight she finally drifted off to sleep, but it was a fretful sleep. Over and over, she dreamed of John in the midst of battle, and after each dream she would awake and find herself sitting up in bed, her heart racing as if she had run a mile. "Dam this awful war,"she said. "It'll get John killed for sure."

John hadn't been killed, but death had come very close, when he was caught up in that god-awful explosion. The hair was missing from his scalp, burned away by the flames of the explosion. His face and hands were covered with huge blisters. His feet were burned badly as well. The pain was almost unbearable, and at times he passed out, which was a blessing, for when he was unconscious, naturally, he didn't feel the awful pain.

Ann was still asleep when the sun came streaming through the tiny window of her bedroom the next morning. If that rogue hadn't killed her rooster, he would have been crowing by now.

When the bleating of her goats roused her from sleep, she sprang into a sitting position, much like a young sapling, suddenly released after being bent to the ground.

Fidgety flew through the air and landed on all four's in the middle of the floor, looking dazed from the sudden flight and such a rude awakening.

"Well, at least this is another day," Ann whispered to herself, as she slid off the bed and slipped her feet into her scuffs. "Fidgety, I didn't mean to throw you onto the floor. I must'a been dreaming. I'm sorry. Really I am."

The cat looked at her through blazing eyes and let out with a very loud "Meow!"

"I sure hope today's a better day than yesterday," Ann said, cupping her hand around one ear and listened for a moment, and as sure as the sun had risen, it was the sound of her father's wagon. She looked out through the tiny window of her bedroom and saw Willie and his father, Ruffus, coming up the road with the load of corn and fodder they had promised to deliver this morning. "Looks like he's as good as his word," she said.

She slipped into her work shoes and went outside to show them where to put the stuff and they went to work, doing just that. While they were unloading the corn and fodder, she shelled an ear of corn onto the ground for the chickens, fed and milked her goats and brought them some water. "I'll be goin' back with you'ns, after you unload the stuff," she said to Ruffus and Willie, as she walked briskly toward the house with the bucket of milk.

"Fine, Missus Shepherd, we'll wait fer ye," Willie said, wiping the sweat from his forehead with an old dirty rag he pulled from his back pocket.

"We'll be ready when you are," Ruffus said.

Ann rushed inside, strained the milk into the crock pot, poured herself a cupfull of warm goat milk and drank it down without removing the cup from her mouth. She carried the crock of milk down to the branch and weighted it down with a flat rock. When she returned, the men, having finished unloading the corn and fodder, were sitting at the rear of the wagon, their legs swinging like the pendilum of a grandfather clock.

"I want you to keep watch for me while I'm gone, Fidgety. I'll be back d'rectly," Ann said, as she climbed into the wagon and sat down in the middle of the seat.

Not much was said on the way down to the Biddy house. Ann felt uncomfortable sitting between Willie and Ruffus. She didn't mind Ruffus so much, but after the ride yesterday, she didn't put much trust in Willie, but he managed to keep his hands to himself the whole trip. She figured that perhaps his father, sitting on the other side of her, played a part in his conduct.

She scurried about at the Bibby house, collecting her father's clothes and bundling them in a bed sheet. She wrapped his razor and shaving mug in a scarf that belonged to her step-mother. His shaving brush by now had seen its best days, but she took it anyway. She found a tintype in the very bottom of the bureau drawer. It was a picture of a young lady. "Could this be my mother?" she asked herself, looking closely at the young lady's face. "She looks a lot like me!"

Tears filled her eyes as she wondered why her father had never shown the picture to her. "Maybe he couldn't bear to look at her picture because he missed her so much. Maybe it brought him too much pain," she said, as she gently wrapped it in her neckerchief and carefully placed in into her dress pocket. "This has to be a picture of my mother," she said, staring toward the ceiling with tears welling up in her eyes.

After loading her father's personal things onto the wagon, she searched through the barn and found his shovel, mattock and his axe and carried them out to the wagon. Making one last search through the barn, she found his froe, wedged between the logs on the wall of the breezeway. "I must take this," she said. "I'd never leave his froe here."

156

She decided to have one last look through the house to see if she had perhaps missed something. P D's rocking chair was sitting at the fireplace in the front room. Her first thought was to take it with her, but on second thought she decided to leave it, for she knew Cathy would be needing it on the nights when her baby was fretful and couldn't sleep. The rocking chair would certainly be a blessing to her.

Ann felt a special closeness to the baby, almost as if the little girl was her very own, even though she hadn't had the privilege of having a child of her own and couldn't possibly know how it would feel to be a mother. But she was sorry for Cathy, in that she had lost her first husband in the war, and though she hoped Willie would be good to her, she still had her doubts. But she planned to keep a close watch on Cathy to make sure she wasn't being abused.

When she was satisfied she had collected all her father's things, she asked Ruffus to take her home. "I'll take ye home, Missus Shepherd," Willie spoke up, before Ruffus had a chance to say yea or nah. "I'd be more'n happy to do it."

"I'll just go along, too, Son. We'll need to go on over to th house and load up som'a yore stuff. I'd like to git ye moved afore th weather gits bad. Could come a long rainy spell, now don't ye know," Ruffus said, as he held Ann's arm and helped her up onto the wagon.

"Thank you very much, Ruffus. I somehow feel safer when you're along," Ann said, as she rested her hands in lap of her black black dress.

Upon reaching Ann Ridge, Ruffus climbed down from the wagon and reached up to give Ann a hand down. She gathered her father's things and carried them into the shanty. Willie sat in the wagon while his father unloaded the shovel and the other tools. Ruffus leaned them against the rail fence near the gate, and without staying long enough to see if Ann needed anything more, he crawled back into the wagon and off they went, without a single word or even looking back.

When Ann returned to the porch to tell them goodbye, they were going out of sight around the bend, down near Britten Creek. "Well, that was a fast fare-ye-well!" Ann said, as she stood gazing down in that direction.

If this was any indication, it looked as though they would not be spending any extra energy on her, nor courtesy, for that matter. "Well, they don't have to be friendly. I'll be satisfied as long as they pay the rent on time. I can get by without their friendship, but I will expect that money at the very first of the month, or I'll be payin' them a little visit," she said.

"Well, so much for that," she said, as she busied herself with

157

folding her father's clothes into the bureau drawer. She picked up his Sunday shoes and noticed they still carried a shine, for he had always tried to keep them clean and polished. In her mind she could see him on the morning of her wedding day, dressed in that black suit, black tie, and black shiny shoes. Large tears rolled down her cheeks as she sat on the edge of her bed, stroking the toe of one of his shoes with her long slender fingers.

She looked up suddenly when she heard the door creaking open. She was startled at first, but when she saw that it was only Fidgety, a smile came to her face.

The cat had killed a young gray squirrel and had brought it all the way home. "Bring it to me, Fidgety. I'll skin it and we'll have it for supper," she said.

She skinned the squirrel and washed it, cut it in pieces, and put it into the cast iron pot. She poured some water over the squirrel, added some salt and a dab of grease and swung it over the fire. "I'll let it cook while I'm takin' care of the goats," she said, talking to herself.

The cat replied with a meaow, brushing up against her dresstail and curling her long tail half way around Ann's leg. She took the milk bucket down from the wall and as she strolled out toward the little barn Fidgety was right behind her, ready for some warm goat milk.

The sun was already down behind Wildcat Spurr when she finished with the milking and was walking back toward the shanty. She stopped for a moment to listen to the call of an old hoot owl. He seemed to be serenading her from the cliffs, way up in the hollow above her little shanty.

When she walked up the steps, crossed the porch and opened the door, the pleasant aroma of the squirrel, cooking in the cast iron pot, rushed out to meet her. She could hardly wait to stir up some corn meal for a hoe cake. She strained the milk and carried it down to the branch and brought back the crock of milk that had been cooling in the creek all day.

As soon as the hoecake was done, she checked to see if the squirrel was tender and it was. "Let's eat, Fidgety. This squirrel smells mighty good."

She poured some milk into the cat's bowl, placed one of the squirrel's legs onto a plate and sat it on the floor so Fidgety could get at it. They ate until they had devoured everything. The squirrel, the hoecake, and the gravy, everything had gone the way of the gullet. "My! That sure was good, Fidgety. You can do that again, just any time," Ann said, getting up from the table, ready to wash the dishes. "Just any time," she said again.

She washed and dried the dishes and placed them upside down on the table and carried the pan of dish water outside and emptied it onto the red worm bed. Since times were hard and food was so scarce, she had learned that fishing could help put food on the table. She had also learned that dish water encouraged the growth of red worms, and this summer she had some whoppers, some so large they were frightening to her, but not to the fish. She had set aside her old walking stick and cut a longer one from a slinder hickory sapling, one that could be used as a walking stick and a fishing pole as well. She always made sure she kept a piece of twine and a fishhook in her dress pocket, stored inside a tiny leather pouch.

On days when she went over to Bent Oak or down to Deep Gap, she would dig a few red worms, put them in a tin can, add some moist dirt, wrap the can with a piece of cloth to keep the worms from escaping and put the can into the basket she always carried with her when she planned to fish. There was a special spot on Britten Creek where the water was deep and always teeming with fish. That's where she would leave the can of worms, hidden beneath some leaves beside the road in the shade. On her way back from her trips she would stop and fish.

Today was such a day. On her way back from Bent Oak, she stopped at the fishing hole, caught a couple of fish and headed on home, happy in knowing she would have fish for supper.

After supper, and the chores were done, she went outside and sat on the porch for a while, listning to the babbling of Britten Creek. A whippoorwill sang its repetitious song, perched somewhere in the thick underbrush on the other side of the creek. The sounds were soothing, but not so soothing as to keep her from thinking of the terrible things that had happened these last few days. Not so soothing as to remove the pain of losing her father in such a hideous way. She would not forget that. Not ever!

No sound, however pleasant, would erase the pain of missing John. She missed him terribly, and each day that passed without hearing from him, caused her to miss him even more. "I do wish he'd write," she mumbled to herself, as she stood up, walked inside, closed the door, and pulled the latch string inside. "What could keep him from writin' a few words?"

In her heart, she felt she knew why he hadn't written, but she wasn't about to express her feelings with the uttered word. Thinking about it was painful enough, but saying it aloud would be suicide, she thought. "Hope is what I have left and I'll n-e-v-e-r give up hope," she said, as she crawled into bed to face another night of dreadful dreams.

# Chapter

# 10

## John Glares Into The Looking Glass And George Washington Wiggens Heads South

John was facing another painful night as well, trying to cope with the burns on his face, hands, feet, and scalp. However, the nurse who was caring for him decided earlier in the day to try something she thought might possibly ease the burning. "Why not apply soft unsalted butter to his burns?" she thought. "At least it will serve as a second skin, should be soothing, too. After all, since we don't have anything else, I'm obliged to try something," she said.

She placed a bowl of unsalted butter on the windowsill and the heat from the afternoon sun turned it into a soft paste. She applied it to John's burns while it was still warm. It was painful when it was first applied, but when the burns were covered, he felt immediate relief.

His nurse tried to feed him a few bites, but he fell asleep, for he hadn't slept since the explosion. "That's alright, Young Man, sleep'll do you good right now, may do you more good than food," She said, as she turned to dress the wounds of another soldier who was lying on the cot across from him. This young man hadn't been burned but he had lost both legs, just below the knee.

John woke before daylight the next morning and when he reached up to scratch his itching scalp, the nurse took hold of his arm and said, "No, Son, don't do that."

She had not stopped him soon enough, for he had already touched his scalp and realized he had no hair. "What's happened to my hair?" he murmured.

"You were caught up in an explosion, Son. You lost all your hair in the blaze."

"What explosion and blaze? I don't remember no explosion."

"There was an explosion in the trenches, down at Petersburg. A lot of men were killed, but you are one of the lucky ones."

"From the looks'a my hands, don't look like I was very lucky," John said, as he stared at them through eyelids that had no lashes.

161

"I know you were burned badly, but you'll heal with time. It will just take time," the nurse lady assured him. "Here, take some water," she said, holding the cup to his lips.

He managed to take a swallow, but it stung his throat as the water went down. He pushed the cup away and said, "That hurts my throat."

"That fire and smoke must have burned your throat, too, Son, but you must drink some water."

She held the cup to his lips again and after taking another sip, he pushed it away again, saying, "That's all I can stand. Give me a little more time."

Suddenly, John thought of the black button that was torn from Ann's dress while they were building their shanty. He had threaded it onto a piece of string and looped around his neck before leaving to fight in the war. It was to bring him good luck, or so he thought. He pushed aside the lapel of his tattered jacket and felt for the button, but it was gone. "Where's my button?" he asked through blistered lips.

The nurse reached into her pocket and pulled out a large, black button. The string was broken, but it was still threaded through the button hole. "Is this it?" she asked.

"That's it! That's it! Where'd you find it?"

"You were carrying it in your hand when they brought you in," the nurse answered.

"I must have had it in my hand when things flew apart," John said, reaching out to touch the button.

The nurse placed the string around his neck and tied it. It seemed to bring John a great deal of comfort to have his good luck carm back where it should be. "Thank you, maam, for keepin' it for me," he said, as he caressed the black button with his blistered hand.

"You're quite welcome, young man. I thought it must have meant something to you, or you would't have had it in your hand."

"It does mean a lot to me. It's a button from my wife's dress. I've been wearin' it around my neck all through the war for good luck, and up until now I've been spared," he said, as he lay back and closed his eyes.

Days and weeks passed as he lay recovering from his burns. He suffered many setbacks, for it was about impossible to keep the burns from becoming infected. He had large weeping sores on his face, and when the sores finally began to heal, it was obvious that he would be scarred. "When this war's over and I get to go home, will she know me?" he asked himself, as he stood staring into the looking glass.

Leaving the Union Army behind, George Washington Wiggins met with many obstacles on his journey southward. He traveled mainly during the early morning and late evening hours, knowing full well he would be in great danger if anyone happened to see him.

But on one occasion he was sure he had been seen as he passed close by a farm house, for an old man who was on his way to the barn, threw the milk bucket he was carrying to the ground and ran back into the house to get his gun and when he came back outside he fired the gun in his direction and set the dogs on his trail. Wiggens broke into a run and ran until he could no longer hear the dogs chasing after him. Darkness was closing in around him when he finally stopped by a small stream for a drink of water and after drinking his fill, he crawled up under a thicket for some much needed rest and sleep.

The next morning when he awoke, he heard someone calling for help. He lay for a moment asking himself, "Ought I go or ought I no?" But as the call kept coming, he made up his mind that no matter the danger to himself, he must go to the rescue. He eased out from under the canopy of the thicket and crept through the woods in the direction of the call for help. When he came within sight of the caller, he saw an elderly man, pinned between a stump and the base of the tree that he had just chopped down. The tree had lodged on the limb of a nearby oak, kicking back and pinning his leg against the stump.

"Help!" came the cry once more from the elderly man as he stood with his arms wrapped around the lodged tree.

"Mista, wudge lowme ta hep ye?" Wiggens asked, as he cautiously approached the old man.

"I shore would, son. A man in my shape ain't got much choice, now that's a fact," the old man said, his voice quivering as he spoke.

He didn't even seem to notice, or care that Wiggins was a black man. Seems as though under certain circumstances, the color of a man's skin makes no difference at all.

Wiggins stood for a moment, scratching his head and studying the situation. The old man's mule was standing nearby, fully harnessed and hitched up to a singletree. A trace chain was hanging from one of the hames.

"Mista, if ye low my pinion, I blieves dish ea mule a yose'cn pull dish ea tree offa you.

Ize gwine take ishea chain what be hangin round de hames, conneck it to da swingletree, wrop it round de bottom uv dis tree'n

163

yank it offa yo laig," he said, as he unwound the chain from the hames.

He wrapped the chain around the lodged tree trunk, about six inches above the ground and attached it to itself with the hook at the end. He brought the mule around and connected the other end of the chain to the singletree. "We is ready, Mista, ta yank dis hea tree right offa ya," he said. "Soons yo leg be freed, yo mus hump it on up de hill so dat tree don't fall on ya."

"I'll do my best, young man," the old man said, as he cocked his good leg, ready for a hasty escape.

Wiggens clucked to the mule and whacked him across the rump with a brush, and in a single bound the mule humped his back and yanked the tree about three feet away from the stump.

The old man fell backwards onto the ground, but hurriedly worked his way up the hill, scooting along on his backside. He was dragging the leg that had been pinned between the tree and the stump. It snaked along the ground like a loose plowline. "I b'lieve my leg's broke, young man. You'll prob'ly have to tote me ta th house. Ain't no way I can walk," he said, breathing hard as he grasped his injured leg.

"Be mose glad ta tote ye to da house, Mista. But fust, I betta tie up dat leg some, to keep it frum gettin wosen it be now."

"I b'lieve ye got sompum 'ere son. I can tell you got a head on them shoulders."

"Lun it up yondo, fightin in dat wau. I done seed many a po boy, his laig blowed mose haf off. Used what eva we cud pick up ta keepum frum diein," Wiggins explained.

He unsnapped the latchet from the bit ring on the mule's bridle and pulled the line from the harness. He picked up a couple of short sticks from the ground nearby and placed one on each side of the old man's injured leg and secured them with the rope. "I blieves dat'll do it,"he said.

With the old man's leg secured, Wiggens lifted him and cradled him in his arms like a baby and struck out through the woods, leaving the mule stanging. He walked till he came to a clearing. Looking off into the distance he could see a small cabin. "Dat yo house?" Wiggins asked, panting for breath.

"That's it, son. Tain't much, but it's mine," the old man said, clinging to Wiggens, who was now going in a trot.

"Don't drop me, whatever ye do," the old man said. "If ye do, it's bound ta kill me."

"Neva drop ya, Suh. I is got ya. No chanch a me doin dat."

By the time they reached the cabin, Wiggins was exhausted, all sweaty and out of breath, but he stepped up onto the porch and deposited the old man on the bench and leaned him back against the wall. "Leme opum up dishea doa anile stretch ya out on de bed."

The old man let out with a long sigh of relief as Wiggins gently laid his frail frame on the bed.

"If you hadn't a come along when you did, I s'pose I'd a been out 'ere till I died and that's fer shore," the old man said, reaching up to shake Wiggins' hand.

"Sumpum what had ta be did, Mista. What be yo name, noway?"

"I'm Sonner, Sam Sonner. Lived here in this neck'a th woods most all my life. I wuz borned down here about two miles off Broad River, down 'ere close ta Bear Woller. You know where that is?" he asked Wiggens.

"Neva hea uvit," Wiggins replied.

He removed the braces from Sam's broken leg to get a closer look at it and found that no bones had pierced his akin. "You got some likka, Mista Sonner?"

"What you want with likker?" Sam asked. You ain't gonna get drunk on me, are ye?"

"Need sompum what will kill yo pain. Hafta put dese bones back ta gever soz ya be able ta walk about. Dat gonna hurt a plenty."

Sam pointed to the shelf above the eating table. On the shelf sat a large earthen jug in which he stored his liquor. He never allowed himself to be without his tonic, as he called it. Wiggins took the jug from the shelf and filled a tin cup and handed it to Sam. "Hea, Mista Sam, take a swig a dis an I'll set dem bones."

Sam propped up on his elbow, took it by the handle, put the cup to his lips and drank it all down without so much as removing it from his mouth. "You sho does put dat stuff away in a hurry, Mista Sam. You sho does."

"Well, if a man's got somethin' ta do, they's no use foolin' around," Sam said, puckering his mouth as if he had just swallowed a handful of persimmons.

After a few minutes Sam was feeling the affects of the whiskey and Wiggens began the task of putting his leg bones back in place. It was painful to the old man, but in only a short time, the bones were set and Wiggens was binding the broken leg with strips, torn from an old bed sheet to keep the bones in place until they healed. "Dat won't so bad, now wuzit?" Wiggens said, finally getting a chance to sit down.

"Twern't bad a'tall, son. Not bad a'tall. Now't I've told ye who I am, Wh'ont ye tell me who you are?" Sam said, looking straight into Wiggens' big brown eyes.

"I be Wiggens, Geoge Washinton Wiggens. I comes frum Saff

165

Calina. Sumpta, Saff Calina ta be mo perzact."

"Well what ye doin' way off up here, Son."

"I done stolt my way off up noth. Got caught up in dat wau up dao, but I done got my belly full o fightin an come on back down saff whea they ain't no fightin."

"But they's fightin' down here, too," Sam said.

"I knows, but leas I be ta home. 'Sides, Ize got a message ta bring ta Missus Ann Shepud. She live down ere in Poke Couny. Ann Ridge, ta be mo pacise."

"What kind of a message?"

"Hafa tell hu dat hu man done be killed in dat awful splosun, up dau in Vaginua. Blowed mose to kingdom come, I spect. Ain't seed hide no hair uv him since."

"Well, Polk County's still a fer piece from here yet, but I'll tell ye how ta get 'ere. You go out here a ways, out toward where the sun's a settin', and you'll come to a right big river. Now that'll be Broad River. Jist go down 'at river a little ways'n you'll come to a place where ye can cross it, where it spreads out and you can cross it. You'll have ta wade, but you'll have no trouble a'crossin' it. Go on down 'at river a little ways, till ye come to a trail. That's a Indian trail. Cut back ta th right when ye come to it and foller it on around the mountain a good piece till ye come to a creek. Now that'll be Pool Creek. Jist foller that creek on up th side'a th mountain and you'll come ta Jude's Gap road. You'll have ta be mighty careful on that road fer they's times when it'll be full'a cattle er other animals, People from South Ca'lina, drivin' their livestock ta market. I don't think you'll want them a seein' ye. They's no tellin' what they'd do to ye if they happened ta see ye, you bein' a black man," Sam said, as he reached down to rub his broken leg.

"Well, you just stay on Jude, travelin' south and east and you'll come to a place they call World's Edge. If ye could see that fer, I 'spect you could see all th way ta where you're from, down 'ere in South Ca'lina. When ye get 'ere, you could almost see Ann Shepherd's house, if ye knowed where ta look, fer she lives almost due south, there at th foot a'th mountain. Just stay on Jude's Gap road out the crest uv th mountain and bear ta th right when ye come ta th gap and then you'll be goin' down hill after that. When ye come to the very bottom of the mountain, you'll come to a little creek. That'll be Britten Creek. After ye cross that creek, look ta ye right and up on th ridge and you'll see her little house. That's where she lives, there on Ann Ridge," Sam said, as he pushed himself up on one elbow.

"Can ye remember all 'at, George?"

"I thinks Ikin memba dat, Mista Sam. I blieves I can."

"Well Son, if ye 'spect ta get anywheres today, ye better get started."

"Can't leave ya in dis kind uva mess, Mista Sonna. You got narry a soul to take care uv ya. Can't evun walk, much less cook sompum ta eat. No, I spose I betta stay un take care uv ya till somebody come along."

Wiggens knew full well that staying could be dangerous, but he wasn't about to leave the old man alone until he was able to take care of himself, or someone else came along to help him.

"I spect I betta go back out in em woods an fetch yo mule to th house. Sides, he be getin powful lonesome by now," Wiggins said, getting up and heading for the door.

"Wait, Son, they's another thang we need ta figger out."

"What dat be, Mista Sam?"

"They's times when I'll have to go pee, and not only that, but they's that other thang, too, ye know."

"Yeaza, Mista Sam. Many be da times Ize seen dat necessitation wif dem poor boys up yondo. Them, wif they oums blowed off an they laigs ta boot. Cuden do nothin thout yo hepum. Soons I brings dat mule a yose to da house, I spect I betta cut one a dem fauked twigs, soos yokn use it foa a spaia laig,"

"Don't be too long, 'cause I'll be needin' it by th time you get it made, and that's fer sure."

"Wont be long, Mista Sam, not long atall."

Wiggins hurried through the woods, dodging the low hanging limbs and spider webs. The mule was somewhat startled as he approached, but Wiggens was able to calm him down quickly, for he was familiar with the handling of farm animals. He had learned all that when he was a youngster, living on the farm, down there in South Carolina.

He unhitched the traces from the singletree and draped them over the hames. He then gathered up the remaining plow line. He was reaching up to take hold of the mule's bridle when he noticed a small maple sapling. It forked about six feet above the ground. "Dis heall make a fine crutch. It sho will," he said, as he picked up the axe he was about to leave in the woods and chopped down the sapling, removed the small limbs and cropped it above the fork. He balanced it and the axe on his shoulder, reached up and took hold of the mule's bridle, and headed for the house.

He stopped the mule at the edge of the porch and went inside, carrying the crutch with him. He helped the old man into a standing position to see how well the crutch fit. "I b'lieve 'at's a bout got it, George. Let's see if works. I've got ta go NOW!" Sam said, as he placed the crutch under his arm and went hopping toward the door.

"Not a smiggin too soon, Mista Sam," Wiggens said, laughing.

"You're mighty right about 'at, by George," the old man said, hurrying out to the edge of the porch. "Not a minute too soon," He said.

After relieving himself, he took a deep breathed, buttoned the front of his overalls, made his way back into the house and sat down on the edge of the bed. "I 'blieve I could use a bite ta eat, George. How 'bout you?"

"Yeahza, Mista Sam, I blieves I cud eat a bite, mysef."

Wiggens set about, searching through the old man's kitchen for something to fix. He found a dab of corn meal in the bin and there was a smidging of lard in the tin. A half dozen or so of Irish potatoes were in a hand-woven basket on the kitchen table. "Yo jes lay backun rest them bones o yose anile fix up sumpum in a jiffy," he said, as he stirred the fire in the fireplace and raked some coals onto the hearth.

Wiggens spent the next several days with the old man, preparing his meals and seeing to it that he made it out to the outside toilet seat that he had managed to put together. "Why didn't I thank a'this, George? It's put a awful lot a'strain on 'ese old legs a'mine, squattin' out here in'ese woods, ever' time I had ta do my thang."

"I spec we puts off doin sompum longs we can, Mista Sam."

ΟΟΟΟΟΟΟΟΟΟΟΟΟ

By mid-October, Sam was able to get around by himself, even without the use of the crutch, and still none of his relatives, nor anyone else for that matter, had come by to pay him a visit. But this very day, while Wiggens was out gathering firewood, Sam had a visitor, Jim Dunker, from over on Broad River. "What's 'at nigger doin' out 'ere in your woods?"Jim asked, demanding an answer.

"Don't you dare call him nigger, Jim Dunker. That young man saved my life. I wuz out 'ere in them very woods by myself cuttin' down a tree and it pinned my leg aginst th stump and he come along'n rescued me, saved me frum certain death, no doubt. He's been here fer weeks, cookin'fer me and takin' kear'a me jist like I wuz his papa. So don't you go sayin' nothin' hatefull about him," Sam said, shaking his fist in anger. "What'er you so all fired concerned about? You never come by here lest you need to borry sompum."

Jim Dunker, feeling that he had been insulted, left in a huff and

168

didn't look back.

"He'll be trouble. I'm sure uv it," Sam said to himself, as Jim went out of sight, flailing his arms and muttering obscenities and saying something that sounded like, "We'll see about this."

When Wiggens returned late in the afternoon with a wagon load of wood and was unloading it onto the porch, Sam shuffled out onto the porch, looking very distraught.

"What be yo twuble, Mista Sam? Yo looks like yo done loss yo bess frien. Haps you is tiada me bein heah."

"Tain't nothin' like that, George. You're 'bout th best friend I ever had. You saved my life, didn't ye? But I'm afraid we've got big trouble."

"What dat be, Mista Sam?"

"That hateful Jim Dunker come by here whilst you wuz out 'ere cuttin' wood to keep me warm this winter, wantin' ta know what you'as a doin' out 'ere in my woods. He seed you wuz wearin' them Yankee duds. He figgers you're his enemy and besides that, you're black. He hates black folk. He figgers they're th reason we're in this war in th first place."

"Black folk aint stawted no wau. Sides, Ias boan down hea in de sauf. Got no quawl wid no white man. Dat be de reason I done quit de waun come on back home."

"You know that, and I know that, but Jim Dunker don't give a doodley squat about what we think. He hates black folk and he hates Yankees and he'll be back and you can count on it. We'd better pack you some grub un get you out'a here afore daylight tomar. I shore don't want you a gettin' killed, ner nothin' like 'at."

Way before daylight the next morning, Wiggens was up and ready to continue his journey southward. He had packed a hoecake and a baked sweet potato in his knapsack the evening before. There was a chill in the air and a faint light from a waning moon filtered through the trees to the west as the two figures stood on the porch for a moment thanking each other for the friendship each had kindled. They shook hands and Wiggens vanished into the night. The old man shuffled back into the house and closed the door.

It was coming daylight when Wiggens reached Broad River. He removed his tattered shoes and rolled his britches legs up above his knees, preparing to wade through the cold river water. As he waded through the water he was chanting to himself, "I is crossin Jowdan Ribba, I is crossin Jowdan Ribba."

Reaching the farther side of the river, he rolled down his britches legs and sat down to replaced his tattered shoes. When he stood up and

169

was about to head up the old Indian trail, he heard the sound of a musket. It sounded as if it came from the direction of the old man's house. "Jus wondo whut dat mean?" he said to himself, as he walked swiftly up the trail.

He had gone only a short distance when he turned and looked back toward the old man's house and saw smoke rising above the treetops. "Dat sho aint no chimbly smoke, too much fo dat," he said, as he quickened his pace, heading up the mountain ridge.

Tears welled up in his eyes when he began to put together what had apparently happened to Sam and his house, but he immediately put the thought out of his mind and concentrated on the task at hand, that of finding John's wife. He had learned from his mother and father not to dwell on tragedy, but to store it away for future reference and to always look on the brighter side.

As he topped the mountain and headed down the other side, he could hear the water of Pool Creek rushing over the falls beyond the large hemlocks. Above the noise of the falls, he heard something that sounded like children playing. He stopped dead in his tracks and cupped his hands around his ears. "My ears mus be playin a trick oma brain," he said to himself, as he stood perfectly still, listning.

But sure enough, he had heard children, laughing and playing along the creek bank. Sam hadn't mentioned that he could possibly meet up with Indians along the way, but there he stood, right in the midst of the village. Immediately, one of the young boys in the group saw him and ran to alert the elders. "Strange man here. Him face black with war paint!" he shouted.

An old lady with long gray hair emerged from one of the huts and seemed surprised to see him, but in a calm, but stern voice, asked, "What be your name? Why you here? What tribe you from? Why you have war paint on face?"

Wiggens was somewhat overwhelmed with so many questions coming at him at once, but he set out to try to answer them as best he could. "I is Geoge Washinton Wiggens. Ize on my way down to see Miz Ann Shepud. I dun brough news uv John Shepud. He be daid in dat wau up yondo. Kilt in dat splosun. Aint frum no tribe lessun I say I be from cross de big wato. Aint no wau paint on my face. Dis be de culla my mama done gib me de day I done come into dis hea wold.

"How you know John Sherherd? May be you kill him and put blame on other person."

John Shepud bez my frien. We lib like brothas, way down in Souf Calina. Who bez you, Good Woman?"

"Me Lady Owatta. Me herb doctor. Me know Ann Shepherd.

170

She be Owatta's good friend. We gather herbs. She study to become herb doctor, also."

"I spec I betta to be on my way, Lady Watto. Taint safe fao no black man to stan in de same place too long," Wiggins said, as he removed his cap and gave a nod to Lady Owatta.

The young Indian boys formed a circle around Wiggins feining a war dance, pretending to shoot him with their bows and arrows. Owatta scolding then said, "Stop, this be George Washington Wiggens. Him our friend. Him friend of John Shepherd. He also friend to Ann Shepherd. He go now and we say, go in peace."

"Go in peace," the young braves said, echoing her words.

Wiggens nodded again, turned and walked away.

When he reached the foot of the mountain, he expected to see a large stream, but instead hc found only a trickle. It had been a dry summer. Nevertheless, being thursty, he reached down and scooped up some water in his hand to quench his thirst.

'That'll be Britten Creek. After ye cross that creek, look ta ye right and up on th ridge and you'll see her little house. That's where she lives, there on Ann Ridge.' These words rang clear as a bell in Wiggens' head. They were the directions the old man had given him. He looked to the right and there, up on the ridge was the little shanty. He could hear chickens cackling and goats bleating as he walked cautiously up the hill toward the shanty.

Ann stood looking through the tiny window with Fidgety cradled in her arms. "Wonder who he is? He can't be a Confederate, she said, when she noticed that he wasn't wearing the gray. That's Yankee duds he's wearin'."

Fidgedy let out with a loud "Meow" and sailed to the floor when Ann suddenly released her and reached for her pa's muzzle-loader. She opened the door, walked out onto the porch, stopped and took aim at Wiggens and said, "Stop where you are, or you're a dead man. Black or white, I'll kill you if you take one more step. You must be a Yankee or you'd be wearin' grey."

"Ize yo frien, Ann Shepud. I is hea ta tell yo de bad news," Wiggins said, dropping to his knees in a prayerful pose.

"How do you know my name?"

"I knows yo man. He name be John. We done knowed one de uthah since we wuz younguns, livin down dawo in Souf Calina."

"You'd better tell me who you are, if you know what's good for you," Ann demanded.

"My name bez Geoge Washinton Wiggens. Yo man, John, done tolt me all bout yo."

"John mentioned your name in one of his letters, but how can you prove you're who you say you are?"

"Right hea in my pocket," Wiggins said, as he slowly moved his hand toward his pocket.

"Keep your hands where they are," Ann warned.

"Hows I spose to pwove who I is if a cant show yo?"

"Well show me, but take it slow and easy, but if you come out with a gun, I'll blow a hole through your belly big enough to thread a wagon tongue through it."

Wiggens very gingerly slid his hand into his pocket and when he withdrew it, palm up, there lay that pearl handle knife that once belonged to John's great-grandfather. Ann would have recognized the knife anywhere. "That's John's knife!" she screamed. "Where'd you get his knife?"

"Ize done seed him up noth, up whea theys a fightin. Met up wid him twixt de lines. Met wid him one night when they wuznt no fightin goin on. Had dis hea apple in my pocket. Wanted to vide it wid him. Had no way to chop it opum. Den out he comes wid dis hea puil handle knife un say, 'Disheall do it'. An dats how come dis hea knife a hissen hea in my pocket."

"Well, you must a'stold it," Ann said, as she pointed the muzzle-loader in his direction again.

"No, Maam, dat ain de way it hapum. Jes stuck dis hea knife in my pocket frum foce uv habbit. Did not mean to do it," Wiggins lamented, as he dropped to his knees again.

"Pitch it over here and let me have a look at it, but don't you try any tricks. I still have this gun on you." Ann said, motioning him to toss the knife in her direction.

Wiggens tossed the knife to her and as she bent over to pick it up, she noticed the initials, 'J. S.', carved into the handle. "What have you done with my husband? Tell me, and tell me now!" she demanded.

"Twont me, Maam. He done got hissef kilt in dat sploshun up dauh in de wau. Fust dey wuz nuthin, den all uv a sudden de whole wuld wuz aflyin thu de aiah. An Izes sho yo man wuz in amunxt it."

"You mean to tell me that John's dead?"

"Fraid so, Miz Ann. Fraid so."

Ann dropped to her knees, crying. She picked up the knife and held it close to her bosom. "Oh, John! Oh John!" she cried, over and over, as tears cascaded down her cheeks.

Wiggens cried as well. He wanted to comfort Ann, but didn't dare approach her, for he was well aware that she was a white woman and he was a black man. "I is so sad, Miz Ann. I hates I had to deliva

172

dis hea bad news to yo, but I jes had to let yo know."

"I'm sure it took a lot of courage to come all this way just to let me know, George, and I do appreciate it, but I do wish it had been good news. I could have used some good news. Seems like all I ever get is bad news," Ann said, as she wiped the tears from her eyes on the sleve of her black dress. "He was the very last person I had in this whole wide world."

Using the muzzle-loader as a staff, Ann pushed herself into a standing position. "You must be tired and I'm sure you're hungry. What's wrong with your foot? I noticed that limp."

"Taint nutin, Miz Ann. My foot be Jus a little soa frum walkin so fua, I spose."

"Looks like you could use some shoes, too, George. Come on up to the house and I'll see if I can't find you a pair. And you'd better get rid of them Union Army clothes. If somebody was to see you wearin' them they'd kill you for sure."

She walked up the path to the shanty with Wiggens following a good ten steps behind her. When she stepped up onto the porch, she turned and said, "You wait here on the porch and I'll see'f I can't find you somethin' to wear."

While Ann was inside looking for some clothes, Wiggens sat on the edge of the porch. He removed his left shoe and looked at the sores on the bottom of his foot. The sores were blood red and oozing corruption, but when he removed his right shoe he discovered that foot had fared better.

"Here, try these things on and see if they fit," Ann said, returning to the porch with some of P D's work clothes and a pair of his shoes.

When she saw the condition of Wiggens' feet she said, "We'll have to do somethin' about them feet. Go on out yonder to the barn and put these clothes on while I mix up a puoltice for your sore feet."

Wiggens slipped his tattered shoes back onto his sore feet, picked up the clothes and shoes from the porch and eased out toward the barn. He hadn't noticed his feet hurting so badly before, but since Ann mentioned it he became keenly aware of the pain.

The goats blated as he entered the barn, walked over and sat down on the milking stool. Amongst P D's clothes, Ann had included a pair of his patched wool underwear. Wiggens was very thankful for that, for winter was approaching and he was glad to have something that would keep him warm. To his surprise, all the clothes fit very well. Even P D's shoes felt good on his sore feet.

As he sat on the milking stool, wondering what to do with his old army clothes, Ann came out, carrying a pan of warm soapy water and a wash rag. "Here, wash your feet while I mix up some herbs for a poltice, I'll take these old clothes inside and burn 'em. Looks like Papa's clothes fit you," she said, as she walked back toward the shanty with Fidgedy scampering along behind her.

"Dat dey do, Miz Ann. Dey sho do."

Ann returned in a few minutes with the poultice for his sore feet and some clean cloth strips for bandages. "Stretch out on the ground, George, and lay your feet up on the stool and let me doctor 'em. You don't want 'em to get infected. If they do you'll have a mess on your hands, or maybe I should say a mess on your feet."

After applying the poultice and bandages to Wiggens' feet, Ann told him that he would be welcome to stay a few days and he could sleep in the barn, but he would have to watch out for any visitors. "I don't have many visitors,"she said. But you can't never tell when somebody'll show up."

"You sit and rest and I'll go fix you somethin' to eat. It'll take me a while, but I'll be back out here drectly," she told him.

She picked up the wash pan and walked back toward the house, as Wiggens made himself comfortable, resting his head on a bundle of fodder. He closed his eyes while he waited for something to eat, thinking how nice it was to be away from that awful war and how fortunate he was to have someone treat him so kindly, he being a stranger and black to boot.

He was dozing when Ann returned. She was carrying a sheep-skin under her arm, a plate of food in one hand and a cup of goat milk in the other. She startled him when she nudged his leg with the toe of her shoe. He threw up his hands, saying, "I gives up! Sides, I is one a yose. Ize frum de souf."

"It's alright, George. It's just me with your supper."

"O lawd! Though ize a daid man fo shua."

After the shock of the sudden awakening wore off, he sat up, rubbed his eyes, and reached up for the plate of food. "Thank yo, Miz Ann. I sho is hongry. I sho is."

"This old sheep-skin'll keep you warm. The nights have been gettin' a mite chilly here lately," Ann said, as she unrolled the sheep-skin and spread it on the ground beside him.

"I've been thinkin', George, and I've finally decided that it would be a wise thing if you went on your way tomorrow. That is if your feet are well enough to travel. Them blood-thirsty fools'll be lookin' for you. Word'll be out that you're in these parts and there'll be no place you can hide. Wouldn't be a bad idea if you had some kind of a disguise," she said.

174

She scratched her head, staring up at the barn loft as if in deep thought. "I know what I'll do," she said. I'll use some of this sheep-skin and make you a skull-cap. That way you'll look like an old gray-headed man. You can walk with a stick and act like you're crippled. If you happen to meet somebody they'll never be the wiser. Besides, a sheep-skin cap'll keep your head warm."

She sprang to her feet and said, "I'll be right back," as she spun around and raced toward the shanty.

She searched through her sewing things, and when she found her scissors and a ball of strong sewing thread, she hurried back to the barn.

"Let me see now, this part right here should make you a good cap," she said, pointing to the neck portion of the sheep-skin.

She draped the sheep-skin over his back and pulled the neck portion over his head. "This'll work just fine," she said, as she went to work with her scissors, cutting off the neck portion. She trimmed it to fit his head, leaving enough material on each side for the sideburns.

When she finished with the skull cap and placed it on Wiggens' head he was instantly transformed into an old gray-headed man. "Have I seen you before, old man?" she asked him, laughing. "All you need now is a good stout walkin' stick."

Several days passed before Wiggins' feet were well enough to travel, well enough to walk any distance, that is. During that time he kept out of sight when there were visitors.

On one occasion he came close to being discovered when Eli Bailey came for a visit and went by the barn to have a look at the new-born kid goat. When he heard something moving around in the barn loft he convinced himself that it was Ann's cat, but when he walked up to the shanty and knocked on the door and Ann let him in, he noticed her cat, stretched out on the hearth by the fire. "Ann, I heard somethin' stirrin' around in your barn loft. I thought it wuz your cat, but there she is, sprawled out in front a'th the fireplace."

"Got some mighty big rats out there, Eli," Ann said, coming back at him with the only explanation she could think of.

"Maybe if you'd let Fidgety spend some time out 'ere she'd get rid'a some uv'em."

"Maybe so, Eli, maybe so."

As soon as Eli had finished with his visit and was out of sight around the bend, Wiggens eased down from the barn loft and made his way up to the shanty. He eased up the steps to the porch, crept over and gently knocked on the door. "Miz Ann," he called out softly. "Is you in dowa? It be bout time foa me to trabel."

"Yes it's time you were on your way, George. It's too risky for

175

you to stay here any longer," Ann said, when she opened the door.

"I be bout to say de same thing, Miz Ann. I blieves Mista Eli done smelled a rat."

"I've cooked you some bread. It should keep you from starvin' till you can find somethin' to eat along the way. Here, put it in your haversack," Ann said, handing the hoecake to him as she stood in the doorway.

"Yo has been so good to me, Miz Ann. I is neva goin to fogit dat. Neva, longs I lib "

He thanked Ann for the disguise she made for him and for the clothes, and for the 'stout' walking stick. He reached out and touched her hand, turned and walked away. He didn't look back, not because he didn't want to, but because he had tears in his eyes and he didn't want her to see him crying.

"Bye, George Washington Wiggens. Thank you for lettin' me know about John and for bringin' back his pearl handle knife. I'll never forget you for that."

She closed the door and went over by the fireplace and sat down in the rocker. Tears stung her eyes as she sat there caressing John's pearl handle knife and running her fingers over the initials, 'J S'. "My last person in the world, the very last one," she said over and over.

But when Fidgety leaped up onto her lap, purring and licking her hand, she suddenly realized she still had her cat. And then she thought of her goats and the chickens. "Yes, Fidgety, I still have you. I'll always have you,." She said as she stroked her thick fur, listening to the crackling of the static electricity.

After feeding her animals and chickens, she went to bed early, not that she was sleepy, but because she was so saddened from the news of John's death and she didn't feel like sitting up any longer.

Sleep didn't come to her right away, for she lay late into the night, reflecting upon her tragic past. She thought about the fact that she had grown up without a mother, for her mother had died on the day she was born.

Then there was the death of her great-aunt, Isa Biddy, who had cared for her since the day she was born. Isa had been so good to her that Ann loved her as if she had been her very own mother. It was tragic enough that she had lost her great-aunt, but after she died, her father remarried, causing her to have to contend with the abuses heaped upon her by Hassie, her step-mother.

Even though Hassie had been abusive to her while she was growing up, she finally make a change for the better and began treating her more like a daughter, but not until Ann was married and had moved away from home.

Next was the death of her mother-in-law, Mama Sarah. And then only two days after her mother-in-law's death, her father-in-law, Papa Shepherd, was burned to death in his own house, when that old 'Green River boy', Brute Bates, set his house ablaze. Only a few months later her mother-in-law drowned in Britten Creek, when the wagon in which she was riding overturned, pinning her face down in the icy water.

Then on the thirtieth day of July of this year, she and Eli Bailey found her father at the end of a trail of blood at the edge of the woods near his house, killed by a deserter, they believed. His throat had been slit from ear to ear, looking much like a slaughtered hog.

"And now, John's dead, killed off up yonder, fightin' to keep us all safe. Safe from what? Safe from what?" Ann asked herself, while staring into the darkness with tears streaming down each side of her face and onto her pillow. When she finally fell asleep, she dreamed of John, being blown to pieces in that awful explosion.

ᑲᑲᑲᑲᑲᑲᑲᑲᑲᑲᑲᑲᑲᑲ

Indeed, John was there when the blast took place, but he had survived. He had been right there in the midst of it, suffering burns to his hands and feet. All the hair had been singed from his scalp. He suffered deep burns on his face that were sure to leave it permently scarred and disfigured. The nurses kept his face coated with salve and covered with a bandage, leaving only openings for his mouth, eyes, and nose. For weeks, the only food he was able to consume consisted of liquids he was able to suck through a straw.

He hadn't looked at himself in the looking glass for quite some time, for he hadn't really wanted to. But as a nurse approached his bed one morning he asked her if she would bring him a looking glass. "My face is itchin' and I b'lieve I need a shave," he said.

"That's a good sign, John. Itching means your face is healing," the nurse said. "But you're not ready for a shave yet. At least I don't think you are."

"Why don't you take this bandage off and we'll just see," John said, reaching up to touch the bandages.

"Let me finish my rounds and I'll bring a mirror and you can have a look see."

"Thank you, Maam. You're a kind woman," John said.

He grew anxious as he lay waiting for the nurse to return with the mirror. Now that he had finally gathered enough courage to see just

177

how badly his face had been disfigured by the blast, it was now hard for him to wait.

After about an hour of waiting, John began to think the nurse had forgotten him, or perhaps she was staying away intentionally. But when he had just about given up hope she appeared, mirror in hand, prepared to let him have a look at his face.

"John, I'm sorry I was gone so long. I had to help remove a man's arm. But here's that mirror you wanted. Are you ready to have a look see?"

"Ready's I'll ever be," John said, reaching for the mirror.

"Wait. We'll have to remove the bandage first, son," the nurse said, reaching into her apron pocket to retrieve her scissors.

She carefully clipped the bandage with her scissors, removing it piece by tiny piece, but when she reached the inner layers of the bandage she discovered it was attached to the skin. Drainage from the burns had dried and bonded to the bandage. "I'll have to get some warm water and soak the rest of the bandage before I can remove it," she said, placing her hand firmly on John's shoulder, as if to reassure him that everything was okay.

"I'll be back in a jiffy," she said.

In a few minutes she was back and began soaking the bandage, removing it ever so gently, so as not to break the skin. John grimaced and gritted his teeth as she worked to remove the glued on bandage. "I know it hurts, son, but I'm going as easy as I can," the nurse said, as she continued on with a steady hand.

"I know, Maam," John responded through clinched teeth.

When the nurse finally finished removing the bandage, even she was disappointed with what she saw. Large scabs on his face and neck were a prelude to the fact that he would be permanently scarred. His earlobes were missing and the catilage on the top of his left ear was clearly visable beneath a thin layer of regenerating skin. "Well, it don't look so bad," she said, attempting to prepare him for what he was about to see.

John raised the looking glass with his bandaged hand and held it out at arm's length. He gasped as he glanced at himself in the mirror and moved it away quickly. As he moved it slowly back into position, his hand trimbled and tears ran from his eyes, stinging the sores on his cheeks. "My face is ruined. Nobody'll ever recognize me any more," he said, as he lost his composure, breaking down and crying openly.

"It's not so bad, John. You're looking at scabs. They'll go away. Give it a little more time."

"And so will my face," John said, taking one last look at the

178

image in the mirror, before shoving it back into the nurse's hand.

While the nurse was coating his face with salve, she asked him just where we was from. "North Carolina. Polk County, North Carolina to be more exact," John said, reaching up to rub his itching nose.

"Go easy on that nose, son. We don't want to break the skin. That could spell trouble."

"But it itches, nurse."

"It's healing and we want it to continue doing that. Well, when I asked you where you lived, I was about to ask you if you had relatives living there and if you would like me to write a letter for you. Your folks will want to know that you're still alive."

"Nobody'll care if I'm dead or alive when they find out how scarred up I am. Besides, they wouldn't even recognize me. I wouldn't recognize myself any more if I didn't know it was me behind this hideous mask of sores."

"Do you think it's right to keep it from the ones you love? Let alone the ones who love you!"

"Can't help that, Maam. It's my secret and it's mine to keep," John said, his eyes awash with tears.

"Well, just remember, if you need to have a letter written, I'd be more than happy to do it for you."

The nurse went on with the business of taking care of other wounded soldiers, leaving him alone to deal with his physical and emotional scars.

John wrestled for weeks with the question as to wheather or not he should write and tell Ann that he was still alive. But as his face healed the scabs peeled away, leaving deep scars, and a face he no longer recognized, he decided it would be better not to let her know. "If she thinks I'm dead, she can get on with her life. She'll be better off without me anyway," he believed.

# Chapter

# 11

## Ann Goes It Alone

Ann was getting on with her life, but she certainly didn't feel that she was better off by living alone. When she woke each morning, the first thought that came to mind was that she would never be able to see John again. She tried to put it out of her mind, but it grew like a cancer. She began to believe it would comsume her whole body, for she was always tired and she cried often and long. Her cat knew that something was wrong, but of course there was no way a cat could know what it was. Nevertheless, day after day, the cat stayed close by Ann's side, if not in her lap.

"Fidgety, if I didn't have you, I don't know what I'd do," Ann said, as she walked briskly out toward the tiny barn.

"Meaow!" the cat answered.

As she walked into the breezeway of the barn, Ann sensed that something was wrong. She was startled when she saw a note attached to the door of the kid goat's stall. It was written in charcoal on a piece of brown paper. The note read: "Got ye goat. Swhatye git fer lettin at nigger sleep in ye barn. Watch ye step er yull be sarry."

Ann opened the door to the stall and sure enough the kid goat was gone. She sat down on the threshold and cried. She cried for an hour before she was able to pull herself together.

The bleating of Precious and Gracious, her nanny goats, was music to her ears. Her crying stopped as she opened the doors to each of their stalls. She hugged and petted them for a while, before bringing them into the breezeway to be milked. "Leastwise I still have my two nanny goats. I'll kill the fool that tries to do harm to my pets," she said, her face crimson with anger.

"How could anybody know about George Washington Wiggins stayin' here in my barn?" she whispered to herself, as she sat milking the goat. "Whoever it was must'a been watchin' my house."

"Meow!" Fidgety said, sitting on her haunches, waiting for her regular squirt of warm goat milk.

181

"I hear you, Fidgety, here it comes, Ann said, as she aimed the teat in her direction, sending a stream of milk squarely into the cat's face.

Fidgety lapped at the stream of milk, wiped her face with her paws and licked them clean while Ann finished with the milking.

"Good, huh?" Ann said to the cat, smiling.

Steam rose from the bucket of warm milk when Ann walked out of the breezeway into the cold air. The wind was roaring over the crest of Worlds Edge. All the trees were bare except for the white oaks and birches. Hoards of dry leaves were carried aloft by the strong wind, looking much like a covey of quail in flight. Snow and ice crystals, swirling in the wind gusts, stung her face as she hurried up the path to the shanty.

ⅩⅩⅩⅩⅩⅩⅩⅩⅩⅩⅩⅩⅩ

December was fast approaching. In fact, there were only two more days left in November. "Where does all the time go," Ann said, as she looked at the calander on the wall above the little table. "And so many things have happened this year. Bad things. B-A-D things."

She strained the milk into the crock pot and was about to sit down in the rocker in front of the fire when she noticed there were only a few small sticks of wood on the hearth. So instead of sitting down, she walked out to the porch and as she was loading her arm with firewood she heard someone coming up the road on horseback. "That's Willie Ruff. He's two days early," she said, standing bent at the hips, peering down in that direction.

"What brings you out on a day like this, Willie?" she asked.

"Time ta pay th rent, Missus Shepherd."

"But it's two more days till the first of December, Willie."

"What's a couple a days? 'Sides, we could git a big snow and I wouldn't be able ta get it up here in time."

"Well get off'a that horse and come in and warm yourself."

"Think I'll just do that, Missus Shepherd. This north wind'll chill a man clean to th bone," Willie said, sliding down from his horse and wrapping the reins around the porch post.

"Here, le'me carry 'at wood fer ye," Willie said, wrestling the firewood from Ann's arms.

"You can sit here in the rocker, Willie. Draw it up next to the fire so you can get warm."

Willie did as he was told and when he glanced down at the ashes

182

on the hearth, he saw a round object that looked like a penny. It was half buried in the ashes. "This here's my lucky day," he said. "I b'leive I've just found a penny."

But when he reached down and picked it up, he discovered it to be a brass button. "No it ain't no penny. It's a brass button with th letters, 's n', stamped on it."

He didn't realize that he was looking at it upside down, but when he handed it to Ann, she immediately knew that it was a button from George Washington Wiggens' army jacket. "Maybe it's a button from papa's overalls. I burned some of his old wore out clothes the other day," she said, dropping the button into her dress pocket.

She had indeed burned some of her father's clothes, but she burned Wiggens' Union Army jacket as well.

Willie sat in silence before the fire for several minutes, gazing into the flickering flames as if in an hypnotic trance. Ann thought he was dozing, but when he suddenly sprang to his feet, his head narrowly missing the mantle piece, she sprang to her feet as well, dumping Fidgety onto the floor. "Thought you were dozin', Willie!"

"Missus Shepherd, I 'spect I'd better get on home. Cathy'll be worried," he said, as he drew seven crumpled Confederate dollars from his pocket and put them into Ann's hand and pressed her fingers tightly around the money. "I'm much obliged to ye," he said, staring into her eyes for several seconds.

"Thank you, Willie. I don't know how I'd ever get by if I didn't have this money comin' in. What with John up yonder, fightin' in that awful war and not knowin' wheather he's alive or dead."

Willie made no reply. He didn't seem to care one way or the other. He was just that kind of person. After all, he had refused to go and fight. He had made the statement right after the war started that he would hide out in a cave and drink muddy water and eat spring lizards before he'd fight in that "crazy war."

He hadn't had to hide out yet, but there could come a time when he might have to.

As he was about to open the door to leave, Ann asked him how Cathy and the baby were doing. "Oh, they's both fine as frog hair, split three ways," he said, grinning from ear to ear.

Even though he had been prompt in paying the rent, Ann still found it difficult to trust him. For she hadn't forgotten how he had placed his hand on her leg as she sat beside him in the wagon on the day they were carrying her dead father up to the Biddy graveyard. He had claimed his hand must have slipped, but the thought of it still sent shivers up and down her spine. "The things I've gone through in my life are enough to turn any normal woman into a witch," she thought, as Willie stepped outside and she closed the door behind him.

She called to mind the day P D was killed, how a man that could have passed as Willie's twin, came flying up the road in her father's wagon and how he wore that dirty old rag over his face to keep anyone from recognizing him. She remembered that it was Willie who brought the wagon home later that same day, claiming to have found it up near Britten Creek. She remembered how his shirt was covered with blood, and again, he claimed to have wrung a chicken's neck and it bled all over him.

And today she thought he had gone a little far when he closed his hand around her's when he gave her the seven dollars rent money. "Why didn't he just hand the money to me like any other gentleman, instead of standing there staring me in the face like some fool? A lot of things about him don't set right in my mind. "I'll keep my eyes open when he's around", she said to herself, as she sat by the fire with Fidgety resting on her lap.

Before night set in, she went out to the barn and fed the goats some of the corn and fodder that Ruffus and Willie brought up from her father's barn. She couldn't help but shed tears as she halved a hand of fodder, thinking of P D and how his kind hands had stripped it from the stalk and perhaps how packsaddles may have stung him as he carried it on his back and placed it in the barn loft.

"He was a good papa," she whispered to herself, as she devided the fodder between her goats. "Goodnight, Sweeties. Don't let nothin' get you'ns tonight. Call me at the very first sign of trouble," she said.

Snow flurries were still swirling as she made her way back to the shanty, but she could see stars overhead as the large puffy clouds separated, sailing out over the crest of Wild Cat Spurr. "Gonna be a cold night tonight," she said to herself, shielding her face with the collar of her wool coat.

Somehow, she couldn't come to a full realization that John was dead, even though Wiggins had traveled so far out of his way to bring her the news. She so desperately wanted to believe he was still alive.

"George Washington Wiggens says he's dead and I guess I'll have to believe it, but I sure don't want to," She said, as she crawled into bed and stretched out on the shuck-filled mattress.

She snuggled up to Fidgety as they lay beneath the sheep-skin coverlet with the fleece next to their bodies, shielding them from the chill of the night.

Sometime during the night she had a dream. It was the same

184

dream she had had before she and John were married, that of falling in love and of being married in the little log church with creaking shutters. The dream was so vivid she awoke suddenly with her heart racing. Tears came to her eyes when she realized that it was only a dream. When she wiped her eyes on the sleeve of her nightgown the salty tears stung her chapped cheeks. "Oh, pain, when will you ever go away?" she said, as she lay listening to the wind whistling around the corners of her little shanty.

Sleep finally came sometime later on into the night and when she awoke the next morning, a bright beam of sunlight pierced the tiny window of her bedroom, lighting her face and giving her the appearance of a cherub. She shielded her face from the sun's rays as she slid from the bed and slipped her feet into her scuffs.

After unbanking the coals in the fireplace, she added some kindling and soon there was a flame and then a good warm fire. She held her hands over the fire till they were warm, then stepped over to the window of the living room to see if there had been any accumulation of snow during the night. Only a dusting lay in low places out near the barn where the wind hadn't been able to get at it.

She was pleased to see that only a dusting of snow had fallen, but then something strange caught her eye. Hanging suspended from the porch wall plate directly between her eyes and the sun, she saw what looked like one of her game chickens. "What on earth can that be?" she said, rushing outside to investigate.

She found to her dismay, one of her laying hens, hanging from the wall plate by a piece of twine, looped around its neck. On the porch, weighted down with a rock was a note. It was written in blood, drawn from the chicken, "You pay agin fer helpin th enemy."

Ann's hair seemed to stand on end when she read the note. Her next thought was, "Have they hurt my goats?"

She raced out to the barn as fast as her legs would carry her. When she opened the doors to their stalls, she found them safe, but eager for something to eat. "Thank goodness you're both alive," she said, giving each a hug.

Her ball of twine lay there in the breezeway with several feet of it unwound in a tangled mass beside it. "If I could only find out who's doin' this I'd give him somethin' to remember me by," she said, as she stood untangling the twine and winding it back onto the ball. "I've got to figure out a way to scare this fool and keep him away from here. He'll ruin me if I don't do somethin'."

She returned to the shanty and walked up the steps to the porch, and believing the chicken would be safe to eat, she pulled John's pearl-

185

handle knife from the pocket of her apron and cut the twine on which it was suspended. She went down to the creek and brought back a bucket of water, poured it into the black pot and swung it over the fire.

As she sat, tending the fire and waiting for the water to get hot enough to scald the chicken, she searched her brain for something she could do to scare off the scalawag who was trying to intimidate her.

It came to her like a bolt of lightning from a thunder cloud. She remembered her father once used a syrup can to make a "bellower". He had made it to scare off a couple of menacing boys from down in the cove who were harassing his cow and mules. She remembered that he had taken a large syrup can, punched a hole in the center of the bottom with a nail, ran a resined string through the hole and attached it to the nail on the inside of the can. When he pulled on the string and let it slide between his thumb and forefinger, it made a godawful sound. It was enough to scare you out of your britches if it caught you by surprise, especially in the middle of the night and especially if you were in a place where you had no business in the first place.

"That'll work!" she said to herself. "That'll work.!"

A large syrup can was sitting on the floor beneath the kitchen table. It was empty, except for a couple of rusty nails and a handful of wormy chestnuts. She emptied the contents into a bowl, turned the can upside down on the table and pounded a nail through the center of the bottom with the shoehorn that John had managed to save from his father's burning house.

While waiting for the water to boil, she went out to the barn and unwound some twine and cut off a short piece for the pull string of the bellower. She picked up a piece of pine resin from the kindling pile as she came back into the shanty. She threaded the twine through the hole in the bottom of the can and attached it to the nail inside.

After applying the resin to the twine, she gave it a try. One pull on the string and Fidgety let out with a scream as she leaped from the rocker and stood stiff as a poker in front of the fireplace. Every hair stood straight out on the cats body. Her tail, standing straight up in the air, took on the appearance of a giant feather duster. Her eyes were ablaze as she stood staring at the bellower. "Yes, that'll work," Ann said, laughing.

When the water was finally hot enough to scald the chicken, she placed it into the foot tub and doused it with the hot water. After plucking the chicken she singed it over the fire at the fireplace.

After removing the entrails, she washed it, cut it up and placed it into the cast-iron cooking pot, added water and salt and swung it out over the fire to cook. "We'll have us a good dinner, Fidgety," she said, still amused over having scared the cat with the bellower.

After about an hour the cat had settled down somewhat, but she was still leery of the syrup can. "It's O K Fidgety, it won't hurt you. Besides, I made it to scare off that fool that's dead set on causin' us trouble," Ann said, as she stirred the pot of chicken that was now beginning to simmer.

She had a feeling in her bones that the scoundrel that had been trying to intimidate her would be back tonight for more of the same, but she was now ready to give him a run for his money.

A little before sundown, she fed and milked Precious and Gracious and put them into their stalls. She rushed back to the shanty, hurried up onto the porch and into the kitchen where she strained the milk and began preparations for scaring the living daylights out of that scoundrel, whoever he might be.

Talking to herself under her breath she said, "I'll lodge this old syrup can between the logs in the breezeway and hide under my sheepskin coverlet and when that fool comes creepin' into my barn, I'll teach him a lesson he's not apt to ever forget."

Fidgety, brushing up against her leg said, "Meaow?"

"Yes, Fidgety, you can go, too. We'll hunker down under the sheepskin and keep each other warm while we wait for that scoundrel."

Darkness was settling down over Ann Ridge when she walked out to the barn, carrying the sheepskin and the bellower, with Fidgety right on her heels. She placed the bellower between the logs there in the breezeway, then she settled down with Fidgety beneath the sheepskin, making sure she had pleanty of room to pull on the resined string when the time came to do it. Time passed and they waited, and they waited.

Ann was in a doze of sleep when Fidgety stirred at her side. She roused from her sleep and when she did she heard footsteps out passed the barn. "That must be him!" she thought to herself.

Her heart was pounding so loudly she was afraid it would be heard by the intruder. But then, there he was, standing at the entrance of the breezeway, silhouetted against the star fllled night sky.

She eased her arm from beneath the sheepskin and grasped the resined string near the bottom of the syrup can and gave it a steady pull.

The bellower let out with a haunting roar that resonated throughout the little barn and echoed back and forth. Fidgety bristled and screamed like a panther. Ann screamed as the cat stiffened, digging its claws into her leg. The intruder stumbled over the milk stool, fell forward, and struck his head on the corner of the barn. He scrambled to his feet and in a few seconds he was tearing his way through the saw briars above the road near the creek. The ripping of his clothes could be heard as he forced his way through the briars. When he finally made his way through the thicket of saw briars and found his footing on the hard roadbed, he lost no time as he raced at top speed in the direction of Deep Gap. Ann listened to the echo of his brogans pounding the hard road until the sound faded into oblivion. She then broke into an uncontrollible fit of laughter, and she laughed until tears ran down her cheeks. "I 'spect that'll teach him a lesson," she said, thumbing the tears from her eyes, her heart pounding from so much excitement.

That was the last time that anyone prowled around her place at night, attempting to do her harm. But a couple of weeks later when she went out to the little barn to feed and milk her goats, she heard a rustling in the stall where her kid goat had been staying before it was stolen. When she opened the door to the stall, there stood the young billy goat, munching on some fodder. She knew it was him from the white blaze on his forehead. The blaze was in the shape of a bolt of lightning. She would have recognized him anywhere. "May miracles never cease!" she exclaimed in astonishment.

She sat on the threshold for several minutes, petting the goat, so glad to have him back where he belonged. "Ba-ah-ah," the goat said, struggling to break away to return to the fodder.

"I'm sorry, little'un, go ahead and help yourself to the fodder," Ann said, as she stepped outside his stall and closed the door.

Saturday, the third day of December broke bright and clear. Ann was short of a few thing, so she decided to go down to Bent Oak to buy "a few things."

After feeding and milking Precious and Gracious and feeding the kid, she threaded her arms through the sleeves of her black coat and wound her wool scarf around her head and face, grasped her walking stick, and struck out down the road toward Bent Oak.

As she walked passed the entrance to Deep Gap road she heard a wagon approaching from that direction. It was Willie Ruff, riding in the wagon that had been handed down from Papa Jacob to PD and after PD's death, Ann had given it to Willie.

"Where ye headed Missus Shepherd?" Willie asked, as he pulled the mule to a stop.

"Headin' over to Bent Oak," Ann answered.

"Well, hop in. I'm goin' 'at way."

"Believe I'll just do that," Ann said, as she hoisted herself up onto the wagon. "How's your wife doin', and Mary Ann, the baby?"

"They's fine, Missus Shepherd, just fine."

"How'd you get that bruise on your head, Willie?"

"I'as out huntin' th other day, fell and struck my head on a

188

rock," Willie said, reaching up to pull his hat down over the bruise.

"Looks like you got quite a whack." Ann said.

Eyeing his frayed coat, she said, "Looks like your coat's been through the war."

Willie seemed a bit embarrassed, but made no reply.

"Just two more pieces to the puzzle," Ann thought to herself. "Could he be the scalawag that's been sneakin' around my house?"

She would hold her tongue till she had more proof.

Nothing else was said until they reached Bent Oak and Willie sprang from the wagon and hurried around to help her dismount.

"Thank you, Willie, that's so nice of you!" Ann said in utter astonishment. For he had never shown that kind of courtesy before.

"It's th least I could do, Missus Shepherd, th very least."

As Ann entered the trading post she asked the proprieter if she had received any mail. "None, Maam, not a scrap," he said, staring at her through his metal-rimmed spectacles.

Ann wasn't surprised, for she was now beginning to believe that John was dead.

"What can I do fer ye today, Miz Shepherd?"

"Do you have any coffee, I mean real coffee?"

"Very little, Maam, and it's high. It's mighty hard to come by."

"Can you spare me a drab?" Ann asked.

"Spose so Miz Shepherd, 'nuffta make a cup er two."

"When's this confounded war gonna be over? Are they gonna keep on till they kill everbody and destroy all we ever lived for?" Ann shouted, unable to control her emotions any longer.

"Can't go on much longer, Miz Shepherd," the proprieter assured her, reaching over to pat her on the shoulder. "It surely can't go on much longer."

ⵣⵣⵣⵣⵣⵣⵣⵣⵣⵣⵣⵣⵣ

But the war wasn't about to be over, at least not for John. The burns on his face and head had finally healed, but he had convinced himself he looked so hideous that Ann could never bear looking at him again. "I'll never be able to go home, even when this war's over," he said , as he stood looking at himself in the mirror.

Since the burns were healed, there was nothing to prevent him from returning to the trenches at Petersburg, but he found it difficult now to find a reason to continue fighting. If he had no hope of ever returning to the one he loved, "then what's left to fight for?"

189

Thousands of his fellow soldiers had simply deserted and gone home. But John wasn't the kind of person to throw down and give up. He had come too far to do that, besides, he remembered the words of his father, "Son, you're duty bound if you're called."

But because so many men had deserted, the Confederete lines were stretched to the limit and beyond. Supplies were pitifully short and the weather showed no mercy on the poorly clad soldiers, some without shoes. This would be the coldest winter in recent memory.

So John found himself hunkered down in the trenches once again, determined to stick it out, for he still felt duty bound. He and his comrades were able to beat the cold by burrowing into the sides of the trenches like groundhogs. They used whatever material they could get their hands on to cover the openings at night, and being underground, the temperature was at least above freezing.

Occasionally, John thought of Wiggens, but when he did, his thoughts were of things of the past, for he felt sure that he had died in the blast. "Maybe he's better off," he said. "At least, he don't have to sleep in the ground like a groundhog."

But George Washington Wiggens hadn't died in the blast and he didn't have to tunnel into the ground at night in order to stay warm, but life was not about to be a bed of roses for him, for he was destined to witness the devestation and destruction wrought by General William Sherman and his thousands of Union soldiers upon his beloved state of South Carolina. Sherman had promised, "It will be one of the most horrible things in the history of the world. The devil himself won't be able to restrain my soldiers in that state."

And so the siege continued into the bone-chilling winter of 1864, a few miles south of Petersburg, Virginia. And John was there in the trenches, in the snow and freezing rain, surviving on skimpy rations and barely enough clothes to keep from freezing to death.

ꙮꙮꙮꙮꙮꙮꙮꙮꙮꙮꙮꙮ

Meanwhile, Ann was doing her best to retain her sanity, at a time in her life when she felt she had lost everyone near and dear to her. She felt there was no one she could call on if she needed help, but for comfort, she drew near to her animals and began having one-sided conversations with them. After all, they were the only friends she had left in the whole world, or so she thought.

Fidgety, her cat, was by ber side day and night, and hadn't she protected her in times of threat or danger? "You're my very best friend,

Fidgety," Ann said, as she lay beneath the covers with the cat nestled beneath her chin, while outside, the cold wind whistled and moaned around the eaves of the tiny shanty.

The wind made haunting sounds, and at times it seemed as if she could hear voices. Once, she imagined hearing John calling out to her and she sat up in bed, listning, but when the winds died down the voices hushed and she lay back and close her eyes.

The howling wind continued late into the night as Ann lay suspended somewhere between wake and sleep, haunted by the voices of the past. Voices of her Father, P D and her great-aunt, Isa Biddy. She heard Hassie, Papa Jacob and Mama Sarah. It seemed as if all those who had passed on were now hovering around her bed, serenading her.

"Ann! Ann!" John called to her as she lay dreaming. The winter wind rattled the front door, waking her from her dream. She bounded from bed and rushed to open it, expecting to see John standing there, but now wide awake, she realized it was only the wind, that cold winter wind. Tears burned her eyes as she climbed back in bed and snuggled up to Fidgety. Later on in the night the wind died down and she was finally able to drift off into peaceful sleep.

It was bone chilling cold the next morning when she awoke. She slithered from beneath the heavy covers and slid her feet into her scuffs. Looking out the tiny window by the fireplace, she could see the old oak tree that had been dead for some time, leaning squarely across the road. It was resting in the top of a small sourwood, bent like an archer's bow under the weight of the heavy oak tree.

"That tree'll be to cut down before it falls on somebody and smashes 'em to smithereens," she said to herself.

As she sat warming herself at the fireplace and sipping on the coffee she bought at Bent Oak last Saturday and gnawing on a piece of hoecake left over from yesterday, she heard the familiar sound of her father's wagon coming up the road. It was Willie Ruff. He had barely enough room to drive the wagon beneath the bent sourwood, burdened with the weight of the oak tree, but only by his bending low in the seat.

When Ann came to the door he said, "You'll need to cut 'at tree down afore it kills somebody."

"Why're you telling me? You've got the wherewithal to do it. After all, I thought you had become a gentleman," she said, as she motioned him to come inside.

"Just come to pay the rent. Didn't know I'as gonna have to cut down a acre a'trees to do that."

"Just one, Willie, not a acre."

"One tree er a acre, what's the differnce?" he asked.

"Enough that I'm sure you'd know, Willie."

"I 'poligize, Miz Shepherd. My old self sneaks in now'n 'en. I'd be only too happy to take that tree down fer ye."

"And I'll be obliged to cook you a good dinner, such as it is, and have it ready for you when you're finished," Ann said, smiling.

"Can ye pull a crosscut saw, Miz Shepherd?"

"Been doin' it since I'as a child," Ann answered.

"Well, don't get too busy, fer I'll be callin' on ye soon's I get that thang on the ground."

Willie took the last sip of his coffee, stood up and walked toward the door. "Better put on some warm clothes. Won't take but a jiffy to get that tree on the ground," he said, as he stepped outside and closed the door.

He reached beneath the wagon seat and grasped the handle of his axe. The sourwood tree was leaning away from him, bending heavily under the weight of the dead oak. He could hear the wood separating beneath its bark. He sank the blade of the axe into the tree about a foot above the ground and stood for a moment, leaning with one hand resting on the tree and staring out in the direction of Deep Gap, as if in some deep thought.

Suddenly, there was a loud pop. A slither of the sourwood, beginning at the place where he sank the axe, split off and sprang up, catching him in the side beneath his rib cage, impelling his body and lifting him high into the air.

He was screaming for help as Ann came racing down the hill. "What have you done, Willie?" she yelled.

"Git me down from here, Miz Shepherd, I'm dyin'."

Before Ann even had a chance to help him, there was another loud pop and the sourwood along with the oak tree came crashing to the ground, pinning Willie's legs beneath it. A gurgling sound was coming from the gash in his side and he was bleeding badly. It was obvious to Ann that he was dying and there was nothing she could do to help him.

As life drained from his bleeding body and his breathing became shallow, he motioned for Ann to come closer. He had something to say to her. She knelt by his side and held her ear close to his whispering lips. "It was me, Miz Shepherd. I'm the one what killed ye pa. I butchered him like a hog. I know ye can't fergive me, but I'm sorry, real sorry. Promise me that you'll see to my little wife and her baby."

As the breath left his body, Ann promised him, "I'll see that they're cared for, Willie. I give you my word."

She held his hand as his face went pale and he closed his eyes in death. She knelt there for several minutes in deep shock, not only for the tragedy that had just taken place, but from what Willie had revealed to her about her father. She had suspected for some time that he was involved in her father's death, but she had no proof.

She felt an anger she had never felt before, but she couldn't let go of his hand. She thought of his wife, Cathy, and the baby and wondered how they could survive, yet again, without a husband and a daddy, in a time when everyone, doing their utmost, could barely make ends meet? "I'll do what I can," she said. "After all, I promised him."

Then she said to herself, "How will I ever get by without the rent money?" but in the very next breath said, "I'll get by somehow. I always have. I'm as tough as anybody else. I'll do what I have to. I'm not about to let myself go the way of the wind."

She rose to her feet, wondering what to do next. "I can't work the crosscut saw by myself. I guess I'll have to chop this tree off of him, she said, as she worked her way through the tangled brush to retrieve the axe.

She first cut two short poles and forced them beneath the oak log on either side of Willie's body, to prevent his legs from being crushed worse than they aleady were. Then she began the task of chopping her way through log, but after a few strokes of the axe, she suddenly remembered, "Papa used to take one handle off his saw and he used it like a handsaw. Why can't I do that?"

She put the axe aside and rushed up to the barn to get the crosscut. It took all her strength to unscrew one of the handles. The saw was still sharp, for it hadn't been used since P.D. last sharpened it. It wasn't easy to work the saw with no one on the other end, but she managed it quite well. In only a short time the gash was well past the midway point in the log. She stopped to make a wooden wedge and pounded into the gash to keep the log from binding on the saw as she completed the cut. When the saw passed through the log, the thee trunk dropped to the ground, but the upper part of the tree settled onto the poles that she had forced beneath it to keep it from crushing Willie's legs. She made the next cut a little further on up the tree, far enough from the first one to allow the wagon to pass between the cuts after she removed that second log. When the second cut was finished, she made a pry pole from a small sapling and muscled the log off Willie's legs and over to the side of the road. After removing the limbs and brush from the roadbed, she struggled to drag Willie's body to the side of the road. She knew she would never be able to lift his heavy body up onto the wagon.

She hurried up to the shanty, climbed into the wagon, guided the mule out of the yard and onto the road. She smacked him across the rump with the reins, urging him into a full gallop. The loose plank in the wagon bed slapped as they went flying down the bumpy road.

"Woa! Woa!" she yelled, as she rounded the first curve, meeting Eli Bailey on his horse.

"Where ye in sich a hurry, my dear?" Eli asked, reining his horse to an abrupt stop.

"Willie's dead!" Ann managed to say.

"Willie who?" Eli asked.

"Willie Ruff. That old dead oak below the shanty fell on him!" Ann said, her voice quivering.

"Where's he at?"

"Up on the ridge below the shanty, Eli."

Ann wheeled the wagon around and followed Eli up the hill to the scene of the accident.

"Looks like he's been stabbed," Eli said, bending down over Willie's body.

"A slither of that sourwood split off and caught him right under the ribs," Ann said, standing behind Eli, peering over his shoulder.

"That must'a been the thang that done it," Eli said, pointing at a bloody splintered piece of sourwood, mixed in with the tangled brush.

"Yes," Ann said. "It had him jacked up in the air for a few seconds before the whole thang come crashin' down on'im."

"Well, now't he's done for, I guess it's up to us to get him down to the Biddy place and tell Cathy that her second man's dead. That'll be a bitter pill fer her to swaller," Eli said, motioning to Ann to bring the wagon closer.

"You git 'im by the other arm and we'll lift 'im up onto the wagon." he said, as he grasped Willie's left arm. It was almost more than they could handle, but together they managed to muscle him up into the wagon.

"Makes me sorry for Cathy. She's had too much grief. She's already lost one man, and now Willie," Ann said, as she helped Eli set the tailgate in place.

The goats had been bleating for some time now, but with all the excitement, Ann hadn't heard them. "Guess I'd better take care of my goats before we go. I dread this trip like the plague. I don't know how Cathy'll handle it," she said.

"Come on up to the shanty, Eli. You can warm yourself by the fire while I milk the goats. Won't take but a few minutes."

"I do believe I'll just do that, my dear. It's a mite airish out here this morning."

Ann came inside after milking and poured some into Fidgety's

194

bowl and strained the rest into the crockpot. There's a dab of coffee left in the pot, Eli, if you'd like some."

"Thank you, but we'd better get on with it. Willie'll be to burry, you know. Take a while to dig 'at grave."

Eli opened the door as Ann covered her head with the shawl. She was carrying the sheepskin under her arm to spread over Willie, thinking it would make it easier on Cathy, when she came out to view his body.

There wasn't much said on the way down to the Biddy place, but Ann's brain was traveling at about a thousand miles a minute. She felt as though a swarm of bees had taken up residence in her head and someone was puffing smoke up her nostrils in order to rob them of their honey. "I can't tell Cathy that Willie killed my papa, it would just about kill her for sure," Ann thought to herself.

"Poor Willie," Eli said.

"Yeah!" Ann answered, in a half hearted way.

They pulled into the yard at the Biddy place and as soon as they eased to a stop, Cathy came to the door, cradling her infant daughter, Mary Ann, in her arms, a child from her first marriage. She looked surprised and immediately asked, "Where's Willie!"

"I'm afraid we have some very bad news for you, Cathy," Ann said, as she bounced down from the wagon and ran up onto the porch.

"I've already had enough bad news in my life, but tell me wha—," Cathy said, cutting herself short, when she saw the sheepskin draped over something lying in the wagon bed. "Is that Willie?" she screamed, almost dropping her baby.

"Yes, I'm sorry to say," Ann said, as she reached to take the baby from her mother's arms. "A tree fell on him."

"I'm so sorry, Cathy, and I can't help but blame myself for it, for I asked him to cut that old oak tree out of the road. But it was just one of them things that happens. Pure accident," Ann said, hugging Cathy with her free arm.

The baby began to cry, seeming to sense that something was wrong. "Don't cry, Baby, I'll take care of you. Shush now, you'll be alright," Ann said, bouncing the baby in her arms.

They had failed to hear Willie's father, Ruffus, ride up on his horse. He dismounted and stepped over to the wagon. When he lifted the the corner of the sheepskin and saw Willie's body lying beneath it he shouted, "Who killed my boy? Looks like he's been stabbed."

"A tree fell on him, Ruffus," Eli spoke up.

"Didn't know trees could stab!" Ruffus yelled.

"If you'll just stay calm I'll tell you how it happened, Ruffus."

195

"Well, tell away," Ruffus said, his face afire with anger.

"A dead oak wuz bearin' down an a little sourwood, 'bout to fall acrost the road up 'ere at Ann's. Willie squeezed the wagon under it an got on up to the house, tolt her't sumpum needed to be done afore it fell on somebody and kilt 'em. Well, she says, 'You got the wherewithal to do it. Why don't you cut it down?' Words wuz said, but Willie finally said he'd cut it down if she'd help'im get it out'a the road. Willie took his own good time about it. He sunk his axe into the bottom a'th sourwood'n stood starin' out torge Deep Gap when part a th sourwood split off and caught him under th ribs and jacked him high into th air. He screamed fer Ann to come'n help him, but afore she could do anythang, th rest a th tree broke off and fell acrost his legs. They wadn't nothin' she could do fer him. With him bein' pinned under that heavy oak and no way she could lift it off. Tweren't no time till he wuz dead," Eli explained.

"It 'as probly that old sharp stick she carries around with 'er that done it, stobbed him with it and drug 'im down there and cut 'at tree down on 'im to make it look like that's what done it," Ruffus said, kicking a clump of dirt in her direction.

"Witch! You witch! He shouted, dangling the bridal reins in front of her face. "You always hated my boy, so you figgerd out a way to get rid of 'im."

"Hold ye tongue, Ruffus, er you'll answer to me," Eli said, stepping up and pushing him out of Ann's face.

"I've al'as thought you wuz a witch, wearin' them old black clothes and draggin' that old black cat a yourn around with ye everwhere ye go!"

With that, Eli popped him in the mouth with him big knurly fist, dislodging his gold tooth and leaving his mouth bruised and bloody. "I said simmer down, Ruffus, Ann didn't do no such a thang. She'd never do a thang like that."

Cathy stepped over to the wagon and took a look at her husband as Ann lifted the black sheepskin coverlet from his body. She began to convulse as tears streamed down her chapped cheeks. "Oh, Willie! My Willie!" she cried.

"To hell with the lot of you," Ruffus said, as he reached down to retrieve his gold tooth from the ground.

"I'll take my boy out'a this mess and burry him myself," he said, dragging the sheepskin off the wagon and tossing it onto the ground.

He climbed into the wagon, slapped Jude on the rump with the reins and took off with a jerk.

Eli, Ann, and Cathy stood staring after him in total amazement as he went flying out the road.

"He don't have no right to take my man off like that," Cathy said, sobbing on Ann's shoulder.

"Let him go, Cathy, let him go. Let him do his thing. After all, Willie's his boy, so let him take him and burry him if that's what he thinks he has to do," Ann said, blotting Cathy's tears on the corner of her black shawl.

"But he's my man," Cathy managed to say between sobs.

"I know, Cathy, but when a person is so dead set on doin' a thing, sometimes it better to just let him do it. Let's go inside. Your baby's gettin' cold out here."

Eli stood rubbing the bruise on his big knotty fist. "Guess I'll have to learn to control my own temper," he said.

He brought in an armful of firewood and laid a few sticks on the smouldering embers, stirred the coals beneath the andirons and soon there was a blaze and warmth.

Cathy sat in the rocking chair in front of the fire for several minutes, crying and cradling the baby in her arms. Ann sat beside her in a straight chair, stroking her arm and assuring her that everything would be alright.

"You're goin' up to my place, Cathy, till you get over this thing," Ann said, touching the baby's pinkie with her forefinger.

"But I can't do it, Ann. You know there's the cow to feed and milk and the chickens and pig to take care of. Besides the baby needs that cow's milk."

Eli interrupted them saying, "I'll feed and milk the cow and take care of the pig and chickens. "I'll even brang th milk up 'ere to ye till thangs git better."

"That's so kind of you, Eli, I'll forever be in your debt," Cathy said, still sobbing.

"That dirty rascal's took the mule and wagon, but you and Cathy can ride my horse and take the baby on up to your house. No use stayin' around here. I'll milk th cow'n feed th pig while you're gone, Ann. You can bring the horse back after while."

Ann helped Cathy gather the things she would be needing for a short stay, then she cradled the baby in her arms and they both went outside to where Eli stood holding the horse's reins. "You can sit behind me and hold the baby, Cathy. That'll keep the cold air off of her," Ann said, as Eli gave Cathy a boost up onto the horse's back.

"Be back in a little, Eli." Ann said, as she and Cathy went racing up the road astride the big stallion, with Cathy snuggling Mary Ann close to her bosom.

197

Eli fed the pig and chickens, fed and milked the cow and funneled the milk into a demijohn. He sat warming himself by the fire till he heard Ann returning with his horse. He picked up the demijohn and stepped over to the door and pulled the draw string inside. When he went outside, Ann slid back behind the saddle. "I'll let you have the front seat," she said, settling down on the horse's rump.

"That's mighty thoughty uv ye, Girl," he said, as he mounted the horse, grasping the handle of the demijohn.

The stallion carried its load with no effort as he galloped up the road toward Ann Ridge. Ann locked her long slender arms around Eli's big belly and in a short time Eli was helping her dismount in front of the shanty, handing her the demijohn.

"Thank you, Eli. You're a true friend. I don't know how we'd get by without you," Ann said, as she walked up the steps.

"Jist glad to do it, Girl. Alus glad to help when I'm needed. See ye tamar when I brang the milk," he said, as he nudged the horse in the ribs with the toe of his boot.

Tears glistened on Cathy's chapped cheeks as she sat near the flickering fire, holding the baby on her lap. "Better let me put some of this lard on them cheeks, Cathy. I know they're bound to be sore," Ann said, as she gently applied the soothing pork rendering to her face.

"I know you're the kindest person I ever met, Cousin Ann. You always know just what to do for a body."

"I'll warm up some of this milk. I know Mary Ann's bound to be hungry," Ann said, as she poured some milk from the demijohn into a small cast-iron pot and sat it on the hearth near the fire. "Twon't take long," she said.

After the baby had her fill of warm milk, she lay sleeping in Ann's arms, as she and Cathy sat before the fire, talking. "I've been thinkin' since Willie died that he had been acting strange here lately. You reckon he had somethin' botherin' him, and if so, what could it have been?" Cathy said.

"Who knows, Cathy? Guess we're all bothered once in a while with one thing or another. We can't read another person's mind, now can we?"

"Guess not, Ann, but I think it 'ud be kind a nice to be able to do it once in a while."

"I 'spose it 'ud stir up a lot of trouble at times if we could," Ann said, thankful that Cathy was unable to read her mind.

Late into the night, as the cold north wind whistled around the eaves of the shanty and long after Cathy and the baby were snoring, Ann lay wide awake, wondering how the war was going and if, against all odds, John could still be alive.

ꙨꙨꙨꙨꙨꙨꙨꙨꙨꙨꙨꙨꙨꙨ

There was no way she could know, but the war wasn't going well for the Confederates, especially in the deep south. For it was at this time that William Tecumseh Sherman was making his devastating sweep through Georgia and South Carolina, less than three hundred miles south of Ann Ridge, burning and destroying everything that seemed to stand in his way.

Likewise, she could not possibly know of John's circumstances, but it was not well with him either. He and his comrades were still hunkered down in the trenches near Petersburg. Many were without shoes and their clothes were rotting away. They were suffering through the coldest winter known in that region for many years. But he was still there and still alive, but scarred in both body and soul. His thoughts were always of Ann, but in a distant kind of way, for he could not make himself believe that she could ever care for a man who had been so hideously scarred. He felt that his appearance had become so repugnant that she could never love him again. So he continued to man the trenches and to suffer through the cold.

ꙨꙨꙨꙨꙨꙨꙨꙨꙨꙨꙨꙨꙨꙨ

Way passed midnight, Ann finally fell asleep, but it was a very fretful sleep, for she kept dreaming of Willie, suspended in mid air, impelled by that splintered piece of sourwood before it crashed to the ground. After each dream she wound stir and mumble: "What have you done, Willie?"

Morning finally came and they were awakened by the baby. She was hungry and uncomfortable and needed her diaper changed.

Ann slid her feet into her scuffs and went over to the fireplace to stir the coals. She soon had a fire going and the inside of the shanty was beginning warming up.

Cathy coddled the baby in her blanket and carried her over to the dining table where she removed the wet diaper, dried her bottom and pinned on a dry one. "You're a cutie pie", she said to her baby, kissing her on the belly.

She sat in the rocking chair before the fire, bottle feeding the baby while Ann made herself busy, preparing breakfast. "Twont take but a jiffy to fix us some vittals", Ann said, as she mixed some

199

cornmeal batter and poured it into the Dutch oven and placed it onto the glowing coals on the hearth.

And sure enough, in a short while there was a steaming pone of cornbread on the table, along with a couple of fried eggs in each of the two tin plates and a glass of goat milk sitting beside each plate. A small crockpot of molasses sat in the center of the table.

"Cousin Ann, looks like you've made us a feast, Cathy said, sliding up to the table with her baby in her arms.

"It's not a feast, Cathy, but let's be thankful we have what little we have, with all them thievin' deserters snatchin' ever'thing they can get their hands on," Ann said, as she pulled her chair up to the table beside Cathy.

"Did I hear a horse nicker?" Cathy asked, sitting perfectly still, her hand cupped to her ear, listening.

"Yes it was," Ann said, when she got up and looked through the tiny kitchen window. "It's Eli and it looks like he's been hurt!"

Cathy placed her baby on the bed and followed Ann as they rushed outside to see what was wrong. Eli was slumped forward in the saddle, grasping the pommel with his right hand and pressing his left hand against his side. Blood was oozing out between his fingers and dripping onto the horse's flank. "What happened, Eli?!" Ann screamed, reaching up to help him down.

"I've been shot. Somebody shot me," he said, grimacing in pain.

He managed to make it up the steps with Cathy and Ann supporting him as best they could. A couple of steps inside the shanty and he collapsed onto the floor. "Who did this to you Eli?!" Ann shouted, as she fell to her knees beside him.

Struggling for breath, he was unable to answer, but before  he took his last breath they thought thought they heard him whisper, "Why, Ruffus?"

"What did he say, Ann?" .

"I think he said, Why, Ruffus, Ann said, as she reached over to smooth his eyelids down over his glaring eyes.

"Well ain't this a fine howdy do? We've lost the very last person willing to protect us from the fools that would like to kill us," Ann said, as her eyes filled with tears of sadness and anger. "I'll put a spell on the very last one of 'em, a spell they won't ever forget, I'll give 'em a reason to call me Witch Ann."

Fidgety jumped up onto Eli's big belly and let out with a loud meow, seeming to reinforce Ann's statement.

"We'll never be able to move him by ourselves. He must weigh nigh onto two hundred and fifty pounds, Cover him with the old

200

sheepskin and I'll take his horse and see'f I can find somebody to help us move him," Ann said.

She slid her sinewy arms into the sleeves of her black coat and wrapped her black shall about her face and neck, rushed outside and was about to mount the black stallion when she noticed Eli's blood on the horse's flank. She reached down at her feet and picked up a handful of leaves and wiped the blood from the horse's flank, mounted, and was on her way in a flash, her black coattail flailing in the wind.

"I'll go down passed Deep Gap and see'f I can meet up with Eli's two nephews" she said to herself, as she sailed along astride the black stallion, looking much like a witch, even without a broom.

She would have to pass the Biddy place on her way down to where Eli's nephews lived. When came within sight of the house she saw Willie's mule and wagon out near the barn. The mule was trying to pick some dead grass from the roadside as she reined the big stallion to a halt. She dismounted and when she examined the wagon she found that the wheel nuts had been removed from each wheel. "Who'd do such a dastardly thing like that?" she said, as she searched through the leaves and dead grass around the wagon, looking for the nuts.

She found one, then two, three and then four. She had found all four nuts. She threaded a nut onto each hub and went inside the barn to search for the wrench. She found it in the box beneath the loft stairs where she remembered her father always kept it. After tightening the nuts she went back into the barn to put the wrench away and suddenly it came to her, "Things are just too quiet around here. Where's the cow?" she said. "And the pig? It's gone too." There was not a sign of a chicken on the place either!

But when she examined the mule, she found him in good shape. "You alright, big boy?" she asked, patting him on the neck. He lifted his head, shifted the bits in his mouth and went right back to picking the dead grass as if nothing had been said.

She left the mule nibbling on the dead grass, still hitched to the wagon. She mounted the big black stallion and they went flying down the road toward Eli's nephews' house. When she reached the house she knocked and an old lady came to the door, opening it slightly. She peeked through the opening and said, "Whachu wont?"

"I'm Lookin' for Eli Baley's nephews, Ben and Buck. You know where they are?"

"They's gone off down to the Tradin' Post. Left early this mornin'. I recken they won't be back till dinner. Who's you, noway?" the old lady asked, with her face barely showing through the small opening between the door and the jam.

201

"I'm Ann Shepherd. I'm afraid I've got some bad news."

"And what may't that be?" the old lady asked.

"Their Uncle Eli is dead. Somebody shot him this morning."

"I've heard talk abou chu. They say't you're a witch and I may't say you shorly do fit the bill, wearin' them old black clothes and ridin' that black hoss and all that."

"Well, I'm not a witch, but I can't help what people say about me. I'll catch up with Ben and Buck at the Trading Post," Ann said, stepping down from the porch, preparing to leave.

"Well, Eli's my old man's brother and chances are you prob'ly killed him yerself with that old pointed stick they say you carry around with you all the time," the old lady screeched as she slammed the door, almost pinching her nose in the process.

Ann mounted the black stallion once more, and he, feeling a bit friskey, was off in a fash. When she came back by the Biddy place, she stopped for a moment to attach the mule's bridal reins to the hitching post in front of the barn to keep him from straying while she went on down to Bent Oak.

When she got to trading post, she walked inside and found the two Bailey boys bellied up to the counter sipping on a mug of home brew. She approached them gingerly and said, "Boys, I need some help. Your uncle's been shot and killed and I need somebody to help me move him."

"The heck you say. We seed him this very mornin'. He wuz alright then," they scowled.

"He's not alright now. He's layin' sprawled out in the front room of my shanty, dead from some fool's bullet,"

"You shore it wuzent you what done it?" Ben asked, cocking his head sideways.

"I'm quite sure it wasn't me. Are you boys gonna help or must I look for somebody else?" Ann said, becoming a bit angry.

"You got any way a haulin' him? That is if we can get him outta yer house," Buck said, after taking another swig of home brew.

"Got a wagon up at my pa's old place. Is that good enough?"

"That'll do till we can get somethin' better," they both said, as they stood up on wobbly legs and made their way toward the door.

"Miz Shepherd, wait a minute! I think I've got a letter here for you," the proprietor said, reaching into the mail basket.

"Good God in heaven, who's it from?"

"Don't know, maam, got no return address on it."

Ann latched onto the letter and examined it, and sure enough there wasn't a sign of an address on the envelope, front or back. She

202

opened and read it: "I met your husband while he was up here fighting in this awful war. He gave me your name and address and I thought I'd write you a letter to see if you had seen him or heard from him. He told me so many nice things about you. I'm sure you must be some kind of a fine lady. It's been quite some time since I've seen him. Please write me and let me know how he is."

The letter was signed, "A friend, Sam Worley."

His mailing address was at the bottom of the page.

"That's strange," Ann said, as she folded the letter and put it back into the envelope and stored it in her dress pocket.

They all three went outside where Ben and Buck mounted their horses. Ann climbed up onto the black stallion, nudged him in the side with the toe of her shoe and of she flew.

Ben and Buck had fallen behind by the time she reached the Biddy place. She had already dismounted, tied the stallion's bridal reins to the rear standard of the wagon, loosened the mule's reins from the hitching post and was climbing up onto the wagon, preparing to head on up toward Ann Ridge, when they finally caught up with her. She tapped the mule with the lines and he headed up the road in a trot, moving to the rhythm of the old familiar flapping of the loose board in the bed of the wagon.

The sound of the flapping board brought to mind the day she was walking down the road toward Britten Creek and met a man who's face was covered with a dirty old rag. "He was ridin' in this very same wagon, pulled by this very same mule. That was Willie Ruff, I'm certain of it," she said to herself.

As she guided the mule and wagon up the ridge to the shanty, stopping with the back of the wagon even with the porch steps, Cathy stepped outside cradling Mary Ann in her arms. "I see you found somebody," she said, as Ann hopped down from the wagon.

"I did. Eli's nephews, Ben and Buck."

Ann invited the boys inside the shanty where Eli lay sprawled out on the floor just inside the door beneath the sheepskin. Fidgety was perched on top of the heap, taking on the appearance of a   sentry.

"Where's he at?" the two boys chimed in unison.

"Under the sheepskin, beneath the cat," Ann said.

"Why's that damned cat settin' on my uncle's dead body?" Ben yelled, pointing at the cat.

"Guardin' him, I s'pose. The cat liked Eli," Ann said.

Buck grabbed hold of the sheepskin, jerking it from the body, spilling Fidgety onto the floor. Fidgety raised her bristles and let out with a loud meow, sprang up onto the bed and stood with her back

203

arched, staring at Buck through blazing eyes.

"Better keep that damned cat outa my way," he said. "That is if you expect us to get Uncle Eli out of here."

"She's not gonna bother you, long's you don't bother her," Ann said, a quiver of anger in her voice.

"Well, just keep her in her place," Buck said with a snarl.

"Me and Ben'll get him by his arms. If you and that other woman there can get him by his legs we'll carry him out and put him in the wagon."

It was easier said than done, but they did manage to half carry and half drag him outside and load him onto the wagon.

"We'll bring your wagon back soon's we get through with it," Ben said, as he and Buck made ready to leave.

"Eli's black stallion's in the barn," Ann said. "You boys can have him when you bring the wagon back."

The Bailey boys didn't say yea or nay either way as they headed down the road toward Britten Creek, with Eli's big body bouncing in the wagon bed.

Cathy was on her knees wiping Eli's blood from the floor when Ann came back inside. "I could've done that, Cathy. You've got a baby to take care of,"Ann said.

"It won't hurt me none to make myself usefull," Cathy said, as she made a few more swipes and struggled to her feet.

"Well, Cousin Cathy, the Bailey boys didn't seem so all fired interested in claimin' Eli's body. They wanted to know if I had any way a haulin' him. I told 'em I had my pa's wagon. I asked them if that would be good enough. They said it would do till they could get somethin' better. I don't know what better they thought they could get. Do you?"

"They seemed a little bit drunk to me, Ann. I sure hope they give Eli a good burial."

"Eli's hat! Where'd you find his hat?" Ann asked, walking over to where it lay upside down on the table. She ran her forefinger along the outer edge of the brim.

"Right here beside the door," Cathy answered.

"Well, I don't s'pose he'll be needin' it any more. I don't think they wear hats where he's going. Besides we may find a good use for it," Ann said, standing steady as a rock, as if in a deep trance.

"I'll go down in a day er two and see what kind of job they've done. I think we owe that to Eli. He was a good man and he sure was good to us, too. He didn't deserve to die the way he did. But the one who did it will have a hard row to hoe. I'll promise you that,"Ann said, as the dark hair on her arms bristled.

It was getting well along in the evening and the sun had already dropped down behind the mountain. It was biting cold and the wind was whipping across World's Edge, bringing snow flurries with it. "I'd better bring in some wood in case it comes a snow tonight," Ann said, slipping once again into her black coat and wrapping the black shawl around her face.

After filling the wood box, she took the milk bucket down from the nail on the wall behind the kitchen table and went out to the barn to feed the animals and to milk the goats. The black stallion nickered as she walked into the breezeway. "I'm fixin' to feed you, big boy, but first you'll need some water. She snapped the lead to the ring on the halter and led him from the stall and down to the water hole at the creek. He was thirsty, for Ann had forgotten to water him because of all the commotion of the day. After he gulped down all the water he wanted, Ann led him back up to the barn and put him back into his stall. She fed him a couple of hands of fodder and an ear of corn. She knew that probably wasn't enough, but she didn't know just how long she would be keeping him and she sure didn't want to run out of feed. "I'll keep you out'a sight for a while, big boy. I've got plans for you," she said.

She went back to the creek once more and filled the milk bucket with water and brought it up to the barn for the goats. "Bet you babies are gettin' thirsty, too," she said as she poured the water into their pans. They were thirsty and they proved it, for they drank it all.

She fed and milked them and hurried back to the shanty. The chickens were okay, for they pretty much took care if themselves with Ann shelling them an ear of corn each morning. They were already in their roosting places, high up in the hemlocks.

Ann strained the milk and filled two tin cups, one for herself and one for Cathy. They sat down at the table and ate a piece of cold cornbread, left from this morning's meal, dipped in the warm milk. Come to think of it, they hadn't had anything to eat since this morning either. They were both hungry, but so exhausted, they could hardly feed themselves. "This has certainly been a day to remember, but better forgotten," Cathy said, as she went slowly toward her mouth with another bite of milk-soaked cornbread.

"We're not apt to forget this day. Ever!" Ann said, raising her milk ladened cornbread high in the air. A chunk of it dropped back into the cup of milk, splashing some onto the table and Fidgety leapt up onto the table to lap it up.

"Not apt," Cathy said.

The next morning arrived with only a fine sifting of snow on the ground. Ann expected the Bailey boys to return the wagon sometime up in the morning, but noon came and went and still no wagon. "I don't believe them boys ever get in a hurry," she said, as she stood for a moment, looking out the tiny kitchen window.

"They've got their own speed, Ann," Cathy said, sitting in the rocker at the fireplace, holding the baby on her lap.

But along about mid-afternoon, they heard that all too familiar sound of P D's wagon coming up the road. It was Buck. His horse was tethered to the rear standard. "Well bless my bloody bones, they decided to bring the wagon back," Ann said, looking down toward Britten Creek.

Buck guided the mule and wagon up the road to Ann Ridge and pulled to a stop in front of the shanty. He bounced down and walked around to the rear of the wagon and was releasing his horse's reins from the standard as Ann came outside. She was about to remind him of the black stallion, but on second thought she decided not to. She figured he didn't want the horse anyway, since he hadn't replied one way or the other, when she mentioned it the day before. He snapped the reins to the bit ring, draped the reins over the pommel, climbed into the saddle and was off without so much as a thank you maam.

"Well, it's too bad he didn't take on any of his uncle's ways," Ann said, as the horse galloped away, carrying him down the road toward Deep Gap.

She unhitched the mule from the wagon and led him down to the creek and after he drank his fill of water she lead him back up to the little barn. Since all the stalls were occupied, she removed his gear and turned him into the lot behind the barn and fed him some corn and fodder. She left the gate to the breezeway open at the rear of the barn and closed the front gate so the mule could come inside during the night if he wanted to.

Halfway between the barn and the shanty, Ann stood for a moment, mulling over the things that had happened over the past several days. She stood steady as a statue, staring up at the crest of World's Edge with her hands resting on her hips. She looked ghostly, standing in the darkening shadows of the evening. She was groping for a plan to bring justice to the man who had killed Eli, namely, Ruffus Ruff, for she was certain in her heart that he was the killer.

Like a vision from the nether-world, it came to her. "I'll bring the old syrup can and rosin string back to life," she said. "I'll stuff a couple of bundles of fodder under my black coat, put Eli's hat on my head and ride that big black stallion down passed Ruffus Ruff's house.

When I pull on that string and the syrup can starts to bellow it'll scare thirteen devils out of the seat of his britches. In the meantime, I'll spread the word that Eli's ghost is on the prowl at night, searchin' for his killer. I'll keep the charade goin' till I run him clean out of this part of the country."

A feeling of contentment spread over her entire body as she opened the door to the shanty, walked inside, closed the door and pulled the drawstring inside. When she sat down in the chair at the fireplace, she was grinning and Cathy wanted to know why.

"I've come up with a plan that'll get even with Eli's killer," Ann said. "I'll get rid of him once and for all."

"How d'you 'spect to do that, Ann?"

"With that old syrup can, a rosined string, a black stallion, two bundles of fodder and Eli's hat. That's how!" Ann said, breaking into a fit of fiendish laughter, taking on the personality and appearance of a wicked witch. She was totally unlike herself.

It frightened Cathy to see her this way, but she soon realized that Ann had taken all she was going to take and she was ready to fight back. She just wasn't going to take it any more.

They sat near the hearth for quite a while gazing into the flickering flames, saying nothing. Then suddenly they both rose from their chairs at the same instant, as one would do when a judge enters a courtroom and the bailiff says, "All rise". They said good night to each other and went to bed.

Morning came, and after Ann kindled the fire at the fireplace, she sat down at the kitchen table to answer the letter she had gotten from Sam Worley. It puzzled her that a total stranger would take the time and trouble to write to her, asking about John.

She wrote: "It's been a long time since I've heard from John. In fact it was last May when I heard from him last. Since then I received word that he'd been killed, but I find it hard to believe. I just don't know what life would be worth without him. So I keep on believing that somehow he is still amongst the living. Thank you for your concern and thank you for your kind words about me. Please write me and let me know if you find out anything about my man's whereabouts. Sincerely, Ann Shepherd."

"You're up mighty early, Ann," Cathy said, as she slid from the bed, coddling Mary Ann in her arms.

"Soon's we eat breakfast and I take care of the animals, I'm gonna take this here letter down to Bent Oak and spin a little yarn while I'm at it,"Ann said, stuffing the letter into the envelope.

By mid-morning she had hitched Jude to the wagon and was on

her way to Bent Oak. She broke into a snicker several times as she rode along, thinking of the plan she had put together to get rid of Ruffus Ruff. "I'll fix him. He'll not rest, long's he's in this part of the country," she said.

As she drove up to the trading post she noticed Ruffus Ruff's horse tethered to the hitching post outside the store. She guided the wagon up beside his horse and wrapped the mule's reins around the next hitching post. She wanted everyone to notice that she was traveling in her pa's wagon, and for sure, she didn't want it to be known that she had possession of Eli's big black stallion, for that would give her whole scheme away. When she walked inside she handed her letter to the man at the counter and said, "I've got a letter here that I'd like to mail."

She noticed Ruffus Ruff standing half hidden behind some horse collars that were hanging on a rack over a barrel of axe handles. He was examining one of the handles, checking it for smoothness and ballance. Or perhaps he was only pretending to be interested in the axe handle while in reality he was eavesdropping on Ann's comversation, hoping she might say something that he could use to incriminate her.

"Sorry to hear about Eli," the man at the counter said. "He sure was a good man."

"That he was," Ann said, and they tell me that his ghost is ridin' that big black stallion at night, searching for the man that done him in. They say he lets out with a haunting call as he rides through the night, calling out the name of his killer.

"Has anybody heard him say the name, besides you?" the man at the counter asked.

"Not that I know of, but I'm sure Eli's killer will know when his name is called," Ann said, glancing toward Ruffus.

"Can I get you something?" the proprietor asked.

"A little can of black paint, if you've got it, and a small brush," Ann said.

"I've got it, my Lady," he said, reaching up to the top shelf to retrieve the can of black paint. He selected a small brush from the tin can on the countertop. "Will that be all, Maam?"

"That'll do just fine," Ann said, placing the small can of paint and the brush into her coat pocket.

"Looks like it's gonna be a fine day," she said, walking prissily toward the door, exploding into a fit of fiendish laughter as she walked outside and closed the door.

"That woman's a witch! They's no doubt about it," Ruffus said, stepping out from behind the horse collars and pitching the axe handle back into the barrel. "I went by poor old Eli's grave last evenin' and who did I see there? Well, It was Witch Ann herself, pullin' a plank from his grave marker. Jist why would she be doin' that? If anybody killed him, it was her. They found him dead in her front room, didn't they? If they's anything to this story about Eli's ghost, he'll be callin' on her. You can count on that."

After several minutes of his ranting and raving the people inside the store lost interest in what he had to say. So he shrugged his shoulders and said, "Huh!", stormed outside, mounted his horse and rode away.

Ruffus had told the truth about seeing Ann at Eli's grave. And it was true that she had removed the bottom board from the grave marker. The words of the epitaph were painted in black on the three boards that made up the grave marker. The words on the top board read: 'HERE LIES ELI BAILEY.' On the second board: 'BORN 1803 DIED 1864.' The words on the bottom board read: 'KILLED BY WITCH ANN.'

Ann knew very well that the statement on the bottom board was untrue and she was determined to correct it, so she pulled the board free. The nails that held it in place were still embedded in the board. When she got back to the shanty, she took the board from beneath the wagon seat, laid it in a level place in front of the barn, and scrubbed away the words with sand and a flat stone. After removing the words she carried the board inside and placed it on the kitchen table.

"Where'd you get that board, Ann?" Cathy asked.

"It was part of Eli's grave marker," Cathy.

"Well, what are you doing with it?"

"Oh, them fools made a mistake on it and I aim to correct it," Ann said, as she reached into her coat pocket to retrieve the can of paint and the brush.

She gave the can of paint a good shaking and pried off the lid with a spoon handle and began her version of what should have been painted on the board in the first place, which was: 'HE WAS A GOOD MAN.' "Now, that's the way it should be," she said, as she closed the can and wiped the brush clean on an old rag.

"I'll put this board back on Eli's grave marker tonight on my way to serenade Ruffus," she said, almost breaking into another fit of laughter, but she was able to control the laughter by placing a hand over her mouth.

"You mean you're gonna sing him a song?" Cathy asked.

"No, silly one, but I'll be playin' his song on the old syrup can."

"You're gonna do that tonight?"

"Sure, why not? They'll be a full moon. Shouldn't be too dark.

209

Just light enough for Ruffus to see the ghost rider when he steps out onto the porch to see what's causing such a ruckus."

The wind was getting up as the sun dropped down behind Wildcat Spurr and a big full moon came up, shimmering through the leafless trees in the east.

Ann applied more rosin to the string of the bellower and gave it one quick jerk. It made such a loathsome sound that it scared the baby and she began to cry. "Don't cry, baby, I won't do it again here in the house," Ann said, as she put the bellower aside and picked up the baby and pressed her close to her bosom. As soon as the baby had quieted, Cathy took her and put her to bed and in a short time she was asleep.

"Well, Cathy, tonight's the big night. It's a night of reckoning for Ruffus Ruff," Ann said, as she slid her slender arms into the sleeves of her black coat. "He'll be headin' for nobody knows where, once this night's over."

"You be careful out there, Ann Shepherd. That man's a killer, so don't you be taking any chances."

"Chance is all we have left, Cathy, ever'thang else is dead, but I'll give him a run for his money. Keep your fingers crossed and your toes, too. If there's any scare in him, I'll bring it out tonight."

When Ann placed Eli's hat on her head, she found it was so large that it came down and covered her ears. "Well, it'll keep my ears warm," she said, as she wrapped her dark shawl around her neck.

As she picked up the old syrup can from the table and headed for the door, she said, "keep the draw string inside tonight, Cathy. You never can tell when some fool'll be sneakin' around. Can't be too careful, you know."

"I'll be up when you get back, Ann. I'll keep the fire blazing."

Ann walked out to the little barn and saddled up the big black stallion and put the reworked gravemarker into the saddle bag. She stuffed two bundles of fodder inside her coat to make herself look as big as Eli. She mounted the big black horse and capped the syrup can over the pommel. A nudge in the horse's flanks and they were on their way, looking very much like the ghost of Eli.

The first task of the night was to replace the missing board of the gravemarker which she did by using a stone found near the grave. It wasn't too hard to replace the board when she finally located the nail holes in the post and aligned the nails in the board with the holes. The moon was so bright she could see the lettering on the board and she read it aloud: "HE WAS A GOOD MAN."

Bitter tears flooded her eyes as she stood for a moment, remembering all the good things Eli had done for her. "I surely will

210

miss you, Good Man," she said, as she mounted the black stallion once more and the horse galloped away.

It was a blustery night. Tree limbs scrubbed against the side of Ruffus Ruff's shack, disturbing his sleep. Downdrafts blew smoke and cenders from the fireplace and out into the room where he lay. He was having nightmares about Eli and how he had shot him just to spite Ann. This went on for quite some time, but around midnight, he was so exhausted he fell into a deep sleep. He roused once, when the wind blew smoke down the chimney and into the room again, but he quickly went back to sleep. He was too sleepy to notice that the wind had blown firecoals onto the floor and into the stack of ritch pine kindling. The house was so open, he didn't notice that the pine kindling had ignighted and set the braided rug ablaze. At first he felt warm and comfortable and by the time he began to really feel the heat, it was too late. When he finally awoke in a stupor, he found himself in the midst of a burning inferno. Half crazy, he staggered through the blazing room, searching for the water bucket. The smoke and fumes from the fire soon overpowered him and he collapsed onto the burning floor.

Ann saw flames shooting high into the air as she came over the hill. She urged the black stallion forward, but by this time it was too late. The shack was completely engulfed. There was nothing she could do to save Ruffus. Her whole plan had been foiled by the blaze, but perhaps it was better this way. A feeling of relief came over her as she sat astride the stallion, but she was soon sickened by the odor of burning flesh, as she sat watching the flames. shooting high into the night sky.

"I'd better not be seen around here. If somebody sees me here they'll say I was the one who started the blaze. They're already callin' me a witch." Ann said, as she turned the horse around in his tracks and headed back up the road as fast as he would carry her.

On the way back to Ann Ridge, she stopped at Britten Creek and removed the bits from the horses mouth to give him a drink of water. After drinking his fill, she replaced the bits and led him up the hill to the barn. She removed the saddle, put him in the stall and fed him some fodder. She hid the syrup can under a tow sack beneath the loft stairs, saying, "Nobody needs to know that I've got this thing,"

As she walked up onto the porch, Cathy hollered through the door, "Who's out there?"

"It's me, Cathy."

"Well, It didn't take long to serenade Ruffus, did it, Ann?" Cathy said, lifting the latch and opening the door.

"He's dead, Cathy. Burned to death in his shack."

"You didn't—" Cathy started to ask, before being cut short by Ann's reply.

"Certainly not. I'd never do a thing like that. The place was all ablaze when I got there," Ann said. "But we best not let anybody know that I was there or they'll accuse of doin' it."

"My lips are forever locked," Cathy said, as she helped Ann off with her coat.

The shock of having things turn out so differently from what she had planned left Ann in wonderment. "Maybe there's a higher power that takes care of things when they get too hard for us to handle," she said, as she settled down into the rocking chair at the fireplace.

As she gazed into the fire she envisioned Ruffus Ruff's burning house. "I had no intention of hurtin' the man," she said, looking up at Cathy, her eyes awash with tears.

"Nobody says you had, leastwise not me, Ann Shepherd!" Cathy said, grasping Ann by the shoulders and shaking her.

"Well, let's hope nobody says so," Ann said, holding onto the arms of the rocker as if she were riding in a runaway wagon.

"It's real late, Ann. Let's get to bed."

"Good idy, Cathy. Why didn't I think of it first." Ann said, bouncing up from the chair like a jack-in-the-box.

Surprisingly, their heads had hardly pressed their pillows and they were asleep.

For the next several days they laid low. They didn't even leave the ridge. They felt sure somebody would come by and tell them about the fire, but nearly two weeks passed before anyone did.

It was about sundown on the nineteenth of December as they were eating supper of goat's milk and cornbread, when they heard what sounded like a cow bawling. They jumped up from the table and hurried over to the tiny window and almost bumped heads as they struggled with each other to get the first look. Their jaws were touching as they pressed their faces against the small window pane. They stared in disbelief at what they saw. It was Cathy's crippled brother, hobbling up the road, leading her cow by a flimsy rope. "Where'd he get my cow?" Cathy screamed, waking the baby.

"Your guess is as good as mine," Ann said, as she lifted the child from the bed, attempting to calm her.

Cathy's brother,Lank, was born a cripple. He walked with a strange gait, like someone almost falling, but breaking the fall with each step. His condition kept him from serving in the war. He had lived with his great-uncle since he was a child.

Cathy rushed to door, open it, and ran outside. "Where'd you

212

find my cow?" she screamed.

"Over't Ruffus Ruff's house. His house burnt down thuther night. Nothin' left but the shed and this here cow. Is she your'n?"

"She sure is, Cathy said. Ruffus must a stole her from down at the Biddy place. That's where I've been living since I married Willie."

"And who's he?" Lank asked.

"Willie? Willie was Ruffus' boy," Cathy said.

"Oh, I heard about that. Ever'body's talkin' about how Witch Ann killed him, but we know it ain't so. She'd never do a thing like that. Ann's heart's as good as gold."

"I've been livin' with Uncle Dody since I wuz a boy, but he died a couple a weeks ago, died the same night Ruffus Ruff's house burned to the ground."

I'm Sorry about that, Lank. I sure am," Cathy said.

Cathy and Lank hadn't seen each other for two or three years, so they were anxious to catch up with what had been going on during that time. "Let's take the cow out to the barn and feed her, then we'll go inside and catch up on all the gossip that's been goin' around here lately," Cathy said.

"Howdy, Cousin Ann, and how've you been?" Lank said, as he and Cathy came inside. "Been hearin' strange talk about you."

"I'm well, Lank, but there's people in these parts whose heads ain't exactly straight on their shoulders and I think they've lost control of their tongues, too."

"Yeah, people, some people, just love to wag their tongues. They can turn a flea into a hound dog, if you know what I mean, Lank said"

"I know exactly what you mean, Lank. You can try to help people and try to be right by 'em, and they'll twist what you've done all out of shape in spite of everything you can do. But what I do is pay 'em no mind and just keep on keepin' on."

"Man's been able to tame just about ever' wild creature they is, but that tongue's a different animal, Cousin Ann."

"We were sittin' down to supper, Lank, when we heard the cow bawl. Won't you have a bite with us? All's we got is goat milk and cornbread, but it goes down good when a body's hungry."

"You're mighty right about that, Cousin Ann. I've had just about nothin' fer sev'al days and I'm powful hungry."

Ann placed another bowl onto the table and motioned Lank to sit down. She pushed the pone of cornbread in his direction and he wasted no time crumbling some into the bowl and pouring milk over it. He ate several bites without saying a word.

"Sorry, ladies," he finally said, wiping his mouth on the sleeve of his ragged coat. "Didn't mean to make a hog a myself, but I was mighty hongry."

"We understand, Lank, stuff to eat's hard to come by these days," Cathy said, twisting in her chair and pushing up from the table to go check on the baby.

"Who's baby is zat?" Lank asked, before shoving another spoonful of bread and milk into his mouth.

"She's mine," Cathy said. Her name's Mary Ann. Toddy Joe Ruff, my first husband, was her daddy. Got hisself killed, fightin' in that god-awful war up north! "

"Mary Ann's a fine name. That's a fine name indeed," Lank said, after caughing to clear his throat of a bread crumb that had gone down the wrong way.

Turning his attention to Ann, he asked, "Where's your man at?"

"He's been up north, fightin' in that god-awful war, too. I hear say he's dead, but I'm not gonna believe it till I get some proof," Ann said, her voice cacking as she uttered the last few words.

"You got a heap a faith, Ann Shepherd. As awful as things have been for them poor boys, it'd surprise me if they didn't all end up covered with about six inches of sod, never to be seen no more."

"Well, thank you for them kind words of encouragement, Cousin Lank. That's the very thing I need to hear right about now," Ann said, looking him straight in the eyes.

"See there, Ann, my tongue's loose again. Sayin' things it shouldn't. I apologize. I oughtn't a said them words."

"Next time, ask yourself if what you're about to say's gonna help or hurt."

"I will, Ann, honest I will. Your man could very well be alive. Can't blame you for believin' he is."

"I guess I best be goin'," Lank said, dropping his spoon into the bowl and pushing away from the table.

"Going? Where?" Ann asked. "You've got nowheres to go and you know it. You'll stay here with us tonight. I'll fix you a pallet right here on the floor. It'll be a heap better'n sleepin' outside in the cold."

"Well, if you insist, but I hate to be a bother to you."

"It's no bother, Lank. After all, you're kin and you're welcome here any time."

After Ann and Cathy finished washing the supper dishes, they all sat in a semicircle at the fireplace for a while, talking. Ann told Lank about Willie's accidental death and how it had left Cathy all alone once again, and with a child to raise.

"How'd you like to come and stay with me, Brother? At least till things get better," Cathy asked.

"Are you sure, Cathy?"

"Sure I'm sure. I'm afraid to stay down there by myself. Besides, I don't want to wear out my welcome here at Ann's."

"You're not apt to do that, Cathy," Ann spoke up.

"In that case I'd be glad to go down and stay with you, Sister. I may be a cripple, but I can still carry my weight. I'll see that nobody harms you," Lank said, balling his right hand into a fist.

Ann spread a quilt onto the floor and threw down a sack of shredded corn shucks for a pillow. When she pulled the sheep skin coverlet from the foot of her bed, dumping Fidgety onto the floor, the cat let out with a loud meaow of protest. "I'm sorry, Fidgety. I didn't mean to disturb your sleep," she said, reaching down to stroke the cat.

The ladies spent as peaceful a night as they had spent in quite some time. That is, except the one time when Lank had to go outside to relieve himself and accidentally closed the door without rethreading the drawstring. At that time Ann was dreaming, and in her dream John had come home from the war and was knocking on the door and calling out to her, but when she awoke she was disappointed to descover that it was only a dream.

"Cousin Ann, wake up and let me in. It's freezin' cold out here," Lank called from outside the door, as he stood barefoot, shivering in the cold night air.

After opening the door for Lank, Ann crawled back into bed and snuggled up to the baby as she lay sleeping between Cathy and herself. The baby stirred, but didn't awake. Cathy muttered something in her sleep and then all was quiet.

As the sun rose the next morning, they awoke to the crowing of the little game rooster, perched on the lower limb of the hemlock tree down below the shanty. The baby awoke as well, for her diaper was wet and she was hungry. "I hear you, Child. I'll put you on a dry diaper and warm up some goat milk in a jiffy," Cathy said, as she pulled a dry diaper from the carry bag beside the bed.

"No need to warm the goat milk, Sister, I've got warm cow's milk right here in this bucket," Lank said, as he came inside with the milk, still steaming in the cold morning air.

"Now ain't you a handy thang to have around," Cathy said, obviously pleased to have warm cow's milk for the baby. "I forgot all about the cow. Can you imagine that!"

They had hardly finished breakfast when they heard a noise outside. "What could that be?" Ann said.

Lank hobbled over to the door and stepped out onto the porch to see what was causing the noise. Out in the yard stood a man dressed in a grey uniform. "Who are you? And what would you be doin' way back in these woods?" Lank asked.

"I'm of The Home Guard," the man in grey said. "I'm out rounding up deserters. "You look young enough to be a soldier. Why ain't you up there fighting for the cause?"

"Do I look like somebody that's fit to fight? How long do you thank I'd last with these old crooked legs?" Lank said, his face turning crimson with anger, bracing himself on the porch post.

"I've had several reports of deserters in these parts. They're shooting deserters, you know."

"How well I know that, Sir. If I'd a been able, I'd a been the first one to join in this here fight," Lank said.

"I can see now that you're in no shape to fight. What might your name be?"

"My name's Lank. Lank Biddy, to be complete."

"Well, Lank Biddy, would you happen to know if there's any deserters hiding out around here?"

"No Sir, I don't. We hate deserters as much as you do, I s'pose. They's always breakin' into our houses and stealin' thangs, and killin', too, I might add."

As Lank and the man in grey stood talking, the black stallion snorted and let out with a loud neigh. "He's hongry," Lank said, looking out toward the little barn. I'd better go out and give him somethin' to eat before he kicks the barn down."

"What kind of a horse is he? He sounds like he's a big un," the man in grey said, walking behind Lank, as he hobbled toward the barn.

"He's a big black horse," Lank said. "He's a stallion. Got a lot a fire, he has."

"I've been looking to buy a high spirited horse. Would you be interested in selling him?"

"Tain't mine to sell. Blongs to my cousin, Ann Shepherd."

"Is she the woman they call Witch Ann?" the man from The Home Guard asked.

"They call her that, but she ain't no witch. Why, she's the most obligin' lady you ever met."

Lank opened the stall door and had barely snapped the lead reins to the ring on the horse's halter when the big horse muscled his way through the opening. "He do have fire, don't he?" the man in grey said.

"Yeah, when ye open that stall door, ye better be ready to get out of his way," Lank said, staggering to one side.

"How much would she take for him?"

216

"Don't don't know what she'd take fer him. Don't even know if she wants to sell him," Lank answered.

"I'd be willing to offer her three ten-dollar gold pieces for him. That is if he's a good saddle horse. Confederate money ain't worth nothin' no more, but gold's always good."

"Ann says he's the best she's ever rode," Lank said, hobbling along, trying to stay out of the stallion's way, as he led him down toward the creek to give him some water.

"How come you ain't ridin' a hoss? Where's your hoss at, nohow?" Lank asked the man in grey.

"Some dirty thief stole him from me last night. I spent the night in the barn loft of that deserted place down the road a piece and while I was asleep some rogue took him and my saddle, too."

"I 'spect you need a hoss real bad then," Lank said.

"I do need a horse and that's a fact," the man in grey said, picking up a stone that Lank had almost tripped over and flinging it down toward the creek.

After Lank watered and fed the horse, he and the man in grey went back to the shanty and Lank ushered him inside. "This here's the lady I've been talkin' about," Lank said, pointing to Ann.

"How do, Maam. I'm a soldier of The Home Guard, and I'm in dire need of a good horse. Hank, I mean Lank, tells me that big black stallin down there in the barn belongs to you. I told him I'd be willing to offer you three ten-dollar gold pieces for him, that is if he's a good saddle horse."

"Best I ever rode," Ann spoke up.

"Well, would you be interested in letting him go? Would you take thirty dollars in gold for him?"

"Give me forty and you can take the saddle, too," Ann said.

The man in grey reached into his pocket and pulled out a small leather pouch, opened it, and retrieved four ten-dallar gold pieces. "It's a deal, Maam, and I'm much obliged to you. You can be sure of that."

"Won't you have a bite to eat. I'm sure you must be hungry," Ann said, pointing toward the table.

"I could use some milk and a chunk of bread. I surely could," the man in grey said, sitting down in the chair and pulling up to the table.

Ann took the four ten-dollar gold pieces, tied them up in her handkerchief and put the handkerchief into her dress pocket. "Thank you, Sir, for the gold pieces. They'll help me make it through the rest of the winter," she said.

When the man in grey finished downing the chunk of cornbread and milk, Ann went with him out to the barn to show him the saddle and to make sure he didn't take anything extra. "Can't be too carefull these days," she thought to herself.

Nobody had bothered to ask the man's name and he hadn't said. So he rode away and they still didn't know hide nor hair about who he was, nor where he was from. But Ann was rid of the big feed-eating horse and had four ten-dollar gold pieces in her pocket to boot. "These gold pieces will do me till spring comes around," she said, patting the bulge in her dress pocket.

These were the first gold pieces she had ever had and she was proud to have them, especially in these hard and uncertain times.

When she came inside after getting the man on his way, Cathy asked, "Did anybody bother to ask him his name?"

"I didn't, Ann said. "Didn't think it was important. I just wanted to get rid of the horse and get the gold."

"Well, I noticed he had one joint missing on the little finger of his left hand," Cathy said. Don't guess there'll be many men walking around in that kind of a fix. Let's remember that, just in case we should ever have to identify him."

"What's in a name," Ann said. "Besides, if he had said he was John Brown, we wouldn't know if he was tellin' the truth or not."

"Guess not," Cathy said.

"Don't you thank we'd better get down to the Biddy place, Cathy? Some rogue'll have everthang you own toted off, with nobody there to guard the place," Lank said.

"Yes, we'd better. If you'll hitch up the mule and wagon, we'll go," Cathy said, as she scurried around, gathering up her things.

Cousin Ann, I sure do appreciate what you've done for me. I do hope I'll be able to repay you in some way, some day."

"Just glad to do it for you, Cathy. I'm sure if I needed help, you'd be the first person to show up."

Lank brought the mule and wagon up to the shanty with the cow tethered to the rear standard and stopped in front of the porch. He held the baby for Cathy while she climbed aboard. When she was up and seated, Lank handed her the baby, all snuggly and warm in the thick wool blanket.

Ann waved as they rode away. She watched them till they were out of sight. Pangs of loneliness shrouded her as she went back inside and sat down in the chair at the fireplace, but Fidgety didn't let her stew in her loneliness, for as soon as she settled into the chair, the cat sprang up onto her lap.

Ann sat for some time, stroking her big black cat. Her mind wandered the paths of her troubled past, ricocheting from one tragedy to another as she sat staring into the flickering flames.

The bleating of her goats plucked her thoughts from the paths of the past and placed them in the present. "Nothin' works better than the duties of the day to clear the cobwebs from the mind," she said, lifting the cat from her lap and putting her down onto the floor. "Let's go milk them goats, Fidgety! Are you ready for some milk?"

"Meaow," the cat said, speaking in cat jargon.

Even though they didn't speak the same tongue, Ann and the cat, as well as the other animals of the barnyard, understood each other when they spoke. They would now be talking more often with each other, since Ann was without human companionship.

Through no fault of her own, all her people friends had been ripped away, one after the other. The only friends she had left were her cousins, Cathy and Lank, and perhaps John. But was he still amongst the living? She didn't know, but she refused to believe otherwise.

After feeding and milking her goats the next morning, she cooked a pone of cornbread for herself and Fidgety. She still had some molasses in the small earthen crockpot, the remnants of what her father had given her for her part in helping with the harvesting of the lassey cane. She had been going skimpy on the servings of molasses, but this morning she poured on a generous portion and completely smother the piece of cornbread. She even dribbled some onto the cornbread in Fidgety's plate. "Now that I've got some money, I might as well use it for the things I need. I can buy more when this is gone," she said.

The cat answered with a long drawn out M-e-a-o-w!

Ann muddled through the day, doing mostly nothing other than sitting before the fire with Fidgety resting on her lap, but along about sundown she forced herself into a standing position and said, "Time to take care of my babies, Fidgety." And again, her cat answered with a loud "M-e-a-o-w!"

As Ann sat milking, Fidgety stationed herself on the fifth step of the loft stairs, moping the goat's milk from her nose and jaws with her front paws and licking them dry.

When she thought she heard footsteps outside, Ann stopped milking for a few seconds. She listened but heard nothing. But when she resumed her milking, A large hand suddenly seized her forehead and drew her head back into an awkward position, but she could see that the last joint of the little finger was missing from the hand. She felt something blunt pressing firmly against her back. She was sure it was the barrel of a pistol.

"Give me your gold or I'll put a hole through you," a voice she recognized from the day before demanded.

219

But before Ann fully realized what was happening, Fidgety sprang from the loft stairs with a hiss, attaching herself to his skull and clawing him across the face. He was caught by such surprise that he released his grip on Ann's head, dropped his pistol, and ran as fast as his legs would carry him down the road toward the creek.

Ann spun around on the milk stool, picked up the pistol, cocked it, and fired off a shot in his direction. The bullet struck a dead limb above his head, ricocheted, and plowed into the ground a few feet ahead of him. "Damn that witch!" he said, lunging ahead like a galloping horse.

Ann only got a glimpse of him as he vanished from sight, but she was able to see that he was not wearing a Confederate uniform, but was dressed in tattered clothing. His crumpled hat lay on the ground at her feet, flung aside when Fidgety made her daring leap. "Well Fidgety, you've done it again. I do b'leive you scared the devil out of that man," Ann said, laughing hysterically.

She laughed so hard that tears came to her eyes and the goat stopped eating and turned to have a looksee at what was happening. "Never mind, Precious, that fool's gone. Fidgety took care of him," she said, mopping her eyes on the sleeve of her black coat.

When she finished with the chores at the barn, she and Fidgety went back inside the shanty. She closed the door and pulled the drawstring inside.

"I s'pect I'd better hide these ten dollar gold pieces," she said. "That fool's liable to come back for another try, soon's he can find a washpot for his head."

But where could she hide them? At first she couldn't think of a safe place, but then she happened to think of her sewing basket and the ball of yarn she kept there for darning holes in her clothes. She would unwind some of the yarn, then rewind it with the gold coins clutched within its coils. After unwinding several turns from the ball of yarn, she accidentally dropped it onto the floor and it rolled beneath the bed. Fidgety pounced on it and chased it around the room as if she were chasing a mouse. Before Ann could stop her, she had left a trail of yarn all through the room, back and forth, 'round and around, under the chairs and around the bedpost, finally stopping beside Ann's chair.

"Thanks a whole heap, Fidgety!" she yelled. "Now I'll have to wind all this yarn back onto the ball!"

She took the gold coins from her pocket and began rewinding the yarn, concealing all but one in the ball of yarn. As the final few feet of yarn jaggered along the floor, Fidgety once again pounced on it, almost causing Ann to drop the ball again. "Stop that, Fidgety!" she yelled.

The cat sprang up onto the bed and lay there with a paw covering one eye. Through the other eye she peered at Ann as if waiting for an apology, but when no apology came, she rolled onto her back and closed her eyes.

Ann put the remaining gold coin into her change purse saying, "I'll go over to Bent Oak tomorrow and buy a few things that I've been needin' for a long time."

She slept the night away with the change purse tucked deep inside the pillowcase beneath her head. The loaded pistol lay within reach on the table beside the bed. And Fidgety? Well, she was curled up beneath Ann's chin like a big ball of fur. Their sleep was not disturbed because the intruder, for one reason or another, didn't return to reclaim the gold pieces.

As she walked through the door at Bent Oak the following morning, her dresstail caught on a splinter that was protruding from the corner of the potato bin just inside the door. She reached down to release her dresstail and overheard two men talking. One man was telling the other: "He'as wearin' old ragged clothes and ridin' a black stallion. Didn't have no hat on his head. Bought some rations and paid for 'em with a ten dollar gold piece, climbed up onto that horse and took off like a blue streak'a lightnin'. Said somethin' about gettin' outa this here hell hole of witches and black cats and crazy people. Looked like he'd been tangled up in a briar patch, 'cause he had scratches all over his face."

"How'er you, Miz Shepherd? Cool morning, huh?" the proprieter said, propping on his elbows at the counter. "Got another letter for you here in the mail basket."

"Who is it from?" Ann asked, rushing up to the counter to accept the letter.

"Looks like it's from that same feller that wrote you the last time," he said, looking at it closely as if searching for fingerprints.

"Well bless my soul if it ain't. Wonder what he's up to?" Ann said, sliding the letter into her coat pocket.

After buying the things she needed, she threw the bag of stuff over her shoulder and struck out down the road, her walking stick clicking as it struck the frozen ground. The sun was almost overhead by this time and the places where the roadbed was exposed to the sun were beginning to thaw. Ann chose to walk in the shaded areas to avoid the red mud of the thawed ground.

She was a fast walker and in a short time she was nearing Ann Ridge. As she walked up the hill toward the shanty, she could hear the crowing of her little game rooster, perched in the hemlock tree out near

221

the barn. Her sheep and goats were bleating, as they peered at her through the openings between the logs. "All's well," she said to herself. "Thank goodness, all's well."

She hurried inside, anxious to read the letter. She stirred the fire in the fireplace and threw on a couple of sticks of oak wood, sat down in the straight chair near the hearth, and with John's pearl handle knife she opened the letter.

"My dear Ann Shepherd," the letter began. "Was so good to hear from you, but saddened to hear about John, but then gladdened to know you hold out hope that he may still be amongst the living. And who would know but God Almighty. A lot of men have died, but some have survived and that's for sure. It's been unbearably cold in these trenches this winter with cannon balls whizzing over our heads, aimed at Petersburg. But spring can't be far away. I saw a flock of geese, just today, on their way north. I could hear them honking over the noise of the guns. You didn't say in your letter how you were doing, but I trust you are well. If you should hear from John, be sure to write me and let me know. I will be waiting for your letter. P.S. Were there many chestnuts this year?"

The letter was signed, "Your friend, Sam Worley."

"How on earth could he know about the chestnuts?" Ann questioned. "John must have told him," she reasoned, as she folded the letter, put it back into the envelop and into her pocket.

The next few weeks were consumed with Ann visiting with her cousins, Lank, Cathy and Cathy's baby, Mary Ann, and vice versa.

She looked forward to spring. Perhaps it would bring about a change in her life. At the least, she could get outside in the little garden spot and plant some potatoes, corn, beans, and the likes of that.

As February rolled into March, the wind picked up and dried the ground, allowing her to spade up a space in the garden spot large enough to plant two rows of Irish potatoes. "A body's got to have taters," she said to herself, as she pulled the rich black earth onto the last hill.

"Why didn't you tell us you were gonna plant somethin'? We'd a been tickled to help you," Cathy said, sitting in the wagon with Mary Ann cradled in her arms, as Lank pulled to a stop there beside the garden spot.

"You scared me half to death, Cathy! I guess I was so busy plantin' these taters that I didn't hear you comin'," Ann said, straightening up and pressing a palm into the small part of her back. "This kind of work takes a bit of gettin' use to."

"I s'pose it does," Lank agreed.

222

Lank held the baby and held Cathy's hand as she dismounted and they all went inside, out of the wind.

"I got another letter from Sam Worley yesterday, Cathy. I just can't figger him out. In his last letter he asked about chestnuts. This time he asked about the goats, even mentioned their names, Precious and Gracious. Now, can you cipher that?"

"Strange, real strange," Cathy said, staring through a hole in the ceiling. She could see blue sky through the opening in the roof, where a shingle had blown away during the brisk March wind. "You've got a hole in your roof, Ann," she said.

"I know, Cathy. I aim to fix it, but I ain't got around to it yet," Ann said, scratching her head. "John left spare shingles out there in the barn. And there's nails out there, too, if I may say so."

"I'll fix 'at hole for you, Ann. I may be a cripple, but I can fix a roof any day," Lank said, flexing his right arm as one would do in driving a nail. "Where's your ladder?"

"Out there in the barn," Ann said, smiling for the first time in quite a while.

"Spring's gonna bring a change, Cathy. I can just feel it," Ann said, as she reached over to touch the baby's nose with the tip of her forefinger.

"I agree, Cousin Ann, and I'm ready for a change. If this hateful war'd come to an end that'ud be a change we could live with."

# Chapter

# 12

## The War Continues

The end of the war was nowhere in sight, and things were getting tougher each day for the Confederate soldiers, stranded in the muddy trenches near Petersburg. Sixty thousand Confederate soldiers had simply walked away and gone home, but John was still there, along with his comrades, choosing to stay and fight to the bitter end. Their lines were stretched to their limits and beyond, and while the Confederate Army was diminishing by the thousands, the Federal Army grew steadily stronger.

The Confederacy was in peril, not only in the north, but in the south as well, for it was at this time that Sherman was ploughing through the south with his hundred thousand man army, laying waste to everything that stood in his way, setting plantation homes ablaze and sharecropper's houses as well, leaving widows and orphans to the mercies of the elements, with little or nothing to eat.

"Granny, why'er they doin' this to us?" Mamie Siler's six-year old grandson asked, as he stumbled along the heavily trodden road with tears streaming down his mottled face.

"To learn us a lesson I reckon, Child, but it looks like we're gonna lose ever thang before we learn it," his grandmother answered.

She reached back and took the lad by the hand and led him down the path toward a demolished farm house. Jeb was hungry, for he hadn't had a bite to eat since yesterday. "Let's see if we can find somethin' to eat here't this house. Maybe they've left a scrap er two," Granny Siler said.

"Sure hope so, Granny, 'cause I'm plenty hungry," Jeb said, as he struggled to keep up with his grandmother.

"Well looky here, Child, they's a cellar to this here house and it's locked up tighter'n th county jail. I bet there's stuff to eat down there," Mamie said, as she walked over to the wood pile and picked up the go-devil. "I'll break the lock off a this here door and we'll see what we can find."

She hefted the go-devil by its hickory handle and with one glancing blow, sent the lock tumbling. "Now, let's see what we can find," she said, as she swept the cobwebs aside and entered the damp and dark cellar. As her eyes adjusted to the darkness she noticed a bin of Irish potatoes on one side and a bin of sweet potatoes on the other. A wide oak board shelf was loaded with jars of preserves, string beans, and tomatoes. "Would you look at this, Child? They's enough stuff here to feed us for weeks to come," she said, as she picked up a sweet potato and handed it to her grandson.

"It sure is sweet, Granny," Jeb said, chomping down on the potato like a horse eating corn.

"They'll taste better roasted, Child."

"Can't get much better'n 'is, Granny," he said, chewing on the sweet potato.

"And would you just look at this?" Granny Siler said, pointing to a tin pail at one end of the shelf. "I bet they's lard in that bucket."

Sure enough, when she removed the lid, the smell of hog lard filled the cellar. "Like you say, Child, it can't get much better'n 'is."

Granny Siler kept the cellar door hidden with brush while she and her grandson made it their home. "We'll stay here till the grub runs out or the owner comes back and runs us off," she said.

ᘉᘉᘉᘉᘉᘉᘉᘉᘉᘉᘉᘉᘉ

Confederate commander, Joseph E. Johnston, made an attempt to stop Sherman's advance at Bennetville, North Carolina, but with only twenty thousand men compared to Shermnan's hundred thousand, made the attempt impossibile.

So Sherman continued to reek havoc on the citizens of North Carolina, as he led his army north toward Virginia to lend support to General Grant at Petersburg, which was still under siege.

With Lee's army dwindling, his defences at Petersburg were on the verge of collapse.

Grant and Lee had faced each other in front of Petersburg for nine long months. Grant extended his lines slowly and steadily to the left. Lee's lines had been forced to stretch, too, but with his army shrinking, it was becoming impossible for his tired and tattered soldiers to hold the line.

Lee, standing near the earthworks, very sparsely occupied by his soldiers, said to his aide, "It has happened as I told them in Richmond it would. The line has been stretched until it is broken. Our only hope now is to move our men safely out of the trenches and to the southwest where we can join up with Johnston in the hills of North Carolina."

But Grant was making every effort to keep him from doing so.

Lee moved first by directing Gordon to make a sudden night assault, which briefly won possession of the earthworks at Fort Steadman, but superior Union firepower quickly drove them off.

Grant counterattacked by sending Sheriden with two infantry corps and twelve thousand cavalry around Lee's flank in an effort to block his exit at the crossroads called Five Forks.

Union soldiers could smell victory and began to fight with a vengeance. On the first day of April, they routed the Confederate division under George Pickett, taking forty-five hundred prisioners. The Confederate soldiers seemed to have no commanders and no orders. They scattered helter skelter, looking for a guiding hand, but found none. Another volley, a new charge by Union soldiers, then with a sullen and tearful impulse, the Confederate soldiers flung their muskets to the ground and surrendered.

When Grant got word of their surrender he simply said, "All right," then ordered an all out attack to begin at four-thirty the next morning, all along the Petersburg line. Relentless in their efforts, Union soldiers drove the Confederates from their trenches, leaving old men and boys as young as fourteen lying dead.

Lee sent a message to Jefferson Davis saying, "My lines are broken in three places. Richmond must be evacuated this evening."

Jefferson Davis was attending a Sunday service at Saint Pauls Episcopal Church in Richmond. His wife and children had already left the city for safe haven farther south. The sexton handed the message to Davis, and as he began to read it, he took on a ghostly appearance as the blood drained from his face. He hurried from the church and ordered that his government be moved to Danville, about one hundred and forty miles to the south. He took only a few belongings with him. He entrusted the heroic marble bust of himself to a slave, instructing him to hide it from the Yankees, so that he would not to be ridiculed.

The Confederate Government was loaded onto a series of freight cars, with each bravely labeled "Treasury Department," "Quartermaster Department," and "War Department." The President and his cabinet boarded last and the train pulled away. One elderly man watching as it passed said, "It's a government on wheels."

As the Union columns entered Petersburg, Lee's army slipped across the Appomattox and headed west, with Union troops at their heels in hot pursuit.

Richmond was in chaos, for much of the city had been set ablaze by retreating Confederates.

On the third day of April, Abraham Lincoln and his son, Tad, arrived at Rockett's Warft aboard a small barge. "Thank God I have lived to see this," Lincoln said. It had seemed to him that he had been dreaming a horrible nightmare for four long years, but now it looked as if the nightmare was over.

Blacks mobbed him, straining to touch his hand. They were laughing, singing, and weeping with joy. Kneeling before him, one man said, "I know I am free, for I have seen Father Abraham and felt him."

ꔷꔷꔷꔷꔷꔷꔷꔷꔷꔷꔷꔷꔷ

Lee moved his exhausted army west, with the Federals in constant pursuit. His first objective was Amelia Court House where he had asked the Commissary Department to have ready for him the hundreds of thousands of rations his men would need if they were to fight on.

Hour after hour in an almost continous battle, the lines were alternately forming, fighting, and retreating. A boy soldier came running as fast as his legs would carry him and was asked by a reporter, who was there to cover the retreat, why he was running and his answer was simply, "I'm running 'cause I can't fly!"

Lee did his best to keep his tired and hungry soldier's spirits up, riding slowly along the line of tangled wagons and faltering men. He rode erect, showing no signs of fatigue. From the way he carried himself no one would have conceived that he so well knew that his army was evaporating and his supplies were almost gone. He could hear his own stomach rumbling, and when he thought of how tired and hungry his foot soldiers must be, his eyes moistened with tears and he felt as though a horse had kicked him in the chest. "Poor lads," he thought to himself.

John Shepherd was one of those tired and hungry soldiers, stumbling along, trying as best he could to keep his footing. The words of his father ricocheted through his brain like the squeaky wheel on the wagon he was trailing. He remembered telling his father about hearing men talking at the saw mill, where he had gone to buy lumber, that men were now being drafted to fight in the war. He remembered telling his father, "I don't want to go, but if they draft me, I guess I'm duty bound to go."

His father's words were: "Yeah, Son, you're duty bound if you're called."

"Duty bound. Duty bound. Duty bound." echoed through his brain. Somehow, it kept him from collapsing onto the ground from sheer exhaustion.

When Lee's hungry army finally reached Amelia Court House on the third of April they were sorely disappointed, for there was not a single ration of food stored there. For one reason or another, Lee's request had never reached the commissary officials, and when he sent foragers out through the Virginia countryside to beg farmers for whatever food they could spare, they returned with practically nothing.

◻◻◻◻◻◻◻◻◻◻◻◻◻◻

On the fourth day of April, Jefferson Davis had arrived in Danville, and though he was ready to flee farther south, he made a bold statement: "No peace will ever be made with the infamous invaders. Our army will fight on. We will now be able to move freely from place to place, and not having to guard cities, nothing will stand in the way of our triumph."

But even as he spoke, one hundred and twenty-five thousand Federal troops were closing in from three sides on Lee's withering army of twenty-five thousand, as they continued their staggering retreat westward. Tired and hungry, they sustained themselves on handfulls of corn, originally meant for the horses. The pursuing Union soldiers were hungry, too, but not because they had no food, but from their eagerness to be in on the kill, they had pushed far ahead of their supply wagons.

Lee's army staggered on, willing to follow their great commander to the end of the world if necessary. But as the day wore on his army began to diminish even further as some famished soldiers left the line of march to search for food, while others simply slipped away to surrender, leaving weapons and bedrolls in their wake.

It is said that a Union soldier came upon a ragged southerner, cooling his feet in a stream. He didn't even look up when the Union soldier said, "I've got you this time!"

"Yes," said the Confederate soldier, "you've got me and a helluva git you've got."

Tired and hungry as their men, commanders allowed their lines to become broken and as they approached a place called Sylers Creek, the Union Army took full advantage of the opportunity and attacked.

Lee's starving men fought with special desperation against all odds. In the heat of battle they killed their opponents with bayonets and with the buts of their muskets. Crazed from hunger and exhaustion,

229

they rolled on the ground like beasts, biting each other's throats and ears and noses. One young Confederate soldier placed the muzzle of his musket to the back of his best friend's head, thinking him to be a Union soldier because he was wearing a Yankee coat, and pulled the trigger.

When darkness set in, Lee and what was left of his army slipped away and headed even farther west. About eight thousand of his men, a third of his army, were missing or had been taken prisoner, but John was not one of them. He and his comrades summoned all the strength left in their bodies as they struggled to stay up with their commander.

ⵔⵔⵔⵔⵔⵔⵔⵔⵔⵔⵔⵔⵔ

Phil Sheridan wired a message to Grant which read: "If this thing be pressed, I think Lee will surrender."

Grant relayed the message to Lincoln and his response was: "Let the thing be pressed."

In the evening of the seventh day of April, General Lee received a message from General Grant saying: "The result of last week must convince you of the hopelessness of future resistance. I regard it as my duty to shift from myself the responsibility of any further effusion of blood by asking you to surrender that portion of the Confederate States Army, known as The Army of Northern Virginia."

One of Lee's officers, after hearing the message read, urged his commander to surrender.

General Lee bristled and asked, "What will the country think of me if I fail to fight on?"

His officer's response was: "Country be dammed! There is no country! There has been no country for a year or more!" Then lowering his voice a bit said, "Sir, you're the country to these men."

ⵔⵔⵔⵔⵔⵔⵔⵔⵔⵔⵔⵔⵔ

As the Confederate Army moved slowly onward, roughly parallel to Appomattox River, Sheridan again flanked Lee's army and captured two trainloads of supplies at Appomattox Station. This brought to an end any hope for food or supplies for Lee's army.

At nightfall, Lee and his weary lieutenants gathered at Lee's headquarters around a small campfire in the woods near Appomattox Court House. There was no tent, there were no chairs, and no camp stools. They sat on blankets or on saddles at the roots of trees, to once again listen to further instruction from their great commander. "We are

230

almost entirely surrounded," Lee told his lieutenants. "We are outnumbered four to one, and as you well know, after loosing those two trainloads of sypplies at Appomattox Court House, our chances of receiving more supplies are slim to none."

Even with only two hundred and fifty men left in one of his divisions, Lee was ready to face about and fight. The few men who still carried their muskets had hardly the appearance of soldiers. Their clothes were tattered and covered with mud. Their eyes were sunken and lusterless, yet there they were, ready at a moment's notice from their commander to turnabout and fight.

Lee's first instinct was to do just that, "I'll strike that man a blow in the morning," he said.

The next day was Palm Sunday. At dawn, just outside Appomattox Court House, Gordon's men drove Federal cavalry from their positions and swept forward to the crest of the hill, but there they halted, for below them a solid wall of blue was advancing, the entire Union Army of Saint James. Lee couldn't go forward, he couldn't go backward, and he couldn't go sideways. He knew it was over. The North had nearly a million men under arms. The South had fewer than a hundred thousand. "There is only one thing left for me to do," he told his aids, "and that is to go and see General Grant, but I had rather die a thousand deaths."

"What will history have to say of your surrendering your army in the field," a tearful aide asked him.

"Hard things," Lee answered. "But that is not the question, colonel. The question is, is it right to surrender this army? If it is right, then I will take all the responsibility."

When John got word of a possible surrender he said to himself, "What'll I do when this here war's over? I can't go home to Ann. Me, with this old scared up face and the bottoms of my ears burned off! I can't do that. I just can't! "

"What did you say, John?" Sam Worley, his buddy asked.

"Ah, nothing!" John snapped. "Just nothing!"

"Didn't sound like nothing to me!" Sam snapped back at him.

"Just thinking out loud," John said. "Think nothing of it."

# Chapter

# 13

## General Lee Surrenders

It was approaching noon when Lee sent a rider, along with a note, into the Union lines carrying a white flag, actually it was a white towel. General Grant and some of his officers were resting in a field when a horseman came galloping up behind them at full speed. The horseman was waving his hat above his head and shouting at every gallop, "A message from General Lee! A message from General Lee!"

Grant read the message to himself, then handed it to his friend, General John Rallins and asked him to read it aloud: "I, General Lee, will order my soldiers to surrender."

Word is that none of Grant's fellow officers looked their commander in the face, but finally after a moment, Colonel Duff, Chief of The Artilery, stood upon a log and proposed three cheers. A feeble hurrah came from the throats of a few of the men, then all broke down and cried.

Grant said nothing and showed no emotion at all. He had been suffering with a terrible headache, but upon receiving the message from Lee, his headache went away.

Lee sent Colonel John Marshall to Appomattox Court House to select a suitable building where he and Grant might meet. Colonel Marshall arrived to find the streets almost deserted, but it just so happened that Wilmer McLean was out for his daily stroll. When he saw the Colonel approaching he ducked out of sight around the corner of a building. "Sir! Sir! A word with you, please. I am here under orders of General Lee," Colonel Marshall yelled.

Wilmer McLean wanted nothing more to do with this war, for he had seen the first battle of Bull Run fought across his front yard and had moved far away to a quiet place where he would not have to experience a thing like that again. But here he was, and it looked as if the war had found him again. "Sir, I am here under orders of General Lee. I am here to find a suitable building where he and General Grant can meet. Lee is prepared to surrender," Colonel Marshall announced.

McLean was reluctant at first, but when he heard the word, "surrender," he perked up and said, "I came to this place to escape the war, but I will be pleased to offer my house as a meeting place if it will bring an end to this bloody conflict. Lee and Grant may use my parlor if they wish."

General Lee looked magnificent in his crisp gray uniform. His engraved sword hung at his side. "I am probably to be the general's prisoner," he explained to an aide as he prepared to mount his gray horse, Traveler. "I think I must make my best appearance."

"You look stunning, Sir!" the aide extolled, gazing at his commander through eyes moistened with tears.

Lee waited patiently at the McLean house for half an hour before Grant arrived.

When General Grant finally showed up, he was wearing a privates dirty shirt. His boots and trousers were spattered with mud and he carried no sword.

When General Grant enter the room, Lee rose to his feet and stood at attention and the two men shook hands. General Lee, being a man of great dignity and with impassible face, was able to conceal his feelings entirely.

Even though Lee was able to hide his feelings, Grant knew his opponent was in tremendous stress, so he did his best to ease the tention by reminding Lee of their meeting once before during the Mexican war. "I haven't been able to remember what you looked like, Sir," Lee said.

The conversation between the two of them grew so pleasant that one would have thought they were two old friends, getting together for a visit, until Lee finally reminded Grant of the reason for their meeting.

"Oh, I'm sorry, General, I guess I got carried away," Grant said. "Well here are my terms. Your officers will be allowed to keep their side arms and personal belongings. Officers and men who claim ownership to their horses may keep them as well. Officers and enlisted men will be allowed to return to their homes. They are not to be disturbed by the United States Authorities."

"Thank you, Sir, you are very kind," Lee said.

General Grant asked Lee how many men were in his army and if they were hungry.

"I no longer know the number, but I am sure they are hungry," General Lee answered.

Grant sent word to the quartermaster to make ready 25,000 rations for Lee's men. "This will have the best possible effect upon my men," Lee said. "It will do much toward conciliating our people."

Colonel Eli Parker, a Seneca Indian on Grant's staff, inscribed the articles of surrender. After the articles of surrender were signed, the two men shook hands again. Lee left the house first, mounted Traveler, and headed back toward his defeated army to share with them the conditions of the surrender.

"I am so sad and depressed at the downfall of my foe. He has fought so valiantly and suffered so much for the cause, but I do believe that cause is one of the worst for which men have ever fought," Grant told one of his fellow officers as he watched Lee ride away.

Union soldiers began to cheer and Federal artillery started to fire salutes. General Grant ordered them to stop, saying, "The Rebels are our prisioners now and we do not want to exult over their downfall. The war is over. They are our countrymen again."

As he approached his camp, Lee allowed the horse's reins to hang loose. His chin seemed to be resting on his chest. When his men began to cheer, he removed his hat and held it in his hand. His face was flush and his eyes were like burning coals. It is said that his men looked upon him with swimming eyes. They closed in so tightly on each side of the path that led to his camp, until there was bearly enough room for the horse and rider to pass. Those who were not so overcome with grief that they were unable to speak, said goodbye. Those who could not find voice, let their hands glide gently along Traveler's flanks. Each group of soldiers, as their great commander passed by, began in the same way with sobs, all the way to his tent. Grim bearded men threw themselves upon the ground. They covered their faces with their hands and cried like children. Even the officers, sitting upon their horses, cried aloud. One old soldier balancing on one knee cried out, "I love you just as well as ever, General."

John Shepherd cried as vememently as the rest of his comrades, for he had not only lost the war, but he had lost the ability to return home to Ann as a whole man. "What am I supposed to do now?" he asked himself.

A crowd of weeping soldiers were waiting in front of Lee's tent when he rode up and dismounted. "Men," Lee said, "I have done my best for you. You are now free to return to your homes, and if you become as good citizens as you have been soldiers, you will not fail. I shall always be proud of you. Goodbye and may God bless you."

Lee opened the flaps to his tent and went inside. "It's all over," he thought to himself.

One of Lee's officers explained the terms of surrender to the soldiers, and after they had received food and rations, the saddened soldiers dispersed and struck out for home.

John seemed in no hurry to leave. He was caught up in the dilemma of wheather to go home to Ann and face the possibility of rejection, because of his tortured appearance, or to settle in the hills of Virginia and start a new life for himself.

"Thought you would have been long gone by now, John."

"Well, same to you, Sam Worley. Why are you still hangin' around here. You've been waitin' for this day for a lifetime it seems," John snapped back at him.

"Just concerned about you, John. I think you've got it all wrong about what your wife will think of your appearance. After all, it's the whole you that she married, not just your face. Besides, you've got all those scars covered and who's to know as long as you keep that beard? Nobody! Come on, I'll walk with you. My home's in Danville. Danville's in the lower edge of Virginia, on the North Carolina border."

"Well if you're so all fired anxious, let's go," John said, reaching down to pick up his bed roll and knapsack.

From the campsite near Appomattox Court House, they headed west toward Lynchburg, but turned south a little shy of Lynchburg on the road that would eventually lead them to Danville. Sam picked up a musket and some ammunition that had been tossed aside by a retreating Confederate soldier. "We may need this for our protection and it's possible we could run up on some wild game along the way, as well," Sam said, balancing the musket on his shoulder.

John should have been happy to be heading home, and happy that the war finally over, but he was so tortured with indecision as to wheather to return home or to settle some place in the hills of Virginia, he couldn't muster a single smile. Chin down, he watched the road pass beneath his feet. He walked at an uneven stride because the sole of one of his shoes had come loose, causing him to lift that foot higher, so as not to trip on the flapping sole. Yet, even with all the torture of indecision, thoughts of Ann crowded his mind. "She's bound to think I'm dead by now," he mumbled to himself.

"Come on, John. We've got a long road ahead of us," Sam said, looking back over his shoulder.

☒☒☒☒☒☒☒☒☒☒☒☒☒

"This horrible war is finally over, and if my man's still alive, he'll be coming home," Ann said to Cathy, as they sat on the little porch, listening to the cackling hens, out passed the barn.

Britton Creek was lapping at her banks from the heavy rain that had fallen the night before. Birds were singing in the meadow. Crows were pairing up and selecting their nesting places.

Precious and Gracious were peeking through the openings between the logs of their stalls, bleating for attention. "I hear you, babies. I'll be right there," Ann said, handing the baby back to her mother.

Yes, and I'd better be getting home. My bother'll be chomping at the bits for something to eat," Cathy said.

She folded the blanket around the baby and placed her on the straw in the wagon bed. She waved goodbye to Ann, tapped the mule with the reins, and away they went.

Ann watched Cathy until she went out of sight, then went inside the shanty to fetch the milk bucket. The goats were still bleating as she made her way out to the barn. As she sat milking one of her goats, she heard someone coming up the road on horseback. She turned around on the milk stool to see who it was, but she didn't recognize the man in the saddle. "Morning, Maam. How might you be this fine morning?" the man in the saddle said.

"I'm fine, but who're you? And what might you be doing out in these parts this early in the day?"

"Heard they was a widder woman livin' out in these parts. Her man got hisself killed up 'ere som'ers near Petersburg, Virginia. So I figgered I'd come out and pay her a visit."

"Well, I'm not a widow. My man'll be coming home in a few days," Ann answered, with a certain sternness in her voice.

"That ain't what I've heard. If you're Ann Shepherd, your man's been dead for some time."

"I've never been notified by any official of his death, and until I do, I'll continue to believe that he's still alive."

"I heard they's a nigger come by here some time ago and told you personal that your man had got hisself killed."

"You'd better watch who you're calling nigger, if you want to stay able to sit upright in that saddle. Besides, he was my husband's good friend. Knew him since he was a boy," Ann said, now showing a tinge of anger in her face.

"Can't blame a man for lookin', but since we have nothin' to talk about, I'll be on my way. No need to waste my time around here," the man in the saddle said, turning his horse about and gouging him in the ribs with his spurs.

"Go, and good riddance!" Ann shouted, as the horse galloped away, carrying the man out of sight and out of hearing. "Am I gonna have to fight off ever' fool and deserter in these parts till my man gets home?" she asked herself.

It seemed as if that was going to be the case, for she was approached many times after that day. It was humiliating to her, for she was interested in no man other than her husband.

"Wiggens could have been wrong about John," she said to herself. "After all he didn't see him dead. Did he? No!"

ⅨⅨⅨⅨⅨⅨⅨⅨⅨⅨⅨⅨⅨ

Two men talked in hushed conversation as they sat on the wooden bench in front of Bent Oak Trading Post. They kept their voices low and paused when anyone came within earshot. "I've come up with a fine plan," the man in the trench coat said to the man sitting beside him.

"And what might that fine plan be," his friend asked.

"You see that woman right there?" the man in the trench coat said, pointing toward Ann, who had just stepped up onto the loading dock and was about to enter the store.

"Yeah. So what?"

"She's a widow woman. She owns a good piece of land and a nice little shanty over there at the foot of the mountain. I got it from a good source that her man got hisself killed up there in Virginia som'ers. Got blowed up in some kind of explosion, 'cept she won't own up to it till, as she puts it, till she gets word from some kind of an official.

"Well, what's your plan?"

"Hold your tater and I'll tell you." The man in the trench coat said, becoming a bit antsy. "I'm that official, or so she'll think. Got a paper right here in my pocket, all fancy and legal looking."

The document read: "Mrs. John Shepherd, I am sorry to inform you that your husband was killed on the 30th day of July, 1864. Nothing was found of his remains." It was signed: "Bureau of Vital Statistics of The Confederate Army."

"What good will that piece of paper do to convince her that her man's dead?"

"Oh, it will. Just you wait and see. I'm heading for a free ride. I'll have it made for as long as I have a mind to."

"I hope you know what you're doing," the friend said, shrugging his shoulders.

"Shush. Here she comes now," the man in the trench coat said, as Ann stepped out onto the loading dock.

"Maam, might your name be Ann Shepherd? And was your

238

husband John Shepherd?"

"What do you mean by 'was' my husband John Shepherd?" As far as I know he's still alive," Ann said, as her face turned two shades of purple.

"I'm sorry, Maam, but I have a document from The Bureau of Vital Statistics of The Confederate Army. Let me read it to you if I may: Mrs. John Shepherd, I am sorry to inform you that your husband was killed on the thirtieth day of July, eighteen sixty-four. Nothing was found of his remains. Signed: Bureau of Vital Statistics of The Confeaerate Army."

"Let me see that document. I can read, or didn't you know?"

Ann snatched the fake document from the man's hand and began reading it for herself. Her hands trembled and tears filled her eyes and trickeled down her cheeks as she read the message and mulled over it for a few moments. "I didn't want to believe it. I just couldn't believe it. I wouldn't believe it, but now I suppose I must," she said, thumbing the tears from her eyes.

"Maam, would you let me see you to your home? You're in no shape to go it alone," the man in the trench coat said, laying his heavy arm around her shoulders.

"No!" Ann said, flinging his arm aside and stepping backward, almost tripping over a keg of nails.

"Are you sure? I have a big horse. I'd be obliged to transport you if you'd let me."

"No thank you! No, I know what grief is. I've had more'n my share. I'll make it on my own," Ann said, stepping off the loading dock and striking out for home.

"I'll call on you tomorrow to make sure all is well," the man in the trench coat hollered to her as she walked swiftly down the road.

Ann didn't look back or respond to his statement in any way. It was as if she hadn't heard him at all. "If he comes, I'll take care of him like I did all them other fools," she said to herself, as she walked swiftly down the road.

Early the next morning she was jarred awake by a loud knock at the door. Fidgety sprang into a rigid defensive stance at the foot of the bed. Her back was arched. Her legs were straight as a poker and the hair on her back was standing stiff as the bristles on a porcupine.

Ann slipped her feet into her scuffs and eased over to the tiny window and peeped out between the curtains. There, standing bold as the cliffs on Wildcat Spurr, was the man in the trench coat. "He's got some nerve, waking me this early in the morning," she thought.

"Who is it?" she asked.

"I'm an agent from The Bureau of Vital Statistics of The Confederate Army."

"Well, why are you out here at this ungodly hour, rousting me from my sleep?"

"Just concerned about you, Maam. You seemed so upset after you read the government statement yesterday," the man outside the door answered.

"I thought I made it clear to you that I could take care of myself. I've been doing it all my life and I can still can!"

"Just open the door and let me speak with you for a moment. Maybe I can be of some comfort to you," the man outside the door said.

Ann pulled the front of her nightgown together and lifted the wooden latch on the door. "Well, If you're so determined, come on in, but mind you, you'd better steer clear of my cat. She's a mite riled and she don't take kindly to strangers,"

"I'm not here to harm nobody," the man said, keeping a wary eye on the cat.

"Have you had breakfast?" Ann asked.

"No, Maam, but I don't want to be a bother to you."

"I'll make a flapjack and fry a couple of eggs. That won't be no bother since I have to cook anyway. Do you drink goat milk?"

"Never drank goat's milk in my whole life, Maam, but I guess this is a good place to start."

The man sat rigid as a dead oak stump, eyeing Fidgety, as Ann went about fixing something to eat.

"Well, here it is, such as it is, Mister. Not much of a choice these days since stuff's so hard to come by."

"I was just thinking, Maam, if you had a man around here, how much help he'd be to you."

"Mister, I think there's been enough said about that. I told you that I could take care of myself, and I can. So slide up to the table and eat your breakfast so you can be on your way."

The 'government' man moved over to the table, making sure the cat was kept in full view, while she gave him her full attention. "That cat gives me the jitters, Maam. Is there no place else it can be?"

"This is her home, Sir, she belongs here."

After taking a bite of egg and sopping the runny yolk with a piece of flapjack, the man took a swig of goat milk from the tin cup, smacked his lips and said, "This here milk's good. I think I'm gonna learn to like it."

As he enjoyed his breakfast the watchful eye of the cat was washed completely from his mind. He began to relax and to set in motion his plan for the day. "Looks like you've already planted something in your garden. Now, if you just had a man around here to help you do stuff, he could plant that garden for you."

With John strongly on her mind, Ann thought how nice it would be to have him here to help her. "Yeah it would," she said. "I mean it would be nice to have my husband, John, here to do things for me, but not some rank stranger."

"Now, Ann, don't you think it's about time to let John go the way of the heroes? After all, he went off to fight and die so you could be free to enjoy this little piece of God's earth."

"I'm sure he's more than willing to fight for the cause," Ann said, "but I feel sure he's not so all fired anxious to die. I'm sure he's looking forward to coming home when this awful war is over. You say he's dead, but after giving it some thought, I believe he's still alive. In a dream last night I saw him, plain as day, stepping up onto the porch."

"You can't live in a dream all your life, Ann. It's time for you to wake up and enjoy the daylight," the 'government' man said, sideling over to where she stood washing the breakfast dishes.

Before she realized what was happening he had her caged in his big bulky arms. As she struggled to free herself, he said, "Don't fight it, Ann. You know you've been needin' a man for a long time."

She tried to bite his arm, but couldn't because of his thick trench coat. He wrestled her over to the bed and threw her down upon it, pinning her arms behind her back. "Either you give in or I'll take what's mine to have," he said, as she kicked and squirmed, attempting to free herself from his grip.

In a flash Fidgity flung herself upon him. She clawed her way up his back and settled down upon his head, taking on the appearance of a skullcap. She dug her claws into his cheeks, clamped her canines onto his nose and held on as tight as the jaws of a steel-trap.

The 'government' man was so caught off guard by the sudden attack that he leapt to his feet and grasped the cat's tail in an attempt to remove her from his head. The cat took a chunk from his nose when she was yanked away. Blood streamed from the scratches on his cheeks and from the gapping hole at the end of his nose.

His 'fine plan' went the way of the wind as he stumbled to the door and made his way outside, clamping his bloody nose between his thumb and forefinger. "She's a witch! She's a witch! She's a witch for sure!" he said, as he struggled to mount his horse. "She's a witch if I ever saw one!"

He kicked the horse in the ribs and in one flying leap they were on their way down the road, and were soon out of sight.

"Fidgety, you never fail me when I need you. I don't know what I'd do without you," Ann said, sitting on the edge of the bed.

"Meaow," the cat's replied.

Ann sat for a moment, mulling over what had just happened.

The bleating of the goats, Precious and Gracious, reminded her that she had other things to think about. "I—hear—you—babies." She said, taking a deep breath between each word. "I'll be right there."

It was about three in the afternoon when the man in the trenchcoat arrived at Bent Oak Trading Post. He had bandages on each cheek and a bloody bandage on his nose. His trenchcoat had blood spatters all down the front. "How did that fine plan of yours work out?" his friend asked him.

"Never you mind how my plan worked out. My horse spooked and took out through a thorn thicket and you can see what it's done to my face. Never got to check on that woman. Don't know as I want to. They say she's some kind of a witch, anyway. Never be able to get a thing out of her. She's too crazy for that. And that cat of her's, she's a devil for sure."

"Well what do you plan to do now?" his friend asked.

"Plan to buy a few things here at the post and head farther south, where I can find somebody who'll listen to me."

After buying supplies, he and his friend saddled up and rode away. They didn't even look back.

ꖦꖦꖦꖦꖦꖦꖦꖦꖦꖦ

"Look at what I've found here, John," Sam Worley said, lifting a pair of shoes high above his head. "Looks to be just your size, too. Luck is on your side. Looks like somebody left these shoes here, right where we could find 'em."

"Let me see them shoes, Sam. I'm tired of walking like a broken down old mule, with a hobble tied to his front leg."

John sat down on a chestnut log beside the road and slipped the sole flopping shoe from his foot. He brushed the dirt away and examined the bruise on the ball of his foot and slid his foot into the shoe. It was a perfect fit and so was the other one. After tieing the laces, he stood up and found them to be very comfortable. "It's pure luck alright," he said, smiling for the first time since before he left Ann Ridge to go off to the war.

They were nearing the end of their first day's journey when they passed through the little town of Lynch, Virginia. Only a short distance beyond Lynch, they came to a crossroads. "This is where we part company, Sam," John said. "I'm going by Roanoke. This road'll take me there and It's the best way home."

"Thought you weren't so sure you were ready to go home, John," Sam said, looking surprised.

"This is the way I went the last time. Besides, I know some folks who live out that way." John said.

"If you know some folks out that way, just who might they be?" Sam asked, in an unbelieving tone of voice.

"Lum and Lailer Luger, that's who. Lum let me borrow his big black stallion on my last trip home."

"Reckon he'll let you borrow it again?" Sam asked.

"P'raps not, since this'll be my last trip," John answered.

"There you go again, John Shepherd. Sounds like you're going home for sure."

"We'll see, Sam. We'll see."

They sat on the bank of Goose Creek and downed a piece of beef jerky before going their separate ways. After saying goodbye to each other, John headed west toward Roanoke and Sam took the south road that leads to Danville.

"So long, Sam. See you in that next war," John said, walking easier now in his better pair of shoes.

"With luck, we won't have another war," Sam said, eyeing John as he went out of sight over the crest of the hill.

With the weight of the war now off his shoulders, John felt a great sense of relief, but the fear of Ann's rejection, because of his battle scars, still troubled him. "Could she ever love me again, me with this old scared up face?"

That same old question plucked the strings of his vocal cords over and over as he made his way west, facing into the evening sun.

As the sun was about to disappear behind the Blue Ridge Mountains, he came to a place that looked familliar. "That's the Luger place right there," he said to himself.

He decided to drop in for a visit. His heart skipped a beat and began to race as he walked up the steps to the porch. He was just about to knock on the door when a woman's voice from inside said, "Who's out there!"

"It's me, John Shepherd. Remember me?"

The door creaked open on rusty hinges and the face of an old lady appeared in the opening. "Course I remember you, John. You stayed all night with Lum and me back in January of sixty three. Come on in here, Son. Lum's not doin' so well here lately. Hain't seed a well

243

day since our boy got hisself killed in the war."

"I'm so sorry to hear that, Maam. That leaves you and Lum all alone now, don't it?"

"Yeah, Son, and it's been mighty slim pickins for us for the last month or two. Run completely out of pork and what taters we have left in the cellar's sproutin' and shriveled so till you can't peel 'em. Been livin' on corn bread'n dried beans for the last several weeks. Hadn't a been for that, I guess we'd a starved."

"I'll get out tomorrow and see if I can't kill us a deer or at least get us some kind of meat," John said, as he followed Lailer through the house and into the bedroom, where the boney frame of Lum lay stretched out beneath an old handmade quilt.

"Well bless my bones, Son. I wuz gist thankin' about you this very mornin', wonderin' what'd come a you. Let me shake yer hand," Lum said, thrusting a trembling hand in his direction.

"Couldn't come this way without stopping for a visit. Your wife tells me you're a little under the weather here lately, but I'm sure it won't last long. With spring just around the corner, I feel sure you'll spring back into action in no time flat."

"Hain't felt right since I got word that my boy'd been killed in that damned war. Knocked the life clean out a me," Lum said.

"I sure can understand that, Sir. I've seen too many men killed in that awful war."

"Well, tell me about yeself, Boy. How'd you manage to come through the war without a single scratch on yer entire body!"

"I didn't, Lum. I got my face all scarred up in that explosion at Petersburg."

"I don't see no scars," Lum said.

"Me neither," Lalier spoke up.

"Can't see 'em through this beard," John was quick to say.

"Well law me, you could a got yeself killed, Son," Lum and Lalier spoke in unison.

"Come might nigh," John said, stroking his beard, happy that it had concealed his affliction.

"Got some dried beans simmerin' over the fire, John. Ain't much, but you're welcome to have some with us," Lalier said.

"It would be a pure delight, Maam. I ain't had no soup beans since that little wife a mine cooked a pot of 'em at our little shanty on Ann Ridge."

"How is she? You hain't said a word about her since you got here," Lalier said.

"Last letter I got from her said she just didn't know what life

244

would be worth without me."

"Well, I 'spect you're in a powerful hurry to get home," the Lugers said.

John told them that he couldn't decide wheather to go home or not, because he was afraid Ann would reject him. "I don't know how she'll feel about these scars," He said.

"Well, they ain't no reason to be afraid a that, Son. Long's you wear that beard nobody'll ever know," Lum said.

"Why no they won't," Lalier said, voicing her oppinion.

"You two have just about convinced me that there's nothing to worry about, but I'll hang around here long enough to get you back on your feet before I go. If I could kill a deer, that'd give you some meat for now and some dried venison for later. I'll even help you plant your corn and taters and stuff in the garden."

"That black stallion a mine ain't no draft horse. Wouldn't pull a plow if his life depended on it," Lum said. "But they's a feller lives down the road a piece. He's got one of the finest plow mules around these parts. I'm sure he'd let us borry it on the days he wasn't usin' it hisself," Lum said, throwing back the covers and swinging his legs off the edge of the bed.

"Where's my shoes and socks at, Lalier?" he said as he threaded his boney legs into his britches. It seemed as if life was returning to him big time.

They sat at the table and ate soup beans until the pot was empty. "Nothin' like good old soup beans," Lum said, smacking his lips.

John noticed that Lalicr no longer set an extra plate for their son. He didn't mention it, for he knew it would be too painful for her to talk about. "Some things are better left unsaid," he thought to himself.

"I'll go and see'f I can borry that mule first thing in the mornin', while you're off lookin' fer a deer. We'll start turnin' ground soon's the sun's up. That is if I can get the mule," Lum said, reaching over and patting John on the back.

Lalier whispered into John's ear saying, "You've rekindled his fire, Son."

John grinned at the thought, for he was now anxious to get things in order at the Luger place an get on home. Ann would surely be longing to see him. For the first time since the crater explosion he was feeling good about himself.

He was up early the next morning and before good daylight he was hunkered down at the edge of the woods, where Lalier told him she had seen deer browsing the day before. Just as he was getting comfortable on a bed of leaves, a large buck emerged from the underbrush, snorted and shook his antlers. John eased the musket into firing position and drew a bead on the buck's rib cage.

When he pulled the trigger the big buck dropped in his tracks with a thud. "It sure does seem like luck's on my side," John said to himself, recalling the words Sam Worley had said about the shoes he had found beside the road.

He left the deer where it fell and returned to the house to get Lum and Lalier's help in dragging the animal home, but before he could get back to the house, he saw Lum coming up the road, leading his neighbor's mule, all harnessed up with the singletree hanging from one of the hames. "Just in time, Lum. I killed a big buck out there at the edge of the woods. Needed somebody to help me drag it home, but that mule can do the job for us."

"You ain't one to fool around, ere ye, Son? We'll have meat today, won't we?" Lum said, bringing the mule to a stop.

"That shore is a big'un, Son," Lum said, as he drew the lasso around the deer's antlers.

He ran the rope through the ring of the singletree and told the mule to git up. The mule, as most mules are, was slow on the takeoff, but once he stepped off, he pulled the deer with very little effort.

They hung the deer by his hind legs from a  beam in the breezeway of the barn. They skinned and dressed the animal and as they began carving it, readying it for hanging in the smokehouse to dry, Lailer came out to the barn carrying a small tin tub. "Cut me off some a that venison and I'll cook up a big mess fer dinner," she said.

"Be glad to, Maam. It's been a long time since I've had a good mess of deer meat," John said, grinning.

Lum smiled and smacked his lips at the thought of having meat on the table again.

After the deer was carved and hung to dry, they went up to the house to wash up. "What's that I smell, Lalier?" Lum asked, as he stood drying his hands on the frazzled towel at the kitchen door.

"Coffee and chickory, Lum. I've been saving it for a special occasion. This is just about as special an occasion as we'll ever get," she said, as she placed  three tin cups on the table and filled them with the steaming coffee.

"Well bless your heart, Lalier. I love you, Lady. You're some kind of a woman. I do b'leive I'll keep you," Lum said, clutching her about the waist and spinning her about the room like a top.

"Careful, Lum. You're liable to strain yourself! You've been laid up fer a while. Remember?"

"All that's ahind me now, Woman. Why, I'm fit as a fiddle, ain't you noticed?" he said, as he let her down gently and planted a kiss on her forehead.

They each sat down at the table and sipped their coffee, savoring every drop.

"Well, Son, I 'spect it's about time we got started breakin' up that ground. I'll take care a them sprouts while you plow, that is if that suits you."

"Yes sir, Lum, I'm chomping at the bits to get started, too. The sooner I get your crop in, the sooner I can be on my way home."

Lum and Lalier frowned at the thought of being left alone again, even though they were well aware of the fact that John wouldn't be with them very long. But he would be there for a few days and they would surely treasure those days. His being there was almost like having their own son back home.

John let the last drop of coffee from the tin cup drip onto his tongue, stood up and began rolling up his sleeves. "Time to hit the fields, Lum. Better get started before it gets too hot."

"Mighty right, Son, we wouldn't want to break into a sweat this early in the spring, now would we?"

"Here, John, this was our boy's straw hat. It'll keep the hot sun off your face," Lalier said, as she wiped the dust from the brim and handed it to him.

The ground wasn't too difficult to break, but since Lum hadn't been able to plant a crop the summer before, several bushes had sprung up and had to be grubbed with the mattock.

Lum did very well the first part of the morning, but as the sun rose higher into the sky, he spent more and more time sitting in the shade at the edge of the field. "You're not givin' out on me are you, Pop?" John said, as he pulled the mule to a stop for a moment, wiping the sweat from his brow.

"Don't you worry none about me, Son. I'll stay ahead a you. I just stopped for a minute to let my breath catch up with me," Lum said, letting out with a little nervous chuckle.

John's shadow shortened and settled at his feet as the noon hour approached. More than half the ground in the field had been turned when Lailer rang the old cow bell, signaling them that dinner was on the table.

"Do ye hear that, Son? Leave that plow a sittin' right where it is and let's get some a that venison. I can smell it from way down here in the field."

"You go on ahead, Lum. I'll be right there soon as I water and feed the mule."

247

"I'll save you a bite er two, Son," Lum said, as he struck off up the hill toward the house.

He couldn't wait until John finished taking care of the mule, for when he came inside Lum was already feasting on the venison. His jaws were bulging as he tried to speak. "I jist couldn't wait fer ye, Son. I wuz about starved fer some meat."

"Quite alright, Pop. Don't you worry, I'm ready to chow down, myself," John said, as he sat down at the table and Lalier loaded his plate with enough venison to feed a giant. "Whoa! Whoa, Lalier! Who do you think I am? Goliath?"

"A workin' man needs to eat, and you sure have been doin' that," she said, glancing over at Lum as he devoured the meat in his plate, looking much like a half starved cave man. "Take your time, Lum, there's plenty more in the pot."

"Can't help myself, Lalier, been many a moon since we had meat on the table."

They all feasted on the tasty venison until they were stuffed. Lum was first to push back from the table. He wiped his mouth on the cuff of his ragged shirt sleeve, cleared his throat and said, "Now you'ns eat up, but me, I've had a plenty. Don't think I could hold another bite."

"Hope it don't make you sick, Lum. Never seed a man eat like that in my whole life," Lalier said, as she pushed back from the table, stood up, and started collecting the eating utensils.

Lum sauntered out onto the porch to catch a few winks before heading back to the field. The call of a bobwhite resonated throughout the meadow as he nodded off, sitting in a straight chair, leaning back against the wall.

"Are you ready to get back at it, Pop?" John asked, tapping Lum on his shoulder.

"Huh! Huh! I reckon so, Son, what time is it? I must a dropped off to sleep," he said, lifting his hat and rubbing his eyes.

"Nigh onto one o'clock I 'spect, Pop. We'd better get at it if we aim to get that ground broke today."

"We'll get it broke, Son. Don't you worry none about that."

And that they did, for by nightfall the ground was all broken, harrowed, and ready for laying off the rows.

Lum spent the next morning visiting neighbors, borrowing enough seed to plant his fields.

John had finished laying off the rows around noon and was up at the well watering the mule when he looked up and saw Lum trudging up the road with a tow sack swung over his shoulder.

"Find any seed, Pop?"

"Sure did, Son. Got enough taters to plant a couple a rows. And enough corn to plant half the field. Zeke Adams let me have about fifty cabbage plants. We'll have some cabbage later on. Got some seed beans and okra, too."

"You must have some mighty good neighbors, Pop."

"We share with one another, Son, That's how we survive. Well, let's get some dinner and start plantin' some of these seeds. They ain't no good till they're in the ground, you know."

"That's right, Pop. You're sure right about that"

John was rather silent at the dinner table. His thoughts were of Ann, wondering how she was doing. Would she be able to plant her little garden? He missed her terribly and longed to see her. He could almost hear the bleating of the goats and the cackling of the little game hens, in the woods near the shanty. "I've got to get back there," he thought to himself.

"John. John. Say, John! Are you alright?" Lalier asked in a raised voice."

John quaked and dropped his fork onto the floor.

"Are you alright, Son?" she asked in a calmer voice.

"Yeah! Yes! Yes, Maam, I'm fine. Just thinkin' about my little woman, wonderin' how she's doin', John said, reaching down to retrieve the fork that had tumbled to the floor.

"Well, after I called you three times with no answer, I began to think somethin' was wrong", Lalier said, breathing a sigh of relief.

"No, I'm alright. Just thinkin' about my little woman," John said, as he pushed away from the table. "Well, let's get them seeds in the ground, Pop. I've got places to go."

"And where might that be, Son."

"Home. Just home," John said, adamantly.

Tears welled up in Lalier's eyes at the thought of John's having to leave. "What effect is this gonna have on my husband?" she questioned herself.

As the two men strolled out onto the porch, Lum looked out onto the plowed field and with a wide sweep of his right arm said, "Just look at it, Son. I couldn't a done it without you."

"Don't know if you've noticed it, Pop, but you can outwork me any day."

"Ah shucks, Son, you sure know how to pull an old man's leg and fill his head full of mud, now don't you?"

They both laughed as they headed down toward the shade of the large maple to pare the potatoes for planting.

They sat cross legged with their backs to the road as they pared the potatoes. They were so consumed with conversation, they failed to hear the horse and rider approaching, until a deep throated male voice immediately behind them said, "Looks like you men are fixin' to plant some taters."

He was so startled at the sudden intrusion that John sliced the leg of his pants with the knife he was about to wipe clean.

"Good God! Don't you ever knock?" Lum said to the man on horseback, without even thinking.

"Sorry, Sir. I didn't mean to startle you. Thought you had seen me coming. Allow me to introduce myself. I'm Jeb Jenkins. I'm part of what's left over from that damned war. My mama and daddy were both killed in it, and our house was burned to the ground. Dang nigh got myself killed, too, up there at Petersburg in that god awful explosion."

"I can sympathize with you, Jeb. I was there," John said, standing up to shake his hand. "I'm John Shepherd and this here's Lum Luger. His boy was killed in the war, too. I'm helping him get his crop in before I head on home."

"That's mighy kind of you, John. Where bouts do you live?"

"North Carolina," John said.

"Quite a ways from here, Huh?"

"A few miles," John said, pointing in the direction of the Blue Ridge Mountains.

"Ye say ye lost yer mama and daddy and yer house, ta boot?" Lum asked.

"Sure did, Sir. This war's left me with nothing." Jeb said.

"Well maybe not, Son. How'd you like to live here with me'n my little woman? We'd be only too happy ta have ye," Lum said.

"Do you really mean that, Sir?"

"Wouldn't a said it if I didn't," Lum said.

"Well, Sir, I can't take the place of your boy, but I sure will try."

"Well, make yourself at home, Jeb. Tie ye horse to that fence post over there and help us get these taters planted. Ader that I'll take you in and let you meet my little woman."

Thank you, Sir. You're a good man. A real good man," Jeb said as he slid down from his horse.

The words John was hearing was music to his ears. He had been concerned as to how Lum and Lalier would fare when the time came for him to go home, but Jeb would certainly fill that void.

"Jeb was my boy's name. You're just like my own boy comin' home," Lum said, looking Jeb squarely in the face.

With that said, they headed out to the field to plant 'taters'. Jeb dropped the potatoes in the furrows as John covered them with the hoe. Lum trailed along behind them picking up roots and tossing them aside and just savoring the occasion, having two young men plant his crop for him.

When they finished with planting the potatoes Lum, as he had rpomised, invited Jeb up to the house to meet his wife.

Lalier was standing at the door when they walked up the steps to the porch. "Lalier this here's Jeb Jenkins. He's gonna take th place uv our boy. He's got th same first name and if I may say so, he looks a lot like him," Lum announced.

"Well glory be! Will miracles never cease?" Lalier said, stepping out onto the porch to embrace Jeb as she would have embraced her very own son. "Come on in this house, Son, I bet you're hungry. We're eatin' high on the hog today. We've got soup beans and venison. How does that sound to ye?"

"Sounds mighty good, maam," Jeb said, stepping back to get a better look at his new mother.

"I'd be honored if you'd call me mom, that is if you don't mind."

"Not a bit, Mom. Not a bit," Jeb said, his face lighting up with a smile that seemed to stretch from ear to ear.

Lalier led the way as they followed her into the kitchen. First in line behind her was Jeb, then Lum, with John trailing along behind. John was pleased that Lum and Lalier had taken so to Jeb. It couldn't have worked better if he had planned it that way.

Lalier set a plate for Jeb, filled it with venison, and poured him a cup of coffee. Lum and John were still full from the big meal they had eaten at noon, but they each accepted a cup of coffee when Lalier offered it.

Conversation at the table was mostly between the Lugers and Jeb, with John getting a word in edgewise now and then. It was almost as if he wasn't even there, so he sipped on his coffee and smiled and nodded his head occasionally, as Jeb and the Lugers acquainted themselves with each other.

"John, have some more of this coffee. I didn't mean to ignore ye. It's just that I never dreamed of havin' somebody come along and offer to take the place of my boy, now don't you know." Lalier said.

"Thank you, Lalier, I've had plenty," John said, pushing back from the table. "I spect we'd better get back out there and finish that plantin' before the rain puts us out of business."

"Now that makes sense. You sure got a head on them sholders, John," Jeb said, standing up, ready to go back at it.

"Jeb, get that old rusty bucket out ere't th barn and fill it up with

251

water. You and me'll set out them cabbage plants while John drops th corn, and when we finish settin' out th plants, we'll commence to coverin' th corn. Lalier, where's that old dipper?" Lum said, handing out orders like a drill sergeant.

Jeb filled the old rusty bucket with water. John picked up the bucket of seed corn from the porch. Lum, after some searching around, finally located the dipper, picked up the bunch of cabbage plants, and they all headed down the hill to the field.

John had dropped corn in four rows by the time Lum and Jeb finished setting out the cabbage plants. They hurried down to cover the corn and were only a few feet behind John when he dropped two grains into the last hill.

"I believe that'll do it, boys. Them bean seed I borried is th climbin' kind so we'll wait till the corn comes up before we plant them. Let'em grow up th corn stalks. We'll wait till th weather warms up some before we plant the okry seed. Okry does better in hot weather," Lum said, as he straightened up, after covering the last hill of corn.

Black clouds were gathering in the west over the mountains and a low rumble of thunder could be heard in the distance. "Not a minute too soon, Pop. Looks like we're gonna get some rain," Jeb said, as he reached over to relieve Lum of his hoe.

"Couldn't a worked better if we'd a planned it this way, Son."

As they made their way up toward the barn, Jeb and Lum walked side by side, chattering like two young squirrels in a hickory tree. John followed a few steps behind them, smiling.

Jeb's horse nickered as they approached the barn and so did the big black stallion. "I spect we'd better water th horses before th storm gits here. Don't you think so, boys?" Lum said.

"Good thinkin', Pop," Jeb said.

John and Jeb hurriedly haltered the horses and led them out to the watering trough, for by this time the storm was getting close. As he shuffled on up to the house, Lum said, "Hurry up, boys. It's gonna storm fer shore."

As they were putting the horses back into their stalls, There was a flash of lightning and at the same instant, a loud clap of thunder that jarred the ground. John looked out passed the barn and saw the top third of a large poplar tree come crashing to the ground. "We'd better get inside, Jeb, before this thing gets any worse," he said, as he and Jeb went racing toward the house.

By the time they reached the shelter of the porch, the rain was coming down in force, but after only a couple of minites, the rain stopped and the sun came out. "Now that's what ye call a pore man's rain," Lum said, looking down toward the field, where only a few minutes ago, they had been planting corn.

"Jeb, that's a nice little horse you've got out there," John said, pointing toward the barn.

"Good saddle horse and he'll pull a plow, too," Jeb said, smiling with pride.

"Well, in that case, we won't need to hold onto that black stallion, will we?" Lum said, looking at Jeb.

Don't think we'll need two horses. Take twice as much to feed both of 'em," Jeb said.

"John, how'd you like to own a big, black, stallion and a saddle to boot?" Lum asked.

"I'd love it, Lum, but I ain't got no money. You know that."

Don't have to have no money, John. Just look at all you've done fer me. You practical brung me back from th edge a death, and look at that planted field out there."

"We'll have to give some credit to Jeb for that, Lum," John said.

"You're welcome to th horse, John. Ye need a better way a getting' home asides walkin'.

"Well, Lum, if you're sure you don't need him, I'd be glad to have him."

"Take him, John, he's yours," Lum said.

Lalier came to the door and said, "Supper's on the table." She was looking directly at Jeb as she spoke.

"And we're ready for it," Jeb said, heading inside.

At the supper table, John told the Lugers that he would be heading home the next day. "Since you've got a brand new son to help you take care of things around here, it's time for me to cut a trail."

Lum and Lalier looked startled at first, but after a moment, a smile began to blossom on their faces. They each realized that John was a very dear friend and he would always be, but they knew very well that he needed to go home. Things had worked so well. It seemed almost like a miracle. They first gazed at John and then focused their attention on Jeb. "It's a miracle for me," Jeb said, a crumb of bread falling from the corner of his mouth as he spoke.

"Tomorrow's the seventh day of June. Sounds like my lucky day," John said. "If I make good time, and I should, ridin' that big stallion, I'll be home by the thirteenth."

His heart skipped a beat at the thought of going home at last. He reached inside his collar and fondled the black button he had worn around his neck throughout the war. He thought of the day when the button was torn from Ann's dress, the day they were laying logs on

253

their shanty. "At last," he said. "At last I'm goin' home."

Early the next morning, Lalier was up, putting together the few morsels that were available and packing them into John's haversack.

"It ain't much, John, but maybe it'll keep you from starvin' till you can find somethin' to eat along the way," she said, as John made ready to leave.

"Thank you, Lalier, you're a kind lady."

After giving Lalier and Lum a hug, he shook Jeb's hand. He thanked Lum again for the stallion and said, "I'll always be geateful to you, Sir". He climbed astride the horse and nudged him in the flanks.

As the stallion carried him down the road, John twisted in the saddle to have one last look at the Lugers. They were all in a huddled, standing there on the porch, waving to him. He gave them one last wave of the hand and then he was gone.

ΩΩΩΩΩΩΩΩΩΩΩΩΩ

As Ann forced herself to become less friendly with people, because of the promise she had made to herself earlier, not to allow herself to get too close to anyone for fear that something tragic would happen to them, they began referring to her as a strange woman.

Some were even calling her a witch, instigated mainly by her uninvited suitors, claiming they had been attacked by her black cat, while they were only trying to be-friend her. These tales, of course, were only lies, told to cover their own mischief. But Ann didn't let the lies bother her, for she knew who she was, and as long as she knew, nothing else mattered.

She went about her daily tasks as usual, taking care of her animals and chickens, weeding and hoeing her little garden, and yes, caring for Fidgety, her 'black cat'. She made regular trips to Bent Oak Trading Post, primarily to check on any mail she might have received from John. Even though she had been told by more than one person that he was dead, she, being a stuborn woman, refused to believe it. "As long as I have hope I have life," she assured herself.

"This is Tuesday the thirteenth, Fidgety. Thirteen's my lucky number. How'd you like to go over to Bent Oak this morning?" she asked her cat, talking to her as if speaking to a human.

The cat answered with a loud "Meow".

"Soon's I get things done up around here, we'll go," Ann said, as she walked toward the barn, with Fidgety, for once in her life, scampering along ahead of her.

After feeding and milking her two goats, and of course, giving Fidgety a squirt or two of milk, she was making her way back to the shanty when she heard a wagon coming up the road. She looked down that way and saw her cousin, Cathy, holding her baby, Mary Ann, with Lank driving the wagon. "Hey, Cousins, it's a delight to see you. It's been a while since I've seen you," Ann said, resting the bucket of milk on the porch and rushing out to the wagon to have a look at the baby. "Well, ain't she growed?" she said.

"Just like a weed," Cathy answered.

"What you doin' out so early?" Ann asked.

"Figgerd on goin' over to Bent Oak and thought maybe you'd like to go along," Lank said.

"How'd you know I'as about to go over there?" Ann asked.

"It could be that we're floatin' down the same old river, Cousin Ann," Lank said, laughing.

"Maybe so, Lank, maybe so. Well, get down and stretch your legs a bit. Let me strain the milk and I'll be ready," Ann said, reaching up to take the baby, allowing Cathy to dismount with ease.

Ann kissed the baby and handed her back to her mother, picked up the bucket of milk and went inside to strain it. Lank and Cathy waited for her on the porch, toying with the baby, as Cathy bounced her on her knee. Lank, being cold natured, had worn a coat, but as he sat in the sun, the coat became a little too warm. So he took it off and hung it over the back of the chair.

"Well, I'm ready," Ann said, as she came outside with Fidgety at her heels. She pulled the draw string to the door latch inside and closed the door. "You'll need to stay here this time, Fidgety. Maybe you can go next time."

The cat collapsed onto the floor and covered her eyes with her paws as if pouting. "I know I said you could go, but I didn't know Lank and Cathy were coming. You'll need to stay here and guard the place while I'm gone."

Fidgety lifted her paws from her eyes, looked up at Ann and hissed. "Next time, Fidgety, next time!"

Lank and Cathy were amused by the way Ann and the cat seemed to communicate with each other. "Strange cat," Lank said.

Lank held the baby while Cathy climbed into the wagon. When he turned to to give Ann a hand up, he looked back toward the shanty and saw her sweeping the path to the gate. "Why're ye doin' that, Cousin Ann? Ain't nobody gonna notice if a leaf or two falls in the yard," he said.

"So's I can tell if some scalawag comes snoopin' around while

I'm gone," Ann said, leaning the broom against the gatepost.

The cat watched as they rode away, then trotted out the trail and sprang up onto the top fence rail and sprawled out.

As they headed down the road on their way to Bent Oak, facing into the sun, Ann reached over and tickled Mary Ann under her chin and the baby giggled. That brought a smile to all their faces. "She'll be talkin' in no time," Cathy said.

"No doubt about it," Lank said. "That's fer sure."

Life seemed so good at the moment. The woods along the road were alive with birds and an occasional squirrel scampered up a tree as they passed by. "Now ain't this nice?" Lank said.

When they arrived at Bent Oak, Ann bounced down from the wagon, hurried up onto the loading dock, and rushed inside to see if there was a letter from John. As soon as she entered the store, the proprietor said, "No mail for you today, Ma'am."

Ann's heart fell when she heard the news, but when Cathy's baby began to coo, a smile came to her face. She tickled Mary Ann's belly and the baby laughed out. "You're a cutie," she said.

"What can I do for you folks?"the proprietor asked.

"Let's see here," Lank said, peering into the coffee bin, to see if any coffee was left in it. "We'd like to buy a little coffee, if you've got any to spare."

"Got a little dab, and I mean a little dab," the proprietor said. "And what I've got's about half chicory."

"Long's it tastes like coffee, that's all that matters," Lank said.

"I can let you have about a quarter of a pound. Hope to get some more in a few days," the proprietor said, as he sprinkled four ounces into the pan on the scales.

"I'll take a chunk of fatback and some flour if you've got any," Ann said.

"Got some of both, Maam. How much fatback do you want?"

"Oh, about two pounds and five pounds of flour,"Ann said.

"Comin' right up, Maam," the proprietor said, measuring out five pounds of flour and pouring it into the bag that Ann had brought along for that very purpose. He cut off a chunk of fatback, wrapped it in a piece of brown paper and laid it on the scales. "That's a little over two pounds, Maam, but we'll call it two."

"Thank you, sir," Ann said, handing him the money.

"Anything else, Maam?"

"That'll be all for now," Ann said.

Two young men were seated at the counter, sipping on home brew, discussing the war and how cruel it had been. Ann Didn't recognize them, but she knew they had been soldiers, for each were wearing a battle worn Confederate cap. Their clothes were ragged and dirty and their shoes were in shambles. She heard them mention Petersburg, so she walked over to where they were sitting and asked, "Did you by any chance meet my husband? His name was John Shepherd."

"I don't know as I remember nobody by that name, Maam," one of the men said.

The other young man sitting beside him shook his head. "Sorry, Maam, we ain't seed him. He didn't get home yet? Hope nothin's happened to him."

"I guess it's takin' him a little longer than some of the others," Ann said, as a teardrop eased down her cheek.

"Are we ready to travel?" Lank asked, as he tapped Ann on the shoulder and pointed to the door.

Ann's tears dried quickly, sitting in the wagon beside Cathy, with the baby cooing and reaching up in a frantic attempt to touch the leaves of the overhanging trees. "You can't reach the leaves, Baby, your arms ain't long enough," she said.

When they reached Ann Ridge and rolled to a stop at the gate in front of the shanty, Fidgety was lying stretched out on the top rail of the fence, enjoying the sunshine. She didn't even look up.

"What's the matter with your cat, Ann? Any other time she'd a been all over you," Lank said, as Ann stepped down from the wagon.

"She's poutin' because she didn't get to go with us," Ann said.

As she looked down she saw large hoofprints there at the gate. She gazed up the path that had been swept clean earlier this morning and saw shoeprints leading all the way up to the porch steps. "What's wrong with you, Fidgety? Are you sick."

Fidgety looked up, stretched her legs, yawned, settled down and closed her eyes.

"Somebody's been here and you act like nothin's happened. Some guard cat you've turned out to be," Ann said, looking puzzled.

Ann invited her cousins in, saying she would fix them something to eat, but Lank declined, saying there was stuff he needed to do.

"Well, Cathy, come back soon and bring that baby with you when you come."

"We wouldn't dream of coming without bringin' Mary Ann." Cathy said, laughing.

Ann reached up and tickled the baby's belly and she giggled. "You're a cutie," she said.

She waved to them as they rode away, then turned and looked at

257

Fidgety, still sprawled out on the top rail of the fence. "You puzzle me some times," she said.

She examined the hoofprints there at the gate to see if anything about them looked familiar and nothing did. She looked closely at the shoeprints in the path and they were unfimilar to her as well. "Wonder who it could have been?" she said to herself, as she stepped up onto the porch and started to sit down in the chair where Lank had been sitting this morning. "Well, he left his coat," she said, pulling a cocklebur from one of the sleeves. "Anyway, it's summer. He won't need it."

She muddled through the remainder of the day, wondering who the uninvited visitor could have been. "Probably a carpetbagger," she figured, "or a scalawag, looking to steal anything he could get his dirty hands on."

By the time the sun went down behind Wildcat Spur she had finished all her chores and had eaten supper. With nothing left to do but go to bed, that's what she did. As she lay listening to the calls of the night birds and savoring the cool breeze coming through the tiny window by her bed, her thoughts turned immediately to John. This was something she couldn't prevent and didn't want to prevent. She loved him and knew she always would. Tears came to her eyes when she thought of him, for she missed him. This night was no different from all the rest, for she lay gazing at the darkening ceiling through swimming eyes.

The woods surrounding the shanty were alive with night sounds. A hoot owl bellowed from somewhere high on the ridge. A screech owl let out with its eerie call, down near the creek. A whipporrwill sang its night song outside her bedroom window.

She was finally lulled to sleep by the various sounds of the night, but it wasn't a restful sleep by any means. Her slumber was interrupted by troubling dreams. In one dream she was standing at the tiny window beside her bed, listening to the drone of an old hoot owl, perched on a dead limb, asking, "Who? Who? Who?"

"I don't know who! I don't know who! I don't know who!" she moaned until she awoke, sitting straight up in bed.

Fidgety stretched her legs and moved over to the other side of the bed. Ann got up and closed the window. "Maybe I can get some sleep if I cut out the night sounds," she said.

Around midnight, she dreamed that someone was pounding on the door and a voice outside was calling her name. The voice was that of John. She sprang from the bed and raced to the door, but when she opened it, no one was there. "Just another bad dream," she said, as she peered out through the darkness.

She closed the door and returned to bed and lay staring into the darkness, breathless, her heart pounding. The dream had been so real. "Why am I having these dreams? John must be trying to tell me something," she said.

When her breathing slowed and her heart stopped pounding she dropped off to sleep again.

Morning finally came, and after fixing herself some breakfast, she went out to feed and milk the goats, but when she walked into the breezeway of the barn, she realized that something was amiss, for a bundle of fodder was lying beside the loft steps and it looked as if someone had used it as a pillow. There were horse droppings and hoofprints at the rear of the barn. The hoof prints looked to be the same size as the ones left in front of the shanty, but there was no way to determine if they were from the same horse. "Who could be doin' this?" she asked herself. "Who slept in my barn last night."

When she checked on her goats, she found that Precious had been milked dry. "That dirty scalawag! I'll fix him if I ever catch him," she said, her face burning with anger.

She fed the goats, milked Gracious, shelled an ear of corn for the chickens, and headed back to the shanty with only half as much milk as she normally would have had. When she stepped up onto the porch, she heard Fidgety meowing and clawing at the door. She opened the door and apologized for leaving her alone. "I don't know what's happenin' to me, Fidgety. I must be loosin' my mind."

"Meow," the cat replied.

Ann poured some milk into the porcelain bowl and sat it on the floor for Fidgety. She strained the rest of the milk the crock. When the cat had finished lapping up the milk, then said, "Let's you and me go out there and grabble some taters for dinner and maybe pull up a bunch of onions or two."

Fidgety was more than ready to go. She was so excited she leapt clean out into the yard, spun around a few times, chasing her tail, then collapsed onto the ground and rolled over onto her back, looking up at Ann, waiting to see what her reaction would be. "You silly cat. What's the matter with you. You've not acted this way since you were a kitten," Ann said, as she stroked the cat's belly with her walking stick.

While Ann grabbled the potatoes, Fidgety patrolled the bushes around the edge of the garden. She rustled up a few birds, but was unable to catch any. "Come on, Fidgety, you can't catch them bird. Let's get these taters washed and get some dinner cooked," Ann said, as she plucked a bunch of multiplying onions from the ritch ground.

Fidgety grappled with spring lizards while Ann washed the

potatoes and onions in the creek, but because the lizards were so slick, she was unable to hold onto them. The cat had failed in all her attempts to catch something, but she didn't seem to mind.

Ann stirred the fire in the fireplace and sat the cast iron frying pan on the tripod over the fire. She sliced some fatback and placed it into the pan to render out some grease. As the pork began to fry, she poured some of the grease into the Dutch oven and sat it on a bed of coals near the fire. She stirred up some corn meal for bread an poured it into the Dutch oven and placed the lid on top and covered it with live coals. "We're gonna have us a good dinner, Fidgety, with these new taters and onions," she said.

The cat didn't answer. Instead, she rolled over onto her back on the floor and closed her eyes.

Indeed, it was a good dinner, for they ate until they were both stuffed. After dinner, Ann got up from the table rubbing her belly, went outside and sat down in the chair on the porch. And where was Fidgety? On her lap, of course. Ann didn't even wash the dishes. "Dishes can wait," she said, as she sat listening to birds singing and a dog barking way off in the distance.

It wasn't long until she was nodding. So she decided to go inside and lie down on the bed and take a nap before washing the dishes. "They'll wait, she said to herself again."

As soon as her head settled good into the pillow she was snoring. Fidgety lay by her side, purring. They slept undisturbed until Ann found herself dreaming of John. She dreamed he was kissing her and his whiskers were tickling her face. She awoke with a start to find it was only Fidgety's rough tongue, licking her on the chin. "Does my chin taste that good, Fidgety? You sure can't be hungry," Ann said, pushing the cat aside and swinging her legs off the edge of the bed. "It must be gettin' late. I'd better get them dishes washed and take care of the chores."

Before she finished washing the dishes, black clouds came rolling over Wildcat Spurr. Thunder was rumbling in the distance. She left the dishes as they were and rushed out to the barn to feed and milk the goats. Yes, Fidgety went along, too. She wasn't about to miss her regular two squirts of warm milk. Ann finished taking care of the animals and was making her way back to the shanty when large drops of rain began to fall. By the time she and the cat went inside and she closed the door, it was getting very stormy outside. Rain began coming down in waves, skittering along the roof, with the sound of a dozen scampering squirrels.

The rain stopped as suddenly as it had started and the sun came out for a few minutes before it slid down behind Wildcat Spurr. Daylight fades quickly on Ann Ridge after the sun goes down. Even though it was still reasonably light outside, it was getting a bit dark inside the shanty, so Ann lit a candle and sat down on the bench beside the table, thinking of the dream she had had about John. It brought back good memories as well as bad. A good memory was of the day they were married. A bad memory was of the day he had to go away to fight in that awful war.

As she sat staring into the flame of the candle she thought she heard a horse neigh. Rushing to the window, she looked out toward the barn and saw a black horse standing in the breezeway. A bearded man was standing beside him. She lifted the loaded musket from the gunrack over the door and went outside, pointed the musket in the direction of the bearded man and said, "I caught you this time, you scalawag. Step out here in the open and let me have a good look at you," her voice trembling from fear and anger.

Rainwater was still dripping from the edge of the barn roof and as the bearded man stepped out into the open, a drop of water caught him of the nose and triclked down into his beard. As he reached up to wipe the water from his nose and beard, Ann said, "Watch where you put your hands, stranger. Remember, I've got this here musket trained on your belly."

The bearded man loosened the collar of his shirt, reached inside, and beneath his whiskered chin, pulled on a string that was strung about his neck and out plopped a large, black button.

"Is that what I think it is?" Ann said, dropping the musket to the ground.

The bearded man stood as still as a dead tree stump. He didn't say a single word as the button swayed on the string.

Staring at the bearded man and the black button, Ann screamed, "John Shepherd, Is that you? Oh, John, It is you!"